"With vividly inventive world building and a fast-paced plot, *The Mirror Empire* opens a smart, brutal, and ambitious epic fantasy series."
Kate Elliott, author of the Spiritwalker series

"*The Mirror Empire* is a fast-paced and exciting read, and the start of quite possibly one of the greatest political dramas I have ever picked up."
Coffee on My Keyboard

"Taking epic fantasy down challenging and original paths. Thoughtful and thought-provoking with every twist and turn."
Juliet E McKenna, author of the Tales of Einarinn series

"*The Mirror Empire* is a fresh, vigorous, and gripping entrant into the epic fantasy genre, able to stand toe-to-toe with any of the heavyweight series out there. I cannot recommend this novel highly enough."
SF Revu

"There's a powerful yet elegant brutality in *The Mirror Empire* that serves notice to traditional epic fantasy: move over, make way, an intoxicating new blend of storytelling has arrived. These are pages that will command your attention."
Bradley Beaulieu, author of The Lays of Anuskaya trilogy

"*The Mirror Empire* takes look at epic fantasy patriarchy & gives it a firm kick in the balls... [It] will be the most important book you read this year."
Ristea's Reads

KAMERON HURLEY

The Broken Heavens

THE WORLDBREAKER SAGA

BOOK III

**ANGRY
ROBOT**

ANGRY ROBOT
An imprint of Watkins Media Ltd

Unit 11, Shepperton House
89 Shepperton Road
London N1 3DF
UK

angryrobotbooks.com
twitter.com/angryrobotbooks
Only one survives

An Angry Robot paperback original, 2020

Cover by Richard Anderson
Edited by Amanda Rutter and Paul Simpson
Map by Stephanie MacAlea
Set in Meridien

ISBN 978 0 85766 562 1
Ebook ISBN 978 0 85766 563 8

Printed and bound in the United Kingdom by TJ International.

9 8 7 6 5 4 3 2 1

For those who dare to dream of better worlds.

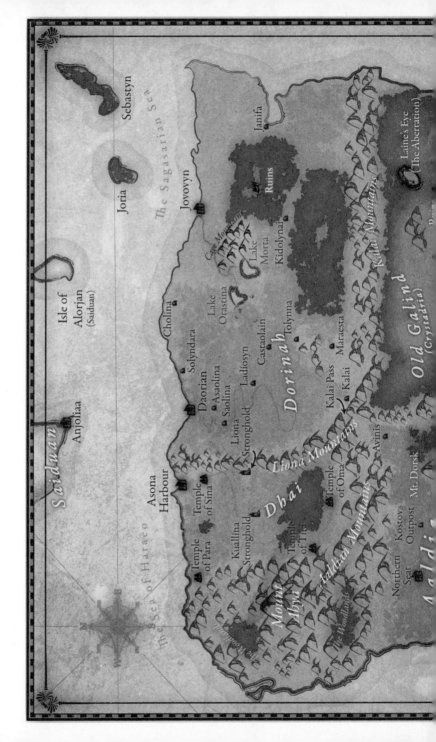

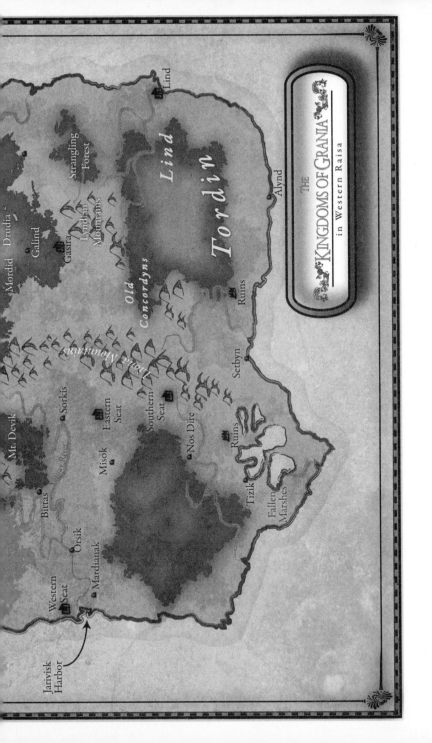

"May your choices be shaped by your hopes, not your fears."
— DHAI SAYING

PROLOGUE

The gnarled old woman carried a box of bones up the mountain. She bent low under the weight. The winking eye of Oma watched her ascent, ever-present in the rippling cerulean sky. Its sisters – violet Sina and twinkling emerald Tira – burned just beneath its glaring red pupil; patient, waiting.

As she climbed, she cursed Oma. A habit from another life. Another world, before all the worlds began to crash together.

At her hip, she bore her weapon: a yellow bonsa branch as long as her arm, infused with the power of Para. It glowed faintly, though Para was still descendant. If the seers were to be believed, Para would enter the sky again sooner than it had in other cycles. Until then, her powers were... limited. Still substantial, but limited.

The bones were a boon. The sole find of any value from her long, disastrous trek over the Kalai Mountains and into the lawless wilderness of warring states in the Tordinian valley to find a bit of ephemera kept safe for two thousand years by a race of slavering, gold-skinned interlopers. The interlopers were dead, burned out, but their storerooms and altars and thrones and the like had remained intact.

Whatever force obliterated them had not returned for a second encounter. Kalinda certainly did not blame them.

She had tumbled through a rent in the fabric between her world and this one the year before, eager to begin again after losing everything. She had been a powerful figure, once. A world had bent at her word. She had promised to save them from the sky.

She had failed.

Now she was the last of her people left alive. And there was some good she could do still. Where she had failed, another might succeed. Hope was a delicious drug; though it, too, could kill, the experience of dying hopeful was far better than the reality of dying in despair. She had seen enough people die of both to know that.

The wind picked up and pushed black thunderheads after her, swathing the satellites in their embrace. She tasted the storm on the air, and moved a little more slowly. The rain would sluice the sweat and dirt from her skin. If it rained long enough and hard enough, she might put down the box and scrub herself with a fistful of sand. It had been some time since she engaged in such civilized routines. It was easy to lose oneself during so much solitary travel.

But the thunderheads brought fine puffs of snow, not rain. The snowflakes clung to her eyelashes. Obscured her vision. Her feet ached. Her own bones protested. Snarls of lavender snowlilies bloomed along the rough path she followed, releasing little white tufts of seed into the drifting snow. The seeds were poisonous if inhaled, so she pulled her scarf over her nose and mouth and picked up her pace again.

The old woman made her way back up over the Kalai

Mountains and across the charred fields of what had once been called Dorinah. She had been through here when it was still ruled by fleshy women wearing jaunty ribbons knotted in their hair while they tugged around their skinny, whimpering men, and slaves on short leads. A filthy people, certainly, like most people, but she missed their easy confidence and airy architecture. She passed villages still smoldering in the early morning light, great temples to their goddess, Rhea, smashed to dust; crimson shards of glass scattered about the wreckage.

She kept off the main roads, though they were certainly areas clearest of creeping plant-life, as the country's new masters still burned away the vegetation from the roadsides to keep them clear. She rested during the height of the day, when Tai Mora patrols could be found on the roads and in the otherwise abandoned streets of the small settlements.

One evening she took shelter in an old hair salon, the mirrors shattered, tattered ribbons collecting in the corners with dust and mice droppings. She caught her broken reflection in one of the larger mirror pieces, and recoiled. Surely no one would recognize her, in this disheveled state? But the Tai Mora had been running reconnaissance on her world for years, as she had on theirs. A few would remember Kalinda Lasa the Unmaker, and how her world had crashed around her, tipped into disorder and ruin by the Tai Mora. She could not risk being recognized.

As Kalinda came to the great forked pass that raked a seam between the Liona Mountains that had once separated Dorinah and Dhai, two Tai Mora scouts riding great white bears called her to a halt. They were hale women, though not quite so fat and satisfied as Kalinda had imagined the

Tai Mora would be here. Spring was a hungry time.

"Where are your papers?" the elder of the two barked.

Kalinda bent her head, and spoke in Tai Mora. "Here, in this box."

"Open it then."

"Alas, my fingers are stiff with cold."

With a huff, the elder ranger slid off her bear and took hold of the box of bones. Shook it. The bones shuddered, making the box tremble. "That doesn't sound like papers."

"I have been collecting this and that." Kalinda murmured the Litany of Breath, seeking the power of distant Para. Her sensitivity to the blue star was unmatched, but the effort it took to find a trickle of its power required the utmost concentration.

The ranger pulled open the box.

Kalinda mimed the Litany of the Spectral Snake and wrapped both rangers in skeins of air. The dark wounds on the women's wrists bloomed with everpine weapons, snapping toward her, but they were too late. Kalinda crushed them both, pinning the weapons to their bodies. Their faces ballooned. Legs kicked. The old woman squeezed the vital juices from their bodies. They burst like spent melons.

The lifeless sacs of the rangers keeled over, spent.

Kalinda grew dizzy. Vomited. Her hands shook with the effort of summoning and directing all that power from a descendant star. For one less skilled than she, holding Para would have been impossible.

Hungry and shivering, she rooted through the rangers' saddlebags and ate everything that appeared edible. The bears, their forked tongues wagging at her and paws churning up the soil, she sent on their way. Traveling by bear would be too conspicuous. She had only made it this far unmolested because few thought to question a poor old woman laboring around with a battered leather box. More fool the rangers, for being the first to tangle with her.

She slept for two days in a blackberry bramble, recovering her strength. When Oma blinked at her the third day, she continued her trek, winding through the ruins of the pass where once a great stronghold called Liona had sealed one country from another. The Tai Mora had carted off much of the building material to serve some other purpose. The Tai Mora were good at that, building their little hives atop the detritus of conquered civilizations. Even the timber here had been cut and loaded into wagons. She passed the corpse of a great bonsa tree lying on its side, the trunk so broad it would take three people standing fingertip to fingertip to span its diameter. The road here was well-trod, much busier than Dorinah, and smelled of tangy sap and moist, thawing soil. Great wagons pulled by mangy dogs and matted bears rolled over the hastily graveled road, moving to and from staging areas for troops and enslaved farmers. Kalinda suspected the Tai Mora were already regretting not bringing more farmers with them.

Kalinda kept her hood up and trudged across the country that was once called Dhai. Those around her called it Novoso Mora now: "Our People Reborn." She passed newly tilled fields and charred groves being cut down by Dhai slaves and their Tai Mora masters, and she wondered how many of them would survive to harvest, let alone survive what the sky had in store for them. The air changed as she traveled through the toxic churn of wooded areas between old clan holds. Warmer, wetter, and yes, she smelled a hint of rot, still, as if the soil were so thick with the moldering dead that it could not help but stink of them.

Up and up she went, finding it more difficult to avoid the press of people: Tai Mora rangers on their white bears; retinues of jistas in purple and red, green and blue robes; Dhai slaves wearing leather collars as they cleared fields of toxic plant life; traveling merchants calling out their offerings, mostly baubles, not enough food; high, garish laughter and jokes about cannibals from mercenaries getting their rotten feet tended by tirajistas – a bustle of humanity far too large for the area to ever support. Where the forests and toxic woods had been, thousands of makeshift tents stood in neat rows along the roadsides, like grave markers.

Kalinda spent evenings sleeping outside the old wayhouses, eavesdropping on the travelers. Hunger was on their minds, and fear of the free Dhai who had taken up in the Woodland. She smiled to hear of that, because any people who could unsettle the Tai Mora were surely her allies. Her allegiance was not misplaced.

To avoid the crush of people near Oma's Temple, she approached it from behind, up through the woodlands, hacking at poisonous balloon flowers with her machete, arms already prickled with a red rash caused by some terrible weed or other. After several hours, she reached a field of dead poppies overlooking the temple proper. The seams between the worlds were soft here; she had learned to sense it. She listened for other travelers in the woods, perhaps those she waited for, but heard nothing but the rustle of treegliders newly woken from their winter slumber.

Satisfied, she dumped the box at her feet and lay in the broken grass and withered flowers and slept another half a day. When did calling on the power of the satellites become so exhausting? Old age was ridiculous. This was a ridiculous time to be alive.

She woke to the sound of soft footsteps. Bird song. The smell of acrid bonsa sap. Crackle of crunching poppies.

"So you came," Kalinda said, and turned to find the girl there, flanked by two very young jistas with dark mops of messy hair. Kalinda had a mind to wipe their mouths and smooth their hair for them. The whole lot of them needed a wash, as did she, which made her appreciate their company all the more.

"I know your face," the girl said.

"It's a time for familiar faces. I know yours as well."

"Is your name Kalinda?"

"It is. And you are Lilia."

This Lilia was in a terrible state, far worse than the one Kalinda had known on her world. The girl before her held a stout walking stick and leaned heavily to one side, favoring her twisted foot. Shiny roundish scars peppered her face, and one of her hands was new and soft, clearly a replacement for one long gone. The other, which clutched the staff, lacked tension in the little finger. She wore an absurdly large bearskin coat, and beneath it a too-big tunic and trousers hung from her slight, gaunt frame. Her eyes were sharp in her sallow face, and dark bruises beneath her eyes made her gaze appear larger, more weary, than that of a woman thrice her age.

Poor child, this.

Behind the girl and her jistas, something rattled in the

bushes. Kalinda expected a dog, or a small bear, but it was another girl, hunched over, eyes smooth pools of flesh, twisting her blind face this way and that, sniffing and tasting the wind. She settled next to Lilia as if they were close companions.

Lilia patted the girl's shoulder with her soft hand. "Did you help me, on your world?" Lilia asked, gazing not at Kalinda, but at the disfigured girl pressed against her.

"No. I ruled that world, before I lost it."

Lilia did not look convinced. "You tried to help me, here," she said. "Was there someone like me over there?"

"No," Kalinda lied, because the truth was always far more complicated. "But I understand your need. And I've brought a gift, as I said in my letter."

"I wondered what sort of Kalinda you were," Lilia said. "I assure you, there are more jistas nearby, should you attempt anything deceptive."

Kalinda cackled. "Oh, child, I could crush the breath from your body in a wink."

One of the jistas stepped forward. The air thickened.

"No, no," Kalinda said, waving her hand. "I'm not here for that. I wanted to meet you personally, to gauge how serious your little rebellion truly is. They complain about you burning their wagons, down in the valley."

"We will do worse than that," Lilia said, "but for now we prefer to be but biting flies. In the days after we fled Kuallina, I promised my people we would take back Dhai. A year later, I'm nearly prepared to make good on that promise."

"Oh child," Kalinda said, "don't you know that now is the time for coming together? Not breaking apart. That's why I've brought you this gift. You will need it, for where you're going. The Tai Mora have found the fifth temple, the People's Temple, long buried beneath the sea. But it's missing a very vital piece."

"How do you know that?"

"Because I'm the one who took the piece." Kalinda nodded to the box. "There is a great warrior in there, and within them, a vital piece the Tai Mora, or some other, would need in order to call on the full power of the satellites from the People's Temple."

"We've been watching their progress," Lilia said, "off the western coast, near Fasia's Point. Is that what they've been dredging up? A whole *temple*?" She shook her head. "Mad."

"Not too difficult, with so many stars in the sky."

"You're giving me this… vital piece? Why? I want to take back the country. I care nothing for closing the ways between the worlds."

"Don't you? The time for worldbreakers is not over, Lilia. It's just beginning. But you can't do this alone."

The girl recoiled. "Don't use that word!" she snapped. "There's no such thing. I've been pushed and pulled by others using that word for me, and it was all a lie. There's no grim purpose, no chosen one, nothing to save us but ourselves and the plans I have put together–"

Kalinda bent and pulled the top off the box. She presented the bones to the girl, triumphant. "What do you say to that, then?"

Lilia stared into the box. The bones were bound tightly in a throbbing, tangled root mass that oozed sticky green sap. Mixed in with it were dried leaves, bits of dead ivy, and a single node of intricate silver-green metal shaped like a trefoil with a tail.

"What... What *is* this?" Lilia said.

"A box of bones."

"I can see that. But this?" She pointed to the silver-green shape.

"It's the symbol for the People's Temple. You recognize it, don't you? I spent weeks digging through old rooms and tunnels, but it was part of the throne, of all things, that gooey silvery throne room packed with bones, and..." She trailed off. Certainly the girl didn't need to know the details.

Lilia rubbed at her wrist. Peered at Kalinda anew. "Are you a... blood witch? Is that why you think you can bring a body back that's this far gone?"

"On my world, yes. But it's not my skill alone. I found this among the detritus of another race, one that can twist a soul's memory into the shape of a root and let it rest for an age – a thousand years, or more – before awakening it again. It was simply very lucky for us that so many died trying to murder them, and I was able to retrieve these bones. Two thousand years of creeping star-magic in that wood, magic foreign even to me, but it has given us a safe place to put this silver piece of the People's Temple. Only you will know it's here."

But Lilia did not seem to hear her. She was staring past Kalinda, across the field of poppies. "When I saw you here, or, my Kalinda here," Lilia said, "so long ago, I thought you were a blood witch. Do you know what that is?"

"I do. The closer a world is to yours, the more alike it is. Your world and mine were even closer than yours and this one."

Lilia came back to herself and staggered forward, the color draining from her face. Her jistas made to follow, but she waved them back. She bent close to Kalinda, and spoke just above a whisper, her breath tickling Kalinda's ear. "Don't talk about what world I'm from."

Ah, of course her little followers wouldn't know where Lilia was from, would not know her mother had bundled her up and stowed her here, slicing a hole between two worlds to do it.

"I know what you are," Kalinda said softly. "I know your mother brought you here from the Tai Mora's world, to save you. And she did more than that. She made it possible for this to end some other way. But you haven't chosen which way, yet. There are many possible futures, most terrible. Some good. You must decide if you truly hate yourself so much that you will murder the people from your own world, or if you will find some other way. I don't envy you that choice."

Lilia pulled away. "What if I don't want this... piece? What if I don't want to go to the People's Temple at all? It's crawling with Tai Mora. I have plans for a different assault, one that will hurt them far more easily."

"You clearly needed aid," Kalinda said, "and I've brought what I could. As I have for you always, haven't I? Some version of me."

Lilia squeezed her eyes shut. Inhaled deeply through her nose. "Stop invoking the name of someone else. You aren't her."

"But I am," Kalinda said. "We all are. Don't you understand that yet?"

"Don't twist my head," Lilia said. "Tell me about who

this is, then. The soul of a great warrior?"

"Oh, it is. I chose the soul very carefully. Of course, for a body this far gone... it does require a bit of sacrifice on your part. It's nigh impossible to bring a body back that's this dead, without some... blood witchery, you understand?"

"Very well," Lilia said. "What do you want for it?"

"It's what you need to give it." Kalinda had already used up a great deal of energy fighting the rangers two weeks before. This last bit of binding would be tricky. Kalinda muttered an intricate litany, one she had not used since she was a girl, and cast a purl of breathy power across the bones. "Now I need you to spit into the box," Kalinda said.

"And... what happens then?"

"That will begin the process of binding."

"Binding... what?"

"This was a very complicated spell, child. I was not alone when I began this journey. I had two powerful sinajistas and six tirajistas with me. All gone now, but all necessary to make this possible. When you spit into the box, the warrior contained within will begin to be reborn, and will be bound to you. But you must spit into the box."

"This is mad," Lilia muttered.

"Let's leave it, Lilia," said the shorter tirajista. "She's just another old woman made addled by all this."

"A moment, Salifa," Lilia said, raising her voice to be heard by those behind her. She lowered it again and said, "Kalinda, I want the truth. About the Lilia you knew in your world."

"I told you, there wasn't–"

"That's a lie. You said your world and mine were closer than this one and mine."

Kalinda hummed a bit, an old lullaby, but Lilia did not react to it. A shame, really. She must not have raised this Lilia as long, here. "I trained you to be a great warrior," Kalinda said, "to fight at my side. To come with me to this world and storm the People's Temple and take control of the transference engine at the center of it and remake the world. I trained you to be a worldbreaker there. You were a powerful omajista, more powerful than any we encountered. You could have seared every one of these Tai Mora in an instant. We had so much more knowledge of what was to come that we could train you from the time you were very small."

"...But?"

"But, yes... there's that, isn't there?" Kalinda's throat ached. She coughed. "But, well..."

"I failed," Lilia said, darkly.

"You did."

"All the knowledge, all the training, and I failed."

"That was a different Lilia. You have made different choices."

"I don't think they're better ones," Lilia said.

"You don't *know* that! None of us does, you arrogant little spithead."

The bones rattled in the box.

Lilia started. "What...?"

Kalinda hefted up the box. Proffered it to Lilia. "I agree with you," Kalinda said. "There is no chosen one, no absolute singular person who can turn the tide. But there are people who *choose*."

Lilia worked her mouth, gaze set on Kalinda, and spit into the box. "Is that enough?"

Kalinda nodded. She put the lid back on the box. "That's good." The box lay inert at her feet again.

"Nothing is happening," Lilia said.

"Patience," Kalinda said. "The warrior will awaken."

"I don't have time to *wait*."

"Tira's tears, child, resurrection takes time. Pack this box into a trunk – three paces long, two paces high – and throw in two handfuls of fertile soil. Leave it in a cool, dry room for… at least seven days."

"And then?"

"Then the warrior will awaken, and will be bound to you. You only become unbound in death, understand?"

"Wait, does that mean… if they die, *I* die? I didn't agree to that!"

"No, no," Kalinda said. "But if you feel pain, they will feel pain. If you are in need, they are compelled to aid you. Come, what do you have to lose, Lilia Sona? Do you already have so many allies that you can turn down a gift from an old woman with a fond memory for who you might have been?"

Lilia stared at the box. She chewed at her thumbnail, the feathery one on her soft, still-forming new hand. "You know what drives me, Kalinda Lasa, what has driven me from the time your shadow found me here, cast out from my world into a field of poppies?"

"I do."

"*Do* you?"

"Of course." Kalinda raised a hand to brush Lilia's cheek, but the girl recoiled. Kalinda would have wept, but she had spent those tears some time ago.

"You continue in the face of the impossible," Kalinda

said, "because you are willing to destroy the world – and even yourself – to get your revenge. I know what the Tai Mora did to you, Lilia, because they did it to my Lilia, too."

Lilia's grip on her walking stick tightened. The little blind girl at her feet whimpered. "It's all right, Namia," Lilia said. "I promise you we will destroy every one of them."

Kalinda held out the box one last time.

At a gesture from Lilia, Salifa took the box from Kalinda's hands. In that moment, a great weight lifted from Kalinda's shoulders. She had done all she could. For this Lilia, and the last.

1

Taigan was already bored with the end of the world.

It had been a year since Oma had risen, its shining bloody face purported to herald some apocalyptic ending for this world and those closest to it. But people marched on, as they were wont to do, scrabbling and squabbling and annoying him. The world kept spinning. He kept living. The promised apocalypse was a maddeningly slow one.

Taigan found it a relief, then, when the naked man fell from the sky.

The body landed with a wet thump a few feet from where Taigan stood at the aft of a great, living Aaldian cargo ship. The body kept its shape... all but one testicle. A single gonad popped free, like a shiny white egg. Taigan had a moment to wonder at the absurdity of that: not just a naked man falling from the sky but that the body had excreted its gonad on impact, like some dim bird shitting an egg.

A jagged tear rent the blue-violet sky directly overhead, revealing the amber-tinged atmosphere of some other world beyond. Dark shapes moved in the wavering rent in reality. The seam rippled, then closed, sealing Taigan's world from the other just as swiftly as it had appeared.

"Poor choice," Taigan muttered, though he couldn't imagine what had compelled this man to shoot himself through a rent in the sky. Certainly, that other world was dying, just as the Tai Mora's had some months before, forcing the few still stuck there to flee to yet another nearby dying world, or perish. Yet, staring at the lonely gonad, Taigan imagined the man might have had a more dignified death if he had stayed on his own world.

The crew shoved the body off the deck, muttering darkly about dire portents and desperate worlds. Birds circled and dived in the water behind them, enjoying the free meal. Taigan had not seen what happened to the gonad, but he suspected it had been a delicious treat for some sea bird.

Taigan lifted his nose to the salty air. Beneath the brine he detected a more familiar scent: the taste of ruin. It was a heady mix of acrid kelp and charred flesh that filled his nostrils even in his dreams. It smelled like home. A home that no longer existed. Perhaps that's why he had been drawn back to this doomed place.

The ship rounded a rocky spur, revealing the source of the smell: the harbor once called Asona, gateway to what had once been the kingdom of Dhai.

Taigan had been present for the harbor's destruction, and remembered it as a smoking heap of wreckage. It was early spring, and the world the Tai Mora invaders had built for themselves on the broken backs of the defeated Dhai was quickly unfurling across the continent, despite the increasing number of interlopers able to hurl themselves from one world to the next under Oma's watchful eye.

The Tai Mora in the harbor lifted great stones using belts of Tira's breath, training vines to set the stones in place. The way they worked reminded Taigan of insects: industrious, poisonous little things with many hands. They may have been the strongest force in the world at present, but Oma's rise had signaled the assault of other worlds. They would need to fight for their supremacy against a great many more enemies in the coming years, if they did not find a way to close the seams between this world and the others.

If that was even possible anymore.

The Patron of Saiduan and his War Minister, Maralah, had believed they could rally enough omajistas to stop the incursion of other worlds, once Oma had risen. But with the Patron dead and Maralah fled, there were few of Taigan's people left to see that vision through. In truth, Taigan was not confident even the Tai Mora could achieve what his people could not. He had spent the last year roaming the decimated continent of Saiduan, killing and fucking indiscriminately. He never expected to be laid low by such increasing boredom. He needed a purpose, like the one Maralah had given him, and all the masters before her. For all his hatred of her, at least she had given him something useful to do.

Here during the end times, Taigan intended to murder as many Tai Mora as possible. Killing was something he was good at, something he understood. It's what he had wanted to do before Maralah sent him out on his mad mission to find gifted omajistas that they could train to become worldbreakers. What a farce.

When he had boarded this ship in Anjoliaa, he clothed himself in an easy illusion, tangling the breath of Oma into a web around him that bent the light and deceived the eye. A breath, a blink, and he appeared to be a shorter, darker man with longer limbs and finer features, the very image of an Aaldian he knew decades ago, when he had sought worldbreakers in that soft little country. For good measure, he wore an approximation of Aaldian clothing, the long robes and elaborate yellow vest of a scholar. He could have done up some glamor to make him look Tai Mora, he supposed, but Aaldian would garner fewer questions and expectations. Holding a glamor this many days when Oma was descendant would have been impossible. Today it was simple as breathing.

The great Aaldian ship slid into port, hugging the pier with its shiny organic skin. The fit little Aaldians sang as they worked, and the hull of the living ship pulsed in time to the rhythm of their tune.

"You see how it loves us," the Aaldian captain said, striding up next to Taigan, boots squelching on the membrane of the deck. There was but one pronoun in their language, though the captain used an honorific that indicated they had borne children. Taigan preferred just the one designation; the five genders in Dhai seemed entirely random in their application, and it confused him greatly.

Taigan said, in Aaldian, "It has been a… relatively smooth trip. I did not anticipate that. The Tai Mora have been ruthless with other races, but not Aaldia."

"The Tai Mora are content to let Aaldians ferry goods," the captain said. "For now. I suspect that will change when the Tai Mora are no longer starving and gobbling up our excess, moldering goods. We came from another place, of course, during the last cycle of the sky, bringing our ships and keeping closely to ourselves. There's no race like ours on their world. We pose no hindrance to them coming over."

"What will you… Will *we* do to turn them back?" Taigan asked.

The captain smirked. "I know you're not one of us," they said. "That glamor can mask your visage, but not your mannerisms, nor your accent. Are you Tai Mora?"

Taigan gave a little shrug.

The captain gazed past him at the crew, busily wetting down the decks with a mix of honey and seawater to feed the ship before letting passengers disembark; the skin absorbed the heady brew in a few moments, and the whole craft shuddered and sighed.

"I had a mind to ask you what's next," the captain said, "if you were Tai Mora. What your intentions are with our people. But if you are not Tai Mora, then… I suppose you know as much as anyone else."

"I couldn't say what the Tai Mora *will* do. But I can point to what they have *done*. Surely their past actions are a great predictor of what the ultimate fate of Aaldia will be."

"Indeed. I have told many this, but they insist it could be different with us. The Tai Mora have sent emissaries to the Five Monarchs promising peace."

"As they did with the Dhai, and the Saiduan before them. And here we are." Taigan gestured to the bustling Tai Mora in the harbor.

"Yes," the captain said. "But perhaps we should wait and see. Give them a chance."

Taigan barked a laugh at that. He could not help it. The optimism of the doomed was the same in every country.

The crew put out the rolling tongue of the gangplank, which slopped into place on the pier, and two Tai Mora customs agents squelched aboard the quivering ship.

Taigan pulled on his hat. "Luck to you, then, captain."

"And to you," the captain murmured, and went to greet the customs agents.

Taigan waited his turn for interrogation by the agents, joining the little queue of other passengers. During his year of self-imposed exile, Taigan had found there were many more things he could accomplish with Oma in the sky – wonderful and terrible things. The Tai Mora probably had, too. That made this trip interesting.

And, above all else, he craved something *interesting*.

When he reached the head of the line, he gave the agents his passbook, which he had lifted from some poor Aaldian back in Anjoliaa.

"What is your purpose in Tai Mora?" the older agent asked.

Taigan said, in Tai Mora, "Visiting a man about a dog."

The agent's eyes narrowed. Taigan poked at her with a thread of Oma's breath to ensure she was not some gifted omajista who could see through his illusion. Omajistas were still very rare, even among the Tai Mora, but caution cost him nothing.

He felt no resistance from the agent; she was ungifted. If she thought him suspicious, it had only to do with his attitude, not his glamor.

Taigan descended onto the battered pier, picking his way across algae-smeared bonsa wood planking quivering with small sea worms. It was high tide, the only time when ships as large as the Aaldian one could dock in the harbor. The three moons as well as the satellites – Oma, Tira, and Sina's shining violet pearl – tugged hard at the oceans. The tides would be worse still when the final satellite, Para, rose.

When that would be, Taigan had no answer, though the chatter among the Tai Mora back in Anjoliaa indicated that their stargazers felt its rise was imminent. All of the stories and legends and texts from the breaking of the world – even the mosaic at the top of the Dhai's Temple of Oma – showed a brief period in which all the satellites would enter the sky. That was the time of the worldbreaking. And here he was, wandering about without a worldbreaker. He had expected far more dramatic things to happen during this momentous time, but without a proper worldbreaker to direct the satellites' power through one of the great transference engines spoken of in the ancient texts, it was just more of the same: war, famine, disease, genocide, drinking, fucking.

Dull as old boots.

The bustling harbor had but one public tavern – a holdover from the days of the Dhai when the country was underpopulated. Taigan's desire for a bath outweighed his desire to avoid the press of people. His new sex organs had only lately appeared, and he had changed the way he thought of himself, once again. He could not say he preferred one set of genitals over another, or a full beard over downy fuzz, or the various rages and flushes that came with the surge of new chemicals in his body. It was all set dressing, to him, just his body, ever in flux. But the new organs were tender, and could use a soak.

Taigan pushed into the common room and sized up its clientele in a glance. The Tai Mora were fanatical dealers in flesh; Taigan found that oddly comforting. He knew the rules of flesh. A mix of mostly Dorinah, but some Dhai, had been marked and put into service to their Tai Mora masters.

Two such slaves served drinks at the battered length of the bar. They wore red collars, which bore misty tails of Oma's breath; some warded piece of chattel management, likely. How odd, Taigan thought, that the Tai Mora Kai, the Empress, had chosen to keep some of the Dhai in service instead of murdering them. Perhaps murdering the last few Dhai didn't matter anymore, as the Tai Mora's world had already disintegrated behind them. What a kindness, then, if Taigan chose to burn down the tavern after he left it. Do them all a favor.

As he finished paying for a room and a bath, two raised voices caught his attention. A stooped Dhai boy exchanged a few words with an older, elegantly dressed man, who was likely Tai Mora. The boy was most certainly a slave, though he wore no collar, and should have known better than to raise his voice in mixed company. The older man hit him. The boy cringed, apologized, and limped out the door as the elder yelled about obedience. It reminded Taigan of his own youth. His frustrated mentor. Like that boy, Taigan had to adjust to a different fate than the one he had desired. At least, over the last few hundred years, that fate had kept him busy.

The young man's gait reminded Taigan of someone. Taigan had lived so long that faces often blurred into one another; it didn't help that all the Dhai looked alike to him. Even the old man was familiar.

Taigan settled into his room – he had requested a single, and paid exorbitantly for it – then enjoyed his bath in the bathing house at the rear of the tavern while the little Dhai slaves laundered his clothes.

As he was getting out of the bath, the boy with the

stooped gait entered, carrying fresh towels. The boy averted his gaze as he drew the water in a nearby tub – most likely for his master.

Taigan scrutinized him. The boy was pretty, though he certainly would have been prettier if he put on some weight and had a few days' rest. Dark circles pooled beneath his eyes, and his hair was lanky and unwashed. The boy noted Taigan staring, and peeked back at him. His eyes widened.

"I was *right*," the boy said. "It *is* you. I knew it. I told Dasai I'd run his bath early, and see if you were still here. To make sure it was you."

"I know your face," Taigan said. "Why is that?"

"Are you *serious*?" the boy whispered, switching to Saiduan. "How could you not remember me? I begged you to take me to Saiduan, to teach me how to fight. You took Lilia instead. And… and *you saved my life*. You don't remember that?"

It came to Taigan, then, that face. "You're Rohinmey," Taigan said, "the novice from Oma's Temple. The one who can see through hazing wards." Taigan laughed at the memory of the boy scattering yams and rice all over the floor when they first met. "That was a strange year. I suppose I'll run into more of you as I head south. You Dhai have a strange way of surviving."

"You're warded? But I can see–"

Taigan shrugged. "A simple glamor. I suppose it's a type of hazing ward. I admit I was uncertain whether those with your gift could penetrate them. A good lesson. I will take precautions among very gifted parajistas like you. Or perhaps simply annoying ones."

"How are you alive?"

"I could ask the same of you."

"What happened to Lilia? Did you take her to Fasia's Point? Or Saiduan? Did you leave her in Saiduan?"

"To... where?"

"She hoped to find her mother at Fasia's Point. It was in the Woodlands, along the sea... The symbol? Oh, it doesn't matter. It was... a long time ago. I was hoping maybe she got out, before... all this. But the Tai Mora are there now. They've unearthed a great temple near Fasia's Point. Or, rather, pulled one up from the sea."

"Ah, yes. I remember a trek through the woodlands, to some cocooned forest that stank of the ocean. I caught up with her properly soon after, but she became more trouble than she was worth."

"Where is she now?"

"I have no idea."

"What did you do with her?"

"That's a very sordid tale. Don't you belong to someone? Surely you have more pressing concerns. Like your own survival. Or your death? I could kill you if you wish. I'm here to murder a great many people."

The boy's face darkened. Poor little Dhai. "No," Roh said. "I intend to live. I'm traveling to Oma's Temple. I told them I can work the transference engines, the ones that help close the way between the worlds."

Taigan started. "What's this? You think you're some worldbreaker? I can assure you that you aren't."

"I told you, we found out how to use the temples, in Saiduan."

Taigan rolled his eyes. "There's no worldbreaker. No guide to show us how to close the seams between things.

We have only ourselves, now, and our choices."

"I told you, I found–"

"Good for you. And where is that find of yours, *now*?"

Roh's face flushed. He bent his head.

"That's what I thought." Taigan found the optimism of slaves wearying. "All lost or taken or destroyed. You know what I wanted to be when I aged? A conqueror. And you, what did you want to be? You wanted to change your fate, yes, I remember. You wanted to be a sanisi. We can't all get what we'd like. We must act with what we've been given. I failed. You failed. Everyone failed. Might as well enjoy ourselves."

"It's not too late. You think once the Tai Mora have access to the power of the transference engines inside the temples that all they can do is close the ways between the worlds? The power they could unleash is far worse than that. They could… break the world. Sink continents."

"Maybe the world needs breaking," Taigan said.

The door opened, and the old Tai Mora man who'd been arguing with the boy entered. Roh turned his gaze to the floor, and Taigan reached for a towel. The old man gave them both a once-over, then barked at Roh to check the bath water, which was nearly overflowing.

"You should be better to the boy," Taigan said, in Tai Mora. "These pretty little cannibals have no experience with servitude."

The old man peered at Taigan, and for a moment he wondered if the man could see through the glamor, but no: he was a sinajista. Taigan could sense that.

"Best he get used to it, then," the old man said. "As should you. Aaldia is next, you know, once we finish with the Dorinah."

"What a relief," Taigan said. "We've gotten so tired of self-rule."

The old man's shocked look made Taigan smile. Taigan reached forward, hand poised to snap the old man's neck.

Roh threw himself between them. "No!" he cried.

Taigan laughed. "They have you cowed already," he said, in Saiduan, and took up his coat. "If you think that old man's status will protect you, you're sorely wrong. All of you are going to die. By my hand or some other."

The old man barked at Roh again, but Taigan was already in the hall. He went upstairs to wait for his laundry. What fools these Dhai were. What a fool he was, to be here to witness it.

He sat on the edge of his bed and gazed at the street below. Why *was* he here? To kill and maim, certainly, because it sounded like a fine way to spend the end of the world. But what if the boy was right? What if there was still a way forward that didn't end in destruction? Taigan had been told his whole life that he was special, gifted or cursed; that his inability to die and Oma's blessing were meant for some greater purpose. But that had come to nothing. He was just an assassin, a sanisi, like any other. If anything, he was simply an abomination, a random result of an infinite number of dice rolls thrown by the gods.

Without Maralah to tug him about as that old man pulled the boy, he had become shiftless. Indecisive. He could not die. Alcohol did not affect him. Poisons worked their way through his system cleanly and efficiently. He had no choice but to live. Maybe he hoped that if he killed enough Tai Mora, one of them would figure out how to kill *him*.

Encountering the boy had made him question too much. Killing was such an easy solution. He could have snapped that old man's neck and the boy would have been free. But then what? Then what, indeed. It was what he asked himself, every day.

Taigan called for his laundry. He pulled on the still-wet small clothes and exited the tavern the way he had come. Lashing out at the old man had been foolish. That man could summon a patrol, or worse, and Taigan had spent enough of his years inside prisons – hacked and slashed and murdered over and over – that he did not relish the thought of going back quite yet, not when he had just arrived.

He moved through the press of people: sweat-slick stevedores, a few Aaldian merchants collecting exorbitant sums for moldering sacks of grain, and above all, the watchful eye of self-styled Tai Mora "guardians", an armed and usually gifted force that he had seen in Anjoliaa as well, all clad in long blue tunics, black armbands, and soft bearskin boots. These were different than the soldiers, something new the Tai Mora had created for policing civilian spaces. The guardians were concentrated at the harbor gates, hands folded over infused weapons, which glowed blue, green, and violet. No omajista-infused weapons, Taigan noted.

As he came into the shadow of the great harbor gates, its massive stones bound by living ropes of blue-green vines, a scream sounded behind him.

Taigan stepped back, reflexively. A body tumbled from the sky. It thunked against one of the bulging vines above and landed ten paces ahead of Taigan, nearly crushing one of the guardians. The body came to rest with an odious sound of burst melon, limbs splayed, limp as a discarded marionette.

The body drew the attention of nearby guardians and numerous gawkers, perhaps some hoping to steal a trifle thrown free of the corpse, others just morbidly curious.

Taigan took advantage of the distraction to pass unmolested through the massive bonsa wood gates. He tilted his head up as he did, and saw that bodies in various states of decay swung from great cages hung on either side of the archway. Tatters of flesh still clung to some of the oldest bones. Fresher bodies teemed with flies. The constant sea wind blew away the stench of them. One body lay pressed with its face to the bottom of a cage, eyeball bulging at him. Just skin over bone, most of the hair gone, mouth stretched wide and silent. As he watched, the eyelid fluttered, blinked.

Taigan trailed his hand over a bit of the twining infused tendrils etched into the face of the doors, which also bore charred scars from the Tai Mora assault. The arch of the gateway soared above him, three hundred paces high, testament to some other civilization, certainly predating the Dhai. The infused tendrils glowed faintly green, and bore an inscription that read, in Dhai: *All who receive entrance are welcome*, which Taigan found absurdly funny as the bodies above rattled in the wind.

Coming through the other side of the thick walls, which were easily thirty paces or more thick, the babbling of the harbor-goers receding, he wondered if he should be offering his services to these industrious people instead of simply killing them. But did that make him any different than the boy, seeking a master to give him purpose?

He was so very tired of losing.

"If you live long enough," his mentor had told him when he was a child, "all the worst this world has to offer will happen to you. But live long enough, and all the good things will happen, too."

If only, Taigan thought. If only.

The sky seethed. Taigan pulled his hat low over his eyes, and entered the kingdom of Tai Mora, still uncertain of his destination, but anticipating a delightfully tumultuous journey.

2

Kirana Javia Garika, Kai of the Tai Mora, Empress of the Known Worlds, and Founder of Novoso Mora had won her decade-long campaign to overtake the mirrored land and bring all but a fraction of her people to safety. She was the most feared sentient being across dozens of worlds.

She had expected that rising to such prominence would make her more cheerful. Instead, it left her anxious and irritable, plagued by dreams of burning worlds that tore away from the blank black canvas of the universe like charred paper, revealing her wife's face, a face whose flesh bubbled and sloughed away, ruined by the force of a searing volcanic wind billowing from an amber sky.

She shivered now under the double helix of the suns, which sat directly overhead. Kirana squinted and raised her hand to her eyes, peering at the great shivering mass her jistas had raised from the bottom of the ocean just off the northeastern coast of what had once been Dhai.

She stood on a narrow sandbar, five hundred paces from the proper shoreline, joined by one of her stargazing omajistas, Suari, and Madah, her intelligence officer. She had tried to keep the number of people who knew about this operation limited, but there were spies in her temples.

Every month her intelligence forces found another traitor and made an example by hanging their bodies up on the harbor gates for all to see. But it had done no good. It wasn't only captive Dhai and Dorinah who had turned on her, which made it worse. The hungrier her people became, the crueler the choices they had to make here, the more her own people sided with those they had conquered. It was the very worst betrayal, to have saved them all from annihilation only to lose their loyalty in the aftermath.

Cold, briny wind buffeted the sandbar, nearly taking Madah, the slightest of them, off her feet. Madah staggered and found her footing, bracing herself by digging her heel into the sandbar. Two scholars and another stargazer huddled nearby, just to the left of the wink that Suari had opened to bring them all here from Oma's temple.

It had been several days since they dredged the thing onto the sandbar, and Kirana was still not used to the sight of it. What had once presumably been a true temple with stone facades and sweeping arches and domes, tamed into being by generations of Dhai jistas, had shed its non-organic trappings, laying bare what she could only call the monstrous pulsing heart of some mythical beast. Like a living leviathan dragged from the deep, the mass of it towered over them, waves breaking around its gooey, barnacled base. The great beast was bound in large, tirajista-trained vines that served as scaffolding for a dozen or more soldiers and tirajistas who worked along the skin of the pulsing mass, seeking an entrance. They had been at it nearly three days, and Kirana had yet to see any progress.

"You've yet to convince me this *isn't* a sea creature," Kirana said, raising her voice above the wind.

"Even a sea creature would have an orifice," Madah said, hugging her arms to her chest. She wore a heavy bearskin coat, and sea foam collected around her slender ankles. "Maybe it's some embryo, going to hatch a beast."

"Five temples," Suari said quickly, consulting a parchment containing diagrams he had laboriously traced from the book they still called *The Saiduan Tome* because they had yet to decipher its actual title – or anything else written in it. The little Saiduan ataisa who had washed up with it had remained close-lipped about its origin and contents, despite the most persuasive efforts of Kirana's interrogators.

The wind caught at the edge of the paper, nearly tearing it in two. Suari clutched it to his chest, frantically rolling it back under his robe. "The symbols on the map in the Assembly Chamber match the locations of each temple. The trefoil with the tail marked this spot. This has to be the primary engine. The one where the power of the satellites is concentrated, the one a worldbreaker can use to manipulate the heavens. We are still working out the precise language in the book, of course, but the symbolism is clear. This temple, on the original map in the book, is sitting on a whole continent, in precisely this location, relative to the rest."

Kirana waved at him. "Yes, I've heard this," she said. "Logically you're correct, but look at the fucking thing."

"I understand," Suari said. "I'm sure once we're inside–"

"And when will that be?" Kirana asked.

"I'm afraid, I still... we still have no timeline, I mean, unless you, Madah–"

"Don't dump this on me," Madah said. She turned to

Kirana. "We got it up from the bottom. Suari and his scholars said they'd know what to do with it after that. This has got to be it, because there's nothing else down there."

"So it's either what we're looking for, or what we're looking for doesn't exist," Kirana said.

"Precisely," Suari said, as if she had said something particularly insightful.

Not for the first time, Kirana wished she had left him behind, and raised up some other omajista with the knowledge necessary to navigate this moment. Too late to start over, alas.

Everyone who could be evacuated from her world had been, in the days after she took Oma's Temple and obliterated what remained of the free Dhai in the valley. The few who could not cross over to this world because their doubles still lived on Raisa had to be moved to a secondary world, one that wasn't disintegrating quite as quickly. Those displaced souls included her own wife, Yisaoh, and their child, Tasia. It was a bitter reality, a decision that wrecked her heart and her ego, and it kept her up at night, after the nightmares roused her. Where could she move them next? For how much longer?

Patrol after patrol had spent the last year murdering Dhai in the valley and in the Woodland. They arrived with hundreds of bodies, at first. Then dozens. Then one or two a week, until Kirana feared the Dhai survivors had left the continent entirely, taking the shadow versions of her wife and child with them. She sent her patrols to the east and south. Someone had to know where this world's Yisaoh and Tasia were. She had put an exorbitant price on the heads of both.

Finding this beast of a temple had been easy, comparatively. The logistics of moving it and keeping it intact, far more difficult. But Madah was good with logistics. She, at least, was worth the trouble. The lands of Dorinah and Dhai were at capacity, with more people coming through each day, and feeding them all and carting away their waste was a logistical battle. Madah had dumped the last few waves of refugees from their world into Saiduan, but they had little knowledge of local flora and fauna, and the land was not fertile enough for intense agriculture. Anything forced from the soil by tirajistas was of notoriously poor quality, devoid of nutrients, like eating sawdust. It filled the belly, but the body wasted. Kirana had brought them all a very long way only to face the reality that another wave of Tai Mora would be dead before the spring crops matured.

Kirana rubbed her fingers, still bearing the sooty texture of the air in the secondary world where her wife and child remained with a limited force, sealed up in a crumbling fortress along the equator, the last place there with a somewhat bearable atmosphere. That world was fading too, just as hers had. Soon Raisa would be the only nearby world safe for any of her people. Soon she would be out of options.

She raised her head to the sky again, peering past the suns to the steady, steely gaze of the satellites. "How much time do we really have to gain access to this thing?" she asked. "It took us months to break into the chambers under the other temples."

"Well, this, you see, here," Suari came up beside her, pulling out his parchment again; it crackled in the wind.

He pointed to a figure at the center of a dais marked with the trefoil with the tail, which the scholars had worked out as the symbol for the People's Temple. The figure at the center, they knew, was the Worldbreaker. Four additional marks ringing the Worldbreaker were color-coded, and presumably where a single jista who could draw on the power of each star was to place themselves relative to the central core. But there were two more figures with longer written explanations that still baffled her scholars. Suari pointed to the figure that held a raised hand to the outermost circle, presumably the skin of the temple. "This figure here is no doubt meant to be a Kai, one the temples recognize. Perhaps we could try–"

Kirana loosened her glove. "It didn't work on the others."

"It's worth an attempt," Suari said. "Perhaps it has been long enough, your power great enough now, unquestioned, that these beasts will recognize you as Kai."

Kirana sneered at the great pulsing blob. She tugged off her glove and walked to the edge of the sandbar where the creature had been beached. It gave off a distinct odor, this close: not unpleasant, but still sinister, promise of both birth and rot. She found a smooth stretch of skin, greenish-black, bare of barnacles, and pressed her hand to it.

The skin of the thing was moist and almost hot: fleshy and comforting, like pressing one's fingers into the mouth of a slick and welcoming womb. It pulsed beneath her, a slow, steady rhythm, like a heartbeat. She waited, pressing more firmly, but the skin of the thing remained unchanged, as did the beat of its body.

Kirana grimaced and wiped her hand on her trousers.

All she wanted to do was hold her wife. Cradle her young daughter. Create somewhere safe for them. And this is where it had led her.

"And it's impervious to all our weapons?" Kirana asked, turning back to Suari. "Even the infused ones? The ones we used at Liona, too?"

"It is," Madah said. "I even had the sinajistas bind together the same offensive spells we used at the harbor."

"You never answered my question," Kirana said to Suari. "How much time do we have?"

He shook his head. "Certainly fewer than one hundred days. The numbers in the Saiduan tome were much easier to translate than the words. A different script, and–"

"I'm aware," Kirana said. "I don't care for the details."

"As with all things to do with the satellites," Suari said, "there is a range. Once Oma enters the sky, Tira and Sina follow soon after. Para is due a year later. And once all four are visible, we have only a few hours to ensure our jistas are in place at all four temples. It's a narrow window in which they can harness all that power, but once they have grasped it, well... all signs we have deciphered thus far indicate that we may be able to draw on that power until Oma descends again. That's nearly twenty years of power. Imagine!"

"Oh, I have imagined it," Kirana said. She followed the girth of the beast up and up and up. She stood in its shadow; it was so tall that this close the thing blotted out the sky. "But what's most important to me is using that power to close the seams between this world and any others. I won't have anyone usurping me. That's our ultimate goal. Understood?"

"Of course, Kai," Suari said.

"This one doesn't like me either," Kirana said, dismissing the blob. "Take me back to the chamber beneath Oma's Temple. Walk me through that again. I want to begin choosing which jistas we assign to each temple."

"Yes," Suari said, "though I must remind you it's a bit... unstable. The temple, the beast at the heart of it, which I assume must be similar to this one, continues to be unimpressed with how we gained entrance."

"I don't care if I piss them off," Kirana said, "so long as I get what I want."

Suari put away his diagrams. He raised his arms and muttered a little omajista litany. The existing wink closed, and another snapped open. Orange light poured from the mouth of it, punctuated by the soft muttering of scholars. Kirana caught a glimpse of the scholars working on the other side in the Assembly Chamber of Oma's Temple, consulting airy illusions sketched in the air above the great black walnut circle of the center table.

"I'll stay and oversee this," Madah said. "Give it another hour and see if I can think of some other approaches."

"I want an update in this evening's daily report," Kirana said.

Suari walked to the edge of the wink and gestured for her to enter. The omajista on the other side was already making her way to the wink. Current protocol was to wait until an omajista was in place on both sides before stepping through. Having an omajista on each side had reduced the number of accidents due to Oma's fickle nature. However, it meant that the vast majority of her omajistas were constantly engaged in managing the flow of traffic from far-flung regions of her empire. It was not a popular use of them, according to the last few line commanders engaged in conflicts across the Saiduan continent and island of Grania, but it was hers to make. Transit of food stores and supplies was more important than mopping up resistance outside of Dhai.

The wink wavered. "Kai?" Suari said, "We're ready for you."

Kirana stepped through and into the Assembly Chamber of Oma's Temple. Suari followed her, and together they crossed the bustling room and descended the long tongue of the grand staircase, passing libraries full of researchers, stargazers, and parajistas, all sorting through the temple's many records in search of old plans, instructions, and diagrams like the ones that had told her about the hidden chambers beneath the temples, the ancient guts of the transference engines that the Dhai had called home for centuries.

The old records confirmed that Faith Ahya and Hahko, the Dhai founders, believed the temples were gods capable of channeling the power of the satellites. Kirana had always believed the ancient living holds of Saiduan and the temples of Dhai were magicked things created by sinajistas and tirajistas in some distant time, to capture the power of the satellites. But seeing the naked heart of them dredged up from the ocean floor made her wonder if they were older and more alien beings, harnessed by some old civilization for this purpose.

She broke into the foyer, Suari at her heels, and passed the great domed meeting room where the temple garrison went through their lessons in reading and arithmetic. She heard them chanting the equation for determining the trajectory of a projectile.

The guard at the basement entrance admitted her and Suari. She went past the bathing chambers and storage rooms to the second level of the holding cells. Most of the cells were full – the first level was where they kept their own troublesome people, those caught fighting or left locked up until they were sober enough to beg forgiveness for transgressions.

The second level was for the people who most assuredly were not theirs – Dhai who required further interrogation, a few suspected Saiduan spies, and at least half a dozen scouts from other worlds. The scouts were giving them the most trouble, because once they had been squeezed of information, all they could do with them was kill them and bury them in the pits. They were far too fervent about protecting their little rebel leader, a girl they called Light. And there was no reforming someone else's cultist.

The next level of guards let them through after confirming her ward and the week's password. She did not expect a brute attack this deep into the temple; it would be a clever double agent ruse, no doubt, hence the changing passwords.

They reached the very lowest level of the temple, or the level they had believed to be the lowest until consulting the Saiduan tome. On this level was a massive chamber filled to bursting with twisted tree roots. Kirana's scholars had found a plinth at the center of the twisting maze. The stone obelisk was carved with the symbol for Oma, and a tattered flame fly lantern lay nearby, as if someone had come down and… not come up again.

What work had been done on this level prior to her arrival was uncertain. Her stargazers and scientists had yet to reveal its purpose. She was far more interested in what lay *beneath* this level.

Ahead of her, a mound of rubble coated with a thick, oozing liquid lay piled up next to a gaping wound in the floor. Light beamed from below, emitted by dozens of flame fly lanterns.

Suari went on ahead of her, sweeping away the fluid on the floor with a searing tail of Oma's breath.

"I hope that stops, eventually," Kirana said.

"Vital fluid," Suari said. "The wounds keep leaking. They are difficult to keep open. Forcing ourselves into these chambers without a Kai…" He cleared his throat.

"Hopefully we won't need to much longer." She was tiring of his obsession with the temple's rejection of her title.

The months of jista assaults to penetrate this cavern – which they had found clearly marked in the Saiduan tome – had driven two jistas mad, and a cave-in had killed another. The temples were not meant to be hacked apart. They were nearly indestructible, which was why she ultimately turned the inhabitants to her cause instead of trying to take them by force. The Dhai could have locked themselves up in the temples and resisted her for years. Better to have traitors on the inside who would open the doors for her.

"I've put another ward on it," Suari said. He descended the ladder ahead of her.

The dusty air made her sneeze. As she mounted the ladder and started after him, the temple trembled again. A dollop of the gooey fluid tangled into her hair. She dropped the last foot to the floor and lifted her head.

The flame fly lanterns only revealed portions of the room, which was largely circular. The walls were the same warm green material that made up the skin of the temple. It was warmer here than above, and the walls throbbed like a beating heart, just like the blob on the sandbar. All along the circumference of the room, the skin of the temple had been scarred with raised symbols, elaborate characters that the scholars said was possibly a very old form of Dhai, but in the month since they had finally breached these levels of each temple, none had managed to decipher it.

Her scholars and stargazers clustered at the center of the room, where four bulbous plinths surrounded a low altar. With the light concentrated there from their lanterns, Kirana could see a great white webbing draping from the ceiling, connecting all the plinths to the temple itself.

Kirana approached the center of the chamber, walking across the spongy floor. A fat copy of the Saiduan tome sat at the center of the stone altar. One scholar stood over it, muttering. Kirana had already had two copies made and sent to scholars in Caisau and Anjoliaa, which were far faster journeys when one had access to omajistas and their powerful winks. Two more scholars worked at a chalkboard on the far side of the room, writing out characters and equations.

All three scholars lifted their gazes from their work and stared at her like animals spotted by a predator.

"Kai," said Himsa, the eldest, sitting next to the book, her voice breathy and urgent, "we did not expect you this early in the day."

Kirana stepped up to the altar. As she did, it began to glow, blue-green, like some living fungus. She gazed at the great round face of it. At the center was the Dhai symbol for "Kai."

She could not help herself. She pressed her hand to the center of the altar. She was, of course, the wrong Kai. The altar did nothing, as it had done nothing the last dozen times she placed her hands on it.

"Have you chosen which jistas will be posted here?" Kirana asked.

Orhin, a tall and gawky older stargazer with a habit of tugging at one eyebrow, said, "We recommend the most powerful are posted to the People's Temple. The other chambers – here – we believe that so long as those who stand in the correct niches can call the correct star, that should be sufficient."

"I'd like more certainties and fewer qualifiers like 'should,'" Kirana said.

A young scholar called Talahina had moved away from the others, and stood in front of the plinth with Para's symbol at the base. She was a distant relative of Yisaoh's, and didn't often speak without being spoken to.

"What do you see?" Kirana asked her.

"I'm just… concerned," Talahina said. "I'm sure you have heard, we have just one hundred days, at maximum–"

"I know the timeline," Kirana said.

"If Almeysia had done her job correctly–" Suari began.

Kirana waved a hand. "She did her best to sabotage that plinth she found above, tangled in those roots. But it wasn't the lowest level, clearly. And she never would have gotten down here on her own. She would have needed

Ahkio, or our resources. Alemeysia was a distraction, at best, and a poor one. She failed in convincing the temple I was Kai. Let's leave that in the past."

"Perhaps you could let us speak to the ataisa again." Orhin did not meet Kirana's look as she said it, only stroked at his brow.

"We tried that," Kirana said. "Several times."

"It was some time ago," Himsa said. "Perhaps the ataisa has softened. If we tell hir how far we have come now, since we last spoke–"

It annoyed Kirana that Orhin used the Saiduan pronoun for the child, but nothing in Tai Mora fit what the Saiduan was. "You put far too much faith in a Saiduan slave. Have you no confidence in yourselves?"

"We are confident," Talahina blurted.

"What do you think, Suari?" Kirana asked.

"It could not hurt to show the ataisa what's on the sandbar," Suari said.

Kirana held out hand. "Give me a copy of the book."

Orhin snapped up the one he was consulting and handed it to Kirana. "Empress."

"Stay here and work," Kirana told Suari. "I have a meeting with my mother soon. I can visit the ataisa on the way up."

Kirana left them. She heard their voices behind her, low and urgent. Occasionally one of them would inform on another, hustle their way up to her quarters

The sinajista guard bowed to her. Kirana went up two more levels, to the proper gaol where she had kept the little ataisa who had brought her the Saiduan tome. Unwillingly, of course, but brought it all the same.

Inside, the two ungifted guards on duty played screes, a popular Dhai strategy game. They unlocked the cell she pointed to.

Kirana pulled up the wobbly three-legged stool and sat in the narrow slant of light that spilled into the cell from the doorway.

The ataisa was chained to the far wall, hands and feet given just enough chain so that ze could relieve hirself in a bucket in the corner, which was overflowing.

"I'll get them to empty that out," Kirana said. It had been several weeks since she last visited, as the smell nauseated her and she'd had far more important business to attend to. Kirana called to the guards, "Is ze eating?"

"Some bread, a bit of mashed yam," the heavier woman said.

"Water?"

"We have to make her. Won't do it on her own. Wants to waste away."

"Well, that won't do."

The ataisa did not flinch in the onslaught of light. Hir hair was matted, mostly on the left side, and what remained of hir tunic was in tatters. Hir body bore a curve of breast and a curl of cock; one of those born with a mix of sexual characteristics. Kirana had thought of the ataisa variously as a stubborn girl and an annoying boy, but settled into using ataisa because it's what her scholars used. Kirana had tried the more humane way to get the ataisa to divulge information, when her second, Gaiso, first delivered hir to the temple the year before. But the child had grown up in Saiduan. Saiduan made them tough.

"I came to tell you we dredged up the fifth temple,"

Kirana said. "The one central to the breaking of the world, as it's written in the book." She placed the book in her own lap, and rested her hands on top of it, palms down. "I understand your continued resolve. You crossed an ocean with this book. You understood its importance. But we are nearly at the end, here, and your silence buys neither us nor you anything, this far in the game."

Silence. Kirana wondered why she bothered. Perhaps the progress below had made her optimistic again.

"Your silence buys you nothing but more long days of darkness," Kirana said. "Help us. Give us the translation key to the Saiduan tome. Join us, and I'll get you a bath, proper clothes. You can go free, Luna. When we awaken the temples again and close the ways between the worlds, there will be nothing to fear from one another any longer."

Luna raised hir head. The feral look she gave Kirana chilled her, like looking into the face of a wild creature. Busting this ataisa down into hir most basic needs and wants was part of the exercise, but Kirana was always surprised at how easy it was to accomplish. Kirana had gotten information from far tougher people than this one by simply offering them a piece of clothing, a bath, a mango.

Kirana returned the stool to its place inside the doorway. She should send one of the scholars here, perhaps someone pretty and young, someone this ataisa could confide in. She tucked the book under her arm and beckoned the meaty guard over.

"Keep hir eating," Kirana said.

Keep eating, keep breathing, she thought, as she went back up through the temple, as if in a dream, an ascent from the very belly of the breathing beast that was Oma's Temple.

She paused on the landing that opened onto the foyer and pressed her hand to the smooth skin of the temple. "I am your true Kai," she murmured.

The beast's skin roiled beneath her. Kirana heard the distant drip of a water clock in one of the garrison offices. The ever-relentless advance of time.

One minute less. One hour less. One day less.

At the top of the stairs, she saw her mother, Javia.

Javia reached for her arm, and Kirana allowed her to take it. They stood with their bodies pressed close, and wandered out into the back gardens, neither saying a word. Kirana missed the family she had left behind; but she had her parents, at least, her cousins, friends, colleagues in arms. They had saved more than she dreamed possible.

As they came to a little stand of early blooming dandy flowers, her mother smiled and said, "Oh, how your brother loved dandy flower tea." Her voice quavered.

"It was peppermint tea," Kirana corrected, gently. Her mother had been making small mistakes more often since her arrival in this world. "It was father who loved the dandy flower."

"Ah, of course, of course," her mother said, patting at her hair. The style was a little different today: two plaited ropes instead of three. "Ahkio lost, and Yisaoh and the children…"

"Not Yisaoh. Or the children. Not yet."

"Are we doing the right thing, Kirana?"

"Right and wrong have no meaning here. There are shades of gray. Always more than two choices. Come, let's eat."

"Did we choose correctly?" Her mother gazed across the garden at a flickering rent in the sky. On the other side, a blazing amber wash. Little bits of ash and char rained over the fire river, localized as a cloud burst. A tea table stood up on a low platform that overlooked the vast chasm of the Fire River, below. Kirana set the book on the table, and manuevered her mother into one of the intricate iron chairs. She poured her mother a cup of the still steaming amber tea. Small tea biscuits lay on a plate at the center, ringed in raw fiddleheads and dandelion flowers. She suspected the biscuits would be dry and dusty, crawling with weevils, but she knew from long experience that dunking them into the tea for a few minutes would make them more or less palatable.

"The other worlds are dying," Kirana said, "or, at best, being transformed. There are no good choices." She sat across from her mother.

Her mother's gaze moved to the book. "Have you been praying?"

"No, it's the foreign book. The guide to how," she gestured at the temple, "all of this works. I was questioning the ataisa again."

Her mother pursed her mouth, as if tasting something sour. "You believe too much in the fist. You will get more flies with honey."

"I already tried coddling–"

"*Show* the child why we are here. What drove us. Convince that child as you convinced me. Love runs deeper than fear." She reached out and touched Kirana's hand. She had been more affectionate, since they came over. Perhaps Javia too understood how lucky they were to be alive at all. "You know that."

Kirana thought of Yisaoh, huffing in the detritus of a dying world. "I do."

Javia waggled her fingers. "We must grow their love, their loyalty. Start with this one."

"That ataisa isn't a flower you can make bloom with some huff of Tira's breath."

"Show the child, then," Javia repeated, and took up her tea in both hands. She sipped, winced. "I much preferred dandy flower."

Kirana said, "We are lucky to have the mint at all." Behind them, the temple sighed.

She lifted her gaze again to the heavens, waiting. Not long, now. Not long at all.

3

Lilia herded the children toward the thorn fence, picking her way through the tangled vines and roots smothering the path. She smelled the boars patrolling the thorn fence before she saw them, a musky, pungent odor that reminded her of another world, another time, before the worlds began to come together. The dozen or so children shrieked and collected around her. She bent and showed them how to fill a shallow dish with blood and feed it to the boars.

"They help protect our encampment," Lilia said, pressing the last few drops of her own blood into the dish.

She handed the bowl to Tasia, the young orphan who had clung to Lilia since the mad retreat from Asona Harbor the year before. Tasia stuck out her lower lip and regarded the yellow-eyed boars as if they were Tai Mora in disguise.

"Go on," Lilia said. The other children held their collective breaths.

Tasia took the bowl and thrust it toward the boars' mucus-crusted snouts. The boars greedily licked up the blood, snorting and squealing for their offspring. Half a dozen spotted piglets came trotting out of the nearby bushes. Tasia's eyes lit up with delight.

"They love it!" Tasia said. "Look at the babies!"

"The thorn fence keeps out the walking trees," Lilia said. She began to rise, painfully, and the little feral girl, Namia, turned her blind face to Lilia and offered a shoulder. Lilia thanked her and heaved herself up.

Lilia's mother once told her that nothing could cross through a thorn fence, but that was not true, and she did not repeat the lie to these children. The fence did help dissuade some of the worst of what the Woodland had to throw at them, and the boars sent up loud, squealing alarms when dangerous flora and fauna approached the Woodland camp that Lilia had founded in the aftermath of the retreat from the burning ruin of Kuallina.

Tasia had grown bolder over the last year. The children had an easier time adjusting to life in the woods than the adults. Lilia had knotted Tasia's hair with ribbons, a style preferred by the dajian refugees that Lilia had brought with her into the Woodland. Tasia tugged at one frayed white ribbon as she watched the hungry boars.

"Mother Lilia," Tasia said, and Lilia did not dissuade her from calling her that, because it seemed to placate her. Lilia knew what it was to miss one's mother. "Are we safe now?"

"Safer," Lilia said. She peered up at the massive cover of the trees, so thick that in the woods below they lived in perpetual twilight. Safer than we were, she thought, but safety and comfort were a lie, out here, a dream.

Lilia had kept the Dhai alive in exile far longer than should have been possible. She knew that. Her people knew that. Even cigarette-toting Yisaoh and smirking Meyna could not argue about Lilia's role in their survival.

Lilia knew the Woodland in a way that even Meyna did not, and using it to their advantage against the Tai Mora had been Lilia's idea from the very start. They only moved to a new area once the Tai Mora patrols had been over it. These days the Tai Mora concentrated their time to the south, scouring the foothills and craggy valleys around Mount Ahya. They were as safe in the north, here, as they ever would be. For a time.

"Why couldn't the boars protect Catori Mohrai?" Tasia asked, fingers sticky with blood.

Lilia tugged at Tasia's frayed ribbon and retied it. She took a few deep breaths to calm herself. Anxious panic often overwhelmed her during the strangest times. It had come more often the last few months. "They can protect us from enemies outside the fence," Lilia said, "but not enemies already inside."

"Are there a lot of enemies inside?" Tasia asked.

"I don't know," Lilia said, mindful of the other children.

"I thought we were safe in the Woodland," Tasia said, "safer than in the valley."

"We are, love." Fleeing to the Woodland had been their only option after the Tai Mora invasion. They had no access to Asona Harbor, and trying to climb over Mount Ahya and into Aaldia would have killed the old, the children – and the infirm, like Lilia, would never have managed it.

Even in the Woodland, Mohrai, the Kai's first Catori, never seemed to fully recover from her difficult pregnancy, and Yisaoh, with the loyalty of the Garika and the Badu clans, had a voice that grew stronger over the weeks and months instead of weaker. Meyna – parading around the young child she insisted was the chosen Kai – was in hale health. It was Mohrai they finally lost, and Lilia admitted that she sometimes dreamed it would be her own death next. Maybe all of them together, in one Tai Mora raid. The fear gripped her again; a racing of the heart, a sense of impending doom.

"Are you scared?" Tasia asked.

"No. Are you?" Lilia half-smiled at her own lie, because her guts roiled even as she breathed through the heart palpitations.

"Sometimes."

"We have each other," Lilia said. "I won't let anything happen to you."

A single tirajista, Salifa, stood a few paces distant, watchful for semi-sentient monstrosities from the woodland. She met Lilia's look, warning her that the conversation was being followed with great attention by the other children.

"We should go back," Salifa said. She wasn't much older than Lilia, only a novice when they fled Dhai and still not a proper Ora, but she bore an infused everpine weapon and carried herself like she had been born into the militia, puffing out her chest from the post at the fence. Her left eye sagged in its socket, gray and bleary; like the film of a rotten lizard's egg. She'd lost the eye to a bone tree not long ago, and it was still in the long process of regenerating; a possibility only with Tira in the sky. She wore a single white ribbon around her throat.

"Salifa is right," Lilia said. "You've spent enough time above ground today."

The children protested. Lilia herded them ahead, thunking her walking stick like some old woman. The children went before her, easily navigating the deliberate maze of trees and scrub that hid the entrance to what had become their semi-permanent settlement the last few months.

Lilia rubbed at her face with her soft, undersized left hand. A tirajista had cut the hand off and begun to regrow it the year before; there were a great many of them taking advantage of Tira. Lilia had been unable to grip anything due to a bad break and worse recovery. She had considered doing the same with her leg, but could not have afforded the time it took to heal. The hand was enough of an ordeal. The leg… the leg could wait until this was over.

Namia kept at Lilia's side, her ever-present shadow. Salifa, too, hung back, eying the children forging ahead as if they might sprout wings and fly away.

A rustling caught Lilia's attention, and she shrank away from the snapping violet tendril of a feeding lily. Salifa jumped between her and the lily, severing its trembling head neatly with her everpine sword.

"Li," Salifa said, "let me walk between you and the wood, here. The tirajistas haven't been through to clean it out this morning."

"It's all right," Lilia said. "I saw it."

But Salifa remained between her and the edge of the path, mouth forming a thin line. Lilia sighed.

"This is a dangerous place," Salifa said, "and not all of that danger is from the trees."

"Mohrai died eating a hasaen tuber. It's been known to happen."

"I knew this truce wouldn't last," Salifa said.

"If someone deliberately harmed Catori Mohrai, there's no proof of it. It's best we continue to work toward our goals. Who is Catori, or Kai, doesn't matter to the greater cause. You know that. I know that."

"Even with them all married to each other, they are still back-biting and snarling. I wish they were as easygoing as you, Li."

Lilia said nothing. Silence asked to be filled, and the people around her were always quick to fill it. The marriage of Mohrai, Meyna, and Yisaoh had been Lilia's idea, soon after all the fractious groups of surviving Dhai had come together in the Woodland: a difficult, frightening, and fractured time.

"It's the unity of their marriage that saved us," Lilia said. "The Tai Mora seek to fracture us. Remember that. Always. If anyone tries to tear us apart, you must ask why. Who does it serve?"

"I know, I know," Salifa said.

"It could very well have been a Tai Mora agent," Lilia said. The walking, and the conversation, made her wheeze. She slowed and tapped at the mahuan-laced water bulb in her pocket. Her fingers still trembled when she thought about eating raw mahuan instead of the powder, to ease her breathing, but that had nearly killed her. And only living people could get revenge. She often blamed her anxiety on the lack of raw mahuan.

"Surely you don't still think they have agents among us?"

"Why not?" Lilia said. "We certainly still have our own informants among *them*. Why couldn't the Tai Mora have done the same?"

"They didn't expect us to live this long," Salifa said, and the pride in her voice made Lilia wince. But it was the pride that Lilia had used to her own advantage. Salifa loved to feel part of something larger than herself, something important. So many of them did. It made them pliable, easy to manipulate.

Around the next bend, Avosta met them, hand perpetually on the hilt of his standard sword, dark eyes widening at Lilia's approach. He strode toward her, offering an arm though he knew she would not take it. Avosta was another of hers: a former member of Ghrasia Madah's militia, whose gaze often made her intensely uncomfortable. He looked upon her as a god, big-eyed and sometimes bashful.

But he was useful. Like Salifa.

Avosta was a stout man with a pockmarked face and the shadow of a mustache on his upper lip. His hair was knotted back in white ribbons, a style he had insisted she show him how to manage himself. The knotted white hair ribbons had become a symbol of loyalty to Lilia, a sign in their belief that she was divine, or perhaps Faith Ahya reborn... and she had not dissuaded them from that belief. It was among the many reasons the three married Catoris did not care much for her. But she couldn't take revenge on the Tai Mora alone. It required a long embrace with what she had made of herself.

"The children are below," he said. "There were two snapping lilies here. Are you all right?"

"We're fine, Avosta," Lilia said, sighing. "I was the one to tell you all how to spot the lilies, yes?"

Avosta put thumb to forehead, a gesture of respect. "Apologies, Li, I only meant–"

"I understand. Could you give Namia and me a moment to rest?"

"Certainly," Avosta said. "I came to tell you, however, that Caisa has arrived with the week's news."

"She's much earlier than expected."

"She says there have been major developments."

"No one following her?"

"Absolutely not. I give my word on that. I've trained our rangers very well."

"Escort her to my rooms. I'll speak to her after Catori Mohrai's funeral. I need to keep my head clear and focus on this."

"I will, yes." He bobbed his head, but did not move from her path. "Are you... certain you wish to stay here alone?"

"I'm happy to stay with you," Salifa said, good eye widening.

"I'll meet you both at the tables," Lilia said. "We're quite near the village now. I have Namia, and my own gift, and I'm the one who taught you both to navigate snapping lilies."

"You have been so ill, though," Avosta said, "it's been some time since you called Oma. I understand, of course, I just don't want something to suddenly–"

"I'm fine," Lilia said.

Avosta nodded once. "Of course. Apologies."

Salifa put thumb to forehead and followed after him, but both kept glancing back at her, as if Lilia might blow away on the wind.

Big drops of rain splashed against the thick foliage above. Fitting, Lilia thought, that Mohrai's funeral should begin with rain. She waited for Salifa and Avosta to disappear in the stir of others preparing for the funerary feast before she allowed herself a breath. Being some kind of infallible prophet was exhausting.

Beside her, Namia signed, "Noisy."

"I agree," Lilia said. "But they mean well."

Ahead, in the area cleared around the great trees for public events, funerary attendants raced to cover the open fires with waxed linen; it was too dangerous to build stoves above ground, especially this close to their refuge. But the dead did not wait on the weather. They came and went at their leisure; far too many and far too quickly, of late.

Lilia stepped beneath the welcoming arms of a great bonsa tree to avoid the rain, carefully balancing on a tree root to keep her feet out of the gathering puddles. The smell of roasting flesh permeated the air. Her stomach grumbled, tightening into a needy fist of hunger. It had been just four days since the last funeral. But the meals between the funerary feasts were grim affairs. They were all starving for calories by the time another of their number succumbed to disease, age, or starvation. It made it doubly worse, then, that so many of the newly dead were children.

Namia crouched next to her, blind face turned up to the dripping canopy. She huffed at something: the spicy scent of Tordinian tobacco.

"You done indoctrinating the youth?" Yisaoh asked. She came up behind Lilia; the stink of the cigarettes still gave her away. She had kept a small cache of them for "special" occasions.

"Celebrating?" Lilia asked, nodding at the cigarette.

"Mourning, clearly," Yisaoh said, taking a long drag.

"Are you going to speak at the funeral and tell everyone how much you loved Catori Mohrai as your own sister?"

"Mohrai was always a pain in the ass. Her and all of Clan Sorai, really. Meyna is worse, though. Bigger pain. Bigger ass."

"None of us are perfect."

·"I'll be happy to eat Mohrai's finger bones."

"I'm sure your responsibilities will be easier shared with just you and Meyna."

"Only the two of us?" Yisaoh chuckled. "And what about you, our third leg, with her three hundred little followers flouncing about here displaying their hair ribbons like war trophies."

"I never asked them to."

"I never asked the Tai Mora to take over the country," Yisaoh said. "And here we are. Listen, Meyna bedded Ahkio for years, him and half of clan Garika. All respect for that, but it means Meyna is a social climber with increasingly strong ties to what remains of Dhai, and she's the sort who'd murder us both where we stand, probably with smiles still on our faces."

"I have no experience of Meyna in that way," Lilia said, "but she has a keen sense for how to get what she wants from people. That's a useful skill. We both agreed on that."

"I'm watching you, Lilia, and your followers. So is Meyna. Just warning you about that."

Lilia smirked. She could not help it. She rested a hand on Namia's shoulder to ease the burden on her twisted leg. Namia leaned into her. "I'm not a threat to anyone," Lilia said. "I'm just a scullery drudge."

Yisaoh choked on cigarette smoke and burst into a fit of coughing. "That's... a wonderful joke," she wheezed.

A thump sounded in the canopy above. Patter of leaves.

Crackling branches. A single blue-black frog, big as Lilia's thumbnail, landed on the ground at her feet and burrowed into the loam. Snaking green tendrils wavered up from the detritus, in pursuit of it.

"Tira's tears," Yisaoh muttered, gazing up at the canopy.

"Maybe it will be a small swarm," Lilia said.

"I hate the Woodland."

They stood in silence a moment as a half-dozen more frogs tumbled from above. Lilia sighed and asked, "What is it you want, Yisaoh? I need to prepare for this speech."

"I want to know what you're going to say up there," Yisaoh said, "so I can prepare for the fallout if Meyna wants to eat your face off. You think it's me and her with the political headbutting, but it's you she hates. I'm family, painful as it may be for her to admit."

"I'll share a wholesome message about unity."

"You're a hungry little wolf."

"You're seeing the reflection of a dove in a teacup and thinking it's a snake."

Yisaoh laughed. "I haven't heard that one in quite some time. Your mother use that?"

"She did." Another frog landed on Lilia's shoe. One tangled into her hair, gripping tightly with its tiny feet. She brushed it away. "Oma's breath," Lilia said.

The patter of frogs grew louder. Namia snorted and pressed herself closer to the bonsa tree. Lilia did the same.

"Fire and fear, these frogs," Yisaoh said. "The crowd will take it for a bad omen."

"It's the season for it," Lilia said. "With all the warmer weather this spring, we'll see more of them. That's just the cycle of things."

The frogs continued to rain from above, trapping the three of them together under the spread of the bonsa. The frogs hopped across the forest floor, darting in the direction of the baleful eye of Oma. Whorls of snapping ground sage darted from their subterranean nests and dragged the little frogs back under the loam with them. Soon the frogs piled up nearly ankle high, moving like a great wave across the forest, interrupted occasionally by the burst of ground sage. The smell of sage filled the air, mixing with the scent of cooking flesh from the funerary feast.

"Meyna won't start it until this passes," Lilia said. She glanced over at Yisaoh, who had put out her cigarette but still gripped what remained of it. They had come to confide in one another, brought together by their shared experiences in Kuallina at the feast with Kirana, self-styled Kai of the Tai Mora, but Lilia knew better than to trust her completely. Yisaoh had nearly toppled the country by contesting the former Kai's rule.

"You know Meyna is pregnant again?" Lilia said.

"Of course she's pregnant again." Yisaoh spit a bit of stray, spicy tobacco onto the ground. It was immediately overwhelmed by a slurry of frogs, though the worst of the stampede was over. Only the occasional amphibian dove from the canopy now. "It's something she's incredibly good at."

The tide of frogs thinned on the ground. Lilia wiped a few of them off one shoulder, and untangled yet another from her hair.

"I hate this place," Yisaoh said. She kicked at a clump of frogs, scattering them ahead of a snarl of snapping sage.

"It won't be much longer," Lilia said. "One way or another."

"What are you going to tell them, Lilia?"

"What I always have," Lilia said. "That we are strongest when we work together. That there are some of us who understand that the best way to stop the Tai Mora is to strike back against them."

"Retaliating against them is suicide. You intend to march your little followers down into that valley and start killing people? No one here knows how to kill people, not really."

"Someone likely killed Mohrai," Lilia said, "and there are Dhai militia here who fought the Tai Mora next to Ahkio. There are plenty of murderers among us. More importantly, there are those driven to fight back, as I am. Those are the ones that will help me. I've been planning a strike against the Tai Mora for a very long time."

"Any retaliation just murders more of us."

"So will doing nothing."

"A better way to unite us would be asking your disciples to stop it with the white ribbons. And you could stop holding those religious meetings like you're some kind of prophet."

Lilia studied Yisaoh's long face. Yisaoh gazed out over the funeral preparations as the attendants shooed frogs off the tables and swept piles of the dead and dying frogs away from the main speaking area. Sooty smudges darkened the area under her eyes. Her unwashed hair was twisted into a greasy tangle, held in place by old hair picks.

"What are you so afraid of?" Lilia asked. "I don't want to be Catori."

"No, because then you'd have *real* responsibility," Yisaoh said. "I worry every day about all these blighted people. You don't. You see them as pieces on a board."

"Don't pretend you aren't ambitious, Yisaoh. We've known each other too long. You're just worried about Meyna's child being the legitimate heir to the title of Kai, and not one of yours. Consider Meyna's child yours anyway. You are married, and you are kin. It's the same."

"I hate Meyna. More every day."

"If the Tai Mora are going to come here for any of us, it won't be me. It will be you, or Meyna, or Meyna's child, Hasao."

"You certainly have a lot of little birds in those temples."

"You helped choose them," Lilia said. "I share all my reports with you. The Tai Mora need a Kai to access parts of the temple, the parts they believe will close the way between the worlds. That's why they keep coming. They won't stop until they take all three of you, trying to find out which is a legitimate heir the temples will acknowledge."

"Legitimate heir," Yisaoh said, grimacing. "Ahkio wasn't even a legitimate heir. If he was Javia's son, I'll eat my own arm."

"What matters is what the temples think," Lilia said.

"Divinity is lovely," Yisaoh said, "but so far I don't see anything bigger than us, just people like you using divinity to get ahead."

"There's something much bigger than us," Lilia said, pointing overhead. "The sky, and the satellites that inhabit it. If you have any doubt, the proof is there."

"And in the gift the sky gives you?" Yisaoh said.

"Yes," Lilia said, though she could not meet Yisaoh's look. Her stomach ached at the mere mention of her gift. If Yisaoh knew she wasn't gifted anymore, if any of them found out... Well, she could call on her beribboned supporters, she supposed. But how long would they support her if they knew she had burned herself out, that she was no Faith Ahya reborn, just a scullery drudge tangled up in events far larger than herself?

"Just don't mess this up," Yisaoh said. "I got Meyna calmed down, and you making declarations of divinity and power up there isn't going to help relations."

Yisaoh gestured to the Dhai assembling in the little gathering space above ground. It was a rare day that so many left the underground camp of old bladder traps connected by a maze of corridors.

"I don't care that they believe in you," Yisaoh said. "I'd like them to believe in *something*. But in turn, you need to believe in me, and Meyna, and you need to work with us, and go along with what we decide."

"That's fine," Lilia said. "I don't intend to come back from our retaliation."

"Suicide, then? You really intend to die, trying to hurt the Tai Mora? To keep them rooted here with all the other worlds invading?"

"If I die, I die," Lilia said. "If I end myself all this will go away, and I'll take some Tai Mora with me."

"Fool," Yisaoh said. "It won't go away. Only *you* will. It will all still be here, and you'll just be some martyr, a story, until that story dies with the rest of us."

"I've made my choice," Lilia said.

"Doing any real damage to the Tai Mora would take a miracle."

"It's Faith Ahya's ascendance day, Yisaoh," Lilia said, stepping away from the bonsa tree and toward the funerary tables, careful of the frogs. "It's a time for miracles."

4

Daorian, capital of the former empire of Dorinah, was falling, and Natanial found himself inordinately pleased to be a part of it. He wanted to wrap his hands around the throat of the Empress and squeeze the life out of her the way he had squeezed the life out of her daughter. He entertained this fantasy again while sitting on a stinking bear in a cool, drizzling rain while the siege commander yelled at him.

"Head out of your ass, Natanial!" Monshara yelled, smacking the flank of Natanial's bear with her sword as she worked her way down the line of mercenaries and regular soldiers. Monshara, sturdy as a bear herself, with a mane of hair to match, led the Tai Mora assault on Daorian. She rode up to the front where her six thousand soldiers stood in neat rows, armor a little worse for wear, hair knotted, all in desperate need of a wash.

Natanial scratched at his own scalp; he had shaved his head the week before after a breakout of lice among the squad he led. Most of the hundred or so mercenaries he commanded were from Tordin. Their numbers fluctuated depending on how violent their hangovers or how debilitating their gout. He had gathered them himself after King Saradyn's disappearance left a power void in Tordin. Civil war broke out within weeks of the collapse of Saradyn's army. Natanial did not care for any of the people making claims for the country, and left it in search of some nobler battle. The Tai Mora, it turned out, were recruiting fighters to topple Dorinah. Natanial had never liked Dorinah.

"She's chipper this morning," said his second, Otolyn, who sat on a scruffy bear at his right. She was a long, lean woman that most assumed was a man; she didn't correct them. Natanial had only realized it himself when she got to talking about babies of hers back in Tordin, buried in the same grave, all dug by her own hand. She had a good head, a good sword arm, and most importantly, a dry sense of humor.

"Every day is a new day to take down the wall," Natanial said. "Makes me all warm inside, too."

"Those sinajistas in there burned half a battalion last time."

"We're not here to be heroes."

"Here she goes," Otolyn said, gazing after Monshara. "We'll likely sit this one out."

Dawn was breaking; the satellite Sina winked at them, a purple blot along the northern horizon, blinkering there next to Oma and Tira. The double helix of the suns skimmed the east, warming the gently rolling hills which still bore charred skin from their razing the autumn before.

Tordin didn't have many jistas; Natanial didn't have a single one with him. The mercenary groups like his, spread out all across the rear of the assault, were there as a show of force, and a clean-up crew if the Tai Mora jistas ever breached the wall of the city of Daorian, which hadn't happened once in the two months Natanial had been making a living out here as a mercenary for the Tai Mora.

"There they go," Otolyn said.

Monshara's battalions marched toward the walls of Daorian. Two moved off to flank the left, and two more to flank the right. The main force came from the south. Natanial suspected they meant to hammer at the same stretch of the city wall that had occupied them in the previous foray. Hitting it every day meant the Dorinah had little time to shore it up between assaults.

He sat with Otolyn up on a small embankment, their bears snuffling side by side, enormous forked tongues sniffing the air as they chewed their cud. Behind them were his fighters, a bored lot composed mostly of snot-nosed young men, criminals of all sorts, and women fleeing bad marriages and boring farms back in Tordin.

A flicker of movement from the east drew Natanial's eye. As he turned, a force broke into his view, raising the bloody eye of Dorinah on their flags. He was so startled he thought for a moment they had come out of thin air. That was entirely possible during these strange times.

Natanial cursed. Monshara's forces were still engaged at the wall; they had not seen the stealth Dorinah line yet.

"That's a good thousand," Otolyn said, shifting in her saddle to crack her neck. The sound made Natanial's spine tingle.

"Five hundred, maybe," Natanial said. "It would be impossible to get more in by ship with the Tai Mora blocking the harbor."

"Well, they did. Maybe they have an omajista opening a wink?"

"Shit." He gazed up the hill at Monshara's support camp. Flags there were being raised hastily. A horn sounded. But in the heat of the battle below, no one heard them.

Otolyn yawned. "I could use a skirmish to stretch my legs," she said.

"I suppose we should earn our keep now and then," Natanial said. "Call for an arrow formation on my call."

Otolyn signaled the flag bearers to give the order. She followed it up with some enthusiastic shouting, which was one of the reasons she was Natanial's second. She loved a good show, just as he did. There was a collective hiss and mutter of leather and armor, a shifting of melee weapons and snort of bears.

Far across the field, the Dorinah soldiers – bearing long pikes and cudgels – pounded through the mud toward the Tai Mora. Among the tawny, dark-haired Dorinah faces he saw the darker cast and bare scalps of some outer islanders, and suspected these were a force that had been stationed offshore and delivered here very recently. As the force increased its pace, he knew his time for action was running out. He certainly hadn't come this far to simply witness the outcome.

The Dorinah brought down their pikes, intent on skewering the Tai Mora at the walls.

Natanial gave the order to charge directly into their flank.

Dogs were generally faster than bears over distance, but the Dorinah dogs had been running at pace since they landed on the shore. The Tordinian bears had yet to make their paces today. When the call came, the bears leaped forward, roaring.

Natanial urged his bear to the front of the formation. He hefted his ax. His fighters flared out behind him, keeping loosely to the arrow formation. It had been some time since they'd run one of these, but his formation leaders were all intact, and eager. He saw the anticipation on their faces. Grist for the heavens that churned above, crunching them all into fragments.

The Dorinah saw them move, too late. Their soldiers were already locked into their charge. They could not pivot without chaos. One young woman broke formation and was promptly impaled by the soldier behind her.

Natanial raised his ax. His bear leapt. It swatted the legs out from under the nearest dog.

Natanial's mercenaries tore into the flank of the Dorinah. All was a twisted mass of bodies and yelping dogs and bears and flailing women in silver-plated armor. Natanial swung the ax using quick, narrow strokes. The Dorinah weren't ready for close-quarter fighting yet; most had only their pikes. At this range, he could dispatch them quickly.

He tore through gaps in armor, splitting open an arm at the elbow, a neck along the collarbone.

The Dorinah were tough fighters. He had no qualms about cutting their dogs out of from under them. The great animals bit and snapped and snarled. He hacked into the jaw of one and it collapsed, taking its rider with it.

In the confusion, the riders bunched up, so close that many who left their mounts were held aloft by the crush of the others.

Natanial almost lost his seat, but was saved by the same press. He knocked the woman behind him with the butt of his ax to propel himself upright.

A short blade caught him in the back. Nipped shallowly between his shoulder blades. He twisted, catching the woman's arm. The blow rattled her. She lost her seat and the dagger, and plunged between his bear and her own mount, crushed in the mud and blood below.

The sea of riders began to thin as it broke.

Natanial rode toward the walls of Daorian, chopping at fleeing riders as he went. His mercenaries were already on the ground looting bodies.

He didn't see what hit him. The blow came from behind, hard enough to knock him clean from his mount. Natanial dropped into the churned-up soil, dazed.

The breath left his body.

He gasped, struggling for purchase.

A rider bore down on him, pike out. He rolled; the pike slipped past his head, so near he felt the breath of it as it rushed by.

Natanial clawed his way up. The rider turned and bore down again. Natanial stumbled among the bodies, looking for a weapon or a distraction. He spied the tip of a pike and yanked it out of the tangled ruin of a dog and rider.

He pivoted, shoving the pike into the muck behind him just as the rider came at him. She tried to pull away, too late.

The dog yelped, impaling itself on the pike.

The rider shot free, thumping into the ground just ahead of Natanial.

Natanial brought up the pike just as another melee of riders came at him. These were a mix of dog and bear riders. He noted the shiny Tai Mora armor, chitinous like the armor of beetles. The Tai Mora were in pursuit, hounding two Dorinah ahead of them – and directly at Natanial.

He stumbled over the woman he'd unseated just as she came up with a knife. Instead of him, she lashed out at the nearest rider, one of her own, and cut the dog's legs. The dog went down, taking the rest of the animals and riders down behind it.

The tangle of bodies and beasts roiled. One dog, riderless, took off in the direction of the woods. Two of the bears, one with a rider caught in a stirrup and hanging off its left side, ran after it.

The women who remained tussled on the ground. Tai Mora armor at such close quarters hindered movement, and one woman went down immediately under a Dorinah blade.

Natanial slogged toward the remaining Tai Mora, who were now fending off three less well-armed but still formidable Dorinah women. Behind him, his mercenaries were finishing their looting and already withdrawing. He should, too. What was one Tai Mora? There were enough of them.

But he had come here, after all, to murder Dorinah.

Best get to it.

He came up behind one of the Dorinah and swung hard, hacking into her neck. She jerked like a puppet. As she fell the Tai Mora woman met his look, and he realized it was Monshara, the Tai Mora general. Tai Mora did not wear any insignia marking their rank, but he knew her face; she yelled at him often enough.

One of the Dorinah rounded on him. He punched her. She reeled back into her colleague. Monshara dispatched both of them with her weapon.

Monshara stood with him in the bloody wreck of the bodies. They were both breathing hard. Sweat and blood caked her face. She had a bruise darkening one cheek.

"Call the retreat," Monshara said.

He saw her forces moving away from the wall. He thought the line of Dorinah broken, but he was uncertain of her losses.

Natanial found a loose mount, a bear, and rode back to his company where they were still picking among the bodies and killing any who were slow to die. There was no exchange of prisoners in Tai Mora.

"We're falling back," Natanial said.

Otolyn straightened from a body, shaking a silver ring from a severed finger. "Already?"

"Back to camp."

Otolyn grabbed at the head of a woman cloven almost in two. She carved at its skin even as the other fighters mounted up and headed back toward camp.

"Laine's balls, Otolyn, let it be," Natanial said.

Otolyn carved away more skin, making raw, bloody patches, revealing all the meat beneath. Then she stuffed the bloody head into her saddlebag and mounted up.

"War trophy," she said, grinning. "Lot of power and glory to be found on the field."

She rode away, leaving Natanial alone among the dead. He hesitated to go after her, as the grinning skull put him in mind of other trophies, like the ones he had collected for King Saradyn. All that death, for nothing. As all this would be, in the end: little of it mattered, in the great scheme of things. But he wanted so desperately for *something* to matter. Anything.

Perched deep among the dead, he gazed across the dirt and turf churned into mud, thick with blood.

The silence after battle wasn't truly silence at all; the dying often went on screaming and wailing, clutching at their own split bellies and spilled organs.

A woman lying ten paces from him tried to stuff the glistening mass of her intestines back into the hole in her gut. The viscera, a gleaming reveal of the interior of the body, a secret only to be disclosed in the dark of night, was vaguely sexual, and his belly clenched, tightened by the arousal of battle, the twin powers of life and death.

Someone began to sing, a prayer for the dying, her own aria, and that moved him to action. He nudged the bear with his heel. It ceased snuffling at the mangled body underneath its paws and lumbered back toward the staging camp, pausing only to caress the dying with its forked tongue.

5

The funeral guests were a wet, ragged group; only a few hundred of the thousand or so in their camp came topside for the funeral. Too many above ground at once was dangerous. Though the Tai Mora had swept this area before, they often sent out patrols of birds and rangers, and too many people drew both.

The rain continued all through Mohrai's funerary feast. Lilia sat with Namia, Salifa, Avosta, and a handful of other white-ribboned followers, pressed close to her mentor and fellow healer Emlee. Yisaoh and her family dined at the table opposite, and Lilia noticed that Yisaoh did seem to overly enjoy eating Mohrai's finger bones.

"She was skinny, that one," Emlee said, sucking the tiniest bit of marrow from a section of toe. Emlee hunched over the table, hands curled slightly with arthritis. Tirajistas treated the condition once a week, but could not stop the cause of the inflammation, just as they could not cure Lilia's asthma. Chronic conditions resisted Tira's embrace. The body rebelled.

"We're all skinny," Lilia said.

"Yisaoh going to speak?" Emlee asked, as Mohrai's closest cousin mounted the platform at the center of the gathering and began to recite from the Book of Oma.

"I don't think so," Lilia said. "The less Meyna notices her, the better, I suspect."

When he was finished, Mohrai's cousin called on Lilia to speak.

Lilia rose carefully from her seat. Emlee assisted her, and Namia tagged along behind her. A few beribboned Dhai stood when she did, and there was a little hush as Lilia made her way to the dais.

Rain soaked into Lilia's coat and seeped into her shoes. She took her time getting up onto the dais, and waited two long breaths before she spoke.

"On this," Lilia said, "the anniversary of Faith Ahya's ascendance and the death day of our own Mohrai Hona Sorai, I remind you that we've faced impossible odds before, guided by our divine Kai, fueled by our faith in the vision that Faith Ahya and Hahko had for our people as a strong, united force against the evils of war, oppression, and slavery. It is that faith that unites us. And it is that faith that will sustain us, and ultimately save us, in this dark time. Catori Mohrai knew that. I know that."

Namia leaned her cheek into Lilia's good hand. Lilia had shaved Namia's matted hair some time ago; the hair had grown back dark and straight. Braids kept it from tangling again. Half the girl's jaw hung lopsided, as if from some old blow to the face that never healed properly. What had been done to the girl was written on the scars and poor healing of her bones.

What Namia must have endured often came to Lilia in her dreams, only in her dreams it was not Namia it happened to, but Lilia. And then her dreams took her back and back, to the Seeker Sanctuary while one of the Seekers kicked and hit her with a large cane. Taigan's hands on her back. The rush of air around her as he pushed her from the cliff's edge. Down and down. When she woke, she would claw at her eyes, fearing they were gone, and find herself running her hands over the little pocked scars on her cheeks from the birds that had attacked her, thinking her dead.

Lilia smiled down at Namia. "They believe us broken," Lilia said. "But Namia here is not. I am not. You are not. *We* are not. Many of you have joined those sabotaging supply lines and food stores. Your efforts are appreciated. We may be but flies on their backsides, but enough flies can overpower even the greatest beast."

A ripple of beribboned heads raised their open hands high above their heads. Only a few at first; then a dozen, two dozen, more.

Lilia met Yisaoh's gaze; Yisaoh frowned up at her from the soggy feasting table, damp hair stuck to her cheeks. Yisaoh shook her head. Meyna sat across from Yisaoh, back turned from Lilia. She smiled as she conversed with one of her husbands, Hadaoh, arms wrapped around her eldest daughter, Mey-mey, almost five; and the child Ahkio had pronounced Li Kai, little Hasao, nearly two years old. Her other husband, Rhin, studied Lilia carefully, his long face turned down in a grim expression.

Lilia raised her hands. "Let us give thanks to Oma, for the life Mohrai has led, and the life each of us will be forging for ourselves in the days to come."

She led the group in a recitation from the Book of Oma, one of Ahkio's favorites, something he had bandied about Kuallina during their last days there.

It had the desired effect. Those who had not raised their hands joined her in the repetition of the words, the comforting embrace of the known. Even little Namia babbled beside her, humming the rhythm of the words, if not fully articulating them.

When it was over, Lilia limped back to her seat. Her hands trembled, but she fisted them tightly and firmed her mouth. A few of the refugees from the camps in Dorinah approached her, all beribboned, murmuring encouraging words.

She sat back with Emlee and Tasia. Tasia crawled into her lap as Meyna made her way up to the platform hand-in-hand with Hasao.

They ascended the hill together. Though still so young, it was clear Hasao was a relation to Ahkio; she had his deep eyes, the narrow chin, petite features and shiny, silky hair. Meyna must have been triumphant at that; she certainly pointed out the similarities often.

Meyna patted Hasao on the head, then reached into her own coat and took out a small hatchet.

A susurrus of concerned voices rippled through the crowd.

"This is my favorite tool," Meyna said. "Catori Mohrai and I argued often about it. She asked why I carried it, when we are a pacifist people. I told her it's useful for hacking out toxic plantlife. For cutting back the thorn fence. I've used it to enlarge our chambers, below ground. I've cut supple bows for little Hasao's small hands. Yes, it's a useful tool." Meyna lowered the hatchet and came to the front of the platform. Her wet tunic clung to her curvy form; her pregnancy was just beginning to show.

"But Catori Mohrai, and some others among us, they see a hatchet as a weapon, not a tool. They intend to use our greatest strength in the worst possible way. Yes, this hatchet is useful for many things, but it will not take down a bonsa tree. It's not meant for that. It won't carve through stone. You will never lose an infused weapon to it. It serves one purpose, and to use it otherwise would be an attempt to make it something it is not.

"*We* are like this hatchet. Sharp. Versatile. Adaptable. But all that goes away when we apply ourselves to an endeavor we were not designed for.

"Who are the Dhai? We are enduring. Loving. Peaceful. Intelligent. We understand that we must exist in balance with this world, not seek to bend it to our will. We know that our greatest strength is each other. Unity is our strength."

Meyna paused, gaze sweeping the crowd. "This is why I am welcoming Mohrai's cousins and child into my family."

Lilia nearly choked on her lukewarm tea.

Meyna tipped her head toward Lilia, and smiled. Such a broad, knowing smile.

Lilia turned to see Yisaoh's reaction, but Yisaoh was nowhere to be found. Not even a breath of smoke indicated where she might have gone.

Meyna continued, "You have spoken to me about the dangers of the Woodland. We all understood there would be challenges. We also knew it was temporary. While some seek to break us, to throw us into disorder, to muddy our purpose as a people, I have not forgotten who we are. It has been my honor, and Catori Mohrai's honor, to have spent these last few months finalizing our preparations to take the Dhai to a new homeland."

Audible gasps. A few cheers. Cold fear traveled up Lilia's spine.

Emlee leaned in and whispered to Lilia, "Did you know of this?"

"No," Lilia said.

Meyna's infuriating smirk quirked at the corner of her mouth. "This is why I urge continued patience and perseverance," Meyna said. "This is a not a time for rash actions and revenge, but reflection on how far we have come, and how much further we will go, together, in rebuilding the people of Dhai on a safer shore."

The murmurs grew louder: questions about where they were going, and how, and when.

But Meyna hushed them. "Now is not the time. Let us celebrate Mohrai's life today. Trust that Catori Yisaoh and I are bringing you to safety, true safety, on another shore, as Faith Ahya and Hahko brought their people to Dhai. We are not a place, my kin, we are a *people*."

Lilia's mind reeled. Cheers went up.

"To the Dhai people!" someone shouted, and the crowd took it up.

"To the undefeated Dhai!"

Lilia pushed out of her seat, head spinning. Abandon Dhai? Now, when she was so close to taking her revenge? Had Yisaoh known about this? And where in this world could Meyna possibly take them that would be safe? Lilia did not want to leave Dhai; that had never been the plan.

She took up her walking stick, and stumbled away from the feasting, ignoring the attention she drew from the ground for her abrupt exit. Let them see she was displeased.

Namia followed. Salifa got up to join her, and a handful of other beribboned guests, but Lilia waved them away. The optics of Lilia walking out with several hundred others holding high their ribboned heads could have been construed as actively hostile. She was fine with rudeness, but naked hostility when she did not know the full extent of Meyna's plan would do her no favors.

She and Namia descended below ground to their settlement via a painful ladder that Lilia had argued against from the first day, because it meant the old and infirm, like her, suffered needlessly going up and down it when they could have used a ramp. But she was overruled, as the ladders were easier to remove than a ramp. Mohrai and Meyna had focused more on keeping out invaders, without a care for creating a prison for many of their own people.

Lilia's leg ached as she traversed the cavernous underground system of tunnels connecting the bladder traps that went on for nearly two square miles, tucked just beneath the surface of the woodland. Her chest began to tighten with the stress and exercise, and she took a long swig from her mahuan-laced water bulb, hoping to stave off a wheezing fit. Lilia had found the giant subterranean puzzle of mummified traps a few weeks into the exile of the Dhai who had survived the Tai Mora invasions. It had been her idea to reverse the fangs on the dead traps in all but a few heavily monitored entrances, which prevented others from coming down. Over time, they had dug through the shallow wells between the traps, linking them into rooms, corridors, several kitchens, and even a massive gathering space.

She entered the series of rooms she shared with Emlee, Tasia, and Namia, all lit with flame fly lanterns. The flame flies came to life as she approached, disturbed by the heat and movement, giving her enough light to maneuver through the small spaces.

Two jistas had watch over her rooms, and put thumb to forehead as she passed. Both wore white ribbons around their necks. They were twin sisters, Mihina and Harina, long-legged young women dressed in long burlap tunics that made them look like bristling bags of firewood.

"Is everything all right?" asked Mihina, the one with the stronger jaw and the tendency to cock her head every time she asked a question.

"I'm fine. The weather has moved into my chest." She gave a raspy cough for good measure.

Inside Lilia's room, she kept a massive old map on top of a bulbous growth that served as a table. Back against the far wall was a trunk, three paces long and two paces tall. The jistas – Salifa, Mihina and Harina – knew about the bones and silvery green symbol that rested within, but no one else. She had told Emlee it was private, and locked it, just in case. The last thing she wanted was Tasia to begin digging around in it. The box had been set up over a week ago, and in the last day began emitting a strange odor. The room smelled of honey and dead birds.

As she entered, a slight figure stood up from the shadows. Lilia started, so suddenly she gasped to catch her breath. "Caisa!" Lilia said. "I'm so sorry. I completely forgot."

"It's all right," Caisa said, pulling back the hood of her coat.

Lilia pressed her hand to her chest, wheezing. She did

not want to take the mahuan in front of Caisa if she did not need to. "I'm sorry," Lilia said. "Please, yes, let's sit."

"Li?" Caisa said, and came to her side. "May I help you into a seat?"

Lilia shook her head, denying consent. "I wanted to have a look at the map." She coughed. Dug around for her mahuan mixture in her pocket. Only a few swallows left. She needed Emlee to prepare another batch. Lilia took a shallow swallow and motioned Caisa to the table.

The map was Salifa's work, a lovely rendition of Dhai all scratched out in violet ink on a great, pounded sheet of green paper. Lilia had marked each temple, including the sunken one, as well as known locations for the bulk of Kirana's forces: the harbor, the plateau outside Oma's Temple, Kuallina, and the pass where Liona had been. Red Xs dotting the foothills around Mount Ahya indicated where her small groups of rangers had successfully lured and abandoned Tai Mora scouting parties. The Catoris had liked that gambit because it involved no direct violence – they had lost just one of their own people in all that time, and him to a bone tree. It was the terrain that killed the Tai Mora, once the Dhai took them deep enough into the wood. Lilia had instructed her people not to touch one hair on those Tai Mora heads, even as screaming sentient trees popped off Tai Mora limbs and digested them.

Namia came up next to her. She made the sign for death, as if she could sense Lilia's thoughts.

"Not yet," Lilia said. She glanced at Caisa. "I'm sorry. We didn't expect a report this early."

"Is Catori Yisaoh coming?"

"I'm afraid she's indisposed. I'll relay the information to her."

"I came as quickly as I could," Caisa said. Caisa had been part of a refugee group from another temple. She was a lean parajista, freckled and high of forehead. A fringe hid much of the forehead, the glossy dark hair cut in a severe style that mirrored the grim look on Caisa's round face.

"What have they done now?" Lilia asked.

"The fifth temple has finally been raised," Caisa said.

"From the ocean? The whole thing?"

A nod. "It's just the... heart of it, though. It's like a temple with all the trappings of it taken off. Like a beached leviathan."

"What's inside?"

"They aren't able to penetrate it."

"They got into the other temples, though. Any movement there?"

Caisa shook her head. "The temples are still bleeding, where they forced their way through. They groan sometimes, rumble. They aren't happy about it."

"I wish they could do more than rumble. If they haven't gotten inside the fifth temple, then–"

"They've established where the jistas will be," Caisa said. She pulled a waxed cylinder from her coat. "May I?"

Lilia nodded.

Caisa unrolled a few pieces of parchment onto the table. Lilia wrinkled her nose at it. The Dhai did not make paper from the skins of animals or human beings, not like the Saiduan and Tai Mora. The barbarity of it still rankled Lilia.

"I have lists, here, of the jistas chosen for each temple," Caisa said, "for the niches. These are the four jistas of each time, plus a sort of... conduit: a central figure in each temple, that the others focus their power on."

Lilia read over the names, but only a few seemed familiar, like Suari, Kirana's closest jista. They were all Tai Mora. She pondered what they could do with this information. Assassinate one of them? A whole group of them? But surely Kirana would have others ready to take their places.

"Here is the realization," Caisa said. "You see this fifth temple? The arrangements of the jistas are different. This fifth temple, the central figure is thought to be a worldbreaker. That's the person who will wield the combined power of all five temples to close the ways between the worlds. And these other two... these are different, as well. Someone who can enter the temple, maybe a Kai? And another, just behind the Worldbreaker, that must step into this cocoon thing here. For what purpose, I don't know, but the fifth temple certainly requires more pieces."

"They still haven't fully translated the book?"

"No."

"That's something."

"We haven't either, though," Caisa said.

Lilia hesitated. "Caisa, has... has Catori Meyna or Catori Yisaoh spoken to you about our people leaving the country?"

"What? No!"

"Catori Meyna announced it today. I'm concerned that the Catoris are no longer especially interested in what the Tai Mora are doing unless it's directly impacting us here."

"But... it will impact us! If they can get the power of the satellites concentrated at this fifth temple, they could reach you, reach us! From anywhere. There's nowhere to go, when one force has that much power."

"Won't they just use it to close the ways between the worlds?"

"Everyone says that, but I know there's more to it. It's called a worldbreaker for a reason."

The box in the corner rattled. Lilia started. Caisa peered at it. "What's that?"

"Nothing," Lilia said.

"Perhaps you could talk to the Catoris," Caisa said. "I do think there's an opportunity here, before all the satellites enter the sky, to alter our position."

"I agree with you," Lilia said, "but it was difficult enough to get buy-in for an upcoming strike. And with Catori Mohrai dead... Catori Meyna is moving us in another direction."

Caisa cocked her head. "Li, when has anyone ever moved *you* in a direction you did not want to go in?"

"I'll speak to them," Lilia said, "after this offensive. We'll have a better idea then of how much the Tai Mora are shaken by our offense."

"I'll leave these here," Caisa said. "Oh, you should also know that I spotted tumbleterrors over the next rise. The funerary feast may be drawing them. I told one of your scouts who escorted me in, but I wanted to be sure you knew as well."

"Thank you, Caisa. Stay a bit in the guest quarters. Mihina!"

Mihina appeared quickly, as if she had been listening at the door. "Yes, Li?"

"Could you take Caisa to the guest quarters? Ensure she has something to eat and drink."

Mihina pressed thumb to forehead and gestured for Caisa to follow her.

As they left, Namia signed at Lilia, "Change? Plan?"

"No," Lilia said. "We don't know enough."

"Hurt," Namia signed.

"I know they hurt you," Lilia said. "They hurt me too. We'll get our revenge though, Namia. Very soon. Their encampment near Tira's Temple won't be protected during Tira's Festival, just as it was not last year. Whoever remains there for the festival, well. They will meet us."

"Soon," Namia signed.

"Yes, soon. Let's see if the feast is over." Lilia spared another look at the box, which remained still, then moved into the corridor.

She heard the patter of footsteps on the bare ground. Tasia barrelled toward her from around a bend in the tunnel, as if someone had lit a fire behind her. She beamed like a bear with a snaplilly. Lilia had never seen her look so ecstatic. Tasia bolted past Harina and hurled herself into Lilia's arms, nearly knocking her off her feet.

"What is it, love?" Lilia asked.

"The Kai has returned!" Tasia crowed.

Lilia had a moment of dissonance. "The... Kai? You mean the... Catoris? Meyna? Yisaoh?" Oma, Lilia thought, was *Mohrai* alive? With Oma in the sky and the world breaking apart, anything was possible.

"No, no!" Tasia pushed away and began hopping up and down, clapping her hands. "The Kai is here! The *real* Kai!"

A look of dread came over Harina's face. "No, no," she said, touching the white ribbon at her throat. "Tasia, you know Kai Ahkio is dead. Him, my cousins, nearly everyone at Oma's Temple–"

"He isn't!" Tasia insisted, and Emlee came around the bend in the tunnel and Lilia saw the truth in Emlee's face.

"Kai Ahkio is alive!" Tasia said. "We are saved now, Mother Lilia! Kai Ahkio has come to save us!"

"Emlee?" Lilia asked.

Emlee placed her hands on Tasia's head, to settle her so she didn't push Lilia over in her excitement. "There is indeed someone at the thorn fence," Emlee said, expression grave. "Someone who shares Kai Ahkio's face."

6

After a skirmish with the Dorinah, Natanial generally spent the evening drinking with Otolyn and his fighters. But he was less eager to do so this time. The weary lack of progress the last two months had taken its toll on him.

He spent the late afternoon counting up the dead and ensuring their belongings were wrapped to send back home. He visited those who had been wounded, and tended to the morale of the company. By the time he was done, it was dark, and he was thirsty and had a powerful desire to be left alone.

Natanial rode his dog into the little captive Dorinah village, Asaolina, that the Tai Mora had turned into their supply base. The tavern there was lit up like a festival square. Tai Mora crowded the street, laughing and drinking and playing games of chance. Many of the games he didn't recognize. While most Tai Mora had the tawny skin and slight features of Dhai, it had clearly not been a homogeneous country like that of the Dhai. The gathered soldiers spoke a dozen different languages, though all shared Tai Mora in common. The hair colors and textures, heights and body types and features, gave him the impression that the Tai Mora had conquered countries with a wide geographic scope on their own world. The more Tai Mora someone looked, the more likely they were to be someone in charge; that bit of petty blood rule was unchanged from places like Dorinah and Saiduan. Natanial had encountered it himself when he traveled from Aaldia to Tordin. Tordinians had always looked at him with unease and mistrust, a foreign man in a foreign land, no matter how exceptional his Tordinian or how many years he spent in their backward little country.

He found a seat at the bar in the raucous tavern, a smooth granite counter that put him in mind of better days. He ordered a beer from the barkeen, a Dorinah woman who looked like she would rather punch him than serve him. He could not blame her.

A Tai Mora group emerged from the back of the tavern, exiting from one of the private meeting rooms that had once been reserved for local magistrates and officials. Natanial recognized the Tai Mora generals, including Monshara. She was dressed down, no armor, just a long gray tunic and sturdy trousers. One of the few Tai Mora who retained a bit of plumpness in her face, she had the gray eyes and pale complexion of a Dorinah. Her broad nose and narrow jaw made it look like she was always staring down her nose at something that upset her. She had scrubbed away the filth and stink of the battlefield. Her hair was a mop of tangled black curls.

Natanial didn't acknowledge her, but she noticed him. She bid the other generals goodnight and came over to the bar, smelling of soap and leather. He stiffened, uncertain. Tai Mora had been known to praise with one hand and strangle with the other. The pay was good, yes, and he enjoyed being on the winning side, but the unpredictability of the Tai Mora was far worse than what he'd endured under King Saradyn back in Tordin.

"Put this man's drinks on my tab," Monshara said, in Dorinah, placing a hand on his shoulder. She was shorter and heavier than him by a good fifty pounds. Maybe she was getting all of her calories from beer. "You didn't have to step in today to cut off that force of Dorinah. I didn't order you."

He sipped his beer, studying her. Warm and flat, the beer made him grimace. He said, also in Dorinah, "You could dismiss the company for not obeying an order, if that's what you'd like."

"Certainly." Her breath smelled of beer, and her eyes were bright; he was uncertain how much she'd had to drink. "That's because there are very few smart soldiers. Smart soldiers become officers, in Tai Mora, and Aaldia, Tordin, certainly. Which begs the question… why are you just a boot-licking mercenary?"

"You have your own assassins," Natanial said. "They are better than I am. This was the next logical career path for me."

Monshara laughed. She climbed into the seat next to him and ordered herself a drink. "You speak very good Dorinah for a foreigner."

"I've spent a lot of time here."

"Working for Tordin?"

"Now and then."

"You knew King Saradyn?"

"In passing."

"Saradyn ever use jistas?"

"There aren't a good many in Tordin."

"Omajistas?"

"You recruiting?"

"Always." The barkeep brought her drink, and she took a long swallow. "You saw the mess out there. With an omajista we'd have won this campaign eight months ago."

"You do seem a bit… understaffed."

"We aren't a priority. The Empress has other projects. I've asked often for an omajista, but… well. She's preoccupied with her temples, and rooting out little Dhai spies. With an omajista you could open up a gate directly into Daorian."

"Surely you've tried that?"

"We did, a few months back, before you arrived. They had wards up. We think we've successfully removed the wards, but it means convincing my Empress that I won't waste an omajista this time around."

Natanial considered that. He took a long swallow from the beer. A few Tai Mora women began a rousing chorus of some bawdy song. They were not so different from Dorinah, some nights. "I wish you luck with that," Natanial said, "though I do enjoy taking your money until then."

Monshara laughed and thumped the table. "You Aaldians will outlast us all. You are Aaldian, aren't you? That's what your second says. You don't look it. Tordinian, certainly."

"I'm surprised the Tai Mora haven't turned their armies on Aaldia yet," Natanial said, moving the conversation away from his own parentage. He had no interest in commiserating with her about his past.

"No need," Monshara said. "There are no living temples there, like in Saiduan and Dhai, and there's no people on our side that mirror the Aaldians. You're unique to this world. Eliminating you would serve no purpose. The Empress is ever the pragmatist when it comes to genocide. Besides, the war for the world has been won. If she gives us a fucking omajista, I could be sitting on a fucking country estate right now. But she's gotten paranoid. She's walling herself in."

Natanial had spent much of his life fighting the Dorinah and the cruelties they had unleashed here and elsewhere in Tordin. Or perhaps he sensed that once this campaign was done, his usefulness to the Tai Mora would end. How to better position himself for the future? He chugged the rest of the beer and wiped his mouth with the back of his hand. Was he trying to be useful, or was he just selfish, and lonely?

"I know where to find an omajista," Natanial said, the words spilling out before he had time to consider it further. "He could be... persuaded to assist you, I think."

Monshara raised a brow. "And what do you want in return, mercenary?"

"It's been a long time since anyone asked me that. Anyone with the ability to deliver something other than money."

"Other than money? What kind of mercenary are you?"

"I like to work for the winners," Natanial said. "I bring you an omajista, and you keep my crew in work. I want to be close, to be useful. I want a future in the world that's coming into being. That's all."

"I can't guarantee she won't stab you in the back. She's done it to all of us often enough. That's me speaking frankly after a lot of fucking beer."

"It's all right," Natanial said, "I'm used to working with

intemperate tyrants." He asked for another beer to wash away the guilt roiling away in his gut.

He was already a little sorry. But not sorry enough.

7

Anavha laid out the metal letters of type, carefully following the simple styling set out on the proof pages of the pamphlets he was printing. He found Aaldian to be an intuitive language, but even so he was not fluent in it after a year in the country. Some of that may have been that he lived so far from the cities. He didn't get a lot of practice with language; he knew how to write it and read it better than he could speak it. The pamphlets were purely educational, covering local Aaldian politics. He enjoyed reading them as much as making them.

The slanting light of the double helix of the suns poured through the afternoon clouds and illuminated his work area beneath the great open windows. Aaldia was further south than Dorinah, and a little warmer this time of year. He enjoyed cool weather; the summer here had been too hot for him.

"Finished, love?" said Nusi as they ducked through the pale wooden doorway.

Anavha paused in his work to watch them; they were tall and lean, with a great hooked nose and long sloping forehead. Nusi had wrapped their hair up in a brilliant purple scarf. They flashed a smile at him, more a showing of teeth, a grimace, than a smile, really, but he had come to understand that it had the same meaning, among Aaldians.

Nusi ran their hand over his shoulder as they passed and kissed the top of his head. Their touch still made him shiver pleasantly with the memory of how they spent their nights. He tried to focus on the letters, but his mind was off again, warm and yearning in the dark.

Anavha had come here expecting fear. Dorinah was not fond of outsiders, and he assumed Aaldians wouldn't be either. But he knew the language, more or less, and more importantly, he knew how to play the game of spheres.

His last game still hung in the air in the sitting room, a tangle of threaded spheres he had generated himself using Oma, after much practice. He had lost his last game by putting one sphere into another in the incorrect order. The math involved still sometimes puzzled him. But he was good enough to earn respect during the local tournaments.

Distracted by thoughts of the game, Anavha dropped two of the heavy metal character symbols – one for air, the other for smile – and bent to retrieve them. As he did, a motion in the window caught his attention. He straightened.

There was a man outside, watching him.

He caught his breath. The man was tall and angular, with a prominent nose, strong square jaw and powerful forearms. He was bronze-skinned, and had shaved his thick auburn-brown hair; Anavha missed that hair.

Anavha knew him immediately, but blinked several times in shock, because the man was not supposed to be here.

"Was hoping to buy a pamphlet," Natanial said, walking

to the open window and leaning on the frame. He had an easy confidence about him, the confidence of a man who understood his body's strengths and knew exactly how to deploy them. "Heard you're out here preaching about the ills of Dorinah in these rags."

"How did you find me?" Anavha said.

"I admit, I thought you'd stay in the cities," Natanial said, "but I didn't count on you meeting someone like Nusi. I should have. I know their taste."

"You know Nusi?"

"You forget that I was trained as an assassin," Natanial said. "Finding people is something I excel at. Aaldia is also a fairly small country. There aren't many Aaldians who can speak Dorinah. Finding a moon-faced Dorinah boy out here was comparatively easy."

"I thought you agreed to leave me alone."

"I agreed to no such thing," Natanial said, but his eyelid twitched. "Anavha, I wanted to let it lie. I have for all this time. But we have… a cause that needs you."

"I can't imagine anything in Tordin–"

"I'm in Dorinah now," Natanial said, "working with the Tai Mora. They have nearly overcome the Empress of Dorinah in all but one city. Daorian is the last holdout."

"That doesn't have anything to do with me."

"We need an omajista to get us inside the walls. The Tai Mora can't spare one. There's some scheme in the temples that requires a good many of them. When they asked if I knew an omajista, well. There's only you, Anavha."

"I know people in Daorian," Anavha said. "Good people. Daolyn, and Zezili's sisters, her mother–"

"Fine upstanding people who cull and bind and abuse

half their people," Natanial said, "and turn Dhai into slaves."

"The Tai Mora have slaves," Anavha said. "They aren't any better."

"They are stronger," Natanial said. "They are going to win this. And we can be on the side of the winners."

"I guess I'm not surprised that you're so... mercenary," Anavha said.

"I'm practical," Natanial said. "It's how people like us survive."

"Us? We're not alike."

"We're more alike than you know," Natanial said. "The Empress of Dorinah is a creature, not fit for this world. If you had seen what I did... She has monsters inside those walls, monsters from some other world–"

"The Tai Mora are–"

"Not like this," Natanial said.

Anavha firmed his mouth. He wasn't seeing the difference, but Natanial had encountered the Empress of Dorinah's people, and he hadn't. Still, he didn't like it when people treated him like a child.

"I'm staying out of the war," Anavha said.

"You can come right back," Natanial said. "Oma is risen. You can pop back here any time you want by opening a gate – a wink, the Tai Mora call it. I am asking you for a single favor."

"Why do I owe you a favor?"

Natanial raised his brows.

"You were the one who told me that Zezili used me," Anavha said, "that she cut me off from other people so she'd be all I knew. So I would depend on her. But you did the same thing. You kept me prisoner, too. You aren't better."

"I…" Natanial began, and then seemed to think better of it. "We need an omajista. It's the only power they can't counter. They have no defense against you."

"You should go," Anavha said. "I don't want you here."

"Anavha?" Nusi came in from the kitchen, wiping their hands on their apron. "Who are you – oh."

Nusi's gaze met Natanial's, and Anavha saw a look pass between them that he knew only too well. Everyone loved Natanial, foolish though that may be. Had they been lovers?

"Natanial Thorne," Nusi said, and the breathless tone made Anavha's heart ache.

"It's lovely to see you, Nusi," Natanial said. "I admit, though, that I'm here for Anavha. If he will indulge me."

"He enjoys indulging others far too much."

"I know that," Natanial said.

"I'm right here!" Anavha said. "I can speak for myself."

"Can you now?" Natanial smirked. "That is indeed a new development."

"Come inside," Nusi urged. "I have never been known to turn away a weary traveler."

Anavha said, "He should go."

"Nonsense," Nusi insisted. "It's polite. I'll have one of the siblings make up a meal."

They went around to the door and opened it for Natanial. Anavha stood just behind Nusi, as if to shield himself from Natanial's presence. But it was a futile effort. As the door opened, Anavha had the same reaction to Natanial as he always had. Anavha wanted to curl up in his arms and ask for comfort and safety. It made him hate himself because it was a part of him he knew he could never release. He had a sudden, terrible urge to cut himself, an urge he had not had in months. Natanial was an uncontrollable force, and Anavha needed something he could control.

Nusi invited Natanial into the kitchen. Most of Nusi's siblings – the others living with them on the sprawling farm – were out working, but they called in their sibling Giska to help with a meal, and sent Anavha out to the cellar for some yams. He came back to the kitchen to find Nusi sitting at the big battered wood table, laughing uproariously with Natanial. Anavha stopped in the doorway, torn. Was it jealousy he felt? Or something worse?

He stepped beside Giska to help with the meal. Natanial suggested a card game with Nusi, but they demurred and asked instead to get an update on the Tai Mora assault in Dorinah.

"They will come here next, certainly," Nusi said. "Is that what they tell you?"

"They insist Aaldia is inconsequential," Natanial said. "If they want to expand, they will expand north into Saiduan. If they do work with Aaldia, it will be in making them a vassal state, but that's far down the line. They are suffering with their crops this year. They continue to need Aaldia's help to feed themselves. Aaldia has extensive rice and wheat fields. They need that. It's all very well and good to fight a war, but they are losing the peace, and they know it."

Anavha listened closely, but their conversation soon turned to old business. They talked of Nusi's childhood here, and one long glorious summer where Nusi sailed around the world after having their first child. Which brought the conversation back to why the Tai Mora hadn't chosen some other continent besides this one.

"They couldn't have settled in Hrollief?" Nusi said. "Or some eastern country? There are enough wild things there that they could have had the run of the place."

"There's something here they wanted," Natanial said, "something in those Dhai and Saiduan temples. I don't pretend to know what it is. But I know when to hedge my bets. For now, our paths align. I want the Dorinah gone. I want the Tai Mora to see my value. That's the only way to continue on."

"You hate the Dorinah so much," Nusi said, "that you would ask this of Anavha?"

"I hate tyranny of all sorts," Natanial insisted. "I honestly believed in what Saradyn was doing in Tordin, even if I did not approve of his methods. But the Dorinah... well."

Nusi put their long, strong fingers over his, but he pulled his hand away, and smiled thinly. "It was so long ago," Nusi said.

"They continue to do terrible things." He looked at Anavha. Anavha felt heat move up his face, and quickly turned his attention back to cutting up the yams. Had the Dorinah once done something terrible to Natanial?

When the food was finished, they sat at the table together: Nusi and Giska; Natanial and Anavha; and six of the eight siblings, all called in for supper. Natanial laughed and flirted with all of them, and Anavha found himself envious of Natanial's great confidence.

When the meal was done, Natanial helped clean up, and they all moved outside to enjoy the cool evening. Most of the siblings retired to their quarters, and Anavha went to bed as well, before Natanial could ask him more questions, leaving Natanial to argue his case with Nusi and Giska.

Anavha could just hear the murmur of their voices through the open window.

"He belongs to neither of us," Nusi said, voice rising. "When he came here, he was broken. In many ways, he still is. Dorinah twists all their people into one type of broken child or another."

Natanial answered; Anavha knew the tone of his voice, but he spoke too softly, and the tenor of the conversation dimmed.

Nusi came to bed several hours later. Anavha was still awake, staring at the ceiling. As Nusi undressed, they said, "I understand why he frightens you."

"He doesn't frighten you?"

"On the contrary," Nusi said, lifting the covers and pressing their warm, naked body to his. "I always have suspicions about Natanial's motives. You did not seem keen to join him. He talks of murdering your own people."

"I'm not, and yet…"

"Yes, Natanial has that effect on people," Nusi said, stroking his hair, and their voice was as warm as their body. He pressed closer to them. "If you leave us here, you forget all this peace."

"Just because Aaldia is at peace doesn't mean I am," he said. "Maybe I can learn things from them, and bring what I've learned back here."

"If they let you leave, after Daorian is fallen."

"I'm afraid," he said.

"Stay here, love," Nusi said, and they brushed his hair

with their long fingers. The high window was open, though it was cool, and he caught the scent of the fields, the loamy scent of manure and straw; he heard the lone cry of some plains cat, celebrating a meal. "You want me to stay?" he asked.

"What I want is unimportant. As is what Natanial wants. You came here to discover what *you* want. You have power, he is right. But that doesn't mean you're obligated to use it. You have no responsibility to anyone but yourself, and your community. And we are your community, now."

"It seems a shame not to use it," he said. "Oma won't be in the sky forever, will it? They say it will be ten, maybe twenty years. Then I won't be anyone at all anymore. I liked that, when I wasn't anyone special. Just someone… loved."

"Owned," Nusi said softly.

"Owned," he murmured. "I know it's wrong, I know you and Natanial don't like it, but I miss it. I miss other people telling me what to do. I hate having choices, Nusi. Just tell me to stay."

"You know I cannot."

"Then tell me to go."

Nusi laughed. "You miss the point of this exercise."

"I can't decide."

"Then sleep, love. Answers often come in sleep."

"I'm so afraid of the world," he said. "It's collapsing all around us. I want to hide."

"I know. We all do. But…" Nusi sighed. "The gods are not kind. They break the world when they do this dance. We've all known this day was coming. Now we must endure it."

"I don't know if I can... Should I just keep sitting here?"

"You keep trying to get me to make your decision."

"Sorry."

"I'm going to sleep now, Anavha. We'll talk about this over breakfast."

Nusi closed their eyes. Anavha lay watching the shadows move across their face, dimly illuminated by the outside perimeter lights. All this peace, all this quiet.

He lay next to Nusi for a long time, until Nusi's breath came regularly and they shifted away from him in the dark. Then he got up, quietly, and crept outside into the cool air.

Anavha sat on a large chair on the porch, watching the night flies sparkling across the fields. He pinched the inside of his arm, bringing pain, and with it, a sharper sense of the world, an awareness of being alive. Again, he had the urge to take a blade in his hand and cut away his worry and uncertainty, but instead he breathed deeply and closed his eyes. He had longed for control over his life. It was what led him to the cutting in the first place. And he *did* have control over his life now. Nusi did not bind him. He had his own small income from working on the journal. Natanial had made no show of force, and given no indication that he would haul Anavha away if he did not go freely. He did not think Natanial would kidnap him again, not now that he was free of Saradyn and the dream of Tordin.

Which left him here, in his own skin, alone, to make his own decisions. It was not as exhilarating as he'd always hoped. It was far more terrifying. If he chose wrong, he had only himself to blame for it.

A sharp flash lit up the sky, breaking the stillness. He squinted, but the lightning or tear had already vanished.

Out here, he could almost pretend the world was normal. Almost.

He went back inside and slept, fitfully, until the first gray tendrils of dawn woke him. Oma, Tira and Sina winked in the sky, static though the suns were not, their soft light blending to turn the sky a deeper shade of lavender.

Anavha got up before Nusi and made tea. He pulled on a short coat and went outside to see how the sheep had spent the night. He enjoyed living on a farm, enjoyed walking outside to see a long expanse of gold fields in every direction. Their nearest neighbors lived over the next hill, a two hour walk distant.

He went out to the sheep pen to let them loose to graze. The dogs outside the kennel raised their heads as he passed. He had feared them when he first came here, but they recognized each other as participants with the same goal: to protect the livestock.

Anavha opened the paddock and counted the sheep as they came out onto the meadow to feed. He stood up on the rail to get a better look, and something in the distance, on the other side of the large run, caught his eye.

He clambered down and made his way along the brush fence, running his hand along the exterior. He loved the feel of the fence. He had helped Giska and Nusi pull young saplings from the woods just south of here and wend them through the broken patch of fence to mend it.

An object in the distance that appeared to be a pile of rags and brush began to resolve itself into the form of a human being. Anavha came up short just fifty paces distant, staring long at the figure to see if it moved.

When it didn't, he crept closer.

The body was strangely serene. Only the absolute stillness and awkward twist to the torso and left leg made it seem unnatural. There were no footprints, no broken grasses leading to or from the body. Only the bent stems on which it rested.

Anavha gazed upward. The sky rippled ominously. He took a step away from the body, fearful more might tumble from this sky. This was not the first one he had seen. Nusi had discovered three in their fields over the last few months. The Tai Mora weren't the only people fleeing to this world anymore. To his mind, there was enough room for everyone, but was that really true?

He stood among the grass as flies circled the body. The clothing was foreign, the hairstyle strange. This was an alien person, a worldly invader. But he found he could summon up no hatred for them. If his world was dying, he would throw himself into the tears between his world and another, too.

The morning was cool, and he shivered, though from the cold or the body, he did not know. He gazed back at the house. From this distance, the old Aaldian house was like a ship on a great green plain. The Aaldians had such a love for the sea that it should not have surprised him that they built their houses with riggings on which plants could twine their way from the sod gardens that insulated the roofs. The house itself was half-buried in the ground, which protected it from windstorms and the great tornadic clouds that prowled the plains. Carved totems, like those on the prows of ships, bookended the house.

As the double helix of the suns rose over the house, Natanial stepped out onto the stone porch. It reminded

Anavha of the house in Tordin, when Anavha had opened the gate to Aaldia and turned back to see Natanial there, letting him choose his path. Maybe Natanial had not given him a choice at all. Anavha had thought journeying from Tordin would mean escaping the madness, but as long as the world was mad, it would intrude upon his life. Anavha had been fighting himself for so long that he didn't know what it would be like to fight other people. Maybe Natanial was right, and Anavha would only have to open a few gates, help mend the world in a small way, and then he could come home.

Natanial walked across the porch and followed the fence until he stood at Anavha's side.

"You're seeing more of them," Natanial said, nodding at the body.

"I don't want to destroy Dorinah," Anavha said. "It was, *is*, where my family lives. But this… this is what they are trying to stop, aren't they? The Tai Mora? They can protect us from this?"

"There are whole foreign armies of them in Dorinah," Natanial said, "pushing through the soft spaces between the worlds. It's one reason they want Daorian. It's a secure hold, with a good port. The Tai Mora can hold out against these other worlds far longer, in Daorian."

"They'll stop this, then?" Anavha said. "Nusi and Giska, here… we can save this place?"

"It's possible," Natanial said. "I want to keep you safe, Anavha. I want to keep everyone I care about safe, but to do that we need to align ourselves with the Tai Mora. The closer we are to them, the less likely we are to fall by their hand. You understand? It's why I stayed close to Saradyn, because there was no one in Tordin more powerful than him. And it's why I'm with the Tai Mora now."

"You can't really save me if something goes wrong, though."

"I can try."

The body remained inert. Flies crawled at the edges of the eyes. Anavha thought they would have burst, but the eyes were half-open, dull, with just a hint of wetness at the corners.

"Do you feel responsible for my decision?" Anavha asked.

"I always feel responsible," Natanial said.

"If I go with you, I could come back here at any moment. I won't make any promises, or accept any binding."

"I'm all right with that," Natanial said. "Come, let's tell them what you've decided."

Nusi waited for them on the porch, wiping their hands on an old dishrag, expression inscrutable.

"So you are going?" Nusi said.

"I will only be gone a little while," Anavha said. "I'm going to stop all the people falling from the sky. He says I can help."

Nusi opened their arms and embraced him. Anavha cried. He wanted to take it back, then, as he inhaled the scent of them. But he knew Nusi would disapprove if he made a promise and broke it. So he just cried, and then went to his room to pack his things.

When he returned to the porch, Nusi and Natanial were gazing at the sky. Great thunderheads roiled across the lavender expanse. Jagged lightning radiated from the largest of them. And there, to the north, just before the mountain range, a ragged line had opened, a great wound on the purple horizon through which a yellow fog emanated.

Nusi pulled Anavha close and kissed him. He lingered as long as he could, and then he felt a few drops of rain carried by the wind, and he was moving away, following after Natanial.

"Let's see if you're any better with opening those gates now," Natanial said, and gestured to a broad area of meadow well clear of the house.

Anavha held up his hands, because he found that it was easier to focus that way, and called on the power of Oma. He felt the breath of the satellite beneath his skin instantly, and his body was soon suffused in red tendrils of mist. He trembled a little with the pleasure and fear of it.

"Where are we going?" Anavha said. "Which part of Daorian? It needs to be somewhere I've been, somewhere I've seen."

"There's a village just outside," Natanial said, "Asaolina. You know it?"

"Yes."

"Bring us out on the hill overlooking it, there in the south. Less likely to be people there."

Anavha closed his eyes. He remembered Asaolina, because it was where Zezili liked to stop and rest if they were coming into Daorian too late at night. She would tell him it was too dangerous to bring a man into town after dark. They stayed at an inn there, the Copper Maidenhead, and he remembered the way the sheets smelled of lavender and old socks, and the light was always orange, because the flame flies in all the lanterns were dying. The memory overcame him, and for a moment he was back in that tavern, and Zezili had her hands around his throat as she straddled him. They were both covered in sweat, and his fear and desire mixed in that old, heady way it had every time she touched him.

Asaolina.

Anavha breathed in, pulling the power of Oma into his body and neatly knitting and binding it into the shape he needed. He released his breath, and a great spiraling eye opened in the air in front of him. As he exhaled, it continued to open, further and further, until Anavha could see the familiar tiled roofs of Asaolina on the other side.

Natanial whistled softly. "You've gotten much better," he said. His gaze turned up, to the boiling sky. "We best hurry."

Natanial stepped quickly through the gate, and Anavha followed.

Natanial saw Anavha stumble as he came out of the gate and onto a low hill outside Asaolina. Natanial caught him by the arm and hauled him up. Natanial turned to see what had tripped Anavha. As he did, light flashed across his vision. A massive black tear opened above the fields, not more than a few hundred paces away.

And an army fell out of the sky.

The gate closed.

Natanial shivered. This vision of the army lingered; hundreds, no, thousands, descending onto the Aaldian farm like black insects. Whose army? What world? What nation? He had no idea. Everything was coming together. Everything was falling apart.

"Is everything all right?" Anavha asked, and though the gate was closed and Anavha could not see what lay behind them, Natanial kept hold of his arm and propelled him forward, so he could not look back.

"It's fine," Natanial said. "Everything is going to be just fine."

8

Luna had long practice with silence.

The Saiduan had shaped much of the childhood Luna remembered. It was a childhood where others spoke, and Luna obeyed. That childhood had taught Luna about the quiet resistance of hir own silence.

Once Luna had decided not to speak about the book ze had toted across the ocean from Saiduan, it had become easier to give up speaking all together. Luna knew what the Empress had not yet intuited: that the temples could do far more than simply seal away the other worlds from crossing over. They could be used to remake the world. To shatter continents. Sink whole cities. Luna kept hir silence, because it was the only way ze could think to save the world.

Instead, Luna spun stories in hir head, ruminated over deaths, cursed Roh, cursed hir parents, wept over what was lost, soaked in hir anger at all those who had owned hir over these many years.

Luna pressed hir face to the cell floor, half-dozing. Hunger came and went. Starvation was at once like freeing one from the body and reminding one of just how vulnerable the flesh was, how transient. Luna had once lasted thirty-seven days without food. It had been among the best thirty-seven days of hir life, because Luna had been fully and completely in control of hir body for the first time.

They would try to feed Luna again soon. Ze heard them bickering about it.

The voices subsided. Footsteps sounded outside the door, gritty leather soles on stone. Dhai didn't wear leather shoes. That was how Luna could distinguish the Dhai from Tai Mora.

Creak of the cell door. A spill of light. The guards dragged Luna to the table at the center of the cellblock. One of the guards hefted hir onto the bench. Luna was too tired to struggle. Luna expected to see food: rice, eating sticks, maybe a bowl of broth and a spoon. Instead, they stripped Luna down and took hir up two flights of stairs to a big empty bathing room and tossed hir into a massive pool.

The water was so cold, it shocked Luna breathless. For a moment ze was back under the icy surface of a Saiduan river, choking on death. Luna's limbs felt wooden. Ze could not swim. With some chagrin, Luna realized the water was shallow enough to stand in.

One of the guards called from the edge, "Get decent. Scrub up."

When Luna refused, they came in and scrubbed Luna roughly then hauled hir out. Luna did little to help them with their task, even as they pulled a clean tunic over hir head and dragged hir up the never-ending staircase. At the very top, in a chamber dominated by a massive circular table, the Empress of the Tai Mora waited, grim as ever.

On either side of the Empress, two jistas in long robes waited, hands folded.

"Hello again, Luna," Kirana said. Luna had learned to hate her narrow face, the thin lips, the cold black eyes. "Please, do you want to sit? Eat?"

Luna just stared at her.

"I understand," Kirana said. "I have been unfair, wrapped up in my own concerns. People I trust have suggested that you may not appreciate why we have done as we have, and why it's in your best interests to assist us. I know it seems cruel, but it was very necessary. I could tell you, yes, or... I could show you what's becoming of all these worlds that others are abandoning."

She gestured to one of the jistas next to her. "Suari?"

The man raised his hand. The air trembled. Luna felt the pressure in hir ears and pressed hir hands to hir ears.

Something in the air broke.

Luna recoiled. The world split in two. A shimmering hole opened in the air just ahead of hir, very nearly touching the floor. Luna feared that anything going over the threshold that got caught on the lip between the worlds would blink out of existence.

The guard at hir left took hir arm roughly and pushed hir through ahead of him. Luna shrieked as ze went over the lip of the hole in the world – to somewhere else.

On the other side, it was very dim. Luna stumbled into a piece of furniture. The soldier came after hir, one long leg and the arm that gripped hir pressing through the gate and then–

The hole in the world snapped shut.

Luna's ears popped. The fingers wrapped around hir arm loosened. The arm, a chunk of the soldier's left breast, and most of his left leg slopped to the floor, spraying blood.

Luna felt dizzy. Darkness kissed the edges of hir vision.

"Who's there?" A voice in the hallway. A key in the door. Where was this? Another cell?

The smell of the blood tasted coppery. Luna tried to go around the furniture, but hir eyes hadn't yet adjusted. Luna slipped in blood. Fell hard.

Darkness. A moment of consciousness, gazing at blood on hir own hands. Whose blood? Luna had forgotten. Another hand on hir arm. Alive?

Then dark again, a stutter of lost time, and a voice.

"My name is Yisaoh. What are you called?"

Luna peered behind the silhouette of the woman who spoke, and found hirself gazing out dirty windows. Beyond the streaked glass, the light was the color of weak tea. The air smelled of burning trash and tar; the smell lingered at the back of hir throat, so thick ze could taste it.

"I'm sorry for that… welcome," the woman said again. She turned slightly, no longer in silhouette. She was a tall, broad-shouldered woman with a bent nose and generous mouth. Her head appeared too large for her body, as if she carried far less weight than her frame demanded.

When Luna said nothing, the woman, Yisaoh, continued, "It's all right. Talking uses more breath. Would you like to see why? I expect that's what Kirana wants you to see. She told me you were coming. Something must have gone wrong with the wink. It does happen. I mourn the guard. I knew him. We have seen so much death together, and so much hope. But I am heartened that nothing happened to you."

Luna did wonder at the source of the smell. And the hole in the world.

"How is your head?" Yisaoh offered a hot cup of foul-smelling tea. "This may help."

Luna took it. Gagged a little. Hir stomach protested. It had been too long since ze ate or drank anything.

Yisaoh reached for her shoulder, then stopped. "I apologize. You are Dhai. You don't like to be touched, is that right?"

Luna firmed hir mouth. Luna had been born in Dhai, but the culture ze knew was Saiduan. The Saiduan did what they wished to those who were weaker. They were much like the Tai Mora in that way.

"Until Oma begins to respond to the jistas again, we are stuck together," Yisaoh continued. "There's fresh bread downstairs. And it smells better than here."

Yisaoh straightened. Her hands were bony, the veins prominent. The cuffs of her long violet robe shifted and covered them. She went to the door, waited for Luna.

Luna considered Yisaoh's words. The smell of fresh bread. The tea in hir stomach. Ze had seen no soldiers here, just this woman. Was Yisaoh meant to be a jailer? Or was she a prisoner like Luna?

Ze rose from the bed. Drank a little more of the tea. Ze stumbled, and Yisaoh bent to catch hir. Her arm looped around Luna's waist, a temporary bulwark against Luna's own weak body. It felt oddly comforting, after so long in the dark among strangers who hated hir. Maybe this one hated hir too, but in this new air, this new space, Luna could pretend.

Yisaoh escorted Luna through shattered corridors. Crumbled bricks were lashed with mortar and knotted tendrils of plant matter too uniform to be natural. Luna recognized the work of tirajistas. Luna understood that they were… somewhere else. Perhaps on hir world, but most likely not. The air itself felt alien. The way the ground pulled down at hir, seeming somehow firmer. The stones beneath them had melted in places. As they began up a set of broad steps, the hold rumbled, groaning as if alive and in terrible pain. Luna froze on the stairs.

"It passes." Yisaoh gestured for hir to continue. "The quakes usually aren't severe enough to threaten the integrity of the hold. Our jistas have shored it up."

At the top of the stairs was a door. Yisaoh pulled a scarf from a hook, and a pair of goggles that buckled behind the head. She handed another set to Luna. Ze struggled to get it all on.

"You should really eat before we go outside." Yisaoh pulled a bit of hard candy from her pocket. Luna had not seen candy since ze was a child.

Luna's fingers shook as ze took it. The burst of flavor on hir tongue made hir shiver. So sweet! It suffused hir body like some vital elixir.

Yisaoh opened the door.

A blast of black, tarry particles. The stench of burning hair, and something far more foul that Luna could not name. Ze stumbled after Yisaoh, fingers pressed to the scarf around hir face for fear it would blow away in the hot, dry wind.

As they trod across the roof, they left deep footprints in the ash. Luna's curiosity nearly got the better of hir. Luna opened hir mouth to ask what had happened here, but ze had not spoken in so long that no sound came out. Luna coughed.

"Don't breathe too deeply," Yisaoh said. "Here. You can see it just through the cover." She pointed across the roof of the building. Flat roof, Luna noted. Not a place that was used to getting snow, not like Saiduan. A gory orange-black fire blazed in the sky, like a watery eye trailing tears of wispy smoke.

"It's been poisoning this world for years," Yisaoh said. "The one Kirana and I are from is already dead, did you know that? This is another, adjacent to it, very similar. It had a great army as well, one that failed. We had to retreat here to the middle of the world, along the equator. You know what that is? The midpoint of a world. It's the only place still warm enough, here. With the cleanest air. You see? We had few choices."

Luna searched for the rest of the satellites. Low along the horizon, the faint red pulse of Oma shuddered like a tremulous heart. Luna took in the breadth of the roof. Behind hir, squat towers rose into cloudy brown haze. The windows higher up lay open; what was left of the shutters wept from crumbling frames.

Ze coughed, and wheezed, "There is always another choice." Hir voice sounded foreign to hir, after spending so long silent. *Always another choice*, that's what Maralah would have said, when Luna tried to explain why this or that task had not been completed. People with power always believed there were choices for others, but no other options for themselves except the path of least resistance.

"I assure you we explored many options."

Luna gazed at the edge of the rooftop. They were only two stories up. Hir body tensed. It was not a terribly long drop. Could Luna make it? Get away?

Ze was moving before ze realized it. Legs stumbling across the dusty rooftop, toward the edge.

"Wait!" Yisaoh, incredulous.

Luna leaped, hurling hirself into the great black abyss that embraced hir.

The smack of a forgiving surface.

A deep plunge.

Luna bobbed in the water of a shallow moat. Pulled acrid air into hir lungs. Coughed fitfully. Luna splashed toward a dark shape ze took to be the shoreline of the sludgy moat, only a few paces distant. As ze crawled onto land, the air cleared for a brief moment. Ze had every intention of running, of getting as far and fast as hir legs would carry hir, but exhaustion overcame hir again. Luna had not eaten, or moved so vigorously, in some time.

Hir hands sank into the deep mud. Knocked against what Luna thought was stone, but no, this was more brittle. Porous. Luna smeared away the mud on the shore and found half a human skeleton there.

Luna recoiled. Lifted hir gaze. Let hirself sink back in the mud.

Across the whole of the broad valley, just visible below the dirty air, lay piles of bones. Luna's mind could not make sense of it. The wind was warm, but Luna shivered, tucking hir hands under hir arms. Hir damp hair clung to hir face.

Luna gaped at the valley of bones: chitinous rotting helmets, tattered military banners, rusting weapons, the tangled remains of abandoned gear kits, packs and pouches; the sorts of things no living person would leave behind. What had killed them so quickly that they could not flee?

Ze had never been in a place to make life and death decisions for anyone but hirself, though hir Saiduan masters had certainly sent hundreds of thousands to death at a word. Here was a whole army, thousands of people all at once... Who had decided if they lived or died?

Luna heard raised voices. The bark of a dog.

Yisaoh broke through the misty fog, riding a great pale dog, its body ravaged by mange. The expression on her face was pained. She slid off the dog. A girl came with her, tagging behind, and finally, here, a soldier wearing chitinous armor astride a dog as well, her face as sunken as Yisaoh's.

"That was foolish," Yisaoh said. "How far did you think you could go, in your condition? Are you hurt?"

Luna shook hir head. Gazed again to the valley of bones. Yisaoh followed hir look.

"This world's army," Yisaoh said. "The one that failed to make it to yours in time. I know what we did on your world is reprehensible. We are not good people. But what would you have done, in the face of this much death?"

"You should have died," Luna rasped.

Yisaoh brought the girl next to her closer. A simple girl who shared Yisaoh's high forehead and dark hair. "This is my daughter Tasia. She has a double in your world. As do I. We will die here. Does that make you feel better?"

Luna shook hir head.

"Kirana says you can help. I don't know how. But if you can, please... even if you can't save me, you can't save my daughter... closing those seams between the worlds will save the people who did make it. You can decide now. It's up to you. Not Kirana, or me. You."

"That's unfair."

"Nothing about the world is fair."

A gentle trembling rocked the ground beneath them. Yisaoh pulled her daughter to her. "You go back inside with Sorida."

"Mam–"

"Go."

Sorida, the soldier, also protested. Yisaoh was firm. They rode together back to the hold.

Yisaoh bent to help Luna up. Luna accepted her hand.

"There are no monsters," Yisaoh said. "Only choices."

"What just happened?" Kirana yelled.

Suari raised his hands. Scowled. The other jistas milled about like startled chickens.

"I... lost Oma. Give it a moment. It can be fickle, sometimes. One can lose a thread of power on occasion and–"

"Open it back up!" Kirana said. "That little shit is in there with my wife."

"A moment, I–" Suari furrowed his brows.

The air shuddered.

A great moaning roar came from overhead.

"The fuck..." Kirana muttered. She rushed to the broad windows at the back of the room. The remaining guard and the jistas followed.

The satellites still hung in the sky: fiery green Tira to the northeast; purple Sina higher up and further west, and red Oma, a knuckle of dark ochre smearing the sky between them, its orbit taking it nearly as high as the double suns at midday.

But now a great rent had opened in the sky beside

Oma, smearing the rush of its red light, sending shadows across the ground below. The gory black wedge of some mountainous form pushed through the rent between the worlds, blotting out the suns. It knifed toward the ground, like an upside-down peak trying to embed itself into the woodlands.

"What in Sina's maw is that?" Kirana said.

A great cracking made the air rumble. The sky closed. The massive form that had cut through the passage lost its mooring and fell.

The boom came first.

"Shit," Kirana said. She braced herself against the wall.

A rippling quake sent the whole temple shaking. She nearly lost her feet. Dust filled the air, making her choke and cough.

When the shaking stopped, Kirana again gazed out at the sky. Oma winked madly above them. Below, the heaving monolith that had fallen from the sky lay silent and still as the dust and debris it had kicked up began to settle. Its jagged black form towered above the nearby treetops. It was as if Dhai had grown a mountain at the center of the country.

"Kuallina is there," Kirana said. Two of her legions, three of her commanders, were stationed at Kuallina. "Do you have Oma yet?" she said to Suari.

He shook his head; bits of glass tinkled. "Whatever that was disrupted it."

"Then we do this blind," she said. Pointed at the guard. "I need our bird master and the runners. Go."

He went, crunching across the glass. The dappled light had transformed the room, as if she stood in some other place. Kirana shook her head. Staying sane as the world broke apart took stubborn patience.

"Suari, you're coming with me. I want that little ataisa back if we have to rip apart the sky again to do it."

9

Lilia gripped her walking stick so tightly her hand hurt. This could not be, she thought. Not after all this time, after all the work she had done, after how far she had come, after all the delicate alliances they had maintained. Ahkio the coward, the pacifist, was dead, surely? Meyna herself had seen it, wept over it, thrown things and rent her own garments and then happily taken the title of Catori.

Had Meyna lied?

Lilia just inside the thorn fence at the edge of camp, gnawing at one of her new nails; the quick was already exposed, soft as a dragonfly wing. It had become an unconscious habit gnawing away at pieces of herself while her mind was elsewhere.

A few of her most fervent supporters stood a good way distant, Salifa at the head of them, hand on her weapon. Yisaoh and Meyna had tried to keep everyone away from the two men who had arrived at the fence, but the beribboned heads of Lilia's supporters were visible even from the trees. Lilia worried over them, too, and how they would react to the arrival of this man with Ahkio's face. Namia kept close to Lilia's side, nose raised, sniffing the air.

Lilia admitted that one of the men *did* look like Ahkio;

longer hair, leaner face, his eyes more sunken, and shoulders bowed, but it was more than a mere resemblance. He either really was the Kai, or he was another version of the Kai, seeking to throw them into exactly this kind of turmoil.

She kept to one side, letting Yisaoh and Meyna meet the two men as equals. Yisaoh's face was haggard, shocked, but Meyna only stared at the men fiercely. Lilia tried to place who the sly little man next to Ahkio might be. Liaro? The cousin? That sounded right. An average man, with a long pockmarked face and twisted mouth that made it seem as if he found everything around him either terribly funny or mind-bogglingly complex.

Yisaoh already had the nub of her cigarette out. She did not light it, but sucked on the end, contemplative. "I heard you were dead."

"And I heard *you* were dead," said the man who shared Kai Ahkio's face. He folded his hands under his armpits. Both men bore bloody scratches on their necks and faces. Brambles clung to their rough-spun clothing. They were sweat-soaked, in need of a wash, with tangled hair and grubby knees. Lilia suspected that having all your limbs sewn back on – or whatever he was going to propose had happened to him – resulted in some rough living.

Meyna followed Ahkio's gesture. "I saw you die," Meyna said. "Ora Nasaka came down covered in your blood. I hid, but I saw your body. It's impossible that you are our Kai. You are someone else."

"I don't remember any of that," Ahkio said. "I'm afraid there's a good deal I don't remember about the final days of Dhai."

The last time Lilia had seen Ahkio was when he told her he refused to go through with her plan to poison the Tai Mora Empress, back at Kuallina before its eventual fall. Yisaoh had drugged him, and they'd gone around him to hold the dinner anyway. They then tried and failed to kill Kirana on their own. The real Ahkio would remember that, but this one didn't even seem to recall his own death.

"You were supposed to secure Oma's temple," Yisaoh said, "after Kuallina fell. That didn't go very well, turns out. We're all a little mad about that, as those temples could have outlasted any seige. You had only to secure them."

"I'm sorry," Ahkio said. "I... have no memory of any of that, either. I've been–"

"He's been very ill," Liaro said. "It's a strange time."

"How did you find us?" Lilia asked.

Liaro glanced over at her, as if noticing her for the first time. He picked at his lip; an old scab. From what? Had Ahkio hit him? "There's much to explain. We understand that. If you will sit with us, offer tea, and–"

"Your hands," Meyna said, holding out her own.

"You really should be offering tea first," Liaro said, wryly.

"I'm not Mohrai," Meyna said. "Perhaps she would have been more welcoming to potential Tai Mora."

"Where is Mohrai?" Ahkio asked, voice a little high and warbling, like a child's.

"Dead," Meyna said, sharply. "But our child is alive, if that concerns you."

"Our... child?"

"Ahkio, you declared little Hasao Li Kai in the Sanctuary of Oma's Temple. We have dozens of witnesses."

"I don't..." Ahkio shook his head. "I'm sorry, there's

much I don't remember."

Liaro reached over and squeezed Ahkio's shoulder.

"Your hands," Meyna insisted.

"Meyna," Ahkio said, "I'm still trying to understand the state of things here. Where is Tir? Rhin and Hadaoh? Is Mey-mey–"

"Your hands!"

He held them out.

His hands were covered in old burn scars; twisted, shiny flesh that had never healed properly. Lilia heard that he had gotten the scars trying to pull his mother from a burning shelter in one of the old Dorinah camps for Dhai exiles.

Meyna took his hands in hers and scrutinized them; Yisaoh did the same, bending just over her shoulder, though honestly, Lilia thought, Meyna was the one more likely to notice a difference in the scar patterns. The Kai had lived with her for several years.

Meyna pushed his hands away. "I'm sorry, but... you're dead, Ahkio."

Liaro said, "I found him three months ago, wandering up in the hills above Oma's Temple. He was half-mad, living on moss and tree bark. It's taken this long to get his head straight. He's missing great gaps of time. But it's him, Meyna. I wouldn't have spent all this time trying to find you both, and Mohrai too, if I didn't believe it was him."

"There are all sorts of people wandering around now," Yisaoh said. "There's no way to determine if he's truly our Ahkio, or not."

"That's true of anyone here, then," Liaro said. "By that logic no one should be listening to a word you're saying either."

Ahkio waved his hand. "I remember everything that happened here, yes, in this Dhai, right up until the end of summer, before–" He exchanged a glance with Liaro. "Before what happened at Kuallina. That... I have no memory of anything after that. But the rest of my memory is very clear. I remember Nasaka telling me Kirana had died. I remember Ghrasia... Sai Hofsha, the terrible Tai Mora emissary. And I remember bringing all the clans together, and exiling you, Yisaoh, and you, Meyna. I still stand by that."

"Now we're all stuck in exile together," Yisaoh muttered.

"How did he lose this last *year*?" Lilia said. "A whole year? That's... I've never heard of that."

"Exactly!" Liaro said. "A Tai Mora would have had a much better story, wouldn't they?"

Lilia's skin prickled. She did not like any of this: not his face, not his stories, not what this could mean for their carefully negotiated alliance and her plan to hit back at the Tai Mora. The Ahkio she knew had been averse to naked conflict of any kind, and Lilia did not like how Meyna looked at him. There was something between them still, even if it was just the memory of what they had.

"Not just Tai Mora," Lilia said, raising her voice. "There are far more worlds in play now. It's going to become easier and easier for all of us to get replaced by impostors. If Meyna saw him dead, this isn't him. But maybe he's not a Tai Mora, either. Maybe he is from some closer world, one even more like ours. He may not even know he's an impostor himself."

"Liaro, speak to us privately," Meyna said.

Liaro crossed the thorn fence. Lilia drew back a step. The

stink of him carried, this close; the two men desperately needed a wash. Neither had answered how they found the camp yet, and that disturbed her. A patrol stood a few paces distant; the same patrol that had escorted them here. But they should not even have come this close. The Woodland was a large place, and Lilia had worked hard to disguise their presence here and distract Tai Mora patrols into covering other areas.

Yisaoh and Meyna broke away from Meyna's retinue, and Lilia followed them to the lee of a great bonsa tree. From there they could still see Ahkio, Meyna's people, and Lilia's supporters, but could not be overheard.

Rain still dripped from the giant leaves above. Lilia kept blinking to clear her eyes. Namia circled around to the other side of the tree, where it was drier.

"You're convinced of this?" Yisaoh asked Liaro.

"He's the real Ahkio," Liaro said. "Ask him anything."

"Are you the real Liaro?" Lilia said. "We have no way of verifying who either of you are."

"Are you the real... whoever you are?" Liaro said, lip curled.

Lilia said, "Your tone won't gain you any favor here." Her foot ached, and her mind was already elsewhere. Mohrai dead, and Ahkio suddenly alive. It would upset the power balance here. If she wanted to strike back at the Tai Mora, it needed to be now, before all of this was settled.

"He remembers nothing of Kuallina," Liaro said, ignoring her and turning back to Meyna, "or the events leading up to it. Now, here's the strange part. I'm going to tell you something and it's going to sound mad."

"Madder than you do already?" Yisaoh said, digging

into her pocket for another cigarette stub and coming up empty. "This should be entertaining."

"Something happened to Ahkio before Kuallina," Liaro said. "The day he finally locked up Ora Nasaka and booted out Sai Hofsha, he said he did it because he'd come to know the future. He had already seen the day after that one, and whatever he saw drove him to make those two decisions. He had all these outrageous questions that morning, when he came upstairs from the temple basement. Was Ora Nasaka alive? Who was Kai? Did he look the same? Who teaches mathematics? He said he'd gone... back. He went into the belly of Oma's Temple, there among the roots, and pressed his hand to a stone bearing the temple's mark and–"

"And he proved this to you?" Yisaoh said.

"I was there the first time he touched that stone," Liaro said. "The second, he went alone."

"I'm confused," Lilia said. "Did he go back in time the first time he touched the stone?"

"No, he said he met a temple keeper? But the second time, that's when it was different."

"Why would it be different?" Yisaoh asked.

"Because someone sabotaged the stone," Liaro said. "He thinks it may have been Ora Almeysia. Whatever she did, he lost access to this temple keeper, but what the keeper, or the temple, or someone left behind was this... strange ability to leap back a day."

"How many times has it done it?" Lilia asked. "Leapt back?"

"Just the once," Liaro said. "He told me about it, and how inconsequential the day seemed. He wondered why he was given this chance to relive a day that wasn't important. So, I guess he decided to *make* it important, and that's when he decided to put Ora Nasaka in the gaol and kicked out the Tai Mora emissary, as I said. He would never have done those things if he hadn't been rattled. He's telling the truth. I *know* it."

Spittle flecked Liaro's lips. The passion and insistence in his voice convinced Lilia that whether or not this really was their Ahkio, Liaro believed Ahkio's story. Stepping back a day in time certainly wasn't the strangest thing she'd seen or heard since Oma came into the sky.

Lilia noted that they were drawing a few onlookers, despite the threat of the tumbleterrors. "Let's take this to the tent," Lilia said. "We are going to draw the tumbleterrors."

They brought Ahkio and Liaro to one of the above-ground tents that had been set up for the funerary feast. Meyna put a standing order on keeping any more onlookers below ground until their next move was sorted. But Lilia knew enough about the life of gossip to suspect that would do little but enflame the rumors no doubt already circling through the chambers below.

Lilia led the questioning, speaking up before the others were ready. The Tai Mora were interested in the temple basements, Caisa had said. But if they had encountered this stone that Ahkio and Liaro talked about, it hadn't appeared in any of Caisa's reports.

"What else can you tell us about the temple basements?" Lilia asked. "The Tai Mora have uncovered a level below the one you speak of. An old room for channeling the power of the satellites. Did you ever access that room?"

"No," Ahkio said. He folded his hands in his lap and

stared at Namia. Shifted uncomfortably. He touched his hair once or twice; the matted tangle of it pulled away from his thin, pretty face. "Liaro and I found the stone while investigating something Kirana and my aunt Etena alluded to in some of their writings. When I touched the obelisk... I... went somewhere else."

"Like through the seams between the worlds?" Lilia asked. "The way omajistas do? To another world? The Tai Mora world?"

He shook his head. "This was... different. I went to... some other time. The temple, but not as we knew it. A woman was there, calling herself Keeper Ti-Li."

"A keeper?" Lilia asked. "Not a creature, or a beast, or... she said she was a *keeper*?"

"Yes. The keepers are not... the *temples*, I think. The keepers are like... ghosts of people, maybe souls left to watch over the temples. She said she was unstuck in time. Maybe that's why the stone can do what it... did. Ti-Li said the stone had been sabotaged by Ora Almeysia. But I wanted to try and visit her again, to learn more. Back then... I was still hoping to find some way to turn back the Tai Mora, maybe by using the temples."

"What did she tell you about the temples?" Lilia asked.

"She told me the temples were alive, that they are living... transference engines, she called them. She said they were created a very long time ago. Properly controlled, they could be used to harness the power of the satellites."

"Did she say how to control them?" Lilia asked.

"How is this relevant?" Meyna said. "Whatever the Tai Mora are doing in the temples doesn't concern us. We're going to leave Dhai."

"Leave?" Ahkio said.

"A moment, Meyna," Lilia said. "What exactly did this temple keeper tell you?"

Ahkio rubbed his forehead. "It was a long time ago. She… it? She said they created the temples, with living transference engines, to kill something infecting their sky. But they broke it apart instead, and now the pieces travel among all the worlds. She said only the engines could stop it."

"But how?" Lilia pressed.

"She didn't know. All she could tell me was how they broke the worlds, not how to… fix them again."

"Meyna," Lilia said, "Caisa brought us information that–"

Meyna held up a hand. "No more talk of temples. Walking into one of these temples would be suicide at best. The Tai Mora have them warded and guarded. They are teeming with jistas."

"Caisa is still alive?" Ahkio asked. "She was my assistant, for a time."

"She is," Lilia said carefully.

"Please," Ahkio said, "what's happened here since I've been gone? Liaro could only tell me what happened in the valley. There are so few survivors there. So many bodies were burned and buried, like chattel."

"I'll tell you more of that," Meyna said, "once we decide what to do with you."

"There was clearly an Ahkio here for the fall of Kuallina," Lilia said. "If you don't remember any of that, what do you remember? Where did you find yourself? In the Woodland?"

"No. I woke up in the temple. In my own bed, as the Tai Mora took the temple."

"You *died* when the Tai Mora took the temple," Yisaoh said. "You're telling us that when our Ahkio died, you just... appeared? Woke up in his bed?"

"I know it sounds mad, but so does traveling between worlds, doesn't it? All I remember is touching the stone, and then–"

"I've never heard of the temples doing this," Lilia said. She wondered what else they didn't yet know about the temples, if his story was to be believed.

"Lilia, will you leave us?" Meyna asked. "Yisaoh and I have a real history with Ahkio. Let us speak to him alone. Liaro, could you also wait outside?"

Lilia bit her tongue. She hoped Yisaoh would intercede, but Yisaoh only shrugged. "Yes," Yisaoh said, "we will send for you."

Lilia tried to stifle her grimace, and turned quickly so they could not see the shift in her expression.

She limped from the tent and into the clearing outside, and Namia followed. The wood had gone quiet; the tumbleterrors would have scared away most of the sentient flora and fauna. She rubbed her arms.

Liaro stayed near the tent. As Lilia waited, the storm began to clear, and the rain ceased. Namia sprawled beside her in a sudden sunbeam.

Yisaoh finally came out, hands pushed deep into her pockets, and walked over to Lilia. Shook her head.

"What are you going to do?" Lilia said.

"Ahkio can be controlled," Yisaoh said. "Meyna loves the idea of having him beside her. It gives her legitimacy. I could almost wonder if she knew about him, before, if murdering Mohrai was done knowing Ahkio would come back."

"That's... well, I wouldn't put that past her. Couldn't she just... get rid of him?"

"We can't just kill him," Yisaoh said, but there was no judgment in her tone, only a bored resignation. "I couldn't find a lie, when we spoke to him alone in there. He insists he wants nothing from us, to just go back to being a little religious teacher, but you know how people will react to that."

"They'll follow him," Lilia said. "Some will. How many will follow him into some fool scheme? He's not made for these times. He'll lead them to disaster, the same way he led Dhai to disaster."

"No Kai could have stopped this," Yisaoh said. "Not even if our Kirana had lived. There was no way to win this. You can only destroy monsters like that by becoming one, and no Kai was going to do that to the Dhai."

"What about what he said, about the temple?"

"Going back in time?" Yisaoh snorted. "Who knows?"

"The other part. About the temples being transference engines meant to channel the power of the satellites. We intuited that, but he's confirmed it. The Tai Mora are going to harness that power. That's what they're doing in those basements. They are going to figure out how to break the world, and Meyna wants us to just run away."

"Oh, Lilia." Yisaoh sighed. "Always scheming. First you want to murder Tai Mora, then you want to... what? Take over the temples? If you haven't noticed, we can't even feed ourselves."

Lilia gazed at the tent, and Liaro, who squatted outside it, cracking his knuckles. "I want to see what's down there for myself," Lilia said.

"Good luck with that," Yisaoh said.

"I have people in every temple," Lilia said. "Reconnaissance would not be too difficult, or dangerous."

"Are you listening to yourself right now? Hasn't Caisa given you enough diagrams? And it doesn't matter! We're leaving."

"You may be," Lilia said. "I'm not. Not yet." A plan was beginning to form in her mind, one that relied on some of the same logistics as her plan to strike back at the Tai Mora. Infiltrating one of the temples would be a kind of revenge, after all. She considered the sort of damage she could do to them, if she knew more than them, if she took control of one of these transference engines for herself, or sabotaged them.

"I know that look," Yisaoh said. "Whatever you're scheming, don't do it."

"I have a plan."

"Tira's tears. You and your little cultists are going to murder yourselves."

"If we do," Lilia said, "we will be taking a lot of Tai Mora with us. Come on, Namia."

Lilia touched the girl's shoulder, and Namia followed as Lilia headed back to the entrance to their underground warren.

"You and your little cultists can do what you like!" Yisaoh called after her. "You know Meyna will be pleased if you're gone! She's going to hope you all die!"

Lilia did not answer, but glanced down at Namia. "What's the nearest temple, Namia?"

Namia signed, "Tira."

"That's right," Lilia said. "It's been a long time since I

visited Tira's Temple. Let's change that."

"Danger," Namia signed.

Lilia pushed her hands away.

10

Through the wink, back to the battlefield outside the stronghold called Daorian that had eaten so many of Natanial's mercenary soldiers in the last months. Natanial kept his mouth shut as he escorted Anavha to Monshara's tent. He almost told Monshara he'd brought her a gift, and thought better of it. That was something Anavha's wife would have said, some baser evil.

Instead, Natanial presented him as an omajista, the one they needed to breach Daorian's defenses and end the Tai Mora campaign in this idiot country.

"He isn't much to look at," Monshara said, in Tai Mora.

"He's powerful enough to open a wink back from Aaldia to get us here. He has a good shot at opening one for an army."

"I know you're talking about me," Anavha said, in Dorinah.

"You aren't fit for battle," Monshara said, switching to the same language.

"There'll be no battling," Natanial said, keeping his voice warm and even, because at the word "battle" Anavha had trembled like a leaf. "You'll open a wink, a gate, for the army, is all. Monshara will guide events from there."

Anavha reminded him, as ever, of a frightened young animal. He required a soft voice and a light touch.

"I'd like you to find a place for him here in the village, somewhere he won't be disturbed," Natanial said.

"But I want to stay with you," Anavha said.

"I have my people up the hill."

"Then I'll camp with you there."

"You wouldn't like it," Natanial said. "Cold and filthy. Full of violence." He imagined Anavha meeting some of the people he employed.

"I can provide him a room and protection," Monshara said.

"Protection," Natanial reiterated, switching back to Tai Mora again, "not a jail cell. He isn't a prisoner. He'll bolt if you treat him like one."

"I wouldn't dream of it," Monshara said.

"Tomorrow, then?"

"Tomorrow," she said, and gestured for Anavha to go with her.

Natanial could not get the boy's terrified face from his mind.

Natanial knew the smell of war the way he knew the smell of birth. His mother had borne him on a battlefield, somewhere on the outer islands north of Dorinah. Like many Aaldian sailors, she had also done her time as a mercenary, and he grew up with the smell of blood and steel and the sea. Standing outside the Dorinah village, with the stink of the Tai Mora army behind him and the tangy brine of the sea ahead of him, he was brought back to those simpler times. Birth and death, the sea and the land. All that mattered was having a ship, enough to eat, a family, a purpose. Once he had lost all those things, he was adrift. He was here.

Monshara had brought casks of blood with her. Natanial had assumed that would be entirely unnecessary, but he had no idea how powerful Anavha was, or how well he had mastered his gift in the year since he had last seen him. Better prepared than not.

As Monshara led them down the road, both of them astride large black bears, Natanial appraised Anavha, looking for signs of hurt or discomfort. Anavha's face was drawn, but his complexion was clear, and Natanial did not mark any injury. He had dressed in Tai Mora clothes: wide-legged trousers and a flowing tunic and vest that buttoned up the front. The hat he bore was ridiculous, certainly, but the suns were high and hot.

The cart of blood waited by Natanial's side. His mercenaries were lined up at the flank of Monshara's main force. They would not go in after them, but wait outside the walls to clean up any stragglers. Otolyn had grumbled about that, upset at their chances of getting any loot that way, but Natanial was firm. They had incurred enough losses when he disobeyed orders and saved Monshara's last assault from becoming a rout.

"I'll be beside you the whole time," Natanial told Anavha. "We'll stay here and keep it open. We don't go in until it's done."

Monshara waved the cart driver down, and he rolled up the two barrels of blood.

"What's this?" Anavha said, but the driver was already pushing over the barrel, spilling reeking, clotting blood all over the road.

"In case you need a little help," Monshara said.

Anavha wrinkled his nose and raised his hands.

The air grew heavy. The hair on the back of Natanial's arms stood on end. A slight trembling shook the ground, and rumbled across the road, making little waves in the blood.

Ahead of the great army, the air rippled.

Monshara rode her bear ahead, to get in position and ready her troops.

A snarling slash opened in the fabric of the air. From his seat, Natanial could make out a stone room. It could be any place at all, from the look of it, but he suspected it was somewhere in Daorian that Anavha knew. He had heard it was easier to open a passage where one had been.

Monshara waved a scout in, a very brave girl, no doubt, who barreled through with her bear into the stone house.

Natanial glanced at Anavha, but his face was calm. "You've learned much since I last saw you," Natanial said.

"A little," Anavha said. "I had a good teacher here. But mostly... the difference is that the power's here." He nodded at Oma's blaring red eye. "I can feel it, like a heartbeat."

The scout returned and reported to Monshara. They were too far away for Natanial to make out the words, but Monshara waved her soldiers in.

There was only enough room for them to go four abreast, and the pace was slow. The pace worried Natanial, because if there was any sizable counter force inside, they could stopper up the house, or set it on fire, and completely cut them off.

Monshara rode over to Natanial and Anavha. "Can we

open another gate?" she said, clearly thinking the same thing about their vulnerability. "I want to come in at them from several places."

"I could," Anavha said, "but I couldn't hold it as long. This is my sister-in-law's house. Any other place in Daorian... I don't know as well."

Monshara said. "My people are vulnerable here. Isn't there somewhere else? Near the harbor, maybe?"

"I'll try," Anavha said.

"We shouldn't push him," Natanial said.

"He's an adult," Monshara said. "He can tell me what he can and can't do. Can you do it or not?"

Anavha said, "I can." He spread his arms wide. Natanial held his breath and reflexively reached for the hilt of his ax.

Anavha pushed one arm toward the existing gate, and concentrated hard on a spot twenty paces distant. This time, the blood in the barrels began to leak from the seams between the slats, oozing thickly onto the ground. Natanial's skin prickled. The blood rose from the ground, the droplets emerging from the barrels and coalescing into a winding spiral in the air. Monshara's troops, entering the other gateway, paid it no mind.

Anavha bit his lip. Natanial moved to stand near him. "Hold the first one," Natanial said. "That's more important."

"I have–" Anavha said, and then the world shifted.

Natanial's stomach heaved. He lurched forward as the sky itself seemed to move around him. One moment he was standing outside Asaolina, Anavha just an arm's length away, and the next, he was standing in a dark alley. The sky above juddered. Nausea overcame him, and he vomited into the gutter. When his stomach was empty, he drooled bile and turned and saw Anavha lying on the ground a few paces away.

Natanial crawled over to him, dragging his ax with him.

"Anavha?" Natanial patted his cheek. "Anavha?" Screaming came from the streets on either side of the narrow alley. He smelled smoke.

Anavha's eyelids flickered.

"Anavha, where are we?" Natanial said.

Anavha opened his eyes, and Natanial helped him up. Natanial gazed into the sky; still the same lavender of home, so hopefully they had not traveled very far. The stonework indicated they were somewhere within the city of Daorian, but he wasn't sure where.

"I…" Anavha took it all in, his expression as confused as Natanial felt. "I don't know," Anavha said. "I was trying to open a gate near the harbor."

Natanial sniffed the air, but could smell nothing over the smoke. "Let's move," he said. "Stay near me."

"I can take us—"

"No," Natanial said; his stomach protested. "Seven hells, where are we?"

"I don't know."

"What else can you do with these skills of yours? Because we'll need them. Stay with me! The bulk of the force will have marched for the hold. We'll catch up with them. I didn't want you here, but if you're here, we might as well make the most of it."

Natanial drew his ax and followed the sinuous alley. He ducked under an archway and checked both ways before running across a main street. Bodies lay in the street,

Tai Mora and Dorinah, most civilian. One Tai Mora was looting a body. Flames licked at the remains of a storefront. The smell of smoke wafted down the street, coming mostly from the market area. It had been a long time since he was last in Daorian. He had bided his time there getting close to the Empress's daughter, working his way into her good graces and then her bed, before finally murdering her.

As he entered the next intersection, an arrow zipped past his head. Natanial ducked back into the street he'd come from, throwing one arm in front of Anavha and pinning him to the wall. Ahead, a group of Dorinah soldiers and civilians had set up a barricade, holding the street. Two dozen dead Tai Mora were scattered on the other side of the barrier.

"Have you used your gift on anything but winks… gates?" Natanial asked.

"No," Anavha said.

Natanial glanced back into the street and got a quick count of the defenders. The more he pushed Anavha, the more likely he was to find himself severed in half by some ill-timed gate. He swore in Tordinian. Anavha's face darkened.

"I'm sorry," Anavha said.

"Let me think," Natanial said.

Anavha pointed at the storefront at the corner. It had once been a teahouse, and the roof over the outside dining area had partially collapsed, tilting at a dangerous right angle.

"We could duck down there," Anavha said.

"They have arrows," Natanial said.

"The barricades are too high," Anavha said. "See that

angle on the roof? They are firing down at us. The roof will be in their way."

Natanial peered at the angle of the roof, and saw that Anavha was right. "How in Laine's hell did you figure that?" he said.

"Angles," Anavha said. "Giska taught me painting. You start to see angles in things, how the light hits them. So, I noticed."

Natanial took Anavha's hand and sprinted for the building. Those at the barricade yelled and cursed, but he and Anavha were well gone by then, pounding through the next narrow intersection.

He pulled Anavha into the relative shelter of a great wooden door. Twelve paces distant, a woman dressed in a homespun tunic was crying over the body of a dead young woman, which lay mangled in the street, bleeding into the gutter.

Just ahead, a shimmering line of Tai Mora in their chitinous red armor crawled up the road toward the towering fortress at the center of the city.

Natanial went after them, keeping his distance, because neither of them wore anything identifying which side they were on.

"Is there any way for you to locate someone?" Natanial asked as they hurried after the army. "We need to find Monshara."

"She was still at the house, wasn't she?" Anavha said. "I can take you to the house. The gate is there! It should still be open."

"How far is it from here?"

Anavha stopped and stared at the smoking buildings.

A riderless dog wandered out of a teahouse. Abandoned goods littered the streets, and glassy-eyed civilians wandered aimlessly. Most residents were clearly starving. Natanial noted that some of the bodies in the alleys were emaciated, tossed from houses and piled up like bags of sticks. A few had threadbare blankets thrown over them.

"This way," Anavha said, and now he took Natanial's hand and pulled him through the falling city.

They wended down bloody streets, and dodged civilians throwing roof tiles. Natanial caught a big riderless dog and walked with it next to them, using the dog for cover against the persistent rain of objects heaved from rooftops. He had no interest in dying by roof tile.

Finally, they met up with a coterie of Tai Mora soldiers. Natanial held up his hands and called out the name of his company, and they went by them, each still eying the other warily. Around the next corner was a modest stone house, three stories tall. Outside, Monshara sat there atop a large bear, surveying the troops still pouring out. A little sparrow perched on her shoulder.

Monshara waved them over through the lines of soldiers. "We need him at the gates," she said. "We're having trouble penetrating the fortress itself, and I don't want to waste any more time. Can he do it? Something certainly got fucked up back there."

Natanial told Anavha what they needed. Anavha shook his head. "I could, but... I have to close these other two gates first. I'm afraid of what would happen if I didn't. It might hurt people."

Natanial found that strangely amusing, that Anavha cared so much about accidently cutting a soldier in half when the soldiers he had unleashed on his own city were in the process of burning it to the ground.

"Make sure everyone is in the city first," Natanial said. "Then he can close these gates."

"We just got the main city door open," Monshara said, gesturing to the little bird on her shoulder. "I've ordered the rest to come in that way, including your mop-up crew. Mount up and follow me. Give me a moment to order the gates cleared, and you can close them."

Monshara relayed her orders, and after a time, the march of soldiers through the building became a trickle, then ceased. Monshara lined up the force of about seventy fighters and found a second mount for Anavha.

Once ready, she gave the order to close the winks. Anavha must have done something, though Natanial didn't feel the change. Anavha simply nodded and said, "Done."

As the soldiers began to march, with Anavha and Natanial at the rear, Natanial heard a great groaning behind them, then a crash. The stone house collapsed under itself, blowing dust and debris out the front of what remained of the façade.

Natanial kept his ax handy as they marched.

The fight took them up through the city of Daorian and to the tall walls around the central fortress. The fortress of Daorian was not a living hold like those in Dhai and Saiduan. The Empress hated the flora and fauna of the world with such an intensity that she scoured the land as sterile as she could make it each year.

As they came to the wall, it was already under siege, with the last of the city's jista defenders on the walls, and

Monshara's giving them a fiery onslaught.

Monshara wanted Anavha kept to the back of the company, to protect him. It was not until Natanial rode up alongside Anavha to supervise him while he created his gate that he realized Anavha was crying.

Anavha opened a great wink within the walls of the hold itself. It wavered briefly, and a shower of stones came down before the thing solidified. If it wavered while the army went through it, it was likely to kill a good many of them.

Natanial waited at the back with Anavha, ensuring there were as many jistas and Dorinah soldiers killed as possible before they crossed through. When they finally did, he turned to see his own force swarming through the city, easily recognizable by their drabber clothing, their leather armor. They would eat well and be happy tonight.

When the fortress itself was well cleared, Monshara came back for him and Anavha where they waited in the great courtyard below.

"I have something for you to see," Monshara said.

Natanial picked his way after Monshara, Anavha coming behind. They went into the hold and up and up. She led him to the shattered door of a great hall. A little woman crouched in a far corner, face over her hands. A long chatelaine dangled from her waist. Even with her face covered, her dark hair and skinny frame marked her as a dajian, a Dhai slave, and he was amazed one had survived this long.

Among the bodies of the Dorinah lying all around him, he saw a few twisted forms that he recognized from Tordin: the Empress's strange, insect-like people. Some had

survived the great fire there, the one that Zezili Hasaria
ignited in an attempt to stop their rise. He wondered
how many they had killed there, and if these were truly
survivors from that conflagration or simply from some
other nest elsewhere.

"He's here," Monshara said, stepping over a broken beam
and through a charred, splintered doorway so massive
that Natanial wondered what such a thing was doing this
deep inside the hold. Did they expect dogs and carts to go
through?

As he entered, he realized this was the throne room of
the Dorinah queens. The great purple carpet was torn and
stained. Eight dead animals, large as bears, lay in a pile at
his left. It took half a moment to realize that's what they
were.

The body of the Empress herself lay awkwardly on the
steps of her dais, neck broken, her legs canted at a hard
left angle, fingers clenched, mouth set in a sneering rictus.
Someone had disemboweled her and cut her in half, no
doubt to ensure she didn't come back. And he didn't blame
them. Her skirts were askew, and under them he could see
each of her four legs. The cut across her waspish waist had
sprouted various organs, which all looked fairly normal.
She and her kin bled out just like any other.

Monshara pointed at the great silver throne on the
dais. Natanial thought she meant to get his reaction to its
artistry, and prepared an appropriate response, but as he
formed the words, he noticed the man curled up against
the throne, arms clinging to it. Thick black hair, curled and
greasy, hung into his eyes and down his back. His beard
was full, only a little gray mixed with the black. He was

leaner than he should be, and as Natanial approached, he saw the man only had one hand.

While Natanial knew who this must be, his mind took some time to process it. "Saradyn?" he said.

The man raised the mop of his head. His eyes were large, dark, haunted; the same haunted look Saradyn always had, for he saw ghosts.

"You've come," Saradyn said. "It was foretold that you would come. She has seen it!" This last bit he shouted at the ceiling, gaze raised to the sky as if shouting at some god.

"Saradyn," Natanial said. "I'd hoped you were dead with Zezili."

Saradyn fixed a dark, sunken eye on Natanial. "Traitor," he said.

"Perhaps," Natanial said. "But who is it you're working for here?"

"Not for… they are mine. I command them."

"What's he rambling about?" Monshara said.

A clacking sound came from behind Saradyn. The walls began to move, revealing dark shapes twisted into the shadows behind the massive purple curtains.

Natanial brought up his ax. The shadows seemed to peel from the walls and moved toward them. As they came into the light, the shapes resolved into four-legged, green-eyed figures with human faces and narrow torsos.

"Didn't you clear this room?" Natanial yelled at Monshara.

Anavha screamed. Natanial stepped closer to him to protect him. The air shuddered. Natanial's ears popped as the pressure of the room changed.

"I did!" Monshara said. "I don't know where they came from!"

Great gaping holes appeared in the air all around them. One sliced clean through the tip of Natanial's ax, swallowing it into darkness. The tears in the world yawned open like hungry mouths: opaque, like gazing into impossibly deep water.

Natanial froze. Half of Monshara's sword disappeared into one of the black circles, cut neatly in two.

"Don't move, Monshara!" Natanial said. Anavha, too, had quieted, though his face was twisted.

"Control it, Anavha!" Natanial said.

The shrieking figures clacked around and through the holes in the air. Some lost limbs, bits of faces, digits. Others clattered around, regardless. One lost nearly all of its head, and the body meandered on for several paces before falling at Natanial's feet.

Anavha sweated heavily. His hands trembled. "I can't stop it," he said, just loud enough for Natanial to hear him over the figures.

"Fucking amateurs!" Monshara yelled. "Shut it down!"

The black holes became more focused, tight little speckles crawling across the air like demented dust motes. Natanial blinked furiously, as if he could dispel the floating blackness from his vision.

One of the creatures slipped through the maze of tears in reality, a hunk of its elbow missing, the lower arm hanging by a hank of skin. Natanial gouged it in the head with the sheared handle of his ax, running it through the eye.

"Anavha!" Natanial yelled, again, trying to keep an eye on him without bumbling into one of the tears in the world.

Saradyn heaved himself up from behind the throne and stumbled toward Anavha. "These are mine," Saradyn said. "My women! My pets! Mine!"

He stumbled, miraculously weaving in and out of the puckered black holes. Natanial had no interest in losing his own limbs, but Saradyn's rambling, drunken path was taking him closer to Anavha.

Natanial hefted the ax handle, weighing his options. Saradyn was six paces from Anavha. Five.

Natanial threw his ax handle. It hit Anavha squarely in the back of the head. Anavha gasped, clutched at his head, and bowled over. The black eyes winked out. Natanial crossed to Saradyn and headbutted him. Natanial pulled a knife from Saradyn's belt and backed up against Anavha, who had fallen to his knees, still clutching at the back of his head. Blood seeped through his fingers. That could make things even worse.

"Be calm," Natanial said. "Calm yourself the way you were taught. We have this."

Most of the creatures, a dozen in all, were on the ground or barely standing, too injured and stunned to continue. They peered at Natanial and Anavha with their beady eyes.

Seven soldiers came in from the door behind them. One wore the purple coat of a sinajista.

"Burn these things!" Monshara said.

Natanial pointed at Saradyn. "But not him," he said. "Leave him."

The creatures went up in flame. They oozed a thick, oily smoke that left those who remained coughing heavily. Natanial pulled Anavha to his feet and dragged him over to the soldiers, near the door where the air was better, then went back for Saradyn. Monshara leaned in the doorway with the soldiers, being tended by a passing medic.

"Why do you want that mad old man?" Monshara said.

"Saradyn is many things," Natanial said. "But he has one especially useful skill. He's worth taking back with us."

"I don't have time for laggards," Monshara said. "Speak plainly."

Natanial gazed into Saradyn's haggard face: the matted hair, the tangled beard, and the dark eyes – eyes that still held the wild, angry soul of a man Natanial had believed could unite Tordin.

"Your empress needs a way to detect infiltrators," Natanial said, "to see who's from this world and who isn't, to root out all those little spies in her temples. I've seen this man do that. Daorian is fallen. You and I need to remind your empress just how useful we are to her."

11

Luna sat with Yisaoh over tea and half of a biscuit, still shivering with the memory of the field of the dead, though ze had cleaned off the mud and sludge from hir face and changed clothes. It had been over an hour, and still no one had opened a wink to them. They sat in a small alcove in what had once been a very grand hall. Tirajista-trained vines covered most of the windows, but light still cut through in places, illuminating the dusty, intricately tiled floor. The people and beasts that swam across the floor's design were utterly foreign to Luna.

"Does this happen a lot?" Luna asked. "Not being able to call on Oma?"

"More than Kirana would like," Yisaoh said. She offered her own biscuit to her daughter, Tasia, who took it and scampered off into the hall. Tasia had insisted on having tea; a treat, here, Luna discovered. Weak tea and moldering biscuits.

"Do you have many children?"

"Three."

"The others went over?"

"Yes, they are living with Kirana in that temple."

Luna could not finish hir own biscuit. Hir stomach

cramped painfully. The larvae of little weevils waved their maggoty forms at hir from inside of it as ze set down the rest. More protein, ze thought wearily, and washed it down with the rest of the tea. Hir stomach cramped again. Though hunger roared again since ze had eaten, ze knew from long practice that ze needed to go slowly or ze would vomit everything up, or worse.

They sat in silence while the toxic wind rattled the windows and makeshift coverings around the stronghold.

"There are two dozen of us still here," Yisaoh said. "Not a lot, by any standard." She spoke softly, staring into her tea, as if talking to herself. "What are another two dozen dead, after all this blood and sorrow?"

"You destroyed the Saiduan. All of them. For what? For nothing."

Yisaoh sighed. "I cannot make you help us. Nor can Kirana, as much as she would like to believe herself a god."

"You aren't as confident in her anymore."

Yisaoh peered at her. "Perhaps not. She knows that. She knows I question these decisions. As do you, as you have every right to. But Luna… you were willing to die rather than help end all this. What if you chose to *live*?"

The air around them grew heavy. Luna tensed. Hir ears popped.

A slender tear appeared six paces away, beside the large empty hearth, certainly meant for cooking more than heat here.

"Oma has returned," Yisaoh murmured.

The seam widened, and a jista, Suari, stepped through, flanked by two soldiers.

"Consort Yisaoh? You are well?" Suari asked, tentative,

gaze darting about the foyer.

"The child doesn't bite," Yisaoh said. "We had a chat."

"Empress Kirana said to bring hir back immediately, once we held Oma again."

"Where is Kirana?" Yisaoh asked.

"There has been an… incident. Nothing to worry about, consort. But an urgent matter the Empress needed to address."

"There was a time I was her most urgent matter," Yisaoh said, and stood. She offered a hand to Luna. "I'm sorry, but you must go back."

"She will put me in a cell again," Luna said.

"Suari, you will tell the Empress I request that she release Luna when she has helped with the task set her. No more death. No more imprisonment."

Suari's jaw tightened. "Of course, consort."

Yisaoh squeezed Luna's hand. "That's all the protection I can offer you, my word."

"When the ways between are closed… there won't be any more death? No more war?"

"I am weary of war. So is Kirana. We want to raise our family, Luna, as anyone else would."

Luna gazed at where Tasia played in the outer hall, munching on a biscuit as she set her dolls to the task of finding a missing dog, or some such.

Ze nodded, once, not to Yisaoh, but in the direction of Tasia. Then, to Suari, "I will tell the Empress what I know. But only her."

"I understand," Suari said. He glanced at Yisaoh. "I will have her wait in a guest room, until the Empress returns."

Yisaoh inclined her head.

Luna trusted no one. Relied on nothing. But ze had

leapt before, and would leap again.

"If I do this – I want to be free, Yisaoh."

"I know. So do I, Luna. So do I."

"What the fuck is it?" Kirana demanded, raising her spyglass to her eye and gazing out over the plateau, toward the massive mountain that had fallen from the sky.

"We've already gotten birds back, and a runner," said Madah, her intelligence officer and a former line commander. "It's not a mountain, it's some kind of boat."

The spyglass gave Kirana a clearer view of the outline of the great shape that marred the horizon. There certainly was something… organic about it. Something alive, as if some great gnarl-skinned monster slumbered out there in the woods.

"Is the stronghold intact?"

"Much of it was crushed," Madah said. "What wasn't crushed shattered in the aftershocks. The temples have held, though."

"Fuck," Kirana said. She took the spyglass from her eye. "Gaiso had charge of that hold. We had thousands of soldiers and sixteen jistas under her there."

"There are still damage reports coming in from the settlements. There… could be some survivors."

"Fuck! Suari! Where's my wink?"

"Still working on it," Suari called.

"Oma's being fickle," Kirana said, handing the spyglass back to Madah. "Take Mysa Joasta with you and ride out there. I want an in-person report. You may get there before Oma allows Mysa to make a connection again. Bloody fucking satellite."

"Yes, Kai." Madah bowed and hurried across the Assembly Chamber.

Kirana took a deep, calming breath and settled her mind. Tucked away thoughts of Yisaoh and that Dhai girl. Yisaoh could handle the girl, no doubt, but Kirana hated to be cut off from her family. The uncertainty would eat her alive if she stopped to think too hard over it. She went back to her room and spent some time in meditation, clearing her mind. Emotional decisions could wreck them. She needed clarity.

Once her mind calmed, she went to her office and dug through the notes of the accounts her people had gathered from the Saiduan archives about the last rising of Oma and had one of the servants bring them into the Assembly Chamber.

Suari called, "I have Oma again."

As he did, a wink opened just above the Assembly Chamber table. Madah and Mysa peered through. Behind them was the great organic hulk; this close the skin of it was visible, a burnt, scaly black flaking at the edges. It was so enormous it towered outside the frame of the wink.

"Empress, we have a significant force here," Madah said. "They are wounded, shocked, asking for safe harbor. But it's… large."

Kirana jutted a finger at Suari. "Take these two and go retrieve that girl from Yisaoh. Right now!"

Suari opened a wink on the other side of the room.

Kirana fixed her attention back on Madah. "How many?"

"Best guess, several thousand are still alive. Maybe more, once the wounded and dead are sorted."

"They have a leader?"

"Yes, it's one of the near-worlds we've caught scouts from."

"Kalinda? Aradan?"

"No, it's our favorite one. *Gian*."

"Fuck. I should have known. She was the most stubborn. Any idea how many jistas she has?"

"No, but if you recall, she had those fighting bears."

"I do. Let's hope they're dead. How did we miss her building that monstrous ark?"

"I think she'll deal, Empress," Madah said. "They are worse off than... uh, they are unwell. Food reserves at near zero. This was a desperate act. I think her people will parley."

Kirana knew what Madah had nearly said: "They are worse off than *us*." She grimaced. She had two options, here: pick them off now, one by one, while they were weak and newly arrived, or work out some deal with Gian so they could align themselves against the other incoming worlds.

"We'll need to know if this is a single event," Kirana said, "or if she's expecting more. Madah, you have authority to call in as many troops as you need. Tell Monshara I need two of her companies."

"Yes, Empress."

From the corner of her eye, Kirana saw Suari return from the other side, escorting Luna with him. Kirana let out a breath, unaware she had been holding one.

Kirana waved at Mysa to end the connection. The wink closed. She rounded on Suari.

"How did Mysa snag Oma's breath before you did?"

Suari stiffened, hand still on Luna's arm. "I don't know.

It's highly individualized. Perhaps her position–"

Kirana was keenly aware of witnesses to their discussion, and kept her voice low. "She was clearly still in the temple. Yet she was able to bring herself and Madah there, investigate, and open a wink back here before you even felt it return."

Suari raised his voice. "This one has something to tell you, Empress. Something that will please you." He released Luna.

Kirana noted that in the hour the ataisa had been gone, someone had clearly washed and combed out hir hair, and ze had probably eaten something, based on the renewed vigor in the eyes.

"I met your consort," Luna croaked.

"You did. And did she explain our troubles?"

"I'll tell you," Luna whispered. "But then you let me go."

"When my scholars confirm what you've told me is true, yes."

"So I can go, when I give you this? That's what Yisaoh said. She said you wouldn't harm me. She gave her word."

"Well, I wouldn't want to make my consort a liar."

Luna nodded.

Kirana snapped her fingers at Rimey. "Go get the scholars from downstairs. Have them bring the book."

Rimey ran off to the stairs.

"Will you eat something?" Kirana asked.

Luna nodded.

Kirana called for tea; she wasn't going to waste bread and butter on this one.

Luna sipped the tea as they waited for the scholars to come up. Ze would not look at Kirana.

"You met my wife? My daughter?" Kirana asked.

Luna nodded.

"How is Tasia?"

"She seems well," Luna murmured.

Kirana leaned back in her chair. Perhaps she should not ruin whatever spell Yisaoh had cast on this one.

The scholars arrived, breathing heavily, their coats whirling behind them; Orhin in the lead, face bunched up as if he smelled something terrible; Himsa just behind him, trying to match his great stride; and Talahina, shoulders hunched, eyes big, gaze darting all about the chamber. Kirana had never invited them this far up into the temple before. Talahina held the book, and set it onto the table in front of Kirana.

"Show them," Kirana told Luna, pushing the book at hir. And, thinking of her mother, and Yisaoh's endless patience, added, "Please."

Orhin carefully leaned over and opened the page to the section with the temple diagrams. "We know these symbols here correspond with the type of jista."

Luna's fingers trembled as ze put hir fingers to the diagram. "This explains the machines," she said.

"We gathered that," Orhin said. "We need the key for the language. The diagrams – we can puzzle that out once we have the key. You do… have the key?"

Luna met Kirana's look again. "She promised."

"She did," Kirana said. "I do not make promises I can't keep."

Luna pulled a piece of green paper from inside the book and began to write out a series of symbols. "This is the Kai cipher," Luna said.

"We are familiar," Orhin said. "But that doesn't–"

Luna shook hir head. "It isn't a straight translation. That was the trick of it. Roh understood that." Luna's eyes filled. Some other dead Dhai in Saiduan, most likely. "It reads from left to right, not right to left."

"Oma's breath," Talahina swore, "how did I miss that?"

"It's not that simple," Orhin sputtered. "The Kai cipher was considered and discarded! It was nonsense in relation to this text."

"You can work out the title, here," Luna said, "like this." Luna dutifully translated the title of the book, showing the scholars in detail how ze did it using the cipher.

Kirana leaned back, hands behind her head.

Orhin said, "We'll get to work on this immediately, Empress. All three of us. We'll call in help, also, so we can–"

"Excellent," Kirana said. "Luna, we'll need you here a few more days, in case they have questions."

"Yes," Luna said, softly.

Kirana called over one of her guards. "Take this one back to one of our nicer suites, will you? And ensure it gets something to eat."

When Luna was gone, Kirana addressed her babbling scholars, all of them crowing over the book.

"You're a year behind!" Kirana yelled, and pounded her fist on the table.

They quieted.

"Get back down there and get this done," Kirana hissed.

They bowed and hurried off, so quickly they forgot the book. Kirana grabbed the book and threw it across the room. It rattled the far windows, but did not break them.

"Fuck!" Kirana yelled.

Luna knew hir fate when ze gazed upon Kirana's triumphant face. Though the guards took hir to one of the nicer rooms three floors below where they kept their political prisoners, Luna was still aware of hir status. Luna would only be fed and clothed and tolerated until the book was fully deciphered. After that? Kirana would not keep her promise. It wasn't *her* promise, after all.

Luna waited for a guard to return with hir meal. Despite it being a better room, ze still tripped on a loose stone in the floor, barely covered over with a rug.

Ze sat meekly at the end of the bed as the guard entered. A young woman, not much older than Luna, truth be told. Luna could not look into her face. Instead, ze held out hir hands for the bowl and eating sticks.

As Luna's left hand gripped the bowl, ze took hold of the eating sticks with hir right, and leapt at the guard.

Luna jammed them into the guard's eye. She screamed and clutched at her face. Luna lunged and picked up the loose stone from the floor. Turned before the guard had recovered, and bludgeoned her head with the rock. She went down, but Luna needed to make sure she stayed down. Luna hit her a second time, a third.

Luna fumbled with the keys on the bludgeoned woman's keyring. Ze darted into the hall, closed the door behind hir, and tucked the rock into hir pocket. Ze went casually to the main stairwell. Two jistas were coming up from below.

Wasn't there another set of steps? One less obvious? Luna cast about for a doorway. There. Six steps down. Luna breathed slowly, carefully, taking the steps without hurry. Hir hand met the door. Ze pushed inward, and came into a tight, narrow corridor. The servants' stair.

Luna went down another flight of steps, then risked going out into another hallway. Yisaoh had dressed Luna in a plain gray tunic and trousers, which was similar enough to what the other servants wore for hir to slip among them without too much trouble. Luna spied a girl dressed much as ze was, pulling soiled bedding from a guest room. Luna waited until the girl's back was turned and then scooped up the discarded towels from outside the door.

Ze still had the keys with hir, and the stone. As ze came to the main floor, hir breath quickened. Hir hands shook. A dozen servants and various officials and soldiers still moved about the space, many of them heading to the banquet hall for the evening meal.

Luna passed into the foyer. Dusk had fallen. Flame flies droned lazily in lanterns set into niches in the walls. Ze went quietly to the great front doors opposite the grand staircase. The doors were closed. One soldier sat on a stool there, dozing with his head against the wall.

Ze steeled hirself and padded to the sally port set in the larger gate. It was locked. Of course. Luna dared not try the keys; ze doubted the guards would have keys to the main gate anyway. Instead, Luna crossed to the banquet room on the other side of the doors. Voices came from the far end, in what must have been the kitchen area.

Windows lined much of the wall that faced the plateau. Luna set down the towels on a table. Ze went to the windows and worked at the latch of one of them. It popped open, about as wide as hir arm from wrist to elbow. Luna did not have time to hesitate. Ze pulled hirself up onto the windowsill and sucked in what remained of hir stomach and pressed through the gap.

Luna had always been a small person, but the body that housed hir before imprisonment would not have fit. As Luna huffed and puffed out the window, ze realized a year of starving and wasting away in the cell below was all that had made this possible.

Halfway through, Luna got stuck, and considered breaking the glass. The voices from the kitchen grew louder. Luna let out hir breath in a rush and gave one final push.

Luna landed in the garden and crawled quickly through the gardens to the stone bridge that crossed the gaping chasm between the temple and the plateau. Ze stayed away from the lighted path, stepping softly among the flowers and shrubs instead.

The bridge, too, had guards. Two on this side and two on the other; there was a wall around this front garden that had not been there the year before. Luna's heart sank. Ze knew this was the only way off the plateau, as ze had noted all the ways in and out when ze had first arrived.

Luna took the stone from hir pocket and threw it into the bushes on the other side, hoping to call the guards' attention, but neither was bothered. The ones on this side were engaged in conversation, too low for Luna to make out. Maybe they would be relieved soon? Maybe they would go to have a meal and ze could get out when they changed the guard?

To have come all this way and get stuck and captured again when they discovered Luna among the other Dhai slaves was too much to bear.

Luna got up and stepped boldly onto the path. The stones poked at Luna's feet, but on ze went, striding confidently up to the guards. All Luna had left was the confidence of knowing that ze had survived a year in this place, and hir whole life in Saiduan, while these people tried to murder hir. That confidence was enough to make the walk.

The guards saw Luna and ceased their chatter. Fear tangled in Luna's guts, but this was the only chance Luna had, to face them directly. Luna could not spend another night in this cursed temple, waiting on Kirana's whim. Luna approached them holding the set of keys in hir hands, like a totem.

One of the soldiers peered at Luna. The other stepped closer to see what Luna proffered.

"Where did you find these?" the soldier asked, in Tai Mora.

Luna waited until the guard's hands were on the keys. Then Luna ducked between the two guards, kicking up gravel as ze went.

"Hey, now!" the soldier yelled, alerting the two on the other side.

Luna was terribly weak, but not as weak as ze had been a few hours before. The two other soldiers moved into Luna's path, blocking hir from the other side.

With a great burst of energy, Luna jumped onto the railing and propelled hirself forward, balancing dangerously on the supports. The Fire River churned below, a great black snake of death. Luna pitched forward onto the plateau on the other side, narrowly missing the grasping fingers of one of the soldiers.

Luna ran blindly, not knowing at all where ze was going. Following the path would mean following the light, so ze abruptly turned away from heading down into the little settlement on the plateau and instead headed out to the east. The soldiers were in pursuit. They were faster than Luna. They would make up the time in mere moments.

Ze changed direction abruptly and ran up the edge of the plateau, following its long curve as hir body broke out in a cold sweat.

Luna bolted across the plateau, as quickly as hir exhausted, wasted legs would take hir. Ahead, Luna saw the breadth of everpines and verdant bamboo carpeting the hills on the other side of the ravine that split the plateau. How far were those hills... an age, an impossible distance, maybe fifty yards? Maybe more. Luna wanted a miracle. Luna wanted to be free, one way or another, wanted to be able to fly across the ravine and land in those beautiful, lush bamboo.

Ze wanted freedom more than anything else. The guards were coming. They would end hir. Luna's feet tangled in the long grass. Ze had a moment at the very edge of the plateau, two steps, in which ze could turn back.

Instead, Luna jumped, hurling hirself into the great black abyss where the Fire River yawned below to embrace hir.

Finally, Luna thought.

Finally, free.

12

Lilia found Caisa already washed and refreshed, drinking weak tea in one of the small guest quarters in the eastern quadrant of the warren.

"I'd like you to get word to Elaiko," Lilia said, "in Tira's Temple."

"Of course," Caisa said. "It's only a few days' ride from here. What do you want to tell her?"

"Can you send a bird? It needs to be faster."

"I can… That's trickier, but yes. What's going on?"

"I need Elaiko to help myself and two others get inside Tira's Temple. To the basements, those rooms the Tai Mora have uncovered."

Caisa's face lost a little color. "You can't be serious, Li. That's… they are well guarded. The passwords change daily. The–"

"I want to see it for myself."

"It's safer for me to find someone who can go down there," Caisa said. "My contact in Oma's temple has unprecedented access. They can easily–"

"I need to see it," Lilia said. "I know that sounds mad, but…" Taigan had been so sure Lilia was a worldbreaker, that she had some gift that would help them all. Was she getting caught back up in that story? Or did she simply hate the idea of leaving the potential power of the temples in the hands of the Tai Mora? "Meyna wants to leave Dhai. If we abandon the temples to the–"

"Leave Dhai?" Caisa said. "That's... No! Not after all we've fought for."

Lilia leaned forward. "I don't want that, Caisa, but to convince Meyna there's a future here, I need more than diagrams and vague stories from the Tai Mora. I want to see how this works. I want to know if we can somehow wrest this power back from the Tai Mora."

"I... I don't know, Li."

"Caisa? If we leave, then your year of sacrifice and intelligence is all for naught."

Caisa twisted her hands in her lap. "I'll see what I can do," she said. "Three of you?"

"Just three," Lilia said. "In and out."

"I'll try," Caisa said. "I can get word there and something worked out with Elaiko in a few days, perhaps."

"Could we do it any faster?"

"How fast?"

"Two days. The sooner the better."

"Why the urgency?"

Lilia hesitated. Caisa would learn soon enough, she supposed. "A man has come into camp. He says he is Ahkio."

Caisa clapped her hand over her mouth. "Impossible! He was dead!"

"He may still be. We don't know it's truly him."

"I could... I was close to him for some time, I could–"

"Meyna has taken him aside. Whatever happens with

him is up to her and Yisaoh. You understand?"

"Ah, I see."

"Thank you, Caisa."

"Do you think I could see him? The Kai?"

"You could try," Lilia said. "I assume Meyna will be keeping him close."

Caisa stood and wiped her hands on her trousers. "Does this mean your plan to attack the Tai Mora camp during Tira's Festival is… on hold?"

"It depends," Lilia said.

"On what?"

"On what I find out when I visit the temple of Tira."

Ahkio sat across from Meyna in an underground room lit with flame fly lanterns, hands tucked under his arms. Liaro sat to his left, and that was a comfort. It was not so long ago that Ahkio could not keep his own thoughts straight. Simple words still eluded him, sometimes. Liaro had taught him to put on a tunic and heat water for tea. There was a time, after he had fled the temple and begun wandering the foothills around Mount Ahya, that he had forgotten his own name. What a blessing that had been. Truly a gift from Oma.

Meyna looked much the same as he remembered her; the heart-shaped face, the full lips, the only-slightly-less-generous proportions. Even knowing what he did, with all the history between them, he had a strong desire to press himself into her arms and seek comfort. Old habits were difficult to shake.

Her family sat in the next room; Rhin and Hadaoh, Mey-mey, and the new child, Hasao, the one she insisted was his, and he had no reason to doubt it. She looked startlingly like him, much more so than Mey-mey ever had.

"You could have pretended to like me more," Meyna said, sipping at her tea and wincing at the heat. "I'm doing both of you a great favor."

"And we appreciate it," Liaro said quickly. "It went well, don't you think?"

"It did," Meyna said, but her gaze remained on Ahkio, intense and calculating. "How do you feel, Ahkio? Rumors are moving through the camp that you are here. We'll announce it formally, but I wanted to have a private discussion first, since it's mostly been Liaro and myself speaking about this alliance. I need your backing now, the way I've given you mine."

"I'm real," Ahkio said, resenting her assumptions, as if he did not deserve to be here with his own people. "Don't think you're doing a deal with some other version of me. I haven't spoken a dishonest word to you, or Liaro, or any of them."

"I assume nothing," Meyna said. "But our purposes are aligned. If I'm to convince all of these people to board these ships I have acquired and head south, to a new home, I need someone they have faith in."

"I didn't realize the scullery girl, Lilia, had so much power here," Ahkio said.

"Not power," Meyna said, "but... influence. She has been throwing herself and her cult into this mad dance with the Tai Mora for months now. I've heard she plans on a major offensive, during Tira's Festival. No doubt she'll end up getting herself and her followers killed if she follows through with that. After, there will be a place in their hearts here that needs filling. That is where I see you."

Ahkio glanced over at Liaro, who patted his knee, a comforting gesture. Yes, Ahkio needed it, though it pained him to admit it. He wanted to leap out of his seat and run. Why had he come back? He could have wandered the woods indefinitely, after learning what had happened. Murdered by Nasaka's hand, the temple fallen, his people scattered. It was too much.

Ahkio squeezed Liaro's hand. "I just want peace," Ahkio said. "That's all I ever wanted."

"So do I," Meyna said. "Moving our people to a new homeland will achieve that. Will you support that?"

"What other options are there?"

Meyna curled a lip and tried her tea again, sipping carefully. "Lilia wants revenge. She wants to fight. And she doesn't care how many of us her crusade takes down with her."

"The Tai Mora will follow you," Ahkio said softly. "They can find us anywhere."

"They are too busy with their temples and stargazers."

"They *will* follow you," Ahkio said. "They won't rest until we're destroyed."

"It isn't about that," Meyna said. "Once their world died, they stopped murdering us. Mostly they enslave us."

"Then why are they hunting you here?" Liaro asked. "We ran into several patrols."

"Because Lilia is striking back at them," Meyna said. "She has her people go on little raids sometimes, breaking up supply trains, that sort of thing. We are a nuisance."

Ahkio was uncertain if Meyna truly believed that, or if she knew the more likely reason that the Tai Mora kept coming after the Dhai refugees. Ahkio knew all too well what Kirana wanted, because he had refused to give it to her: Yisaoh Alais Garika. And his refusal had led them here.

Liaro must have seen something in his face, because he said, quickly, "We'll certainly be less of a target when we're gone, then. Ahkio?"

"Yes," Ahkio said.

"Good." Meyna stood. "You've already seen your rooms, but would you like an escort back? We'll come for you when the meeting begins."

"We're fine," Liaro said. He took Ahkio's arm.

Ahkio followed him, head bent, knowing he was a bit like a cowed dog and not caring about the optics of it.

When they left Meyna's rooms, Liaro said, "Let's walk. Get some air. Fewer people above ground. And all this dirt makes me claustrophobic."

They went through the narrow halls of the underground refuge and up the ladders to the misty woodland above. A few people passed them, but none Ahkio recognized, for which he was grateful. So many had died, and so many of these were younger people. Few from the temples had escaped, he gathered. Most had either been killed or put into service for the Tai Mora.

Above ground, a few children played near a great bonsa tree. They ducked away when they saw Ahkio and Liaro; clearly they were not supposed to be up here alone. The scent of a few cook fires teased the air.

When it was clear they would not be overheard, Ahkio said, "They will follow us. Kirana won't stop until she has Yisaoh."

"That wasn't a part of this," Liaro said. "We never

discussed that. I told you, leave this to us. You're still... fragile."

Ahkio rubbed his eyes. He wanted to deny that, but Liaro was right. Liaro had seen him at his worst, but still believed in him, more than any of the others. Certainly, Meyna thought Ahkio was some shadow. And maybe... maybe he was? Ahkio was so confused most days it would not have surprised him to discover it.

A soft rumble made the ground tremble, shaking moisture from the trees and spattering them in cold droplets.

Liaro wiped the damp from Ahkio's face. "I love you, you know," Liaro said.

"I know," Ahkio said. "Is that enough, though?"

"You were given a gift from the temple. You got another chance to live. Let's not waste it. Meyna has all of this in hand. I know you two have a contentious history, but they love her here. She knows the Woodland, and though you may not remember it, you did choose her child to be Li Kai. This will set things right. We just need to keep our heads down."

The soil rumbled again.

"What *is* that?" Ahkio asked.

A clanging bell sounded, high and urgent.

"Walking trees?" Liaro said. "We should get below ground."

As they turned, a great roar filled the woodlands around them. Ahkio froze. Great, lashing vines appeared through the tree cover, their creepers wrapping around tree trunks and tensing – *pulling* – something forward that moaned and crashed through the woods.

Liaro took him by the arm and yanked him toward the

entrance to the tunnels. But Ahkio turned back to where the children had ducked off.

"They aren't safe!" Ahkio said, yanking his arm away. He ran across the muddy ground. Liaro yelled after him, but Ahkio could already see the five children breaking cover, running for them.

"This way!" Ahkio said.

The ground heaved again, and one of the children fell. Ahkio scooped him up and took up the rear of the group.

A seething mass of tangled, fleshy vegetation rumbled toward them, yanking itself along with its tendrils. A half-dozen more, smaller but still as wide as Ahkio was tall, rolled behind it, lashing at the understory of the trees, snapping small branches and tattering the great plate-sized leaves of the bonsa trees.

Liaro made it to the entrance of the settlement and helped the first three children down. He ducked into the hole just as one of the fleshy mounds rolled over it, blocking the others.

"This way!" Ahkio yelled to the remaining children. He set down the one he carried and pulled his weapon. Whatever kind of sentient monster this was, they could bleed. They could be killed. He had fought enough of them to know.

The clanging bell sounded again, a different rhythm this time.

Ahkio slashed at the groping tendrils as the massive sphere of vegetation roiled toward him, seeking purchase on his body to propel itself forward.

"Stay out of its way!" a cry from above, a lean young woman with a mop of hair, sliding down from a tree roost with several others. "Grab the children!" she said to her companions, and drew her bonsa sword as she raced toward Ahkio.

Ahkio knew her face; the freckled cheeks and prominent forehead she was still trying to cover with a fringe of hair. He felt some relief, on seeing her. Caisa Arianao Raona, his former assistant, once a Tai Mora – how many knew that? But he felt such joy on seeing her: a familiar figure, one he had fought beside before. The tension in his belly eased, even as the creepers snapped at his legs.

Caisa stopped just short of him, alarmed at the sight of his face, but recovered quickly and put her back to his, weapon raised. "Move around them!" she called, and began heading out of the plants' paths.

They slipped into the narrow strip between the paths of two of the large sphere, slashing and hacking at the tendrils if they came close.

Her companions snatched up the two remaining children and took cover behind a massive bonsa tree.

The roiling forms of the seething beasts rumbled away, lashing and snapping. Ahkio sliced one more heavy tendril before the things cleared the camp.

Ahkio huffed out a breath.

"Tumbleterrors," Caisa said, wiping sticky sap from her weapon and sheathing it. She came around and peered at him. "It's you?"

He nodded. "I thought you were dead," he said.

"Same," she said. "Meyna saw you die."

"It's a very long story."

As the trembling ceased beneath their feet, a few heads popped out from the various underground entrances to the settlement. Along the edges of the paths the tumbleterrors had cleared, a few more fighters stood, weapons out. Many were already making their way toward him.

"The rumors are true!" Caisa called to them. "The Kai is alive!"

There were a few gasps. People began to clamor out of the settlement and gather around him, pressing close, though not close enough to touch him without consent. They marveled at him. He noted all the young people bearing white ribbons in their hair and around their throat.

The bubbling conversation drew more and more people, until Meyna finally eased her way through the crowd to him, calling, "Yes, it's true! It's all true! The Kai has returned to lead us to our new home! There will be a meeting tonight, in the gathering hall, at dusk. We will share our vision with you!"

Ahkio gazed across the crowd and saw Yisaoh staring at him, her hands covered in sticky violet sap and plant matter, face spattered in dirt. When she saw him looking, she gave a little smirk, and put thumb to forehead, mocking.

He winced. He could not stomach Meyna's politicking. He cast his thoughts again to Yisaoh. Kirana would hunt them all to the ends of the world until she was dead. Despair welled up. He had failed at so much. All he wanted to do was save his people. He just wanted to make it right.

But to make it right, he would have to do a grave wrong.

Ahkio shuddered. He was going to start sobbing again. He feared he would not be able to stop.

13

Roh wept at the sight of Asona Harbor. He wept again when he found out Taigan was alive, and that even such a powerful sanisi would join with the Tai Mora. What had Roh been fighting for all this time? Why had he fought so hard to get here, when everything was falling apart?

It had been more than two years since he had leapt onto a ship to Saiduan with his fellow Dhai scholars, looking forward to living a more exciting, less ordinary life.

He had found that life.

The trip down the Saiduan continent with Keeper Dasai, Dasai's secretary Nahinsa, and their retinue, had taken far longer than he had anticipated when he begged them to take him back to Dhai to meet with the Empress. As a sort of magistrate for Caisau, Dasai had business to conduct, and his tall secretary with the lopsided face was equal parts lover, bodyguard, and contract writer.

Much of the business the Tai Mora did here at the end of the great war was dealing in food and human labor. One of those human chattel was Roh. He survived because he knew the Kai cipher, he insisted he was a relation of the Kai, and – most importantly – because Dasai knew that the man who shared Roh's face in their world was already dead. There was no reason to kill Roh to save one of their people.

They traveled by cart through the old gates of Asona Harbor. Its teardown was nearly complete. Roh sat in the back of the cart with the other chattel – scaly chickens, three young boars, and piles of animal skins, silks, and rice destined for Oma's Temple. He viewed the landscape with his gangly legs with their shattered knees hanging over the edge.

From this vantage point he saw the world pass him by after it was already behind him, and after a while he didn't want to look anymore.

His joy at seeing home again did not last.

Perhaps he should have known what was in store when Taigan laughed at him in the bathhouse on the harbor.

The clan squares of Dhai had been burned out. The lift lines cut. The orchards were twisted wrecks. The fire that had pillaged the world the year before had been thorough, and routed much of the toxic plant life between the clans as well. He saw the mangled shapes of dead walking trees, first one and two and then whole families of them.

Wildlife had been caught in the routing as well; bones peeked through blooming spring wildflowers. Not all of the bones were animal, either. From a distance, he saw human skulls. While the Tai Mora had been busy trying to till the ground, and beat back the encroaching new growth, they had not had time to dispose of all the Dhai bodies. Around Kuallina, Roh saw heaped mounds of soil where he knew the bodies of his people had been buried. They had not been eaten or burned, but buried like fertilizer. Thousands and thousands of them.

Industrious groups of Tai Mora and their slaves were shoring up roads, clearing away toxic plants from new fields, tilling reddish soil, and tearing out old, fire-ruined orchards to make way for grape vines.

These changes were sad, almost expected, but not striking. The change that made him gape was far more permanent and unexpected. As they came up the top of the low hills outside Asona, he caught a glimpse of a great black mountain protruding from the center of the country. If he had to guess, he would say it lay near the Kuallina stronghold.

"What is that?" Roh asked Dasai, though he knew better than to speak unless spoken to.

Dasai ignored his outburst, but when he gazed at the great mountain, his mouth firmed.

They stopped at a wayhouse outside Kuallina where the tavern keeper regaled Dasai and Nahinsa with the story of Kuallina's fall to fire during Sina's rise, and the Kai's retreat to Oma's Temple, where he was chopped to pieces by his own people and thrown in the sewer dregs.

"It's said they fished him out, after," the tavern keeper said, making a two-fingered sign that Roh had learned was a ward against the ire of the gods, to the Tai Mora. "Then they ate him," he said. "Those barbarous Dhai." This last was said without a hint of irony.

"What of that black mountain?" Dasai asked. "We've heard rumor of a great upset here."

The tavern keeper lowered her voice. "It fell from the *sky.*"

"Invaders?" Nahinsa asked. "An army?"

"No one's sure," the tavern keeper said. "Flattened the

stronghold there, though, and made a great crater. Rocked the whole country like a terrible earthquake when it landed. Some of it got cut off, you can see, when the worlds came back together. Oma knows how big the whole thing was."

Nahinsa knit her brows. "But how could a mountain–"

"It's no mountain," the tavern keeper said. "It's a living thing. A boat of some kind."

"From the sky?" said Dasai, incredulous.

"Wild worlds out there," the tavern keeper said.

That night, Roh lay on a straw mattress at the foot of Dasai's bed, clasping his hands together, pretending it was not his own hand he grasped, but that of some good friend or lover, someone who could keep him safe. He took comfort in that. The world had changed irreparably, but he wanted to turn it all back. The creature in Caisau had told him he needed to come to Dhai, but when would it be too late? All those conversations felt like dreams, now, the hallucinations of a boy battered and beaten.

What would happen when he arrived at the temple? The creature said he could talk to Oma's Temple when he got there, but what if he couldn't? And what would he have to say to Kirana, this mirror Kirana, the terrible shadow version of the Kai he had known before Ahkio? He closed his eyes and tried to remember her face, but it was all so long ago that all he remembered was the rough sound of her voice.

She had been a very weak tirajista, and he had once watched her coax a vine from between two stones when he was very, very young and Tira was ascendant. He could not remember her face, but he clearly saw the beaded dew on the vine, the little granules of soil as it twirled up and up into the air, the gods made real.

Two days later, they finally reached the Temple of Oma. On the edge of the plateau, which had once been nothing but amber-colored grass, the Tai Mora had constructed a fortified town.

As Roh entered the village, wondering whom they housed here, he saw the familiar chitinous armor of the Tai Mora soldiers. Among the soldiers were the support people, the dog-minders and launderers and cooks and doctors. Roh passed a doctor's tent where a yowling woman was having a poisonous angler thorn, big as a tree branch, yanked from her leg. Roh had never seen anyone survive the sting of an angler bush when Tira was descendant, but with so many satellites in the sky perhaps she had a chance. He wondered if the Tai Mora tirajistas had some song they could use to heal that hurt, or if they had no idea that the woman's life would be over in an hour without treatment.

He expected their presence to rouse curiosity, but no one paid them any mind. Dasai had been someone up north, but he seemed unknown among these people. Many of these soldiers bore little resemblance to the Tai Mora or the Dhai. They were a mix of different peoples who had clearly come from a broad range of far-flung places across the other world. Some bore elaborate tattoos, others had piercings and dyed henna hair, or wore their hair in spiky locks, or slicked against their scalps with white paste or violet clay. They were tall, short, lean, with faces that were long or broad, foreheads peaked or flat, low or tall. He realized he compared the people of every other country

based on how like or different they were to the Dhai. Dhai
was normal to him, and these people were very different.
Perhaps, now, he was the different one. This was the new
world.

Roh noted the few surviving Dhai among the camp. He
knew them by the tattoos on their necks, like his, and the
cut of their gray clothes. They had not yet learned not to
meet each other's gazes. Roh still saw defiance in their
faces. Where had his gone?

"Here we are," Dasai said, as a soldier raised a hand to
slow their cart.

Nahinsa explained their purpose to the soldier, and
gestured to the cart of goods.

"You'll want to see the quartermaster," the soldier said,
and waved them on through a fortified gate and into a
large square. Here there was a courtyard of beaten dirt and
several tents and hastily erected cabins. One was clearly
a kennel, with spaces for bears and dogs separated. A
blacksmith tended a forge, aided by a tirajista who worked
at panels that had the gleam of Tai Mora armor.

Dasai ordered Roh to wait with the cart while he and
Nahinsa went inside to meet the quartermaster. Roh bided
his time, singing an old parajista song softly under his
breath.

"Rohinmey?"

Roh started, nearly falling off the cart. He jerked around
to face the woman who had spoken. She was a lean woman
with a big frame, wide in the hips and shoulders. Her
plump mouth was pursed, and a wrinkled line appeared
between her brows as she regarded him. He guessed she
was ten years his senior, and she bore the neck tattoo and

plain gray clothes of a fellow Dhai. Her thick mane of black hair was pulled back under a broad gray scarf.

For a long moment, Roh did not recognize her.

She came to the edge of the cart and leaned toward him. It was her eyes that decided him, large and dark.

"Saronia," he said. She had lost weight; the roundness of her face and figure were gone, replaced by a stark hunger that only emphasized the lines of her face. He knew Saronia was much closer to his age than she looked. She carried a basket in her arms, arms that had long shiny scars: burn marks.

"What are you doing here?" he said, in Dhai, and it was a stupid question. What were any of them doing here? It was Dhai, and they were, still, Dhai.

She shook her head. "Tai Mora," she said, and continued their conversation in Tai Mora, even though she surely spoke too low for anyone else to hear them.

"We all thought you were dead," Saronia said. "All the scholars sent to Saiduan. Was that–"

Roh shook his head. "It's their Dasai, not ours. Ora Dasai… Chali, the others… No."

"I'm sorry," she said. "It was like that here. We thought Ora Nasaka would protect us, but she just opened the gates! We didn't know what to do. They killed anyone who protested. Stacks of bodies, Roh, so many bodies. You have no–"

"I have an idea," Roh said. He nearly placed his hand over hers, and stopped himself.

She caught his look, and looped his hand in hers. "It's all right," she said, "I consent."

"I'm sorry," Roh said. He looked around to see if anyone

was paying them mind. A soldier at the door of the quartermaster's office was watching them carefully.

Roh got down from the cart, painfully, and helped her pick up the basket. It was full of dirty laundry, and when she'd dropped it, various pieces of soiled linen had fallen in the mud.

"I'm so glad to see you, Roh," Saronia said as he helped her refill the basket. They had not been friends, in the temple. Saronia was from Clan Garika, and she had been a terrible bully.

From the corner of his eye, Roh saw Dasai leaving the quartermaster's office.

"You should go," Roh said. "Let's not draw more attention."

She raised her head, and did not quite look at Dasai, but she clearly noted his presence. She took up the basket and hustled past Roh without sparing a glance back.

Dasai got up into the cart, staring after Saronia. "Who is that one?" Dasai asked. "Someone you know?"

"From a long time ago," Roh said.

"Come now. The Empress has agreed to see us."

The various guards and additional slaves in Dasai's retinue stayed on the plateau while he, Roh, and Nahinsa were escorted across the natural stone bridge that connected the plateau with the small crag of land that bore the weight of Oma's Temple. Roh limped along painfully, conscious of how different his gait was coming back into the temple than leaving it. He followed the height of the temple, up and up, to the familiar glint of the dome. The Tai Mora had torn down the fenced webbing that protected the temple from the plateau and had completely rebuilt the old stone walls. Inside the walls, much of the front gardens would lie in shade. Roh shivered as he crossed through them to the temple door, which was barred.

Roh had never known a time when the doors to the temple were locked.

They entered the temple proper, ushered by the sinajistas, who unwarded doors as they went. The temple bustled with slaves, liveried servants, guards, jistas, and specialists of all sorts. Roh was overwhelmed by the heat and noise of the place. It had never been this busy; Oma's Temple was no longer a place of study, but one of war and conquest and rebuilding. He lingered behind as his party entered the foyer, and pressed his hands to the wall next to the door.

"Beast?" he murmured.

Nothing. Only the subtle warmth of the walls, which he had felt his whole life. Had Caisau been a dream? Had he come all this way for nothing? He racked his memory for some sign, some key piece of information the creature had given him. *The creature on the plateau will know you. Step into her circle and the map will unfold. You are the map now. You are the Guide.*

"Rohinmey!"

Roh started, and hurried after Dasai.

The sinajistas began up the great stairwell. Roh balked. Broke out in a cold sweat. "Keeper Dasai, I cannot. My–" he could not say, "My legs," and choked on the words. But he gestured.

"Could you carry him?" Dasai asked one of the sinajistas. She made a face. "Certainly not."

"You, there!" Dasai called to a big man sitting next to a

lean, petite woman on a bench in the foyer. "Can you help my boy up the stairs? Just a few flights."

The big man rose. He was not tall, Roh saw now, just broad. His scraggly black hair and beard needed a wash and comb; he had the blunt features and stocky build of a Tordinian. He hunched a little as he walked over to them, right arm tucked against his torso. His right hand was missing. The clothes he wore were the simple cut of a servant. Someone had clearly dressed him recently.

The man said something, most likely in Tordinian. Roh didn't speak it, but many Tordinians knew some Dorinah. His gaze was flat and black.

"Please, Father," Roh said in Dorinah. "Will you help me up the stairs?"

"My dogs," the man said, in mangled Dorinah – or, that's what Roh thought he said. "You have? My dogs?" He seemed to be looking at something just over Roh's left shoulder. "Ah, ah," he said. "Your ghosts!"

"He's addled," Roh said to Dasai.

The little woman next to the man got up, peeked around the man; Roh saw she had the beginnings of a beard. She was pale as a Dorinah, and looked as exhausted as the man. She grabbed the man's good arm and said, in Dorinah, "We are waiting for someone."

"Could he take me up the stairs?" Roh asked, but before she could respond, the man was already moving, very quickly.

Roh scrambled back, but the man scooped him up and hefted Roh over his shoulder. Roh let out a squeal.

"Good, then." Dasai waved at them to continue up.

The way was deeply uncomfortable. Roh kept losing his

breath. "Ghosts?" Roh wheezed.

"See you," the man said. "Patron slayer."

Roh froze like a captured rabbit. Who *was* this man?

The little bearded woman came after them, heaving herself up each step, daintily tugging at her belled trousers as she went.

When they got to the top Roh asked to be put down, and the man – surprisingly – obeyed.

They stood just outside the open door to the Assembly Chamber. The sinajistas announced them.

The Empress stood at the Kai's seat at the great circular table of the chamber, one foot on the chair, pointing at two travel-worn visitors Roh took to be soldiers. Behind her were two slaves, waiting on her whim, and several jistas and councilors of some kind.

Roh expected her to look much more like the Kirana he had known during his time in the temples. But this woman was wiry, with a harder mouth and flat, intense eyes. No glimmer of mirth or mercy there.

She did not acknowledge them for a full minute as she continued speaking to the soldiers. "I thought I had Daorian murder all their jistas. How did this one escape, Monshara?"

The woman soldier, Monshara, said, "He was unknown to them at the time. Natanial, tell her of–"

"It's good he did escape," the lean man, Natanial, said. "You'll need him for the end."

"But Saradyn? Ghosts?" Kirana rolled her eyes.

"It's complicated," Natanial continued, "you should see–"

At the name *Saradyn*, the man who had carried Roh grunted and yelled something in Tordinian. The sinajistas surged forward, but the soldier inside turned, and called them back.

"No! Leave him. Saradyn isn't terribly dangerous anymore." Natanial crossed over to the big man, Saradyn, and took him by the elbow. Presented him to the Empress.

"Where is she from?" Natanial asked, in Dorinah, pointing at the Empress.

"No ghosts," Saradyn said.

"An easy guess," Kirana said. She gestured across the room, to Roh. "And him, the boy, there? Does he have ghosts?"

Saradyn let out a great guffaw. "So many ghosts!"

Kirana folded her arms. "I'll test him, then. He only sees these... *ghosts* from people of this world? That's how he determines who is from this world and who is not? What is a ghost?"

"I have no idea," Natanial said, "but yes, he'll know instantly if someone is impersonating one of your people."

"A fine gift. We've been sweeping the temple for spies for the last six months, and still have leaks."

Natanial bowed stiffly.

Kirana waved him away. "Take the jista downstairs. Is that her?"

"Him," Natanial said. He gestured at the bearded woman – man – who had followed them up. "This is Anavha."

"I don't need to speak to him," Kirana said, lip curled. "Just keep him here. Suari?"

One of the jistas behind her came forward. "Get this omajista warded and bound."

"Wait," Natanial said, "warded?"

"Of course. Every jista working in this temple is bound to me. Monshara, get him a drink. Take that Saradyn man with you. I'll send someone into the foyer to collect you and get you settled. You!" One of the servants from the back came forward. "Escort them to the eating hall."

The servant led the group away: Natanial, clearly still unhappy, and Saradyn, babbling. Natanial said something to Anavha as Suari advanced, something low in Dorinah that Roh couldn't quite catch, as Kirana bellowed for Dasai to enter.

Roh hurried after Dasai and Nahinsa.

"Keeper Dasai," Kirana said, "you took your time getting here."

"It did not occur to me how quickly things were moving," Dasai said, "until the last few months. I've brought this boy with me, a relation to the old Kai. He knows the old Kai cipher."

Kirana smirked. She pulled her leg from the seat of the chair and sighed. "The Kai fucking cipher. You're a little late on that. We already have the Kai cipher! We wheedled it out of some little Dhai washed up from Saiduan. And we're reading it correctly, now. We don't need your boy."

Roh felt his face flush. Who else would know the Kai cipher? "There's a book!" Roh blurted. "A guide to breaking the world. I–"

"Quiet!" Dasai demanded. He raised his hand.

Roh shrank away, but Kirana waved Dasai off. "We have the book," Kirana said. "The Dhai child brought it to us."

"Luna?" Roh breathed.

Kirana peered at him with greater interest. "You knew that ataisa?"

"But have you translated the book?" Roh continued. Was Luna still here? he wondered. "Have your people

memorized it already? Because I have. I know what it
says. I know how to close the ways between the worlds, so
no more mountains fall from the sky, so no one else will
threaten your sovereignty."

"She already told us–"

"Luna told you the cipher," Roh insisted. "But I translated
and memorized the whole book. How much time do you
have, Empress? Enough time for them to translate the
whole book?"

Kirana moved to the other end of the table. She picked
an open book from near a stack of others and slid it over
to him.

Roh approached the table. As he did, he noted its great
circular shape, and the old mosaic map of Dhai peeking
from beneath the scattered papers and writing instruments
and various cups and jista concoctions. He had never paid
much attention to the floor here, but he did so now. A
great ring of the temple's exposed flesh circled the floor
beneath the table, inlaid with blue and green mosaic tiles
along the border.

Step into her circle.

Roh stepped onto the ring of the floor, pressing himself
against the table to manage it, and took hold of the book.
He paged to the end of it, pointed to the complicated
diagrams, the Worldbreaker there at the center of the
diagram.

"You need a key," he said, "a worldbreaker, and a guide."

"I am Kai. Surely that's good for something."

Roh shook his head. "Not here. Not to these temples.
The temples are the beasts, living things. They have long
memories. They remember who the Kai really is. And

honestly, the Kai doesn't have much to do with controlling the mechanism, unless they are gifted, or take on the role of the Worldbreaker."

"Then I will burn the temples the fuck down."

Roh felt the floor beneath him soften.

"Then you will be burning a long time," he said, and he felt himself sinking, dissolving, and he smiled for the first time in many, many months.

The temple swallowed him into a comforting black embrace.

My Guide. You have come home.

Roh felt weightless. So much darkness. He could not speak. But he heard the creature thrumming in his bones.

Oh dear, it said. *You have come alone. You need the Key and the Worldbreaker. I cannot take you to the People's Temple without them. Come back with them when Para is risen.*

Wait, wait! Roh wanted to shout, to explain, but the creature went silent.

And Roh stumbled from the darkness – and into light.

14

"There are tumbleterrors out there," Emlee said. "You haven't forgotten them? They've had sightings ever since the funeral."

"I haven't forgotten," Lilia said as she packed her things. She had endured nearly three days of waiting while Caisa worked with her contacts inside Tira's Temple to plan an infiltration. Ahkio's heroics with the tumbleterrors had sent the camp into an uproar. In some ways, that was good. It meant fewer people paying attention to Lilia and her supporters. Meyna kept Ahkio very close; he was never alone, always with either Meyna or Liaro. Lilia had a terrible feeling about all of it; a knot of dread had formed in her stomach, and she had not slept well.

Harina and Mihina had already gone off to gather those who had agreed to join this particular mission. It had been a popular one, among her people. Everyone wanted the chance to ride and work beside Lilia.

"There's one thing I need before I go," Lilia said. Emlee must have seen something in her face, because she recoiled.

"That bit of Hasao's blood I asked you for."

Emlee firmed her mouth.

"You must trust me, Emlee. I could bring the whole

child, but I'm not. That blood I asked you for yesterday is all I need. Ahkio said the temple responded to him. It recognized him as Kai. If Hasao is recognized as Kai by the temple, I may be able to understand or access something in Tira's Temple that the Tai Mora have not."

"There is always one more thing you need."

"Emlee."

"You ask too much."

"I will take it myself, then."

The box in the corner rattled again. Lilia shivered. It had been doing that more often the last few days, but she dared not open it. Kalinda hadn't told her to open it, and she was honestly beginning to fear what might be inside.

Emlee frowned at the box. "You should cast that into the sea."

"Let it alone," Lilia said. "The blood? Do I need to get it?"

"No, you are terrible with children. And Meyna will murder you if you approach her."

"Tasia and Namia–"

"They are hardly children. None of the children here have been allowed that. They grow into useful appendages for you, too quickly."

"Will you help or not, Emlee?"

Emlee turned out her kit of vials and potions and took out a small jar usually filled with balm. "There's not much," Emlee said. "It was a routine check I did on the child, and Rhin was close the whole time. Had to say she slipped. She was not happy about it, and nor was Meyna, later."

Lilia stuffed the jar into her pack. "Thank you, Emlee."

"Whatever you're searching for, I hope you find it," Emlee said.

When Harina and Mihina returned, Lilia joined them, and Namia followed. But Tasia, alerted from the front room, ran after her.

"Where are you going, Mother Lilia?"

"Hush, I have an errand. I'll be back in a few days."

"Namia is going! Why can't I go?"

"It may be dangerous."

"Then it's dangerous for Namia too."

"She's older than you."

"I'm just as tough."

Lilia stroked the girl's hair from her face. "I know. But I need someone to look after Emlee. Can you do that for me?"

Tasia pushed out her chest. "I know you're just saying that because you don't want me to go."

Lilia considered how many times her own mother had told her that, and she had completely believed her. Simpler times. "You know I'll come back."

"Everyone says that, but it isn't true."

Lilia could not kneel, as it would be painful. But she bent low and kissed the girl's forehead. "I know it isn't fair," Lilia said, "but you must stay with the others and hide, like a snapping violet."

It was only as Lilia turned away and shuffled down the corridor with Namia, Tasia snuffling behind them, that Lilia realized those were the last words her own mother had said to her before she lost her forever.

But Lilia did not look back. She could not look back anymore. Only forward.

She made her way through the underground camp with Namia, sticking to little-used passages. They went through the emergency route, the long, snaking tunnel that came up in a great stand of willowthorn trees well out of sight of the aboveground staging area.

The other two members of the group waited there: Avosta, arms folded, chest puffed out, and Salifa, who had the drawn look of someone who had either recently vomited or was going to very soon.

"Let's proceed," Lilia said as Avosta passed over the lead of a lean dog for her to ride. Dogs were faster than bears, though bears tended to do better in the woodland. Lilia needed speed, now.

"We go southeast," Lilia said, "following the Fire River, to Tira's temple. Everyone is comfortable with the plan?"

A few nods. Avosta's was the most enthusiastic.

"I'm just… I'm still worried about you going," Salifa said.

"Then it's a good thing you are coming with me," Lilia said. "I promise you, we will blend in. No one will notice us. Those temples are crowded."

"And warded, though," Salifa said.

"Elaiko, and her people there, will take care of that," Lilia said. "Trust that we have worked this out, Salifa."

Salifa gave a little nod. "It's just an awful lot of Tira's power I'm going to have to draw. It could alert them."

"It's far enough away from the temple proper," Lilia said. "Elaiko tested it. Come, now, Salifa. We are going to do a very brave thing."

They camped that night just above the Fire River in a wet glade that smelled of everpine and loamy soil. Lilia slept fitfully, and woke even more tired than the day before. A break in the trees let her sit and gaze at Oma, blinking there in the sunrise, its sister satellites glowing just as brightly.

"Are you all right?" Avosta asked. He had the last watch of the evening, and came over to her from his perch at the edge of camp. A snarl of vines caught at his boot, and he used a small knife to pry it off before it tried to sink its hungry tendrils through his boot and into his flesh.

"Just trouble sleeping," Lilia said. She pointed at Oma. "What if someone told you that the satellites used to be one thing. One object? And it was split apart?"

"I would say that whatever did that was very powerful."

"Where would such a thing have come from?"

Avosta shrugged his large shoulders. "Perhaps it was constructed by jistas. Or by the gods, by Oma itself."

"Oma creating itself?"

"People create other people, don't they?"

Lilia hugged her knees to her chest. "I like puzzles," she said. "The sky is the biggest puzzle of all, though, isn't it?"

"I don't think about it much," Avosta said. "There's no point in agonizing over something you can't control."

"I'd like to control it," Lilia said. "I'd like to have control over far more than I do."

"You have an impact on many of us," Avosta said softly.

Lilia leaned away from him and struggled to her feet, leaning on her walking stick. Namia, beside her, wiggled in her sleep and let out a soft sigh. "Thank you for coming, Avosta," Lilia said. "I know it's a very dangerous endeavor."

"So is being alive," he said.

Salifa woke and yawned. "You two are very loud," she said. "Let's eat."

When the party had eaten and struck camp, they continued on through the woodland, following an old game trail littered with dozens of different species of carnivorous plants. Biting hydraflowers and snaplillies sought out their flesh; the bears flicked their enormous forked tongues and ate the furious flora as they went on.

Lilia knew they were near to the temple when she saw a swarm of dragonflies moving parallel to them; the cloud was so large that the light dazzled Lilia's eyes, reflected from their many wings.

She paused to watch them, entranced.

The ground rumbled. Lilia tensed. Insects dropped from the trees and pattered to the forest floor.

"What was–" Salifa began as they halted their dogs.

A great cracking sound filled the sky. It echoed across the woodland. Startled birds took to the air.

When the trees stilled, Lilia let out her breath. The dragonfly swarm broke apart and flew higher into the canopy until they were lost from view.

"An earthquake?" Avosta murmured.

The bears snarled and snuffled.

"I don't know," Lilia said, casting her gaze to the treetops that hid the sky. "They don't usually make sounds do they?"

"I don't like this," Salifa said.

Mihina and Harina shared a look, and rolled their eyes.

"Let's keep on," Lilia said. "We're close." If the heavens fell on them, she didn't want to be caught sitting here gawking. She would rather die *doing* something.

Tira's Temple came into view through a startling break in the trees. A slant of sunlight blinded Lilia briefly. She squinted and raised her hand. Perched atop a cliff in the river valley below, the temple appeared to bloom from a snarl of rock wrapped in flowering vines and great sprays of early spring petals. The temple proper was immune from the encroaching woodland. The green-black fist of the temple shimmered. Its foundation spanned two branches of the river, and water gushed mightily beneath it. The gardens around the temple teemed with life – delicate green shoots and gnarled branches fuzzy with new growth. Unlike Oma's Temple, there was no army camped here, though some force had burned out a great deal of the woodland along the main road that led into the Dhai valley, and had clearly been camping on a blistered black patch of ground not long before.

"I heard it fell quickly," Avosta said, bringing his dog up beside Lilia's. His greasy hair lay knotted against his scalp. "Most of the Oras were called to Kuallina," he continued, rubbing absently at his pocked face. "It's said Elder Ora Soruza and a handful of novices were all they left to defend it."

"A terrible business."

"Did you live in Tira's Temple?" he asked. The others were still coming up the low hill. Salifa was singing to the biting bugs, teasing little carnivorous plants into snapping up the pesky insects.

"No," Lilia said, "just Oma's Temple."

"Did you have people there you cared about?"

Lilia shifted uncomfortably. It could be an innocent question, but Avosta always tried to get too close. "A few, yes."

"I lost many," he said. "Was there... a lover?"

Here it is, Lilia thought. She turned over her answer carefully. "Once," she said. "Her name was Gian." Both of them were Gian, she wanted to add, but that would overly complicate things, and he would want more answers. It had been some time since she said Gian's name aloud.

"Did she perish?"

"Yes," Lilia said. "I... made a mistake. A miscalculation. She suffered for it. I live with that each day."

"I'm sorry," he said.

Lilia waved biting insects away from her face. She turned in her seat to see how close the others were. Nearly there. "In any case," she said, quickly, "they kept a few of the drudges and jistas, but warded them."

Avosta grimaced. "Dirty people."

"They are," Lilia said.

"Well, show me where the crossing is," Salifa said.

"We need to distract the Tai Mora patrols first," Lilia said. "Namia is going to round up the patrols. Mihina, you'll be waiting above that valley choke, there, as we discussed." She pointed to a narrow way between two steep hills just below them. "When the patrols are cornered there, you'll set a fire behind them, trapping them in the valley. Harina, you will accompany Avosta and me up into the temple."

"And Namia? How is she going to escape those patrols once she gets them into the choke?" Harina asked.

"Namia will go up that tree." Lilia pointed to a tangle of vines around a slender sapling. "With all their armor on, they won't be able to follow. Namia and I went through this with Caisa the day before we left. She knows what's expected."

Namia signed at her, "Death."

"Hush," Lilia said, rubbing her shoulder, "not yours."

"They will see you are gifted, Lilia," Avosta said. "You and Harina. They can spot jistas immediately."

"It's all right," Lilia said. "There's a way to mark us as gifted, but warded to the Empress. Salifa, you'll need to train a vine up across the river that carries us up the back side of the temple."

"I got that," Salifa said. "Just show me where. I'm going to need to focus Tira's breath at the base, make it harder for anyone inside to notice it."

"Good," Lilia said. "Once we are in the garden, Elaiko or one of her people will have proper clothes. We will change and proceed to the belly of the temple."

"You're certain of this contact?" Harina said, exchanging a look with Mihina, who shrugged.

"As certain as I am of all of you," Lilia said. "Elaiko has been providing us with information from Tira's Temple for months now. Salifa, I'll want you to maintain your position at the base of the cliff. We'll need your help to go back out that same way."

"What if I'm found?"

"My hope is they'll be concentrating on the fires that Mihina will be manipulating out here in the woods," Lilia said. "If they aren't, do your best to maintain the vines and save yourself. We'll slide our way down if we have to."

Lilia said, "Namia will start rounding them up now. She knows to bring them here once the evening snaplillies open and release their scent. That's when we will begin our climb, so we need to be in position before then."

"This requires a lot of luck," Salifa said.

"Not at all," Lilia said, "it just requires all of us to follow the steps exactly. No mistakes."

Lilia told her mount to sit, and reached out to hug Namia. "You'll do well," Lilia told her.

Namia signed, "Victory."

"That's right," Lilia said.

Namia scampered off through the trees, her form looking small and frail against the monstrous trees and massive tangled vines and shrubs.

"Good luck," Lilia said to Mihina. "Remember, you want to draw the patrols, but don't burn down the wood."

"I'm ready," Mihina said. "I was going to be the one to do far worse to the Tai Mora during Tira's Festival, remember?"

"You may, still," Lilia said. She urged her bear back up and pointed toward the sound of the river. "Let's keep on. It's getting hot."

Avosta kept pace with her, and Harina followed with Salifa at the very back, the four of them keeping to a single-file line in an attempt to disguise their numbers. They stopped twice at the sound of patrols in the far distance, and kept low and silent until they passed.

As they came down the rocky ridge that descended to the rear of the temple, Lilia had them tie-off and muzzle the bears. Going down the steep trail was hard on Lilia's leg, so Avosta carried her. She did not complain. She had a very long way to go yet, and tiring herself out this early wasn't going to help any of them.

Dusk helped mask their approach. Lilia caught the smell of the snaplilies before the others. She hoped Namia did, too.

A gushing branch of the Fire River separated them from the cliff on which Tira's Temple perched. Salifa kicked the rocks and muddy tendrils around them.

"It's going to be very obvious," Salifa said, squinting

across the river in the dying light. "Anyone who looks down will see a great tangled vine bridge."

"Our hope is they don't look down," Lilia said.

Salifa chewed her lip. "Lots of hope seems to be required in this entire plan. Li, are you sure–"

"I'm sure," Lilia said. "For me, Salifa. Please. I need to see what they have uncovered. I must see it myself."

Salifa sighed. The air thickened. She closed her eyes.

All around them, tremulous new shoots sprang from the soil. They tangled together and began moving across the water, growing thicker and darker as they met the cliff on the other side and began to tease their way up.

"Start across now," Salifa said, gaze intent on her creation. "I'm going to lower it into the water behind you to mask it. Lilia, here, take hold."

Lilia grabbed the leafy tine of the vine with her good hand. It wrapped around her waist and over one shoulder and scooped her up, out and over the bridge. Lilia let out a little gasp. The others were snarled up into the plant's arms behind her. Lilia was passed from one tendril to another across the whole span of the blue-black water. The plant dumped her into the mud on the other side. She lost her breath a moment, and worked hard to regain control of her breathing. She lifted her head, and stared up and up at the vast distance they still had to travel up the side of the cliff.

Avosta and Harina arrived, and they began the ascent as the bridge of vines behind them sank just beneath the water. The curling tendrils along the cliff clung to their arms and waists and legs, offering handholds and braces, and a little bit of extra help to climb.

Still, Lilia was gasping by the time she was halfway, and had to stop to take a swig from a mahuan-laced water bulb at her hip.

The others slowed to wait for her, but she waved them onward. It was almost full dark now. The lights of the temple were a beacon.

Lilia knew she was close when the lights from above finally illuminated her handholds as the gentle insistence of the vines continued to propel her upward.

Avosta, already at the top with the others, held out his hand and pulled her up the rest of the way. Lilia leaned against him, trying to catch her breath.

A great bone fence, twice as high as they were tall, confronted them.

"What now?" said Harina. A slight drizzle began to fall. Lilia worried about the rain and the fire that Mihina needed to keep kindled, but an overcast sky would further protect their approach and escape.

Lilia wished for Namia up here, in the dark, as Lilia's night vision was not excellent. Namia could have guided them by sound and smell alone.

"We should see a break in the fence here," Lilia said. "Let's look for it."

They tramped around in the dirt until Harina found a broken, out-of-place bone that they could push out of the way.

"I'll go first," Avosta said. When he indicated it was clear, the rest of them followed.

Lilia led them through a great maze of bones to a long-dead bone tree at the center. Lilia had been to Tira's Temple only a few times, but Elaiko had given good directions. The paths were lit with blue phosphorescent lichen that sent up little puffs of spores as they trod across them.

At the base of the dead bone tree, a little Dhai woman Lilia recognized as Elaiko stood hunched, seeking shelter from the rain. Elaiko hugged her arms to her chest. When she caught sight of Lilia, she darted forward. Like the other Dhai who had been made slaves, she wore some kind of collar, and drab gray clothes, like a scullery drudge.

"You're here?" Elaiko whispered. "All of you? I could only get three outfits. Only two collars. Oh, wait, there are fewer of you than I expected."

Lilia frowned. "Yes, we had to leave very quickly. Avosta, stay here and guard our retreat. Harina, you'll come with me."

"I'm Elaiko," the woman said, by way of greeting, to the others. "I'd so love to offer you tea, but the circumstances–"

"That's quite all right," Lilia said, as she began to shed her clothes. The cold bit into her bare skin. She rucked on the too-big drudge clothes, already damp, as quickly as she could.

"I should go with you," Avosta said.

"We need that break in the fence kept clear," Lilia said. She did not look at him, but was keenly aware that he was staring at her as she dressed.

"Quickly, quickly," Elaiko said.

Lilia didn't hear anything, but Elaiko kept looking toward the temple. "Is everything in place?" Lilia asked.

"Yes," Elaiko said, "but you must put on the collars, quickly."

Lilia handed one of the collars to Harina, and took the other herself.

Harina wrinkled her nose, but she took the collar. "These aren't live, are they?"

"No, no," Elaiko said. "That isn't how the wards work. The wards that keep us from injuring the Tai Mora… those are written into our skin. These are simply a marker that it's been done. A shorthand, you could say. If you attract no attention, they will look away, assuming you are warded."

Dressed and collared, the little party started off after Elaiko. "Go back to the fence!" Lilia called to Avosta. He hesitated another moment, but finally complied. She let out a sigh of relief. She needed their love, yes, but more than that, she needed their faith and their loyalty. Love was more fickle than faith. It worried her that Avosta might love her more than he feared her.

Elaiko led them through the bone tree maze and into the rear temple garden. Here, the way was lit with flame fly lanterns. They came inside through the kitchens. The heat and noise assailed them; the drudges were preparing the evening meal. Rice and tender spring shoots, and meat – the smell of the meat made Lilia recoil a little. What animal were they cooking? The Tai Mora love of flesh outside the funerary still disgusted her. They went in pairs, Elaiko and Harina up front, and Lilia behind.

A passing cook yelled at Elaiko, "She wants tea upstairs! Where have you been?"

Elaiko started. Froze. Babbled, "Yes, of course," and went for the tea tray on the big table at the center of the kitchen. Harina lingered with Elaiko. Lilia did not want them going in groups larger than two.

Lilia kept walking, and Harina came with her. The temple layouts were all virtually the same, but she had gone over a rough map of this temple's interior provided by those in the camp who had been there. She was confident she could wait for Elaiko in the foyer if they ducked into the scullery stair. They needed to pick up laundry, and it was a good place to rest and get a sense of their bearings.

Lilia stepped up into the foyer and headed right, passing under a low arch and into the scullery stair. The mouth of the laundry staging area lay open; all the drudges brought laundry from the levels above here, where another set of drudges were usually tasked with bringing it to the proper laundry facility in the basements.

Two drudges were already inside, dropping off laundry. They nodded as they headed out, but one narrowed her eyes, clearly suspicious that she had not seen them before.

Lilia went to the back of the room where it was darker. She shifted a load of laundry toward Harina as she entered. "Let's get ready."

But just as she cleared the threshold, a dark figure blotted the light. A Tai Mora soldier blocked their path. Pointed at Harina. "You, there. Come with me!"

Lilia froze. She needed a very quick story.

Harina, though, was already moving, so fast Lilia did not catch the flash of the knife, though she saw the blood immediately. Harina bumped into the Tai Mora and whirled him around, so now the Tai Mora stood in the laundry room. It was a solid hit that could still have been construed as accidental.

"My apologies, so sorry," Harina said, wiping at the Tai Mora's shoulder, a sleeve. The Tai Mora pushed her away, still so flustered that he was oblivious to the blood pumping onto the floor.

Lilia became alarmed at the amount of blood. She backed up against the bundles of dirty laundry along the rear wall.

"Out of my way!" the Tai Mora insisted, but then Elaiko was there, with the tea, her mouth a wide O.

The Tai Mora slipped in his own blood and went over. He became aware of the pump of blood. His eyes widened. He gasped. But he was already bleeding out. Even as he pressed at the pumping wound, he was going into shock.

"Stay out of the blood!" Lilia hissed at Harina, but it was too late. She was on her knees, holding the Tai Mora down. Blood soaked through her trousers and smeared her hands. A few drops peppered her face.

Lilia hefted what was left of the laundry bag with her good hand and gingerly stepped across the piles of blood-soaked laundry.

Harina became aware of her own bloody clothing. "Sina's maw," she muttered.

"You can't go out like that!" Elaiko said, gaze darting back into the hall. "Quickly! Someone else is coming."

"Stay here," Lilia said, low. "Clean up. Change your clothes. You know where we're going. Follow us."

Harina grimaced, but nodded.

Lilia went into the corridor with Elaiko and closed the door to the laundry closet, leaving Harina with the body.

"If anyone walks in–" Elaiko said.

"I know," Lilia said. "We must keep moving. Ah, your shoes!"

Elaiko made a little peeping sound. Lilia handed her a towel from her bag, and Elaiko scrubbed at her bloody shoes.

Elaiko hissed something. Lilia turned just in time to see two more drudges heading toward them, up the scullery stair. Lilia moved out of their way. The two gave them an interested look, but kept moving.

Elaiko bustled out of the scullery stair and into the foyer. Lilia hurried after her as fast as her limp would take her. The basement doors had a single guard, who opened it to them after asking the day's password. When the door closed behind them, Lilia murmured, "They change the passwords every day?"

"Yes," Elaiko said. Her hands trembled so hard the teacups on the tray rattled. "All the temples now, at the Empress's command. You can't get down here without the daily password. There's been a great deal of activity. Are you… are you sure we can–"

"Courage," Lilia said.

Elaiko pursed her mouth and said nothing. The teacups still rattled.

Lilia dropped the laundry off inside the steamy laundry bay on the first basement level, then continued after Elaiko to the second set of doors.

"Here," Elaiko said, gesturing to an open storage room. "Stay here until I call. There's never more than one person bringing tea. Only authorized people here."

"Still your trembling," Lilia said. "It will be all right. Try not to look at them." Lilia wanted to add, "Because you will give it away!" but did not. Elaiko was already too shaken. What if they didn't drink the tea? If they needed violence here, Lilia would have to turn back. She did not think she had the strength in her one good hand to injure, let alone kill, anyone.

Lilia ducked into the storeroom. But she could not help but peek out and watch Elaiko taking the last long walk to the two guards at the second set of doors. Elaiko offered up the tea tray to the two guards. One gestured at her to set it on the pedestal near them. Elaiko set it down, clanking and trembling only a little, and started back down the hall. She met Lilia's look.

Lilia turned back to the storeroom. She looked through the barrels and boxes until she found the plain burlap bag that Caisa had Elaiko smuggle in the day before. Lilia was relieved to find it. She opened it and dug through the tubers until she found all three of the plain, shelled hazelnuts at the bottom of the bag. She stuffed them into her pockets.

Elaiko met her there and shut the door. She let out her breath, and began to cry. Lilia did not know how to react. She made a comforting noise, but stopped when Elaiko continued to sob.

"It will be all right," Lilia said.

"No, it won't! What have I done?"

Lilia recognized it, then, but still had no time for it. Elaiko had never committed violence before.

"Maybe they won't drink it?" Elaiko said.

"You need to hush."

"What if they drink it?"

"That was the plan."

"I have to–"

Lilia could not help it. She grabbed Elaiko's sleeve. "No. We stick to the plan."

The clatter of teacups. Someone swearing. A cry.

Lilia held Elaiko's sleeve and met her look, daring her to try to pull herself away.

A thump and crash in the hall. Elaiko finally slipped from her grasp and went to go and see what had happened. Lilia limped after her.

The guards lay heaped upon one another. Broken teacups and poisoned tea lay spilled all around them.

Lilia grabbed the keys from the belt of the nearest one, who was still moaning and retching. Doors in the temples were not built with locks. This one had been attached to the door by the Tai Mora, a simple padlock. Lilia unlocked it, but the door resisted her.

"It's warded," Elaiko said.

Lilia pulled one of the little hazelnuts from her pocket and shoved it under the door jamb.

"Stand back," Lilia said.

Elaiko moved behind her.

The innocuous looking hazelnuts were fused with a powerful twining of sinajista and tirajista spells. One meant to explode with great force when triggered.

A whisper of power made the air heavy. Lilia's ears popped. She shifted back on one foot, unsure herself of what she would unleash.

A low pop. A thread of searing red light. When Lilia looked back, a quarter of the door had sheared away. Lilia pressed at the door and it swung open. The light from the hall illuminated a short flight of dark stairs.

Lilia pocketed the keys and grabbed the nearest guard. He was heavy. Elaiko just stared at her.

"Help me!" Lilia said.

Elaiko stumbled forward. Together, they pulled the comatose bodies down the short stair and rolled them into an open storage room. These rooms were usually overflowing with barrels of goods, but were now empty; the Tai Mora had far more bellies to feed than the Dhai.

Their movement awoke the flame flies in the lanterns hung just inside the doorway. When the bodies were pushed aside, Lilia took up a lantern and headed further down the corridor to the next set of steps. Elaiko hurried to catch up with her.

"What if they–"

"Keep moving," Lilia said. "One more level. I've seen the temple diagrams."

The next door required only a key. She found the right one and stepped into the cavernous space. No more corridors, just a massive chamber filled with what appeared to be tangled tree roots, great fibrous monstrosities. Lilia swung the lantern toward another source of light coming not from above, but below.

Some industrious force had torn up a great section of the floor, and a soft blue light emitted from the gaping hole.

"How did she even get down here?" Lilia said. "This took them so many months."

"It was terrible," Elaiko whispered. "When they broke through the floor the temple... moaned. And bled! I thought it would fall around us!"

Lilia poked her head through the hole in the floor to confirm there was no one in the chamber below. She handed Elaiko the lantern and climbed down the ladder precariously pushed against the rim of the wound in the floor.

"Come down!" Lilia called. "I need a light."

As Elaiko came down, swinging the light with her because she had two good hands, the great room came into focus.

Lilia gaped.

The chamber was far larger than her descent made it

seem. The ceiling stretched far above her, a perfect dome decorated with twining vines and figures that she thought were geometrical until Elaiko raised the lantern. The twining designs were stylized Dhai characters, glistening wetly as if made of something organic. The air here was much warmer than above. The walls themselves pulsed as if alive.

A massive pedestal took up the center of the room, ringed in four more, all skinned like the walls and trembling faintly.

"Well, here it is," Elaiko said. "You wanted to see it. You need to be quick, though. The guard makes rounds again in an hour. We need to be well gone ahead of that."

Lilia placed her hand on the shimmering green walls. Where the Tai Mora had breached the floor, the wound oozed with a gooey amber sap. Lilia sniffed at some of it that had dropped to the floor: tangy everpine and something more fetid, perhaps fungal. She dared not taste it, but the thought occurred to her. She stepped away from the wound and turned, lantern high.

The pedestal at the center of the room glowed an eerie blue-green. Had her light triggered something within it? She approached and gazed at the great round face of it. There, at the center, was the Dhai word for Kai. Was the Kai supposed to stand here to trigger... whatever was supposed to happen? Surely they would only want... But as she rubbed away the dust and dirt, the symbol became clearer. Not Kai, but something far more abstract: a simple circle with two lines through it. Where had she seen that symbol before? Lilia sneezed at the dust. Tira! Yes, it was the symbol for Tira's Temple that she had seen on the mosaic map of Dhai laid into the round table in the Assembly Chamber.

The puzzle drew her. The intricate symbols, the niches, the glowing light: it was a strategy game.

Lilia dug into her pocket. Pulled out the little container of the child Kai's blood. She rubbed again at the Tira symbol at the center of the pedestal, looking for instructions of some kind. Instead: an intricate pattern of raised metal tiles. As she ran her fingers over them, they lit up, bright blue. She moved her fingers the other way, and they lit up, bright green. She tried a few combinations, tapping at the tiles as if they were keys on some instrument. The pattern was easy to recognize. She tapped in the correct sequence her third try, and all the metal tiles sank into the pedestal. The center, too, sank with it, and from beneath each side a shiny device rose. It clacked together: two plates of some substance much like that of the temple walls. The two plates formed a human face devoid of detail, as if stretched from the mold of a newborn babe. Lilia was not entirely sure what to do next.

She pressed her hand to the face.

It glowed green, faintly, then dimmed.

Nothing else happened.

Elaiko made a little startled noise behind her. Lilia glanced back to see the woman already had one hand on the ladder, as if ready to flee. She did not blame her.

Lilia uncapped the canister of coagulated blood, which was now the sticky consistency of thick mud, and rubbed each of her right fingers into it, then smeared some on her palm for good measure.

She pressed her hand to the face.

A brilliant blue light blinded her.

Lilia yelped. Leapt back. Pressed her hands to her face.

A shushing roar, like the opening of a great dam, filled her ears. Elaiko screamed.

Then silence.

Lilia opened her eyes.

The face, fully aware now, animated, the ghostly features dancing across the mold, peered at her. Said something in a language Lilia did not recognize.

"Get away from it!" Elaiko cried.

Lilia waved her away. "Who are you?" Lilia asked the face.

"Who are you?" it countered. The voice did not come from the mold, but from all around them. It made Lilia shiver.

"I…"

The face trembled. The misty countenance blew away, like a cloud in a storm. The rushing of water sounded again, and the face disappeared back into the pedestal, which closed behind it.

"What was–" Elaiko began.

A shimmering form grew out of the pedestal. Lilia took another three steps back until she bumped into Elaiko.

The ghostly specter wore a long flowing robe and had knotted hair tangled with green ribbons and bits of glass or stone. It did not stand on the pedestal, but floated just above it, and the gaze it gave Lilia was glacial.

"Who are you to try and destroy me?" it demanded.

"We weren't," Lilia said. "You are… you're… what are you? A temple keeper? Like… Ti-Li? The woman unstuck in time?"

"I am the creature. The temple keeper is no more. With Oma's rise, the temple keepers were no longer captive here. They were able to escape to their own times. They have left only the creatures, the beasts. I am the Creature of Tira. What are you? You are not Kai, though you have summoned me."

"Just… Lilia. We were here… you know how to stop people coming here? From other worlds? These worlds are all coming here and killing. They are–"

"Oma has risen."

"Yes."

"Why have you injured me?"

Elaiko said, "The Tai Mora broke in here, not us! They're trying to stop others from entering our world. They're going to use you to do it."

"I wanted to speak to you," Lilia said, "to see if it was really true, that the temples were alive."

"Of course we are alive," the creature said. "More so now that Oma is risen. Why are you still tangling with other worlds when you could simply send them back to their world yourselves with the power of the engines?"

Lilia came forward again. "We could… send back the Tai Mora? To their dead world?"

"Of course. All things are possible, if the creatures work together. We could sink the continent, if you willed it. If the Kai… but… No, you are not the Kai."

"No, but I know where she is," Lilia said.

"You can do anything you like," it said, waving a hand. "You could reshape oceans. Break the world. Sear the sky."

"But I don't want to do any of that," Lilia said. "I want to get rid of the Tai Mora."

"And you could do that," the creature said, curling a lip. "But that is far less imaginative than I'd hoped. All they ever want to do is kill."

"How?" Lilia asked.

A great amber light filled the room, bright as daylight. Lilia shielded her eyes.

A roiling mist bubbled up from the floor and slowly formed a massive series of elliptical rings on which rode twinkling orbs of all sizes and types: greens, blues, reds, swirling with orange waves and flaky white patchwork. The orbs moved along the elliptical orbits, all spinning and sparking. It was like a massive orrery, so tremendous that its dimensions clearly exceeded the size of the room. Many of the misty parts ended abruptly in the walls and ceiling.

"When they made us," the creature said, "we broke the worlds apart. This was not their intended purpose, but it was the final result. Infinite worlds. Infinite timelines. So very many choices. Things go wrong in many of these worlds. What none of them understood, then, was that when their worlds began to break, they would feel compelled to come home, to Raisa, here, where it all began."

A misty blue-green orb was faintly visible all around the creature, as if she were standing now inside a soap bubble. "No single person has the power to move and shape the worlds," the creature said. "There are five great machines, our engines. These temples. Each driven by the power of those who can call on each satellite."

"Five?" Lilia said. "The People's Temple? The Tai Mora have dredged it up."

"Yes, the fifth temple was lost to you after the last rising of Oma. The temple of the People. When the other beasts are equipped with the proper bearers of the satellites' powers, the People's Temple will be fully activated. It will have enough power to do… whatever you like. Send all of those from the other worlds back to their own spheres within the orrery, if that is your wish."

"This temple," Lilia said, "the People's Temple. How was it lost in the first place?"

"I can only tell you what your predecessors spoke of in my presence. Faith and Hahko believed the power too great, that using it would corrupt the society they were trying to build, inciting violence and hatreds and powerful rivalries. They believed the cycles should be maintained, that it was not their place to alter them. I suspect this is why they ensured the temple was forgotten."

"Wait," Lilia said. "You're talking about… Faith Ahya? And Hahko? The first Kai?"

"You *met* Faith Ahya?" Elaiko said. "But… but I have so many questions!"

The creature waved a hand. The misty image of the orrery blew away, curling up like smoke. The white lights dimmed, leaving them under the glowing blue of the creature alone in the dark, musty chamber. "I can tell you only what I know from times before. You have made a mess of everything, cycle after cycle."

"Not this cycle," Lilia said. "We're going to do it properly this time."

"What are you talking about?" Elaiko said. "We have to stop what the Tai Mora are doing here. We have to… I don't know! Burn the temples? Prevent the Tai Mora from getting in? Seal these back up? You heard what it said! They could break whole continents."

"Don't you understand?" Lilia said, turning to her. "We don't have to wait for anyone else to reshape this world, to make things right. *We can do it ourselves.*"

15

Taigan had seen many strange things in his extended life on this strange world, but the great half-severed ark jutting up from what was once the stronghold of Kuallina was among the most impressive in his memory.

He had meant to make his way directly to Oma's Temple, but he had been close enough to Kuallina on his ride up that when the mountain fell from the sky, the tremors took him from his stolen mount. The terrified creature wisely ran in the opposite direction while Taigan found his footing on the newly buckled turf. That slowed him down considerably.

This far inland, he found more Tai Mora soldiers, including many clearly recruited from countries beyond Tai Mora. That made his journey far easier. He murdered a soldier who was about his height and tugged on the ill-fitting uniform. This let him release his glamor, which had increasingly become an annoyance.

While he still got looks along the road, riding the Tai Mora bear outfitted in the red and purple livery of whatever guard or regiment he was supposed to be from, a simple hazing ward made it more difficult for them to recall him. A neat little trick, the hazing ward. They had the added bonus of being nearly impossible to detect by another jista unless they actively sought it out. That scullery girl's mother had been clever to use it.

The mountain intrigued him. The stir of soldiers around the area drew him in. He left his bear corralled with others and took up a perch in a collapsed heap of bonsa trees to oversee the activity.

The double helix of the suns had begun to set. From where he sat, the suns cast the looming shadow of the mountain over his position. The air cooled quickly as the light was drenched from the world. From this vantage he observed that the mountain was an organic ship of some kind, like those sailed by the Aaldians, but fully enclosed, as if meant to travel underwater – or through the air, he supposed, as this one clearly had. He wondered if omajistas had hurled the thing through the rent in the sky. Creating a tear that large and moving an object of that size would have taken a good deal of power and resourcefulness. And clearly not all of the ark had made it intact. The top of it was shorn neatly, as if the gate had closed too soon behind it.

As he observed the comings and goings of the soldiers setting up the perimeter, he saw a tear open in an area designated for such travel just below. It was staked off by itself, the boundary set with red-painted stones warning others not to tread into the space for fear of being suddenly split apart like the ark.

A woman came through; tall and lean, wide in the shoulders, with a long sloping nose and the dead-eyed stare Taigan had always associated with Maralah. Several soldiers hurried to her side once she cleared the stone circle, including a broad-hipped woman in a long red robe that would have marked her an omajista even if Taigan had not seen the subtle play of the satellite's breath around her. Was this a general of some kind, then? Behind her came a young bearded man; Taigan saw the blooming red mist about him, as well. Another omajista. How many did the Tai Mora have? He half-expected them to keep coming through the tear, one after another after another, but it was just the two: the female general and the male omajista.

Taigan followed their progress as they met with a small delegation under a hastily erected tent. The meeting intrigued him. He slipped from his perch as dusk settled, and kept to the edges of the activity.

As the general and the omajistas moved together toward the ark, flanked by half a dozen soldiers, he followed in the shadows, seamlessly inserting himself into the rear of the retinue. His hazing ward would cause their gazes to flit right over him unless he asserted himself.

They stepped through a massive split in the skin of the structure and into a dim underbelly lit with brilliant green phosphorescent lichens. The glow transformed the group into something otherworldly, which was perhaps appropriate.

The group picked their way through corridors scattered with broken glass and some gooey vital fluid leaking from the broken skin of the great craft. The party came upon two omajistas, one who appeared Dhai, another who could have passed for Saiduan. They wore tattered blue robes smeared with the brownish secretion from the walls. One bore a wrap around her head, which Taigan found odd. An injury? Could they not heal themselves?

"Wait until we announce you," the tall, Saiduan-looking one said. Her accent was Dhai.

The other passed directly through the skin of the craft behind them. The skin seemed to thin to admit her, then thicken again as she passed. Very clever. He liked the cleverness of these people. When she returned, they were admitted. Taigan lingered still at the back of the group, wondering how much longer he could keep up the ruse. The dimness helped.

He crept through just as the door began to thicken again behind the Tai Mora group, and kept to the back of the new room, clinging tightly to the shadows. It was dim in here as well; the only light was the phosphorescent flora lining the tops of the walls and a single flame fly lantern at a table in the center of the room. The room itself had, perhaps, once been grand, before the crash.

The table was partially cracked, and the walls here oozing just like those in the hall. Scattered goods – clothing, weapons – lay stacked against trunks that had burst their locks on impact, or in drawers that popped open despite stops that had clearly been designed for shipboard life.

Six more people waited inside, five of them in boiled leather armor shot through with silver, clearly there to protect the sixth at their center. She was a wiry woman, with her left arm held against her chest in a sling. Taigan noted the hands belied her age: strong hands with slender fingers slashed with fine white scars and discoloration that indicated bare-knuckled fighting. Her dark hair was pulled back from a handsome face which Taigan at once found deeply familiar, though it took him a moment to place her. Something to do with a lip curled at Taigan, as if Taigan were more dangerous than she. It was the same look the woman now turned on Kirana; distaste on the lips, but a hint of fear in the eyes.

Ah, of course, how could he have forgotten that sneer?

"I take it you are Gian?" Kirana said, nodding at the sneering woman, whose face smoothed at being so critically considered.

"Chief Commissar Gianlynn Mursia," the woman corrected. "Only my mother and my consorts call me Gian, and you are neither."

"We have come to know you by the moniker."

"And you are Kirana, the tyrant."

"Empress," Kirana said, "if we are using titles. Kai is also an appropriate title. But come now, you and I are not so different that we should be formal. We want the same things, and we have done much to achieve them. Few other worlds have been as successful as ours, not even this one."

"I heard they fell without a fight," Gian said.

Taigan prickled at that. Saiduan had fought them for years, admirably and honorably. And not so honorably, when the fight called for it.

"Those who remain are pacifists," Kirana said. "But you and I are clearly not. We have both achieved much. Your ark is an incredible feat of engineering. I understand your intentions may be similar to mine. To find a home. To begin again."

Gian watched her.

Kirana continued, "I know you are in a sore place. You would not have agreed to see me, otherwise."

"My people won't be slaves."

"Nor will I ask that of you."

"You're a flesh dealer. A tyrant. There is no compromise with flesh dealers and tyrants. You chose to build an army ten years ago, when the worlds began to fail. You chose to murder and destroy. We chose to build an ark. We chose to save what we loved, not murder an entire world. We are nothing alike."

"There are plenty of places on this world for you," Kirana replied. "You don't need to settle here. What I offer is, perhaps... a truce. We are looking to seal the ways between the worlds. Surely you understand that the more worlds that come after us, the more contentious our settlement here will become. Constant war. Strife. Famine. Famine, especially. But you and I, together, pooling our resources – we can close the ways."

"Impossible. No one's done it. Not during any cycle."

"We have the knowledge. I simply need... a few more jistas. Omajistas, especially."

"You cannot buy them! We are not–"

Kirana held up her hand. "I'm not seeking to buy them. I am, truly, offering you the chance to work together. You can be free of us, after. If you will but... *tolerate* us, as we will tolerate you, for another month, two at the very most, until Para has risen. You will need that time to recover here, anyhow. If we are to be temporary neighbors, we best work together."

"We are not helpless, you understand. If we must defend ourselves, we will."

"I don't doubt that. And I know you by reputation. We have certainly kept an eye on your people, though we were uncertain what this... monstrosity was for. There are more like you, as you know. Aradan, Kalinda, Sovonia, and those are just the leaders of the worlds closest to us, those who will find it easiest to cross over."

"Kalinda failed," Gian said. "Her people cast her out and dissolved into strife. That is one less."

"That still leaves us the two knowns, and a limitless number of unknowns. My people and yours don't need war. We need to settle here. There is still space, for us. But not for many more of our size."

"What do you offer?"

"Peace," Kirana said, spreading her palms, and Taigan sneered at the sight of it. Peace? "But we have a very short time frame in which to achieve it. And I will be bold: it would assist us greatly to have you as an ally and not a foe."

Taigan was taken aback at that. This was the nation that had destroyed the Saiduan. He remembered the fallow fields he had passed on his journey south, the thin faces. He smirked, then, because he knew precisely their position. They had won the battle, but not the war. The world was still poised to eat them, and he was so terribly thrilled at the idea that, after all this time, they would die of starvation that he could barely contain his mirth.

"We can discuss it," Gian said. "We are not tyrants, so I must consult our people."

"I understand. Until then, my omajistas and tirajistas would be pleased to assist with any injuries."

"That won't be necessary."

"As you wish, however, I–"

"Our gifted are not permitted to harm, or to heal, unless they are protecting themselves or another from certain death."

An awkward silence descended.

Taigan could not help it. He snorted.

Gian whipped round and met his look, steeling him with a gaze that said she clearly saw through his ward. Ah, yes, a parajista, likely – not a powerful one, but one did not have to be powerful to see through hazing wards, if one had the gift for it. His curiosity had made him a bit careless.

"Who are you to judge us?" Gian said.

Taigan sketched a little bow. There was some movement among Kirana's retinue. Kirana narrowed her eyes. In the dim, perhaps, his features were not apparent, but he was tall and dark, and he knew only a few of her people this close to her would be foreigners like him. Taigan waited them out. He could bluff as well as this foreign empress. To admit he was an impostor here, among one she wanted to align with, was to admit her own security was faulty. Taigan merely inclined his head.

Kirana exchanged a look with one of her omajistas. "Yours may not be permitted," she said, shifting her attention back to Gian. "Ours can. The offer is open. I'd like to invite you to a meal, the two of us, perhaps." She indicated the mess around them. "Somewhere outside, in the open air. It's a lovely world."

"I'll send word."

Kirana tipped her chin. "Good." She waved her people out with her, and spared another look at Taigan. Taigan could not help the smirk that crept up his face. He would very much like to murder her, but it was true that she was the only one prepared to close the ways between the worlds. He would just have to deal with another Kirana if she failed, and the mere thought exhausted him.

Taigan did not linger, but followed after them, weaving down the corridor until he found a large crack in the hull. He slipped into it, and waited there in the empty corridor. Wait long enough, and they would forget about him, and hardly recognize his face, foreign as it was among these people.

But even as he prepared to leave the great ship, Gian herself blocked his way back into the hall. Two omajistas stood with her, and another he could guess was a sinajista. The omajistas already had threads of Oma's breath woven into elaborate spells.

Taigan instinctively reached for Oma. The power pulsed beneath his skin. The air grew heavy. He pushed out a defensive litany, the Song of the Proud Wall, and began to shape the Song of Sorrow, a devastating spell no one had yet countered.

The omajistas responded; their casts were not ones he recognized. Something of the Song of the Water Spider, perhaps, twisted with the Song of Unmaking, as if they sought to distract him long enough to cut him from Oma's source.

Taigan wove a defense just as they deployed a second round of casts, these utterly alien to him. His defensive shield burst under the onslaught. He was just fast enough to buffer the blow with a counter spell, but the shockwave heaved him across the corridor and into the next room. He smashed against the oozing wall, widening the weeping wound that glugged essential, sticky fluid over him.

The omajistas pursued. Taigan sliced through the hull with a great burst of Oma's breath and leapt out onto the buckled ground. He spun a glamor as he ran, but realized the threads of his own power would give him away to the omajistas. They could see him if he held a spell. He dropped it and darted into the maze of fallen trees, following the descent of the land to the water below.

He shrugged off his armor, retaining only the linen tunic and trousers beneath, and dove into the water. Taigan might not be able to die, but he was not fond of pain, generally, and these omajistas had spells he had never encountered before. It was entirely possible they could cut him off from Oma and torture him endlessly. He had experienced that a great many times, and did not enjoy that either.

Taigan let himself float down the icy river, keeping his legs ahead of him to cushion his encounters with the rocks. After a time, he rolled over and made for the other side of the river. He was numb, but knew from long experience that his body would combat hypothermia with ease.

The air, too, was cold; early spring was a terrible time to take a dip in a river. He gazed upstream to see if he could make out signs of pursuit, but there was nothing. No threaded tendrils of Oma, no shouts, no figures. He called a touch of Oma's breath and warmed his clothes enough to dry them, then struck out further down the riverbed. Paused.

A noise? A breath. Someone, something, very close.

He drew deeply on Oma, preparing for the Song of the Mountain, an offensive spell instead of defensive.

Taigan twisted on his heel and brought up a great ball of Oma's breath over his head.

"Oh!" a slender boy said, shrinking back into the undergrowth.

The boy seemed familiar, even in the dim light; it took Taigan a moment to realize it wasn't a boy, though it had been years and several genders since he had last seen this little ataisa.

Both he and the ataisa had belonged to Maralah, he through binding, Luna as a piece of property won in a game of chance. It seemed absurd to see the ataisa here in Dhai, after all that had happened, as absurd as seeing some version of Gian fall from the sky in an ark. But surely there would be Saiduan refugees in the south, little clusters of holdouts who had succeeded in fleeing before Anjoliaa was taken?

He saw no tendrils of power around the ataisa, and no other figures.

"You are Luna," Taigan said. "Are you alone?"

Ze nodded, shivering. Taigan noted the damp clothes, and how Luna leaned hard on a great branch ze had taken up as a walking stick.

"You're injured."

"I jumped into the river."

"From where?"

"Oma's Temple."

"That is quite a trip from here."

"I followed the river."

"How did they find you, child?" Taigan asked, genuinely curious.

"I fled from Shoratau."

"Ah, yes. Who else? Roh, that child, he escaped as well. How curious."

"How did… Yes, he did. And Kadaan! He was alive, a year… maybe more, ago. He got me out of Anjoliaa."

"And how have you survived here all this time? You were a slave?"

"I could understand how to power the temples, the

beasts that can channel the satellites. And close all these–" Luna gestured behind hir, toward the ark "–seams, you know. Their Empress does not like people just falling out of the sky and taking what she thinks is hers."

"How is it done, then? Powering the beasts? I heard from a little bird that you found the book you sought in Saiduan."

Luna took another step back. "Are you working for them? I should go."

"I work for myself and my own purposes, now. I belong to no one. But you? Where will you go? Saiduan is destroyed. The Tai Mora own the world. The knowledge you have is useless without allies."

"I've already told them all they need to know to figure out how to use the temples to focus the power. They don't need me."

"That makes you terribly expendable. That's hardly a mark in your favor."

Luna frowned. "Some days I wanted to destroy them all, did you know? Maybe we should. Maybe that's better. If we keep doing this again and again..." Luna tilted hir head at him. "I'm tired of being afraid. Aren't you?"

"I trained as a sanisi long before you were born," Taigan said. "I was burned up eighteen times in various attempts to kill me. I have been hacked to pieces twenty-seven times. Maimed and mauled and broken and left for dead more than I can count. I know fear, and I know pain. I fear most that I will never die, that this is my punishment, that the gods doomed me to this for some terrible wrong I committed on some other world. Who is to say? But here is what I know, little Luna, little satellite. Without fear we are the humble herbivores lumbering on the plains. We are a flash of light in the sky. Without fear to drive us we never become what we are meant to be."

"What about love?" Luna said.

"What about love, yes," Taigan said. "Love is the fear of dying alone. That's all."

"That isn't true."

Taigan held open his hands, palms up. "If you are going to run, then run into the woods, Luna," he said. "Run and run until you're eaten by some bone tree or trapped inside a bladder plant. Run for fear of what could be. But that is what the herbivores do. Run and run, until mortality catches them. I chase, Luna. I chase, always."

"These temples, these machines," Luna said, "can do more than just close the ways between worlds. They could decide to use it in many ways. They could decide to destroy not only this world, but millions, trillions, an infinite number of others. If I give you that information, or give it to them, then I am complicit. All I gave them was the code, cipher. The other… well, they won't find out what else it does, besides close the ways between the worlds."

"Why not?"

"I tore out the appendix."

"You… what?"

"When they captured me. I knew they would take the book, once they realized what it was."

"Taigan laughed. "Where is the appendix?"

"Gone, thrown into the sea."

"So no one will ever know?"

Luna hesitated. Ze opened hir mouth as if to say something, and thought better of it. Ze shook her head.

Taigan wondered if ze told the truth, or obfuscated to make hir case for freedom stronger.

"I'm going to build some other life with the Dhai," Luna said. "With the appendix gone, well, we're as safe as we'll ever be, I guess. They could still figure out how to break the world, I know. But I did what I could to stop it."

"The Dhai? Why those pacifists?"

"There are still free Dhai, in the woods. I've heard that all along the way here. The Woodland Dhai are free. They have a rebel leader, Faith Ahya reborn. They have evaded the Tai Mora all this time. Maybe they can use what I know. Or not. Maybe they could help hide me."

Taigan felt a twist of... what emotion was it? Surely not hope. "Faith Ahya? A little girl in a white dress, her face covered in scars?"

"I don't know. But she is very powerful. She leads the rebel Dhai in the woods. They wear white ribbons, that's what people say. They are going to take back the country."

"If there is some resistance of Dhai," Taigan said, "perhaps they *will* be interested in what you know. If the temples truly are the source of power, if they find themselves a worldbreaker, well... we could destroy a good many Tai Mora this way."

"You don't want to help the Dhai!"

"No, I came here to kill Tai Mora, and it seems that could be a possibility if we are the ones wresting control of the temples. Do you know where the Dhai are? The Woodland is dangerous."

"I'll manage."

"I have traversed that wood," Taigan said. "I can help you survive it."

"No tricks. A partnership between the two of us."

"There can be no partnership between a sanisi and another."

"Well, there is now. New world, new rules."

Luna was right, of course, and Taigan did not think hir cowed for a moment. Taigan recognized that having a Dhai-looking companion could get him there among the rebel Dhai to see what they were truly composed of. Perhaps he could trade that information for an audience with the Empress. And though Luna may not tell him or Kirana how to close the seams between the worlds, it was entirely possible Luna would tell the Dhai. And if Luna did, Taigan would be listening.

Living as long as he had, had taught him patience. His only concern, as he gazed at the dying light outside, was that though he had patience, the sky did not. The sky was going to keep moving, and he knew that once Oma left them in twenty years, they would be stuck with whatever new neighbors had muscled their way in over the decades. Time was not quite as infinite as it had been. Oma waited for no one. Least of all him.

"I don't believe you," Luna said.

"I can heal your little leg, Luna. I can dry your clothes. We can indeed be partners."

"Why?"

"I always did prefer the underdog. And there is no dog more under-served than you."

Luna glanced at hir leg, and Taigan knew then that he had hir. Taigan smiled broadly. "Let's go see what the Dhai in the woods are up to. I suspect they will be just as eager to murder the Tai Mora as I am, bless their little pacifist hearts."

16

A clattering of footsteps above and behind them. The smell of everpine and dust. The temple rumbled around them.

Lilia shivered. Elaiko squeaked.

"Someone is coming!" Elaiko said.

"Yes," the creature said. "I'm afraid our time is limited. You should find the Guide. The Guide can bring you to the People's Temple."

"Who... who is the Guide?" Lilia asked.

"We need to get out!" Elaiko said. "Is there another way out? Can you help us?"

The creature gestured to the walls. "Step through," it said. "I can take you to any other part of this temple. But only the Guide can step from one temple to another."

"Who is the Guide?"

"The Creature of Caisau chose the Guide. The Guide is close. I feel him near. The Key, also."

"But... the Worldbreaker?" Lilia asked, and it came out more desperate than she intended. She had learned to hate that word.

"When the three come together, you will know. The heavens themselves will draw them together."

"But, who–"

"Choose," the creature said, shaking its beribboned head. The image of it stuttered, shifted, purled away and reformed, like a brilliant aurora. "The Worldbreaker is the one who *chooses*. Anyone can stand at the center and direct the mechanism. 'Worldbreaker' is a poor translation. Better, perhaps, to say the figure who controls the flow of power that is channeled to the People's Temple is a world-*shaper*. The Worldshaper, once in place, is the one who chooses what to do with all that power. And there are many choices. So very many."

"But…"

A flicker of lanterns cast great shadows from the weeping wound in the ceiling. Raised voices. The air heaved and compressed. Lilia gasped, like breathing underwater. Shouting. The Tai Mora had found the bodies. The heavy air lifted.

"Please!" Elaiko hissed, grabbing Lilia's sleeve.

"Does the Key know what, who it is?" Lilia asked. "Can the Key be anyone?"

"The Key was chosen long ago. The Key will be unique, able to bear the full power of the satellites."

"So the Key isn't the Kai?" Lilia said.

"The Kai can gain you access to the People's Temple," the creature said, "and converse with the temple creatures, as you have done with me. The Kai can gain access to these chambers, yes, without all this… ruination that the interloper has brought." The creature paused, cocking its head as if listening to the patter of feet above them. "I fear your time here is short. You are nearly found. I see it in your face, though, don't I? I see your desire, to shape the world."

"I'm no one," Lilia said.

"None of us are," the creature said.

"Please!" Elaiko cried. "Can you get us out of here? Can you... someone get us to the back gardens? Please, they will kill us!"

"Can you take us... away?" Lilia said. "To the back gardens here in the temple?"

"If that is your wish," the creature said, and gestured to the wall.

"Wait!" Lilia said as Elaiko tugged at her sleeve and the Tai Mora soldiers mounted the ladder above, shouting, the air heavy now, like soup. "How will I find them, the Guide and the Key?"

"They will find you," the creature said. Its image broke apart again. Dimmed.

"Quickly!" Elaiko said, running for the oozing walls. She pressed her hands to the wall, but nothing happened. She wailed. "Oh no!"

"You must go together," the creature said, its voice distant now.

"Take my hand!" Lilia held out her hand, and Elaiko took it.

A shout, from just behind them. The tickle of power; a tendril of Sina or Tira or Oma, seeking to hold them.

Lilia pressed her hand against the skin of the temple. The warm pool of it gave beneath her fingers and sucked her forward. She gasped and held her breath, yanking Elaiko with her.

The moment was nearly instantaneous. Darkness. Warmth. Then she was falling onto cold stones. Elaiko landed on top of her, driving the breath from her body.

Lilia gasped.

A few paces away, a young Dhai man sat on a bench drinking directly from a flagon of mead. He gaped.

"Hush," Elaiko said, waving a finger at him, "or I'll tell them you're stealing."

He continued staring, mouth still open, as Elaiko helped Lilia up. Lilia huffed in a breath, still starving for air. Elaiko was already moving, though, saying, "It's all right if I help you? We must hurry."

Lilia wondered where Elaiko's courage had come from.

"Which way?" Elaiko asked as they came to a branch in the bone labyrinth. "I've gotten turned around! Oh no!" Lilia pointed, and they continued on, Elaiko half-dragging her, until they came to the broken bit of the fence.

Avosta peered out at them. "Lilia!" he called, relief in his voice.

But it was Elaiko who shoved herself through first, and he got out of her way. Then reached out to help Lilia.

"Harina?" Lilia asked.

"She isn't with you?"

She shook her head.

"Harina knows the way out," he said. "We all knew the risks. We need to get you out of here. Is it done?"

"I got what I came for," Lilia said. She had seen the temple creature herself. "Ahkio was telling the truth. And… there's much more to discuss. We'll talk about it at camp. I need to see the Catoris."

Avosta led the way to the cliff side. When Elaiko saw how they would travel back down, she nearly turned around. But there were more lights and noise from the courtyard, and Lilia knew they would send out jistas soon.

If jistas found them out here, they were done.

Avosta went first, sliding down the great vine until he reached the point where a massive leaf curled, which broke his rapid descent. Then he stepped off, slid again, and called back up at them. "Come on! Hold tight!"

Lilia slid after him, wrapping her arms around the vine and holding tight to the wrist of her new hand with her stronger one to ensure a good grip. Elaiko came last, so quickly she nearly squashed Lilia's head during several descents.

Lilia came down heavily on the marshy ground below. Her breath was ragged. Avosta held out his hand and she took it. He looped an arm around her waist and helped her to the vine along the rushing water as Elaiko squelched after them.

"Do you see her?" Lilia asked.

"No. If Salifa is still there, it will be difficult for her to see us, too. We need to get into the water."

A little moan escaped Lilia; she was convinced it was Elaiko, but no. "The last time I swam across a river it was full of sharks," she said.

"Only fish, here," Avosta said, "but the water will be cold. Hold on to me."

She wrapped her arms around his neck as he plunged into the water. Elaiko shrieked as she followed.

Lilia gasped at the cold. The current pushed them against the massive length of the vine, and Avosta used the heaving current in their favor for a few steps, until the bottom of the river sank away.

She clung to him as water rushed over her, threatening to pull them beneath the vine and off and away. Lilia dug into her pocket for the bag of warded hazelnuts, hoping to reduce her weight, and the current snagged them, rushing them off and away downstream.

Elaiko grabbed hold of her tunic. "Help me!" Elaiko said.

Avosta grunted. The rushing water bubbled around them. His head went under, taking Lilia with him. Lilia nearly let go. They were just halfway across; she could see the other side. Where was Salifa?

Elaiko sagged behind Lilia, letting what felt like her whole weight yank her back.

Avosta lost his grip. All three of them rushed backwards, caught against the heaving vine. Elaiko twisted her hand into Lilia's tunic. Grabbed the vine with her other hand.

"I can't carry you both!" Avosta said, spitting water.

Behind them, billowing waves of red light began to creep down the cliff, tangling with the great vine. The smell of burning plant matter wafted over the river. The jistas were searching for them – and burning the vine-bridge behind them.

Lilia released her hold on Avosta and hooked her stronger arm through a tangle in the vine. Avosta, free of them both, clawed forward another few paces and reached back for her.

"Let go of me, Elaiko," Lilia said. Her fingers were numb. She felt only the dull pressure of Elaiko clinging to her shoulder. "Grab the vine. Let go."

The smell of burning grew stronger.

"Let her go!" Avosta said. "Come on, Lilia!"

Lilia tried to pull herself forward. Elaiko lost her grip on her and clung to the vine. Lilia crept forward. Her arms burned. She could no longer feel her fingers.

Avosta stretched to reach her. "A little further," he said. Elaiko splashed behind her.

Lilia grabbed his fingertips. The vine shuddered. She turned and saw the great red wave of fiery light engulf the vine on the other side of the river.

"No," Lilia breathed.

The vine snapped. Broke free of the other side. Lilia howled and clung to it with her good hand as best she could. The force of the water whipped the vine downstream with a savage jerk.

Avosta lost his grip and disappeared beneath the dark waves. Elaiko screamed. Lilia closed her eyes and held on tightly, riding the push of the water. She hit several rocks, a dull ache. The vine rolled up against the bank. Lilia's feet met the shallow bottom and she hauled herself over the vine and up onto the bank on the other side. She collapsed in the mud, shaking violently.

Elaiko crawled up beside her and began to sob.

Lilia sat up. "We don't have much time," she wheezed, and patted her pockets. She found her mahuan-laced water bulb and took a great swallow.

She did not wait for Elaiko, but continued further up the bank, breath still coming too heavily. She sank down again, defeated. She needed the rest. Closed her eyes. Focused on her breathing.

"Where is that man?" Elaiko said. "Did he... did he make it across?"

Lilia gritted her teeth. She heaved herself up, using a low hanging branch as leverage, and tottered forward. She shoved Elaiko, startling them both. The shocked look on Elaiko's face was so satisfying that Lilia did it again, and again. Elaiko shrank away.

"You fool!" Lilia said. "You absolute cowardly fool! You could have drowned all three of us. Avosta was worth three of you!"

"I'm a fool? Me? What did we learn in there, really? That someone is going to break the world? How does that help us?"

Lilia reared back to push her again. Elaiko caught her by her soft new hand and twisted it. Lilia cried out, stumbled, and fell to her knees.

Elaiko released her. Took two steps back. "You aren't anything special," Elaiko said. "Ora Nasaka thought she was special too, and they murdered her all the same."

"None of us are special," Lilia said, panting. "There are no special people. No one chosen to save us. We're stuck in some long cycle of death and destruction begun thousands of years before we were born, and it will go on thousands of years after, unless we stop it. Not anyone special. Just *us*, Elaiko. You're right. I'm not important. Nor are you. But we found something out today. We found out how to murder the Tai Mora and take back our country. We found out how to use these temples our ancestors built to save ourselves. We may not be special, but *that* is."

Lilia waited a moment in silence while Elaiko caught her breath, then slowly rose to her feet, pushing out her twisted leg to get better leverage. Even so, she nearly went over again. She turned away from Elaiko and started up the long, winding path to the cover of the woodland above where the dogs would be waiting, if her luck held.

After a few moments, she heard Elaiko come after her with great plodding steps. The misty red light did not cross the water, but what was left of the vine continued to burn, shedding red-black embers of itself that sailed through the air, dipping and spiraling before extinguishing themselves in the water.

"Lilia? Is that you?"

A figure at the top of the trail, still a hundred paces further up. Lilia squinted. "Salifa?"

"Yes, come, I'll help you–"

"Don't use your gift! They are watching from the temple!"

Salifa came down to meet her. "I can help," Salifa said, "put your arm around me."

Lilia looped her arm around Salifa's waist, grateful for the help. "Who is this?" Salifa asked. "Where are the others?"

"This is Elaiko," Lilia said. "She has a ward. You'll need to remove it before we go much further. Just… wait until we reach the dogs. I want to be able to move quickly if they see you."

They reached the place where they had left the dogs: two more than they needed with Avosta and Harina missing.

"Tie them behind," Lilia said. "We meet at the rendezvous point. If they make it out, they will see us there."

"I'm so sorry," Salifa said. "What happened? Were you successful?"

"We were successful," Lilia said, and she turned to Elaiko, daring her to say something, but Elaiko only shivered atop her mount, cold and miserable.

"Will you please take off the collar?" Elaiko asked.

Salifa reined her dog next to Elaiko and twisted a few breaths of Tira's power that neatly untangled whatever weave they had put on the collar to keep Elaiko from drawing on her star.

"Another parajista," Salifa said, nodding. "All right. We could always use another jista, even one with a descendant star."

Lilia turned away so neither could see her grimace. "Let's hurry," Lilia said. "The sky waits on no one."

17

Taigan thought it quaint that the Dhai had retreated to the Woodland. Perhaps it was inevitable, but he kept imagining them pushed further and further west, until they were caught up against the sea. He envisioned them hurling themselves off the cliffs and dying spectacularly in a grim pile of broken bodies and squalling babies.

He had always enjoyed his vivid imagination.

Taigan suspected they had moved far north, and his interrogation of the local Woodland Dhai confirmed that. He had followed Lilia across the Woodland to a fingerling peninsula that jutted into the Hahko sea before, in pursuit of her and her little girlfriend, the first Gian, the one he had hated less than the second, and certainly the least of all three of them. That Gian had some sense. Lilia's fondness for that area made it the first he considered. She would be less likely to bury herself in the foothills of Mount Ahya, though that would have been the strategically smarter choice. That would have also been the first place the Tai Mora looked, and from what he gathered, where they were spending most of their time rooting out small bands of Dhai that Taigan suspected were likely decoys.

Luna ate little and spoke less, which he would have

considered a blessing if he had not been so starved to hear Saiduan spoken. For a year he had traveled across Saiduan, holing up in little abandoned towns to see what he could do with Oma now that it had risen. He had great fun with that for a few months, but one could only raze so many villages and dismember so many wayward livestock before growing bored.

When he had sought out company, there was little to find but Tai Mora. Unlike in the Dhai valley, they had kept few Saiduan slaves. Once they had their people and armies through, and their world imploded, there was no reason to kill more Dhai, or anyone else, for that matter. All of the doubles in the Tai Mora world who could arrive had already come over. And someone here had to do the filthy work of farming. In preserving her armies, their Empress had had little time to save her farmers. She was a lord with armies aplenty, but no one who knew how to weave a basket.

Being a warlord was one thing. Being a leader was entirely another.

The trek through the Woodland was as awful as he remembered it, though he was prepared for many of its horrors this time. The swinging bone trees, the curling tendrils that signalled a bladder trap, the dreadful little tree gliders that would dart forward and steal food straight from one's mouth – all of these he could navigate much more easily than before.

It was not long before he found the tracks of a scouting party. He and Luna followed those for a few days to a tree-based camp of what he realized were Woodland Dhai, not refugees. They shouted the two of them off, and deployed a sticky fence that would have trapped them if not for Oma's fiery breath at his call.

"I'm surprised there are this many left," Luna said as they continued their long march toward the sea.

Taigan worked ahead of hir, burning vegetation with little tendrils of Oma's power. He delighted in watching the nasty little plants begin to curl and char and drop. He crushed them under his feet as he walked, and found it deeply satisfying.

"They won't be able to gather in groups of more than a few hundred," Taigan said. "They won't want to draw on their jistas, either. That would be like drawing a great target down over themselves."

"But… aren't you doing that, then? By clearing the brush that way."

Taigan frowned. "It's not much power."

"And you enjoy it."

"I enjoy it immensely."

A few days later, Taigan found signs of another scouting party. This one was much less careful than the first. Despite the tree cover, he could smell the sea. He heard the scouting pair because they were arguing about food – a common topic among everyone during these hungry times.

"How will we approach them?" Luna whispered as Taigan caught his first sight of them through the trees.

"They aren't gifted," Taigan said. "It will be easy."

Taigan tied up the two young scouts with a few threads of Oma's breath and marched down the little gully to them. They could not have been much into their teens. It was almost too easy.

"I'm here to see the little rebel girl in charge," Taigan

said. "She is an old protégée of mine. I assume you are led by this rebel girl, the one with the limp?"

The terrified scouts took some persuasion, but eventually led him and Luna to a large thorn fence that encircled what appeared to be little more than a handful of tents. Something about the whole arrangement seemed off. Was this a forward camp? Surely no one lived here.

He felt the air compress around him, but he had already put up a defensive shield. He noted two tirajistas up in a tree a few paces distant, and neatly cut them off from their satellite using the Song of Unmaking. One of them squealed.

"I'm not here to harm anyone!" he called. "Tell your Kai that Shao Taigan Masaao has brought some information that you may all find quite useful."

A flurry of movement at his left. A young runner bolted from one of the tents and disappeared below ground. Ah, of course. Underground. Taigan grinned because he recognized Lilia's thinking in that. Ever the pragmatic strategist.

It was nearly an hour before anyone else approached them. Taigan released the two young scouts, who hopped the fence and sprinted away. Taigan sat on an old downed tree next to Luna.

"You really think they'll let a sanisi in there?" Luna said.

"They will meet me."

"What if they don't? What then?"

"I make them meet me."

Luna grimaced. "You are just the same."

"Dire times call for–"

"No, you have always been mean. That's why Maralah loved you and hated you."

"What do you know what Maralah thought?"

"She told me. You frustrated her."

"Good. You know what it is to be compelled by her, against your own wishes."

"Yet you would do it to these Dhai."

"You have a bleeding little heart for a Saiduan," Taigan said.

"I don't think I'm Saiduan. Not Dhai either. Is that possible?"

Taigan shrugged. "Many foreign slaves exist in the spaces between things. I was never like anyone else."

A slender, pock-marked man with a mean little face approached them a few minutes later, coming up from the camp with a line of jistas positioned behind him. Taigan kept a thread of Oma's breath just beneath his skin, in case he needed to cut them off in addition to the tirajistas still powerless in the trees.

"I'm Liaro," the man said. "The Kai's cousin. He's asked you to tell me of your first meeting with him, to confirm your identity."

"I had an audience with him in Oma's Temple," Taigan said. "Though he spoke little and his elders spoke much. I informed him of the importance of finding a gifted omajista, someone we thought could act as a worldbreaker. Your Kai was not terribly pleasant to me."

Liaro nodded. "We would ask that – as a show of good faith – you release your hold on our Oras and novices and let them draw upon their satellites again."

"Will that get me an audience?"

"It will, if you would permit them to shield your power in his presence."

"You realize I am just as deadly without Oma as with it."

"Which is why this is merely a show of good faith."

"I permit it," Taigan said.

Liaro waved back at the line of jistas. Taigan released the Song of Unmaking, and let go of Oma's breath. He felt the combined weight of several jistas immediately and inexpertly attempt a Song of Unmaking on him. The air went heavy, then lightened as they became satisfied with their work.

It was not a true fix; Taigan could still sense Oma, and knew that if he applied himself, he could break their clumsy spells. But it seemed to satisfy them, and that's what he wanted.

Liaro led Taigan and Luna back to the circle of jistas. They surrounded a tent which had the flaps of the walls rolled up so that the people sitting around the table inside were clearly visible.

Taigan recognized the Kai first, a pretty young man even with his sad eyes that had dark circles beneath them. Another was familiar, probably Yisaoh, the daughter to one of the clan leaders. He had moved through Clan Garika on his journey to the temple, and she had made a nuisance of herself. The other woman, with fiery eyes, slightly bent over the table, and a large man and skinny man who stood just behind her – either lovers or bodyguards, perhaps both – he did not know.

"Shao Taigan," Ahkio said.

Taigan inclined his head. "You live."

"As do you. This is Catori Yisaoh."

"We met very briefly."

"I remember you," Yisaoh said, curling a lip. She had

something in her hand; a cigarette butt, unlit. Where were they getting Tordinian cigarettes out here? "You were skulking about Garika."

"I'm glad I'm memorable," Taigan said.

"And this is Catori Meyna."

"Two Catoris?" Taigan said, amused. "I'm surprised there aren't more. Always good to have redundancies."

"There were," Yisaoh said, coolly. "Catori Mohrai has died."

"That sounds very tragic," Taigan said.

Luna was already tugging at Taigan's sleeve. "What is it?" Taigan asked.

Ze stared at Yisaoh. "She… I'll tell you later. But, it's important."

"Who is this with you?" Meyna asked.

"I'm Luna," ze said. "Taigan and I know each other from Saiduan."

"You said you have information?" Ahkio gestured for them to sit.

The weight of the attention from the circle of jistas made the air thick. Taigan sat across from the Kai, and Luna sat next to him, balling up hir hands into fists in hir lap.

Taigan leaned back in his chair and observed the three figures at the table. Yisaoh leaned away from them. Ahkio's hands trembled slightly, and he pulled them from the table. Meyna was most confident. She had the intense black stare of a woman with a plan she was already in the midst of rolling out.

When he spoke, it was to Meyna. "Luna was working with a number of your scholars in the north. Ze discovered what it is the Tai Mora want with the temples, and how to use them."

"We know the Tai Mora have plans to close the ways between the worlds," Meyna said. "But that's none of our concern."

"Isn't it?" Taigan said. "I bring you the knowledge of how to do far more than that."

Meyna shook her head. "It's not in our interests, what she's doing. We have come to a decision to leave Dhai."

That surprised him. He looked to the Kai, who nodded. "Meyna and I discussed it at length. This is not a conflict that is winnable if we want to remain true Dhai."

"Pacifists, you mean," Taigan said. "That is true."

Ahkio nodded. "We have already committed many crimes in the face of this conflict. If we want to continue, to rebuild, it is time for us to leave Dhai."

"I can't imagine that is going over well with those who follow little Lilia."

Meyna and Ahkio exchanged a look. Yisaoh snorted and tried to light her cigarette stub with a fire pod.

"Lilia is no longer with us," Meyna said. "Even if she were, she is not a Catori. Her wishes have no part in the decisions we make here."

"Dead, then?" Taigan said.

"Dead to *me*," Meyna said. "Her actions put all of us in danger."

Taigan rolled that over. Interesting. "How do you intend to get away from the Tai Mora?" he asked. "They have you pinned here against the sea."

"We are not trapped," Meyna said. "I am working with the Woodland Dhai, and some Saiduan refugees who washed ashore over the winter. In return for helping them rebuild their ships, we will go with them."

"A fine and simple plan," Taigan said, "if you trust Woodland Dhai and the Saiduan."

"We share a common enemy," Meyna said.

Luna raised hir gaze from hir lap. "You can't outrun the Tai Mora," she said. "They'll find you, if they want to. And what they could choose to do to the world with all the power they could wield… it's far more than just keeping other worlds from coming here. They could reshape everything. Grow a mountain right out of the ground, or have the sea wash you away, wherever you are. You can't run."

Meyna said, "What's your name again?"

"Luna."

"Luna. You speak with a Saiduan accent, Luna."

"You speak with a Dhai accent."

"This is Dhai, you silly little thing."

"Best tell the Tai Mora that, then."

Taigan smirked. He wanted to pat Luna's precious little head. "If we cannot work together, then we will part ways," he said.

"And how do I know you won't give us up to the Tai Mora?" Meyna said.

"What motive would I have for that?"

"You could be their emissary."

"I invite you to attempt to stop me from leaving. It would be a very fine show. Your people have had, perhaps, a year to train your little Oras and novices in the fighting arts. In my country, we did not separate our physical fighters from our gifted ones. And I have been fighting for longer than anyone in this whole blighted little refugee camp has been alive."

"We aren't refugees," Ahkio said. "This is our country."

"You are refugees," Taigan said. "This is not your country. The sooner you all understand that, the easier it will be on you. By all appearances you've sat about here squawking and arguing and doing nothing for a year but dying, getting picked off by Tai Mora. It's a wonder any of you are still alive at all. One raging case of yellow pox comes through here and the temples, and you're all dead, finished, the Dhai race extinguished. You are already a memory, a footnote in some history book."

"Then why are you here?" Ahkio said.

A cry came from behind them. Taigan peered around Ahkio and saw a young girl burst through the line of jistas. She could not have been more than five or six years old, a fat-cheeked girl with dark hair, soft chin, and luminous eyes.

Yisaoh hurried over to her. "Go back, Tasia."

"Is she here?" the girl asked. "Is she back?"

With the others' attention shifted, Luna leaned toward Taigan. "That woman, Catori Yisaoh, and the child. I've seen them both before."

"All Dhai look alike."

"No, on another world. Where that woman, Kirana, is keeping her family."

Taigan raised his brows.

Luna lowered hir voice further. "The names are even the same. Yisaoh, the Empress's consort, and Tasia, one of the Empress's children. They can't come over."

"Interesting," Taigan said.

Yisaoh passed the child off to one of the jistas, who took her back below ground.

"I apologize," Ahkio said. "The children get restless."

"I've no doubt," Taigan said.

"If you believe us bested already," Ahkio continued, "why bother with us?"

Taigan snorted. "I didn't come for you. I was looking for the crippled girl. She had more sense and more backbone than the rest of you. A pity." He stood. "If you will do nothing to alter the course of this cycle, then we are working at cross-purposes. I will find other allies."

Luna sighed.

Ahkio stood as well. Meyna turned to confer with the men behind her. Yisaoh gave up trying to light her cigarette and stuffed it back into her pocket.

"It is a shame Lilia isn't here," Ahkio said. "I know the two of you did not get along, but she had become a great ally to you."

"Oh it's fine," Taigan said. "She has a head for strategy, but it's true she has been far less useful since she burned out. I had hoped, however, you all would share her determination to stop the Tai Mora instead of running from them. I suspect she's off doing something you don't approve of, like finding a way to murder a bunch of Tai Mora."

There was a strange shift. Yisaoh blurted, "*Burned out?*"

"At the harbor," Taigan said. "Ages ago. You didn't know?"

Meyna shook her head. "You must be joking. The dajians worship her."

"Don't use that word," Ahkio said.

Yisaoh said, "Lilia *isn't gifted*? Is this a Saiduan joke?"

"Not gifted! That drink-addled roach!" Meyna said.

Taigan considered his options. Holding the entire camp hostage while waiting for Lilia – especially if she were to die on whatever escapade she was on – would be an exhausting exercise. And if she had no power to move these people, that wouldn't be useful to him, either.

"You said something of Saiduan refugees here," Taigan said. "Where? They have more fight left in them than the Dhai."

"You are welcome to speak to them," Ahkio said, "but you'll find that they, too, are done fighting. Another two days northwest of here, near the sea. They have the natural harbor there warded, though, a hazing ward to keep out the Tai Mora who are working further up the coast."

"We'll be on our way, then."

Ahkio walked with him and Luna to the thorn fence. Taigan considered it entirely unnecessary. As they came to the barrier, however, Ahkio said, "Did you ever find the person you were really looking for? The one you thought Lilia was?"

"No," Taigan said.

"Then perhaps the Tai Mora haven't either. Maybe all this knowledge is for nothing, if they don't have the right people."

"Like a Kai?"

"Yes. The temples are closed to this Kirana. She isn't the true Kai."

"You've been under the temples?" Luna asked.

"Yes," Ahkio said. "But there were no devices under there, no... engines. Just..." He shook his head, as if dismissing his next words as too ludicrous to utter. They must have been outrageous indeed for him to hesitate after all that had happened. "I wish you luck finding your allies," he continued. "But all we want now is to live peacefully."

"Living peacefully requires war," Taigan said. "In Saiduan the word for peace could be translated as, simply, the time between wars."

"I've never believed that. The Dhai haven't fought a war in five hundred years."

"You forget the Pass War."

"That was defensive."

"It was still a war, Kai Ahkio. I fear you and your people are dancing about in circles pretending you can come away from this time in our history utterly clean and without guilt. But you have not and you won't."

"Goodbye, Taigan," Ahkio said.

Taigan tipped his chin at Ahkio. "Goodbye for now, Kai Ahkio. Though I think we are not yet done."

Taigan stepped over the thorn fence, and helped Luna after him. He nearly broke the terrible Song of Unmaking spell right there, to show them his power and how bad their defenses truly were, but waited, instead, until they dropped the song and he could access Oma as easily as breathing, once again.

"You think we can convince other Saiduan to help us?" Luna asked.

"I'm uncertain," Taigan said, "but I'm not really doing anything else. If we do not find allies soon, I may simply burn that whole temple down myself. Doesn't that sound like fun?"

Luna was quiet a moment, then, "It does, actually."

18

Lilia arrived at the meeting point with Elaiko and Salifa just as the first hint of dawn tickled the horizon. She was exhausted and achy; she nearly fell asleep twice on her mount. She scanned the shallow rise of the meeting point as they broke through the trees, hoping to see Harina or Avosta. The smell of smoke still permeated the air, though there was no sign of the fires that Mihina had directed to draw out the patrols.

She had barely begun the ascent, Salifa and Elaiko trailing, when Namia howled and bounded down the hill toward her. Namia clapped her hands and patted Lilia's leg in the stirrup, signing frantically, so fast Lilia could not make it out.

"Slow down," Lilia said. "What is it?"

"Success," Namia signed. "You?"

"Yes," Lilia said. "We had success. You kept the patrols very busy. Thank you."

Namia beamed, which looked more like a grimace on her ravaged face.

Mihina came to the edge of camp, wringing her hands, staring off behind them. "Is this all? Where's Harina?"

"We were separated," Lilia said, sliding down from her

258 THE BROKEN HEAVENS

bear. "We lost Avosta in the river, too, but… it's possible he just washed downstream. I'd like to wait for them, just in case. This is Elaiko. Our contact inside. She was… very helpful." The last part, Lilia had to force out.

"The patrols are far from here," Mihina said. "Do you think they noticed you in the temple? Will they send parties out?"

"I think it will be some time before they realize we escaped," Lilia said. "They won't know how we got out."

"How did you?" Mihina asked. "And why isn't Harina–"

"There was a scuffle," Lilia said. "Blood. Not hers, but… she stayed behind. I think she'll circle back. There's no reason she shouldn't have gotten out as well."

Mihina offered them hard bread and raw tubers. Lilia sat back against one of the trees, and ate gratefully. She fell asleep listening to Salifa and Mihina speaking in low tones, discussing the reconnaissance.

"Was it worth it?" Mihina said, very softly, as Lilia fell into the warm, gauzy arms of sleep. "My sister–"

"I don't know," Salifa said. "Let's see what she has to say back at camp."

A snap. A hiss. The sound of a man huffing up the hill. Lilia snapped awake, disoriented, the tangy smell of everpine in her nostrils.

Avosta struggled up the rise. He leaned against a tree for support. He shivered violently.

"Mihina! Stoke the fire!" Salifa called.

They got Avosta out of his wet clothes and under a dry blanket. Mihina was able to dry his clothes quickly with a few tendrils of Sina's breath. It did not take long to warm him up.

"You're alive," he said to Lilia.

"So are you," she said.

"Harina?"

She shook her head.

Avosta wiped at his eyes. "I thought I was done, there, for a time."

"I'm glad you were not," Lilia said.

"We should…" Salifa glanced at Mihina. "I'm not sure how much longer we can risk waiting."

"I'll stay," Mihina said. "Another day. Please. She could still find her way here."

"I understand," Lilia said. "I'm so sorry, Mihina. Stay a day, but if it gets too dangerous–"

"It's always dangerous," Mihina said. "Being Dhai is dangerous."

The smaller party mounted up and left camp just as the suns reached the midpoint in the sky. Salifa hung her head, shoulders slumped. Elaiko nervously started at every breath of birdsong and flick of viney tendril.

Avosta rode up next to Lilia and asked, low, "Li, I'm sorry to ask, but what did we achieve there that we could not have learned from Elaiko, or some other Dhai already in the temple?"

"She was a slave there," Lilia said. "Was it right for us to depend on her for everything?"

"That isn't what I meant. Harina was–"

"She will make it out."

"But what did we–"

"We discovered how to defeat the Tai Mora," Lilia said. "Once and for all. You knew this was about getting information. We have that information now."

"*I* don't."

She glanced at him sharply. His tone was still soft, but she did not like the shift in his face: the pensive brows, tight mouth.

"Do you trust me?"

"You know I do," Avosta said. "I have faith in you. But… you would never lie to us, would you?"

"I'll never lie to you," Lilia said firmly. "You can trust that. Only great tyrants refuse to change course when they receive new information. What we've learned is that there's no need to attack any Tai Mora during Tira's Festival. We can strike back at them far more effectively if we take over the People's Temple. That one is the Key. That's where everything is going to happen."

"All right," Avosta said.

"Trust that I'm working on what's best for all of us," Lilia said. "I believe in the Dhai. I believe in a future for us."

When they arrived at the thorn fence surrounding the Dhai camp, most of their supplies were gone. Lilia wanted a long soak in a stone tub. They had left without much warning, sneaking away before Meyna or Yisaoh could argue, and Lilia did not expect anyone to be waiting for them. She was surprised, then, to see so many people above ground that afternoon, centered on the meeting tent.

When they came over the fence, Liaro came out to meet them. His hair was washed and braided back, his clothes clean, the cuts and bruises he had sustained on his journey mostly healed. The sly smile he gave Lilia as he took her dog's lead made her shiver, though she could not say why.

"The Kai wishes to speak to you," he said.

"Good," Lilia said. "I have some things to say to her as well."

"Not the Catoris," he said. "The Kai."

Ah, Lilia thought, so that had been decided.

Yet it was not Ahkio, but Meyna who was striding across the muddy ground as Lilia told her bear to sit and dismounted. Lilia took up her walking stick just as Namia caught up to her. Walking stick in one hand, Namia on the other, she turned to face Meyna as the birds cooed overhead.

"You," Meyna said, "are an unconscionable liar. A charlatan. A con!"

Avosta slid off his bear and moved in front of Lilia. "What are you talking about?" he said.

"Your little scullery girl! Has she told you what she is? And here you all are, back from what, endangering all of us? Getting yourselves killed? How many of you actually left? You've lost some, Lilia. As I expected."

Behind Meyna, Ahkio hung back at the entrance to the tent. Lilia did not see Yisaoh anywhere. A good number of jistas were present, though, and a few of her beribboned followers. Did they fear Lilia would lash out at them? What *was* all this? Something had certainly shifted in her absence.

"We've been engaged on a reconnaissance mission," Lilia said coolly. "You will be interested to hear what we've learned. There is a way to destroy the Tai Mora and take our country back."

"This isn't our country," Meyna said. "Kai Ahkio and I have decided on the best way forward. We are leaving Dhai. You've known that for days."

The air was heavy. Lilia's ears popped.

"What *exactly* is happening here?" Lilia said, low.

Yisaoh came up from below ground. Lilia watched her carefully. Her face was grim.

"What's going on, Yisaoh?"

"You lied," Yisaoh said. "And we are not keen on being deceived. Not the Kai, not my fellow Catori, and certainly not all the people you've pretended to love while you deceived them."

"I've never lied–"

"Don't," Yisaoh said. "You told us you were gifted. You told *me* that."

Lilia felt heat move up her face. "I... I am. I have been ill, that's all. I've never lied."

"Taigan was here," Meyna said. "Not an hour ago."

A slow, piercing knife of dread crept up Lilia's spine. "Taigan? An... hour? How did you...?" She gazed back at Ahkio, still cowering there behind the tent flap. He would have recognized Taigan. "Are you *sure*?" she demanded, staring hard at Ahkio.

"If what that sanisi said isn't true," Yisaoh said, "show us."

"Li," Avosta said. "What are they talking about? You flew! You are our light!"

"We were easy to fool, weren't we?" Yisaoh said. "No omajistas among us, so no one would be able to see if it was you using your gift. How many of those little jistas with you have done your work for you? They aren't even proper Oras, they are so young! And you used them."

"I didn't use anyone," Lilia said quickly, voice breaking. Salifa was moving forward, her mouth a wide O of astonishment.

"You said you wouldn't lie!" Salifa said.

"It's not true!" Avosta said. He glanced back at Lilia, on his face an expression of absolute conviction. "You are gifted! Show them! You wouldn't lie about *that*."

Lilia felt trapped: her own people behind her, and Meyna and her new friend Ahkio ahead, with Yisaoh already sneering and turning.

"Faith Ahya was never gifted," Lilia said loudly, "and nor am I. Not anymore. I'm sorry you still thought that. The Tai Mora took that from me as they have taken your country from you." She met Avosta's look. "I'm so sorry. It wasn't… I didn't lie, I just… I didn't tell you I lost it. I was ashamed to burn out. If you thought I was not gifted, would you have followed me? Risked your life?"

"Yes," he said gruffly.

"Then I apologize," she said. "I was a fool. But Meyna, listen," and she raised her voice again. "This changes very little, doesn't it? You and Yisaoh are not gifted. Ahkio is not gifted. Most importantly, it doesn't change the truth of anything I am going to tell you."

"But you've already lied!" Salifa cried. "Li, we trusted you. You lied about this. About this of all things! Harina gave her *life* for you!"

"She should be exiled," Ahkio said, coming out from under the cover of the tent, hands trembling. "There is too much lying, too much–"

"You aren't even the true Kai!" Lilia said. It burst from her.

The blood rushed to his face, darkening him further. "Perhaps there are some here who would question my claim, but yours is in no doubt. You are an ungifted scullery girl."

"And you're a bully," Lilia said. "Some petty shadow from some other world taking advantage of these people!"

Namia whined softly next to Lilia. Lilia wanted to comfort her, to tell her it was all right, but words were running from her mind: all her arguments, her disassembling.

"Enough," Meyna said. "Lilia, the Kai and I have already spoken about this. We discussed it with many of the people here. For your dangerous actions and deplorable lies, we have seen fit to cast you from the camp. You are putting too many of us in danger."

The proclamation landed like a stone. Lilia felt it in her gut. She opened her mouth to deny it, but Avosta was staring at her, and Salifa was crying quietly. Elaiko simply gaped, fingers twisting the frayed hem of her tunic.

"How is it you take him in so easily," Lilia said, pointing at Ahkio, "and toss me aside? I've sweated and bled for you here. We are–"

"Your schemes have done nothing but tear out the hearts of those who love you," Meyna interrupted. "You disappoint us all again and again. And far from striking back at the Tai Mora, all your little missions and raids have done is make us bigger targets. It's time for you to move on."

"You are going to regret this," Lilia said softly.

"Go," Meyna said, "or I will have my Oras escort you."

"I would like to say goodbye to Emlee, and Tasia," Lilia said.

"No," Meyna said. "Take the dog and whatever you have with you and go. Don't come back here. Go now, before someone changes their mind."

Lilia lost her voice. She felt numb. Namia wailed and

clutched at her arm. Lilia managed a quiet, "Shh, hush," sound to soothe her, but she could not look at any of them. Not Salifa or Avosta, and certainly not Elaiko, who had broken out of servitude only to witness Lilia's ostracism.

"I'll... I'll at least see her to the edge of the camp!" Salifa said.

"No," Meyna said. "I'm sorry, Salifa, but if you walk away with her, we'll have no choice but to consider you a danger as well. This woman lied to you. She will lie to you again."

Salifa's eyes filled. Avosta offered an arm, and she nodded, said, "Please hold me," and he did.

Lilia took the reins of her dog and stepped back over the thorn fence. Namia started after her.

"No, you!" Meyna said, and grabbed Namia.

Namia snarled and snapped at her. A great tangle of vines burst from the soil and ensnared her. Namia shrieked.

"Leave her alone!" Lilia said.

"Go!" Meyna said. "We'll release her when you're well gone."

"This is mad," Lilia said. She tugged at her dog's lead. "You're power mad, all of you."

"But... you can't go!" Elaiko said. "You don't... I..." Another snarl of vines curled up between them. Elaiko shrieked and stepped back.

Lilia limped forward, tugging her dog after her. She had no idea in which direction to go. There was no other place for her. What of the other refugees? Could she turn back and gather them? Call to Emlee? Namia was still shrieking. Ahkio and Meyna had cut her off, kept her from going below for this reason. Banished her while she was separated from most of her allies. She kept moving, urging herself to think.

She got onto the dog and led it through the brush in circles for some time until she could no longer hear the sound of Namia's screaming. She only stopped when she grew thirsty. Lilia had the dog sit, and dismounted. She rested along the side of a narrow creek bed. The great dog lay down beside her and put its massive head in her lap. She sobbed.

"I don't know what I did wrong," Lilia whispered. Though it wasn't true. There were many things she had failed at, and many more she would have failed at, if she stayed. Ahkio and Meyna would be too terrified to risk carrying out the kind of complicated scheme that would be required for them to take control of the temples: a Key, a Guide, and a Worldbreaker! Like some riddle. They would never have believed her.

A snapping sound from the woods. The dog raised its head, let out a low growl. Lilia tensed, expecting a wild bear, perhaps, or a boar. Instead, three men approached her, men she recognized from the camp, men aligned with Meyna.

"Come quietly," the eldest said. "Catori Meyna has another fate for you."

"I don't understand."

They took hold of her. She cried out only once, at the shock of being so roughly handled without consent. They knotted a bit of cord around her hands and slung her unceremoniously onto the back of the dog.

"What are you doing?" Lilia huffed. "Where are you taking me?"

She did not have far to go to find out. After only a few minutes, they pushed her off the dog. She fell in a heap. Raised her head.

A massive bone tree sat at the center of a sparkling white clearing strewn with bleached bones. It was an ancient tree, as wide as Lilia was tall, a grim, rippling thing made from the bones of its own prey. Large bear skulls and the delicate skulls of treegliders made up its base; long, snapped tibias and fibias bound by pale, clotted sap and the tree's fibrous tendons made up its branches. The bare crown of it did not so much reach for the sky as dominate it, a crown, a throne to some dark god.

And there, a few paces from the ring of pale bones at the edge of the clearing, stood Meyna. She held the lead of a dog. Two jistas were with her, both full Oras that Lilia recognized. Meyna did not look away as Lilia gazed at her.

"Is this what you did to Mohrai?" Lilia called.

Meyna said, "No. Unlike you, we aren't all murderers. This is something else. More personal. I meant what I said, Lilia. You are far too dangerous to the Dhai, alive. You have endangered us. And you would continue doing it. I know that, because I understand you, little Lilia. I was you, I think, when I was very young. Always seeking attention. Trying to find my place. But I've found my place now, Lilia."

"Don't do this," Lilia said.

Meyna shook her head. She gestured to the men who held Lilia. "Give her to it."

Lilia screamed loud and long, so loud and long she startled the dogs, which began to bark.

The men hauled Lilia up and tossed her into the bone-white clearing, well within reach of the snarling branches of the bone tree. Lilia landed with a crunch onto the discarded bones of the tree's prey, her nose filling with the faint scent of rot. She wriggled forward, moving as quickly as she could, knowing it was already too late.

The creaking of bones. Hissing. A searing pain in her shoulder.

Her body jerked upright, lifted high, high in the air. A knotted limb of the bone tree jutted from her left shoulder, a limb made from cast-off bits of bird bones twisted together with its gooey, poisonous sap. The sap mingled with her blood and spattered the pale ground below as the tree pulled her into its crackling embrace.

A second bony limb stabbed through her lower left side, just above her buttock. She screamed again. Wheezed. Gasped. She tried to find her mahuan with her one working arm. Lost her breath. No more screaming. Gasping. Like a speared fish.

The tree shivered in excitement.

Sunlight from above blinded her. The canopy here was thin, as the bone tree's poison killed any plant life that came too close. She swung her head, trying to see Meyna and her kin.

"This isn't… necessary!" Lilia gasped.

"I assure you it is," Meyna said, and it frustrated Lilia that she could not see her face. "I know you too well, Lilia, far better than Ahkio does. You won't sit around in the woods feeling sorry for yourself. You'll scheme something up. Play the martyr. And we are done with playing games, you and I. We are going to get out of these woods. No more raids. No more secret excursions. You want revenge.

You want to fight a force you cannot win against. You care nothing about the people here, and what's best for them. I *do*."

"This is… a terrible…" Lilia said, but it came out slurred and soft. Her head swam. The poison was making her stuffy-headed already. Relaxed. Her breath came a little easier. How funny.

Dark patches moved across her vision. Numbness crept up her fingers and toes. Her wounds still throbbed, but it was very distant, like an achy tooth. She had a fond memory of watching Taigan dangling just like this, speared by a bone tree. What would have happened if she chose to leave him there? Would she still be here? Was this always going to be the end for her?

Anger burned in her belly. She struggled. But her body would not respond.

She wondered if this was how her mother felt, welded to the top of that great mirror, bound to it until death, until Lilia destroyed her. Until the world destroyed Lilia.

A sharp pain seared through her sternum. She gasped. Bent her head. But there was no visible wound. No gnarled bone branch pushing through her.

The poison, maybe. The poison doing its final work.

Oma, Lilia thought, you have a grim sense of humor.

19

Death was overrated.

But then, so was recovery.

She had done enough of both to know.

She had been mangled, mutilated, infected and left for dead before. The second time wasn't any more fun than the first. The injuries themselves were far worse this time, of course. Or perhaps she had forgotten how excruciating the infected wounds from those wily court predators had been. The mind had a habit of dampening the details of trauma over time, surfacing them only when violently triggered.

Her mind processed her surroundings slowly, as if moving through treacle. Close quarters. Warm. Very dark. Cramped. She lay with her knees tucked up to her chest and her arms squeezed tightly against her sides, and there was something… pulsing and moving around her and… through her. Something slick and alive. She began to tremble violently.

She kicked out. Met resistance. She was in a very small space. Kicked again. Wood. A trunk? What? She began to rip at the slimy growths sticking out of her body. As she pulled them free, she felt a great sense of both pain and relief, like yanking out a splinter or a bad tooth.

More kicking. Spitting. Huffing. Then she pushed up, and the ceiling gave way. Her space filled with dim blue light. She yanked away more of the growths as she tried to sit up. They were some kind of vine. As she pulled them out, her body released pale amber streamers of ooze. Her skin closed quickly around the wounds, almost instantly. She marveled at it. How incredible.

A sharp pain in her sternum made her double over. She tipped her head over the end of her enclosure – a box? a trunk? – and heaved and gagged, nauseous. Blackish vomit spattered across the floor. She clawed at her chest, at the source of the pain, and felt a cold, raised lump in the center of her core, just below her breasts. She pressed her palm against it, triggering another wave of pain. The raised mark had three curved edges and a long tail. Her body broke out in a cold sweat.

She peered at the great round room. It that smelled of musty loam. *Underground?* Like a cairn.

Disoriented, she tried to get out of the trunk, and stumbled over the lip of it. Crashed onto the floor.

"What's this? Oh!" A voice. Footsteps, soft.

"The fuck?" she muttered, trying to raise her head.

"Hush now," a soft, airy voice.

Fuzzy images: a smear of red cloth, a distorted face. The dim orange flickering of flame flies.

"How did you wake me up?"

"I didn't. You were a box of bones."

"A what?"

"You were not awakened. You were recreated. That's what she told me, anyhow. And it appears it was true."

"Sounds complicated."

"It was."

"What's the catch?"

The fuzzy image resolved itself as the figure leaned over her, showed its teeth. A little old woman with sagging jowls and loose, bare skin on her arms that hinted she had once been much more substantial. Puffy white hair crowned the skull, shot through with moss and tiny branches. Perhaps a spider. Probably lice.

"The catch," the old woman said, "well, there is one, I think. You are bound to her."

"Who is *her*?"

"She isn't here. They exiled her."

"I've already died a few times. Who's to say I want to live?"

"Oh, I think you want to live."

"Who the *fuck* are you?"

"I am Emlee."

Her sternum ached again. She gasped. Rubbed at the raised mark again; not a mark, no – there was definitely something just under her skin, *inside* of her, pressing against her guts. She had a sudden urge to get above ground and go... there. That direction, behind her, whatever compass direction that was. Why? But the compulsion lingered. The thing in her chest burned coldly.

"You have any clothes, Emlee?"

"Yes, one moment. You feel something?"

"Yeah, cold."

Emlee brought her trousers and tunic, all very plain and musty, full of moth holes. Her body began to ache in earnest, a painful ache, like an itch that needed scratching.

There was some place she needed to be.

"I have to go," she said. "Thanks."

"Shoes?"

She looked at her feet. Good looking feet. Clean nails. Good skin. For the first time she truly regarded her hands. Smooth skin there, too. No scars. No blemishes. That wasn't right. There was something about her hands that she could not remember… this wasn't right.

"What the fuck happened to me, really?" she said.

"I don't know. You'll have to ask Lilia."

"Why do I know that name?"

Emlee shook her head. "I don't know. She didn't tell me."

Her stomach ached. "I have to go. I need to go." She ran past Emlee, following the desperate urge of her body.

She sprinted past startled children and skinny, malnourished Dhai faces. What had happened here? Where the fuck was she?

Up a ladder. Across a clearing. Over a narrow thorn fence. She burst into a sprint. Her body worked beneath her, free and tireless. The damp ground thumped under her bare feet and it felt good, so good, to feel the cool air against her skin, and the breath heaving through her fresh lungs. *I'm alive, I'm alive!* she thought. But why is that strange? Why is it so strange to be alive, as if she would be anything else?

She ran and ran, compelled to go north, following a little stream. This deep in the woods, there was little light from the moons or the satellites, but she found that she could see fairly clearly. She continued on, hungry to find what compelled her, but still not tired.

As she came to the edge of a milky white clearing, the itching ache across her skin and deep in her sternum began to subside. She gazed across the clearing and realized it glowed white because it was full of bones. And there, hanging from the great bony limbs of a twisted bone tree, was a body.

She stepped confidently across the clearing. When the tree reached for her, she simply snapped off the branch, easily as snapping a twig. Her hand did not even hurt. It tried again. She snapped it off. Again, and again. She grinned. It was a fun game.

She broke off every branch of the tree but those that held the body. Then stepped back to regard it. A lone bird sat atop the tree, just above the body, eyeing her as if she would steal its meal.

"You alive?" she asked. The girl was very familiar. Twisted foot, a soft new left hand, and a forgettable face covered in shiny little scars. Was this Lilia?

The body's eyes opened.

"You Lilia?" she asked.

The girl gave a sluggish nod. "Yes. You…" Her eyes widened. "You aren't… No."

"What have you done to me?"

"I don't… know?"

"I was in a fucking box!"

Lilia huffed and gagged. She thought the girl was having convulsions, a stroke, but no, she was laughing.

"The box… it was *you* in the box…" Lilia said. "Oh, Oma, you think you're so funny."

"Why is it…" She stopped. A thunderous understanding came over her. A tree. A mirror. This girl's scarred face. She sank to her knees. "Oh no," she said.

"I didn't know," Lilia said. "I didn't know it was you in the box. You were supposed to be some great warrior."

"I hope you didn't overpay."

Lilia wheezed again. "Please get me down. This tree is killing me."

"Why should I, after what you've done?"

"Because we're bound, that's what Kalinda said. If I die, you die."

"Maybe I want to die."

"Do you?" Lilia huffed. Closed her eyes. "How many times do you *really* want to die, Zezili Hasaria?"

Zezili pressed a hand to her own throbbing shoulder. A searing pain began to work its way into her back. The same places Lilia bore injuries.

"I chose to die," Zezili said. "But it was under false pretenses."

"So get revenge," Lilia said. "That's what I am going to do."

"If I get you down from there, what's next?"

"I have no idea."

"What if I just want to murder everyone who wronged me?"

Lilia huffed and snorted. "I can help you with that."

20

Anavha sat at the end of a large bed that took up most of the narrow room that the man called Suari had shoved him into. A slim window gave him a glimpse of the world outside, but only just. It didn't make it feel less like a cell.

He was already shivering, clutching his hands in his lap, conflicted about what he should do.

Natanial had told him he would be free, not some slave. He hadn't understood much of what was said with the Empress, but getting hauled off by Suari and shoved into a room, alone, with no explanation, did not bode well. He desperately wanted to trust Natanial, but who was Natanial next to the Empress? How much power did he truly have? Anavha knew he had a very limited amount of time to make a decision, and the knowledge of that made him sweat.

He always waited too long, until it was too late. Zezili would have been bold. Zezili was always so good at making decisions.

The wall in front of him trembled. Anavha shifted his gaze and stared at the rippling surface. Was this another quake, like that one when the mountain fell from the sky? No, he wasn't shaking. Just… the wall…

A boy tumbled out of the wall.

Anavha shrieked and leapt onto the bed.

The boy on the floor groaned and rubbed at the arm he had fallen on. He sat up. It was the boy from the foyer, the one with the broken knees who spoke Dorinah, like all the Dhai seemed to.

"How did you get in here?" Anavha said.

"I… Oh no," he said. "This wasn't how it was supposed to go. Dasai… he's going to murder me. They're going to kill me for this. Sina, take me swiftly."

"What are you talking about?"

"Keep your voice down," he said. "Please. They are going to be looking for me. And when they find me…"

"What did you *do*?"

The boy struggled to his feet. Anavha got up and helped him.

"Thank you," he said. "I'm Roh. You're Anavha?"

Anavha nodded.

"Did you understand what they were saying, up there? About warding you?" Roh asked.

"No. They just threw me in here and–"

"They are going to ward you like they did me," he said. "You will be bound to the Empress. You won't be able to hurt her. Betraying her will cause pain. It's terrible. I want to… do terrible things, but I can't… I can't…"

"Natanial said nothing bad would happen to me. He'd protect me."

"That soldier up there? He's a mercenary," Roh scoffed.

"He's looked after me–"

"Has he? If you had not believed that, where would you be right now?"

Anavha sat back on the bed, distraught. He would have been home in Aaldia, cooking or curled up in bed with Nusi. "He said I was free. It was my own decision."

"Well, I'd make another decision on your own, now," Roh said. "I need to find a way out of here." He went to the window, peered out. Tried to shove his shoulder through, but it was far too narrow. "Do you have any extra clothes?" he asked. "Maybe I could–"

"I can get us out," Anavha said.

"How?"

"I just... I don't know where we'd go. Home, for me, but... people are falling from the sky. Natanial said if I joined the Empress, I could stop it. Now, I don't know..."

"Listen," Roh said, and he took Anavha by the shoulders and peered at him. He was a beautiful boy, Anavha saw, sad and broken, with large eyes and long lashes, skin dry and flaking from too much stress and sun, but very pretty nonetheless. Anavha knew very well what those with power did to pretty boys. "There's a Dhai resistance. You know who the Dhai are? Before the Tai Mora came–"

There was a shout from the hall. The sound of pounding feet.

"Where exactly are these Dhai?" Anavha asked.

"What? I... I don't know. The Woodland? Somewhere."

"I can only take us to places I've been," Anavha said. Roh's frantic movement and warbling tone made him anxious. "Well, sometimes I end up... elsewhere, but that's if something is wrong. But I've gotten very good at taking myself places I've been."

Roh ceased his pacing. "Where in *Dhai* have you been?"

"We arrived on the plateau, out there, near the camp

with all the soldiers in it."

"Directly onto the plateau?" Roh gaped. "You… you opened a wink? You're an omajista!"

Anavha winced. He still did not like that word. "That's what they say. I suppose so. I can't get to other worlds, though, just… this one. Places here."

Roh went to the wall and pressed his forehead against it. Then his palms. He murmured something in Dhai that had the reverent tone of a prayer of thanks.

"All right," Roh said. "Can you take us to the plateau?"

"But, there are soldiers there and–"

"From the plateau, you'll be able to see into the valley, right?"

"I… suppose, yes."

"Then you can wink us into the valley. And from the valley you can see–"

"Woods. Oh!" Anavha considered that. "You are very clever."

"I know," Roh said. More shouting from the hall. "Can you hurry? What do you need from me?"

"I don't… I'm not sure…"

"You can always come back," Roh said. "Please. I can't."

His eyes were so very beautiful. Anavha nodded. He stepped away from the bed and concentrated on the terrible Tordinian poetry, as Coryana, the teacher Natanial introduced him to, had taught him, and as he had practiced all this time.

The air split in two. On the other side was the broken yellow grass of the plateau, and a sea of soldiers inside the temporary barracks and outbuildings just a few paces distant.

Roh said, "Do we just–"

The door burst open.

Anavha gasped. The wink wavered.

Roh heaved himself forward and tumbled through the rent in reality. Fell face first on the grass on the other side.

Two of the Tai Mora guards pushed into the room. Anavha leapt after Roh. Grabbed him and helped him up. They began to run across the grass, Anavha half-pulling him.

Roh grimaced, clearly in terrible pain. "Close the wink! Close the wink!"

But Anavha was too startled. He kept running. The guards came through after them, and behind the guards, someone else, a hulking beast of a hairy shadow.

Saradyn pushed the two Tai Mora out of the way and began to gain on Anavha and Roh.

"What does he want?" Anavha hissed.

"Open another!" Roh pointed. "The valley, there, open another!"

"I can't see–"

But the edge of the plateau came into abrupt focus. They were moving too fast now. Anavha heard the thundering of Saradyn's great feet. The heaving of his breath. The Tai Mora, too, were coming. More and more pouring from the wink that Anavha was still too flustered to close. He needed to let go of the threads, release the… Oh no, they were at the edge, he needed another wink. Concentrate, concentrate, another spell…

"Anavha!" Roh yelled.

They came to the very edge of the plateau. Anavha gripped Roh's hand tightly and bent the world.

A wink appeared, a jagged slash opening there at the edge of the plateau. Anavha and Roh crashed through it, so fast and hard they smeared up dirt and loam on the other side. Anavha lost his breath.

"Close it!" Roh gasped, crawling forward. "Close it and open another!"

Anavha could see nothing but dirt and trees. Heard the rush of the river. He could not get his bearings.

"Anavha!" Roh pulled at him.

Anavha rolled over just in time to see Saradyn leap through the wink after them. Saradyn babbled something at them. Anavha tried to concentrate, tried to untangle the threads of Oma holding the wink open. At least a dozen Tai Mora were rushing toward them across the plateau, only paces away now.

"Anavha!" Roh tried to heave himself up.

Saradyn took hold of him. Roh squealed, but Saradyn only righted him and said something, something that made Roh's eyes big.

Anavha concentrated on the wink. Focused on the little breaths of red mist. The first of the Tai Mora was close enough that he could see the sweat on her face. The hunger in her gaze. She lifted her wrist, and a willowthorn sword spiraled out, coming straight for Anavha's face.

"Let it go!" Roh said.

The wink went out.

A severed hunk of the willowthorn sword landed at Anavha's feet. He collapsed in the dirt, panting. "That was–"

Saradyn yanked him up. "Go," he said, in Dorinah.

"We need to keep moving," Roh said. "How many more of those can you do?"

"I… don't know," Anavha said. "I'm dizzy. I need to… eat."

"Away," Saradyn said, pointing up the hill.

"I… can't," Roh said.

Saradyn gestured for him. "Up!" he said.

Roh clambered onto Saradyn's back. Anavha was a little jealous. He was so tired of traveling.

"Just to the top," Roh said. "They will be coming down after us. We can rest over that rise, until you get your strength back."

Anavha found that his hands were trembling, but Saradyn was already moving, carrying Roh, and he feared being left behind. Anavha glanced back once, at the severed bit of willowthorn in the mud.

By the time they reached the top of the rise, Anavha was out of breath. They hunkered down on the other side. Saradyn hummed something, some Tordinian song no doubt. Roh rubbed at his own knees, wincing.

"How much do you know about your friend Natanial?" Roh asked.

"He helped me, that's all."

"How did you meet him?"

"That was… well, it was complicated."

"How do you know Saradyn?"

Anavha grimaced. "That's also complicated. It's a very awful story."

"We have a few minutes."

"Well… it was… a misunderstanding. Natanial kidnapped me and took me to Saradyn. Saradyn used to be some kind of king, in Tordin. Now he's very mad though."

"Lot of that going around," Roh said. He eyed Saradyn.

"What's all this he says about ghosts?"

"He can tell who is from this world and who isn't, that's what Natanial said. He can see people's… ghosts. Images from their past, I guess."

"Natanial kidnapped you and you still trusted him?"

"He… let me go."

Roh shook his head. Muttered something in what was probably Dhai. "Let me know when you can open a wink again. We have to keep going."

"But where?" Anavha asked. "No one knows where these rebel Dhai are, do they? If they did, the Empress would have found them."

"I have a good idea we won't need to find them," Roh said. "They'll find *us*. But it's likely to be north, near the coast. That's where I'd have gone, if I were Lilia."

"Who is this Lilia?"

Roh looked away, off into the woods. "She was my friend."

"Is she still?"

"I don't know. But it's worth the risk to find out. Are you ready?"

Anavha closed his eyes and reached for the burning thread of Oma. Took a breath. Held the power beneath his skin.

"Yes," he said.

21

"I was supposed to protect him," Natanial said, slogging his way through the rolling grass of the plateau, the jistas and guards from the temple just ahead of him, Monshara grumbling beside him. "Now he's gone, Saradyn's gone, that little boy is gone. That's not on me. That's on your empress and her temple's terrible security."

"She's going to be pissed," Monshara said. "That boy could traverse through the temple like a specter."

"I should never have brought him," Natanial said. "I failed him. I went after him for foolish, selfish reasons. Just like Zezili."

"Maybe he's just gone home," Monshara said. "I'm the one here looking like a fool. She'll want my head."

"This is such a fucking nightmare."

The Empress herself met them in the front garden. She was yelling at the jistas about securing the temple against omajistas. When her gaze found Natanial she stabbed a finger at him.

"Here we go," Monshara muttered.

"The two of you," Kirana said, "come with me to the Sanctuary. Right now." She brought two soldiers with her, ones he recognized from upstairs, and several more he took to be jistas of one type or another.

The Sanctuary was a marvel; Natanial hadn't seen anything like it in all his travels. The great dome of glass filtered the light of the double helix of the suns. The bloody red eye of Oma stared down balefully, precisely centered over the stained-glass representation of the satellite that had been worked into the ceiling... how long ago? Another cycle ago, perhaps, many cycles, the first cycle, if the rumors were to be believed. They had built these temples knowing exactly where Oma would appear in the sky.

Altars to the Dhai gods, the satellites, still ringed the central pedestal. Stone lanterns circled each altar. There was an ancient library here, filling the eastern stretch of the room, and dozens of tables piled with books and papers and diagrams.

An old man waited for them, hands stuffed in the pockets of his tunic.

"Empress," he said immediately, and made to cross to her, but she held up her hand.

"Hold there, Dasai," she said. "Close the doors, Monshara."

She did, leaving the four of them alone in the great space, their voices echoing. Natanial was very aware of his own breath. He let his gaze travel up the green skin of the temple to the domed glass again, shielding his eyes from Oma's light. The other satellites were visible, Tira and Sina, at the outer edges of the dome.

"You all brought a good many messes into my temple," Kirana said. "All at once."

"I apologize," Dasai said, "but as you can see, the boy

can converse with these temples if we–"

"I get it," Kirana said. "Monshara, you can see you're not the only one I'm pissed at. That boy shouldn't have been able to channel. Suari should have put a Song of Unmaking on him. That's his fuckup and I'll have words with him. Dasai, I want you out of here. Pack up your little friends and get back to Caisau. I've no need of you here."

"But Empress, this boon–"

"You brought me *nothing*," she spit. The temple seemed to tremble at that, but it may have been Natanial's imagination. "You are creeping perilously close here to being suspect. A year it took you to get here, after you knew what he was?"

"It's very complicated. I–"

"You have your own little flesh deals, yes," the Empress said. "I know about your scheming in the north. I know that you're looking to consolidate power. I've no time for that. Madah? Oravan? Light him up please."

"This is–" Dasai sputtered.

Madah flicked her wrist, releasing a willowthorn sword that wrapped around her wrist and pressed back against Dasai. She maneuvered him away from the tables.

The air heaved.

Dasai burst into flames. He shrieked, once, long and loud, bringing his arms up even as the flesh seared away, curling his arms into long claws. The body collapsed, still simmering, mostly charred bone and papery flesh, sizzling fat. The smell made Natanial's eyes water.

"And you," Kirana said, rounding on Natanial and Monshara.

Monshara said, "I have ever been loyal. You know that."

"I do," Kirana said, folding her arms. "It's why you're alive. But you," she said, jabbing a finger at Natanial. "You I don't know. Monshara says it was your idea to bring that boy here, and the old man."

"I honestly thought it would help your campaign."

"And why do you want to help me, Tordinian? Or are you Aaldian?"

"A bit of both," Natanial said. "I'm a mercenary. That's true. I like to align myself with the strongest players."

"And that's me."

"Yes."

"And when it's not any longer?"

Natanial gave a small shrug. Monshara grimaced, as if he had just agreed to become a human torch, and maybe he had.

"You want to work for me?" Kirana said. "You ward yourself to me, or I light you up like I did Dasai."

Natanial peered at the smoking ruin of the old man, considering his options. He had chosen to put himself here, at her mercy, so he could survive until the end of all this. But in return, who would she have him destroy next?

"I want to find the boy, the omajista," Natanial said. "I want to live through this breaking of the world, and I care enough for him that I'd like him to live, as well. Let me do that, and I'll do anything else you'd like."

"If he's intelligent, he winked himself off to Aaldia or Tordin," she said. "Be happy you're rid of him. An omajista one cannot control is worse than no omajista at all. Trust me in that. I can offer you protection, but frankly, running after that boy would be a fool's errand."

Natanial gazed up at Oma again, turning over his limited

options. Bound was better than dead. He had made worse pairings. Saradyn had not been his finest moment, either.

"All right," Natanial said. "I'd like to bring my soldiers over. Pay them, and they'll be as loyal as I will."

"Fine," Kirana said. "With Daorian in hand, both of you are worth more to me scouring the Woodland for a few... key individuals I have been seeking for some time. A child, calling herself Tasia. And a woman called Yisaoh. Both Dhai. I have portraits for you. We've found that it's better to have small but well-trained groups working in the Woodland. We've met nothing but disaster trying to move larger units. Those fucking plants eat them like candy."

"Tordin has similar issues with plant life," Natanial said. "I can help Monshara and her soldiers navigate the Woodland."

"Excellent," Kirana said. "So you'll be useful after all. Let's get you warded, and get you your soldiers. What is a useful mercenary without his soldiers?"

As the Empress's omajista advanced to ward his loyalty to the Empress into his flesh, Natanial took a knee, and wondered if he would ever get the smell of burning flesh from his nose.

22

Zezili snapped away the remaining bone branches. She had to pull out the bones that had skewered Lilia's shoulder and belly. The wounds did not bleed out, only oozed a greenish sap or pus. Zezili supposed the tree preferred to preserve its prey and feed off it slowly, like a spider.

"Hey, can you hear me?" Zezili asked. "I need you awake. I don't know where the fuck I am."

"It's fine," Lilia muttered. "It's fine."

Zezili spotted a thin line of blood on Lilia's forearm – she must have created it when she pulled her down.

She had a strange compulsion to clear it away. She pressed her lips to the wound. Sucked at the blood. The blood came away sweet. So sweet! Sweeter and more delightful than anything she had ever tasted before.

She pulled herself away from the wound, suddenly dizzy. She scrambled further from Lilia, overcome with revulsion. Had the tree done something to the blood? Zezili headed for the trees. She got eight paces before she felt the pain in her sternum again. The urge to go back, the feeling that if she continued on her own, she would die horribly, rent limb from limb.

"Fuck you!" Zezili yelled at the sky. But no one answered.

Not Rhea, not her daughters, certainly not the woozy Dhai girl.

"This is a rude fucking joke!" Zezili yelled. She picked up a skull from the field of bones and threw it into the woods. "Fuck you! Fuck you! I chose to fucking die!" She threw a few more until the gesture was no longer cathartic. Then went back to the girl.

She yanked Lilia up, as easily as if she were a bag of yams, and headed into the woods with her. Zezili wasn't thirsty, but the girl probably would be, and the wounds could do with a wash. Bonded, were they? Well, she couldn't just let her die then, she supposed.

Zezili sensed water before she saw it: a metallic taste at the back of her throat. Had she been able to sense water like that before? Surely not.

As she turned to head toward it, she noted a movement at the corner of her vision. Two young men, Dhai probably, as they did not wear armor. They bore plain metal blades, not infused weapons, which was something.

"Who are you?" one of them shouted, older, bearded, the one in charge. "You put that girl back! She's no concern of yours."

Zezili placed Lilia back on the ground. She could not help it: a grin split her face.

They must have understood that grin, because they bolted from her.

Zezili pursued them, humming all the while, a neat little ditty from some puppet show. The men slid in the mud. One knocked into a tree. She caught them easily, in three paces, before her sternum even began to ache.

She took the oldest by the beard and headbutted him. His eyes crossed. He fell. She broke his neck cleanly.

Looked about for the other one.

He was scrambling up rugged terrain backwards, sword out, sweating profusely. "What are you?" he said. "Wh– What?"

"I don't know," Zezili said. She grabbed the flat blade of the sword and twisted it from his hands. A quick flip of the sword, a thrust, and she skewered him neatly through the heart.

He spit blood. Shuddered. She twisted the blade. Blood spurted across his chest. The blood was so very beautiful.

Zezili straddled the body and pressed her hands into the blood and brought it to her lips. It smelled divine. She tasted it, and like the girl's blood it was sweet. So very, very delicious. She cut the man's jugular and cupped her hands beneath the wound, grinning at every flesh spurt of blood. She drank the blood like water until her belly was full and her whole body tingled.

Only when sated did she become aware of her bloody hands. Her sticky face. "What the fuck am I doing?" she muttered. But the blood had made her feel more... alive. Strong. She squeezed the man's neck, sending more blood into her cupped palm, and took it back up to Lilia. She cradled the girl's head with her other arm, and brought the blood to her lips.

"Hey, you hear me?" Zezili said. "Drink."

She wet Lilia's lips with the blood, made her sip at it. Lilia coughed once, grimaced, but then she drank it down as greedily as Zezili had.

A beat, no more than a moment, and Lilia opened her eyes, gaze clear now, not muddled. At the sight of Zezili, Lilia's eyes widened.

"Tira," she breathed, and blood wet Lilia's own chin. "What have you done?"

"You feel better?" Zezili asked. "You here?"

"You look… like an animal. Did you murder–"

"Are you well or not?"

"I… yes… did you…?" Lilia touched her finger to her lips; the finger came away bloody. "Did you feed me… blood?"

"It worked, didn't it?"

Lilia turned over and spit.

"How are your wounds?" Zezili asked. She checked them; they were still pus-filled and oozing, but not bleeding out. "Not a cure-all, then. We have to get you some real care. Where the fuck can we go? You've made a lot of enemies."

"I've made enemies? You made far more enemies than I did."

"Yeah, well, this isn't Dorinah we're in, is it? What day is it? What month?"

"I only know the Dhai months."

"And?"

Lilia told her.

Zezili sat back on her heels. It felt like she'd been punched. "I've… been gone… a year?"

"Your face is different. You look… younger. No scars."

Zezili pressed her hands to her smooth face. She had a dim memory of gazing into a mirror after the cats came at her, her swollen right eye, the jagged rent, the lopsided smile, and her fingers… Rhea, she had lost fingers. No, more than that. Saradyn. Saradyn had taken her *hand*. But this girl knew nothing of that. They had last seen each other in the other world, when Lilia broke the mirror, yes.

She must be talking about her other scars, the battle scars, the ones that Zezili had borne so long she had thought herself born with them.

She pulled her hands away and stared at them again. They were whole. No scars. No missing digits. Two smooth, perfect hands.

"This is a miracle," Zezili said. "A fucking Rhea-blessed miracle. What *am* I?"

"I don't know."

"Someone brought me to you... in a box? That's what... some woman said, when I woke."

"Emlee? Yes. You were supposed to be some great warrior, from Kalinda."

"I don't know who Kalinda is."

"I'm not sure how she found you, or why she was looking. I'm sorry. I... didn't know. I just... needed allies."

"Whatever way you could get them."

Lilia nodded.

"It got you stuck up a bone tree," Zezili said.

"I don't regret any of it."

That was the dumbest thing Zezili had heard the girl say yet. "Then you're a fool."

"You said you want to kill the Tai Mora."

"Who doesn't?"

"I can help you, like I said. We need to go west, until we reach the sea. Then north. There's a great temple there. Something that can help us push them all back to their world."

"Their world is dying."

"Yes."

"You intend to just... send them all back. Murder them all the way they've murdered all of you?"

"You have a better idea? Where did you get all this blood?" Lilia gestured at Zezili's stained face and tunic.

Zezili snarled. "What if it hadn't been me?"

"What do you mean?"

"If it was someone you didn't know. Someone else who wanted to die. Would you have done it?"

"I needed allies."

"You're no better than any of us."

"If you really wanted to die, you could have left me up there. You would have died soon enough."

"I don't know if that was possible. Your blood is delicious, but the idea of murdering you makes me seize up."

"Well, that's a relief."

"Is it? I'm sure it will work the other way. You can't kill me either. If I can ever die. I don't know. That's depressing."

"I'm sorry. I didn't ask how it works."

"Where is the woman who did it?"

"Kalinda? I don't know. I'm sorry."

"No, you aren't."

"Well, maybe I'm not. I needed an ally, and you were a terrible monster. Maybe this is what you deserved."

"Fuck you."

"You're always so angry."

"You aren't?"

"Of course I'm angry. But I don't sit here complaining about it."

"Fine." Zezili stood. "Let's get moving."

"You'll come with me?"

"You haven't given me much choice." She tasted the remnants of the sugary blood on her lips, and felt a craving she could not name.

23

Roh and his companions fled across the Woodland, to the sea. He knew the Woodland more by reputation than experience, and the reality of the snapping, buzzing expanse of them overwhelmed him. On the Saiduan tundra, he could often see all the way to the horizon. Here, each jump brought them into a dense thicket of woods. The massive trees and twisting greenery got him turned around. Anavha had to stop several times to gaze back at where they had come to ensure they really were still heading north. Even the suns were difficult to see, here. The few glimpses of satellites he managed were obfuscated, fuzzy and indistinct.

It was their sixth wink in two days when he finally smelled the brackish promise of the sea. But still no sign of any Dhai, rebels or otherwise.

"We haven't seen anything but plants," Anavha said, shoulders sagging. He began to sit down, but a nest of creeping phlox wept toward him, and he darted away. "Are there any people at all here? Did this wood kill them?"

"I don't know," Roh said. He had given Anavha the same answer four times in the last hour. "Unless you can–"

"No, I'm too tired for more winks. Can we rest?"

"We rested an hour ago. Not yet."

"It's easy for you to say that because you aren't even walking."

"If you think being lugged around is a comfortable way to travel, you are mistaken."

In truth, Roh was relieved to be out in the open air and on his own. He worried often about his ward. Could Dasai use it to track him? To compel him to go back? So far he had noticed nothing different, but that didn't mean anything.

Something flickered ahead. He tried to look around Saradyn's shaggy mane. The man stank terribly.

A bird hooted, unnaturally loud.

Roh tensed, peering into the tree cover ahead of them. A figure came around the nearest bonsa tree, holding an infused everpine weapon ahead of her. More figures slipped from the trees, six of them in all: three small, tawny Dhai and three tall, dark Saiduan.

Saiduan? Roh thought. That was not what he expected.

"We aren't armed!" Roh shouted, and squeezed Saradyn's neck, said to him in Dorinah, "Be still."

A Saiduan woman – taller and older than the rest – stood a little apart from the group. Her hair was knotted against her scalp. She had a broad mouth, deeply lined skin, scarred knuckles… She looked familiar, but Roh's mind refused to place her. Everyone started to blur together, when there were two or three or more of everyone.

"What motley crew is this?" she said in heavily accented Dhai.

"Let me down," Roh told Saradyn.

Saradyn grunted and complied. Roh limped forward,

hands out, palms up. "I am Rohinmey Tadisa–"

The woman hissed and spoke rapidly in Saiduan, "No, you're not. Is this some joke?"

"It's not," he said, also in Saiduan.

"Who are these others?" she asked. "You bring them from the north with you?"

"Anavha, an omajista–" When she raised her weapon, Roh shook his head. "He is harmless, but he has a great skill. He can travel by wink – make gates – to anywhere he's been before. The rest of those omajista things... I don't know if he even knows them."

"And the brute?"

"Saradyn. Mad, but he can tell you who's from this world and who isn't."

"How do I know anything you tell me is the truth? By all counts, you should be dead. They killed those Saiduan scholars. I was there."

"Who are you?"

She looked puzzled. "You don't recognize me? Do I look so different, no longer dressed in black? I did cut my hair." She smirked.

"Oma," Roh said. "This isn't–"

"Possible? Perhaps. Yet, here we are."

"I thought you were dead, Shao Maralah."

"It appears we both sought safety by appealing to the sea. Alas, my ships ran aground a few weeks back."

"But... how did you... why...?"

"That is a very long story. First, I need to know you aren't one of them, hiding behind a familiar face."

"I have a ward," he said. "Can you remove it?"

"I already did, the moment my first scout saw you. They

can track you with those wards."

"I don't know how to prove who I am," Roh said. "What questions you could–"

"Tell me about Kadaan," Maralah said, and Roh felt heat move up his face.

Maralah laughed. "That will do. Come with us. We could use a few more jistas. We have much to discuss."

The Woodland Dhai camp was too new to appear as if it had grown from the surrounding vegetation. Roh knew very little about the Woodland Dhai, except that they had rejected the prescription that the gifted be taught inside the temples to become religious leaders and teachers. As a rule, the Dhai either sorted out their differences or parted ways, and the Woodland Dhai had lived up in the hills on their own for nearly as long as Hahko and Faith Ahya had been dead and the new Kai established the temples as places of learning for the gifted.

This camp appeared to be a nomadic one. The shelters were all lean-tos wrapped in padded swathes of old bonsa leaves. Woodland Dhai stared at their party as they passed. The older Dhai bore blue tatooed faces and dressed in a motley mix of cast off fibers and animal skins. Unlike the valley Dhai, the Woodland Dhai ate meat. The idea still made Roh a little nauseous. The ground was sandy; the sea lay below them, churning in a dark cove that stretched back and back beneath them. A few Saiduan were walking up and down a winding path long worn into the stone they camped on.

"It leads below, to our ships," Maralah said, following his gaze. "We pulled them into the cavern below, to hide them from the Tai Mora while we work. They are not far from us, here, busy with something they dredged out of the sea. We sleep in the caverns below, but these Woodland Dhai were passing through. I told them they draw too much attention, and they pretend they don't understand my accent."

Anavha kept close behind him, uncertain, gaze downcast. Many of the Dhai here would be able to speak Dorinah, but the predominant languages were Dhai and Saiduan, and he could speak neither. Roh felt a little sorry for him.

"I have news from the temples," Roh said, to Maralah. "I was hoping to find someone who could help us. I heard there were rebel Dhai out here. Thought maybe we could be allies. But these are Woodland Dhai, you said?"

She grimaced. "Yes, you can see their tattoos. And you will see it in how they treat you. They are not fond of valley Dhai any more than Saiduan. Apparently they come here once a year to harvest blue stones from the sea. There are Dhai refugees around, including a camp south of here that wants to partner with us to leave the continent. I'm unsure if they are who you're looking for, though."

"Are you in charge here?"

Maralah laughed at that. "I'm in charge of my people, but certainly not these Woodland Dhai. No one is in charge of them. Some talk louder and are esteemed more. I can point them out to you. But they are at best a bickering collective."

"What are your plans here?"

"To leave. Do you want to eat?"

Roh was indeed hungry, and wanted both food and a bath, but the urgency had overcome him among all these people. He wanted to tell them everything, and see if they could help him puzzle out what the temples had told him.

"Is there…" Roh considered the stories he had heard traveling through Dhai, about a rebel leader with a twisted foot, all dressed in white. "Do you know if there's anyone here called Lilia Sona? Or someone who knows where she is? I heard stories about–"

Maralah came up short. "Lilia Sona. Now that's a name that continues to haunt me."

"You know her?"

"I sent Taigan to Dhai to find a worldbreaker. He hoped it might be her."

"That was *you*?"

"Yes." She waved a hand. "A lifetime ago. We gathered a number of young people, hoping one of them would turn out to be gifted enough to act as a worldbreaker, once we understood how to harness the power of the satellites when Oma was risen. All that work for nothing. We still ended up–" a darkness passed across her face as she surveyed the cluttered camp, "–still ended up here."

"I don't think it's too late."

"Good for you. I'm out of the business of changing the world. I just want to die old." She conferred with a group of Saiduan. A young Woodland Dhai was with them, thumbs stuck in her belt, parroting back some passable Saiduan.

"I can show them the springs," said the young Woodland Dhai. Her head was shaved, displaying the full breadth of the tattoos that covered her face and scalp. "I'm Naori. I want to work on my Saiduan. And my valley Dhai!"

"Good," Maralah said. "Thank you, Naori. Roh, when you are clean and fed, there's someone else who wants to see you."

"Are you sure there isn't anything we can do now?" Roh asked. "Anavha could–"

"Could what?" Maralah said, coolly. "Take us home? No, I'm sure a soft Dorinah man like him has never been to Saiduan. Yes, I know how traveling gates work, when they are used to travel across this world and not another. Could he take us to where we were going? No. I'm sure he hasn't been to Hrollief either, which is where I pointed those ships before the storms captured us. And I admit I'm annoyed that you have any fight left in you, boy. Let it go."

"But I think… I think we could–"

"Then you are delusional. Drunk on hope." She pointed at Saradyn. "Be sure you wash him, first. He has the stink of a fucking bear." She left them and followed after two more Saiduan woman descending the long tongue of the cavernous pathway that led below.

"Don't mind her," Naori said. "She has struggled a long time. Her people are dead. You knew each other, though? Was she kind to you?"

"She didn't do any of this," Roh said, though he did not gesture to his legs, or his other scars, physical and mental. "Not to me, anyway."

Naori cheerfully showed them around the camp and took them down another well-worn path to a bubbling hot springs. "My people, clan Kosilatu, we come here every year for bluestones, and to soak in the hot springs."

"Does your clan… Do you know about rebel Dhai living here? Valley Dhai? Refugees?"

"Oh yes," Naori said. "There are several camps, but like us, most of them move."

Roh sighed. The faint smell of sulfur permeated the air around the hot springs. Saradyn pulled off a boot, filling the air with a far grimmer stench, and dipped his foot in.

"Ahh!" Saradyn said, and began to strip off his grimy clothing without any urging.

"I can find some clean clothes," Naori said. She laughed at Saradyn. "Him, though? I don't know. He's too broad for anything I have. I'll see."

Roh stripped, heedless of the others, but Anavha hung back. "What is it?" Roh asked. "Don't you want to get clean?"

"When you're through," Anavha said, face reddening. Roh found that amusing. Was it something about being Dorinah?

Naori met them back at the camp with clean clothes for Roh and Anavha, both Saiduan cuts, so they were too long. Roh helped Anavha with the hems.

There was tea, and mashed tubers, a vegetable broth of leek and early spring shoots. Much of it was tasteless, but it was filling, and that's all Roh wanted.

"What are the Saiduan doing here?" he asked Naori. "She said they were going somewhere else."

"To Hrollief," Naori said. "They were some of the last of the Saiduan, but their ship washed up here last month."

"What of the rest of the Dhai?"

Naori gestured to the woods around them. "There are many camps. Some are resisting. I heard Catori Meyna and Yisaoh lead a good number of them. Maralah says they will meet her here and head south to Hrollief as well."

"What about the Kai?"

"We had thought him dead."

"Had?"

"There's been a rumor he's taken back up with Catori Meyna, and Yisaoh. I got the impression the Saiduan were bickering about that. My Saiduan is still… so-so."

Roh watched Maralah, who was working at the other side of the camp, helping three other Saiduan heave a small felled tree back down through the looping path to the sea.

"Maralah was one of the most powerful sanisi," Roh said. "She was… at the right hand of the Patron. It's just… strange to see her like this."

"She is as human as you or I," Naori said. "She bleeds and sweats, I can tell you that. My clan understands this." She snorted. "All Woodland Dhai understand this. Power, titles, things… we are each of us only a disaster away from losing everything. Best to live without anything. Enjoy each moment as it takes you."

It was evening before Roh got a chance to speak to Maralah again. He had fallen asleep after eating, and it was well into dusk when he woke; the largest of the three moons, Ahmur, was full. The smaller moons, Mur and Zini, were only slivers in the night sky. The satellites were more difficult to see at night, as if the suns' rays illuminated them, made them brighter during the day the way they made the suns bright at night.

The sound of the sea was loud, but not loud enough to drown out Saradyn's snoring, beside him. Anavha sat near one of the big fires, where a trio of Dhai were telling stories. The firelight played across Anavha's eager face. He was rapt, like a child, though he probably couldn't understand any of it. Maralah stood near the fire, apart from the rest, drinking something from a cup made from a hollowed out seed the size of Roh's fist.

Roh stretched and limped over to her. The night was cool. He rubbed his arms absently.

"You're awake," she said. She offered him the cup. "Aatai?"

Roh shook his head. "Where did you get it?"

"We brought cases of it with us. Only a few left, though, at the rate my people drink it."

"How many came with you?"

Maralah gazed at the fire. "We had fifty-seven, when we got on the ship. We have thirty now."

"I'm sorry."

She drank deeply from the cup. "War of attrition. The Tai Mora have won it. We have plenty of room for your people on the boats, though. I suppose there's that. Imagine, a little settlement somewhere of Saiduan and Dhai, trying to make some life together. Who would have dreamed it?"

"You should know that we found the book," Roh said. "The one you and the other Saiduan were looking for, that tells us how to use the temples to close the ways between worlds, and... much more, besides. Luna and I translated it."

Maralah continued to stare at the fire. The reflection of the flames flickered in her eyes. "It doesn't matter now."

"It may not matter to Saiduan, but it matters to Dhai."

She said nothing.

Roh gazed across the fire to the rest of the camp. Low voices from the side of the Woodland Dhai. The twang of some stringed instrument from the Saiduan circle of makeshift tents. A few dozen. All Maralah was able to save. No wonder she was bitter.

"Do you really want to leave all that power to the Tai Mora?" Roh asked. "The power of the heavens themselves?"

"I won't be here to see what they do with it."

"Do you think there's a place in this world, or any of them, that she can't reach?"

"I'm not a threat to anyone."

"Neither were the Dhai."

She rounded on him. Her dark gaze was piercing, and he saw the sanisi in her, then: the old Maralah – the one he had first spied dancing in the courtyard with Kadaan – the woman who had commanded great armies and had the ear of the most powerful man in the world.

"You don't know what you're talking about," she said. "You were always an arrogant child."

"They need a key, a guide, and a worldbreaker," Roh said. "All focused on that fifth temple they dredged up north of here. I can get a small party to the People's Temple from any other temple."

"You need more than that," Maralah said. "I've seen the diagrams. The Dhai, Meyna, showed them to me."

"Oh," Roh said. "You… but if you know, then–"

"Who is this key, Roh? And a worldbreaker? And when you have them, remember that every temple needs four jistas, and a fifth to stand at the center of them and act as some kind of living conduit. How many jistas do you have? I haven't kept up with what your new Kai, or Empress, or whatever she calls herself has been doing, but your people here have. She's filling those temples with her jistas and putting all of her pieces in place. You are already too late. Her people are there."

"But–"

"Be reasonable," Maralah said. "I know it's newer for you, but understand that I've been through what you have. I've seen my country destroyed, its people decimated. I had hope once too. It nearly destroyed all of us."

Maralah shifted her attention to two Saiduan men making their way over with another bottle of aatai. "Ah, here we are," Maralah said. "Look who I found for you, Kadaan."

At that name, a thread of icy fire bit through Roh's belly. He stared.

The men came into the flicker light of the circle of fire, and there he was – Kadaan Soagaan, whom Roh had last seen fighting for his life in Shoratau. The Shadow of Caisau. By all rights, he should have been a ghost, too.

Kadaan was thinner, wiry, and his hair was much longer. A new scar puckered the skin under his left eye.

"You are a sight, puppy," Kadaan said. Roh's mouth went dry. He had no idea what to say.

Maralah glanced from one to the other and said, "You look like men who could use some aatai." When Roh still didn't respond, she took hold of his shoulder, squeezed it, and bent over him. She whispered, "Oma is fickle, and grants us few choices to save what we love. Stop fighting, Roh. Stop fighting and live again."

24

Zezili hated everything about the woods. The insects. The loamy smell. The crashing and chirping of the birds and tree gliders. She itched and sweated, but was still not thirsty, and hadn't had to pee or shit the entire three days they had trekked through the woods. Maybe that was why she wasn't paying attention to her footing anymore.

They had come to the edge of the Woodland the day before, and were following the great ridge of the plateau where the trees and brush had been thinned by storms and poor soil. The sea smelled of death, and brought with it a cool wind, but this far up, it didn't bother Zezili much.

Lilia walked much more slowly, so Zezili paused to let her catch up for the hundredth time. She didn't remember where exactly she put her feet, only that when Lilia got near enough, she pushed off on one foot to begin again, and the ground crumbled beneath her.

"Fuck!" Zezili yelled. She reached instinctively for Lilia. Caught her sleeve.

The two of them slid down the ravine together, rushing toward the beach. They landed in a tangle, covered in sandy soil and rocks. When the rolling stopped, Zezili found herself dizzy and damp. She raised her head and saw a marshy grassland, and sand beneath her fingers. The stink of the sea was much worse here. She stood, wiped herself off, and peered over the grassy dunes. She caught the sparkle of the wine dark seas.

Lilia moaned.

Zezili helped her up. "You alive? Anything broken?"

"I'm leaking," Lilia said, pulling her hand away from the oozing green pus at her shoulder."

"I think we're close," Zezili said, "if you were right about–"

"Oh," Lilia said. She gazed north, out past Zezili's shoulder.

Zezili turned.

A thousand paces up the beach, a massive, decaying beast lay on its side, like an old snoozing dog. The wind was blowing in from the sea, but it was only a matter of time before they caught the stink of it.

"Is that recent?" Lilia asked.

"How would I know?"

"I just wondered."

"It's not rotten, not bleached from the suns. Not picked clean. I guess it's new."

"How can you see that?"

"Easily. You can't?"

Lilia frowned.

They walked along the beach, keeping to the less sandy soil near the edge of the cliff because it was easier to navigate. The wind picked up, sending cool, lashing mist at them. Zezili didn't mind it, but after a time, Lilia was trembling with cold. Zezili wanted to offer something – a blanket? But they had nothing. Lilia's lips were flaking and parched, though she did not complain.

Zezili realized how ill-equipped they were for a journey of any length. How long had it been since Lilia ate anything? Zezili had had nothing since the blood, and she still felt strong, though there was a pang of longing when she thought about how sweet the blood had been.

"Maybe there's something worth eating in that carcass," Zezili said.

Lilia make a retching sound and spit up a little bile.

"You don't know. Come on." Zezili knew things were bad when she felt like the optimist in the group.

They made it three more paces before Lilia collapsed. It was all very sudden. Zezili stood over her, and Lilia was completely out. Zezili sighed then simply picked her up and carried on.

She drew closer and closer to the dead thing, until she could make out the curve of a great harbor carved into the cliffs just behind it. The salty spray of the waves kept churning up to the mouth of the cave and then stopping, spraying upward as if meeting some invisible resistance. Some jista illusion? Perhaps.

Soon she found footsteps along the beach, coming from the direction of the curved harbor. If she squinted, she could just see a few dark shapes moving on top of the cliff. She paused just as three figures appeared from the mouth of the cave, seemingly from thin air. They scrambled across the broken stone, heading toward her. From a distance, she could not make out if they were Dhai or Tai Mora. Surely they were too tall and dark for either?

Three was not too many. She could murder them all if she had to. But what she needed was water for her annoying little ward.

As they caught sight of her, they reached for weapons. Infused blades. The air pressure remained stable. Not jistas, then.

"I need help!" Zezili called in Dorinah, which was likely useless, but she hoped the tone would carry. "I need help. Water?" She curled her lip when they continued to look confused. She went on, in Dhai, "Water? Not armed."

The figures were a mix of people – two Saiduan and a Dhai, all bundled against the cool weather. The Dhai moved ahead of the others. Carrying a body, perhaps, made up for her terrible accent. She was clearly someone in distress.

The Dhai took Lilia from her. Zezili tried to tell him it was fine, no, she could do it, but honestly, it was good to have her hands free. Her stomach ached briefly as Lilia moved away, but they did not go far, and Zezili continued to follow. "Water? Food, probably. Oh, a bone tree! You know–"

"We know about bone trees," the man said, in Dorinah.

"I can speak Dhai too," Zezili said.

He narrowed his eyes. His gaze swept the beach. "Just the two of you?"

"Yes."

"Come, follow us."

Zezili kept her mouth shut and followed them along the coast and back into the curve of the rocky harbor. The closer she got to the invisible barrier that broke the waves, the clearer it was that it was a jista-created thing. When she stepped through it, she came into a deep, cold cavern. Two battered ships rested in the back of the cave where the heavy stones had been beaten to fine gravel. A jet of light pierced the gloom, projected from a break in the cavern

ceiling that illuminated a path worn into the rear of the
cave that went up and up and up to what she assumed was
a camp, above.

The Dhai took her past the great ships. The sound of
hammering and hauling, the scrape of leather on stone,
filled the cavern. The air here was heavier; jistas must be
working somewhere inside the ships.

They climbed the path at the back of the cave and came
up into the light. A scattering of tents stood amid a stand
of young bonsa trees. There were clearly two camps – one
closer to the woods that was mostly Dhai, and another,
scrappier camp made of tattered old sails and scrounged
wood that mainly housed Saiduan. Interesting. Possibly
these were among the last Saiduan still alive in the world.

The Dhai brought Lilia to an open-air tent on the Dhai
side of the camp, one where several other patients were
clearly convalescing. Yet it was a Saiduan who came up to
them and gestured to an empty cot, said to Zezili in Dhai,
"What happened?"

"Bone tree."

The woman showed her teeth. "We've had a few of
those. I'm amazed she's still alive. Do you need anything?
You look–" she gave Zezili a searching stare, "–well. You
seem very well, actually."

Zezili was taken aback at the kindness. No weapons.
No obvious jistas menacing her. If they had an illusionary
ward below, they were certainly fearful of outsiders. But
not her, apparently. Or Lilia.

"I'm good. Great. But she's... She needs to be all right."

"Is she your lover?"

"What? Oh, fuck, no. I hate her."

"Oh. Um. All right, well, come and have some tea. I'll attend her."

Zezili walked over to the next tent where a long table was set up. Three fires blazed nearby, one with tea and two with some kind of bubbling stew. She didn't want either and still found it bizarre no one here had interrogated her yet. Maybe they were all busy working on the ship. Maybe she didn't look dangerous? The second idea bothered her. Did she not look dangerous anymore, with her clear skin and lack of scars and all her limbs in place? She wondered if she could find a mirror. Zezili sat at the table where a few Dhai were having tea. They tried to make conversation, but she didn't want tea and she didn't want to talk.

"You know where I can find a mirror?" she asked.

"The infirmary," one said.

"Maralah may have one," said another.

"Who's Maralah?"

"Tall Saiduan woman, older. Very growly. Makes a face like this." The man scrunched up his face as if he tasted something sour. The others laughed.

Zezili didn't want to get too far away from Lilia. The trouble with not being used to pain and discomfort anymore was that when it came, it bothered her more than it probably should have.

She wandered back to the infirmary instead, and asked the Saiduan doctor for a mirror.

The woman returned with a palm-sized mirror framed in silver. It had once had a handle, but it had been broken or seared off.

Zezili held the mirror back as far as she could and scrutinized her face. She barely recognized herself. Some younger version of who she had been stared back, all soft skin – hardly a wrinkle or a crease, and certainly no scars. The Empress of Dorinah's cats had left her with a monstrous visage, and seeing herself as she had been when she was newly recruited into the woman's army brought with it a wash of both good and terrible memories. Her marriage to Anavha. The fights with her sisters over him. The estate the Empress granted her, and the dajians who were as useful to her as her dogs. Daolyn. What had ever happened to Daolyn, that eager little gem of a dajian? She had made the best coats.

Lost in memories, she hardly noticed the image passing behind her: a tumble of brown hair, a handsome curve of a familiar face.

Anavha.

Zezili closed her eyes. Opened them. There, staring back at her in the mirror, was Anavha. Tall and still very thin, bearded now, but hardly enough to hide who he was. He looked freshly washed. Big brown eyes. They widened as she met his look in the mirror.

I am imagining things, Zezili thought, but she turned anyhow, her heart catching.

And there was Anavha.

She opened her mouth, but no sound came out. What was there to say? How was this possible?

He took a step back. That couldn't be right. Why would he fear her? He was hers. Like the dogs, like the dajians… Dajians like Lilia, like these people who had taken her in and fed her, more fool them. Right?

Anavha gaped. His face flushed. He grabbed at his coat, as if trying to shield himself from her.

"It's all right," Zezili said. She held out her right hand, her perfect right hand, good as new, as unmarred and far softer than it had been on their wedding day.

"No!" Anavha said, and he ran.

Zezili's heart ached.

25

Natanial had chosen his side, mostly freely. But choosing and being contented in that choice were very different things. While he had been unable to sleep since the Empress of Tai Mora had warded him to ensure his loyalty, Otolyn had snored softly and serenely ever since crossing over with his force of fighters. The Empress had access to more jistas, many of them loyal to a woman called Gian. The extra jistas meant more traveling from woodland hill to woodland dale, popping to and from areas where they had limited intelligence about a Dhai presence.

Natanial was not keen on stealing or murdering children, but the Empress's orders were precise, and he understood her reasoning, even if he didn't agree with it.

"A woman and a child," Monshara had said after they left the Empress's presence. "She didn't tell you it's her woman, and her child."

"I don't understand."

"Shadows," Monshara said. "She wants us to find them so she can kill them and bring her version over."

"Surely she's had any number of people pursuing them?"

"Of course. But we have good intelligence now. A captive rebel from Tira's Temple who broke in an interrogation."

"The first to break?"

"Of course not. Just the first to break who actually knew something. Biggest camp we're clearing yet."

Natanial stood with her now in a slight clearing as a new pair of winks opened, giving their forces a view of a few simple tents and the old, scattered remains of large bonfires. It certainly didn't look like over a thousand people lived there. How they were supposed to root out a single woman and child from this rats' nest was a mystery, but Monshara had taken charge of this one.

"They're underground," Monshara said. "That's what the intelligence says."

"You going to drown them out?" Natanial asked.

"No, no, Natanial. We'll burn them out, like rats."

Natanial could not help but wonder if Anavha was somewhere there, huddled underground with the unwashed refugee Dhai. If he was, there was a good chance he could save himself. The Empress had been right, though. Anavha was not a complete fool; he would have gone home, to Aaldia. Natanial certainly hoped so.

"Not very sporting, is it?" Otolyn, his second, said from behind them. She was still on the other side, waiting for her own wink to open. She was due at the opposite end of the camp where they had found a secondary exit. She still carried that damn Dorinah head with her, like a talisman, dangling from the back of her mount.

"Hold the commentary," Natanial said.

"This better pay a lot," Otolyn said.

"When the fire starts, you'll smell it," Monshara called back. "Kill them as they come up for air."

"Here we go," Otolyn said, and moved away from the

frame of the wink and toward her own squad.

Natanial moved left, and Monshara went right; their respective forces joined them, spreading out quickly over the ground of the clearing. The jistas stepped into the circle made by their two forces: two sinajistas and a tirajista. The response from the Dhai came quickly, far more quickly than Natanial had anticipated.

A trembling wave of tumbling vines erupted from the ground. Even as Natanial reined his bear back, the Tai Mora sinajistas were countering, sending waves of flame into the writhing plant life. Smoke billowed into the air, caught up in the tree canopy. Bits of ashy leaves rained over them.

An onslaught of arrows fell from the trees, one wave, then a second. The sinajistas burned them out of the air, but a few got through. One took their tirajista in the shoulder, and she went down.

"Should have brought more jistas," Natanial muttered.

Monshara called another wave forward from a new wink gaping at the center of their forces. Six more jistas moved onto the field, this time placing themselves squarely behind Natanial's mercenaries. To the Empress, his people were little more than a human shield for her gifted troops.

Natanial started a count, wondering how long the Dhai here could truly outlast them. No doubt this show of strength was meant to delay them so the others could flee out the far exit, but Otolyn and her troops would be there waiting for them.

All he wanted in this moment, as the next wall of fire came down on the camp, burning away the tents above ground and swirling into the underground tunnels, was to have a little farm in Aaldia like the one where he had found Anavha. The little farm that had almost certainly been destroyed behind them, the way he was destroying this settlement.

I made a stupid mistake, he thought. He hadn't been able to see any other life but this one, his fighting arm directed by the most powerful person around him.

Dhai began pouring up from the ground.

Natanial held his fist high, cautioning his troops to stay still. As if they needed encouragement to do nothing! But if one of them dove into the fray now for easy killing, they would only put themselves in danger of getting pummeled by their own sinajistas.

The smell of burning flesh and hair, green wood, and the tangy bleed of bonsa sap filled the air. Cries, shouts, yes, some of those too, but mostly he heard the crackle of the flames and the hiss and pop of heat-expanded water and sap exploding from the vegetation.

The bodies kept coming up. They had likely found Otolyn's troops at the rear exit. Those who were not trampled would be suffocated by the smoke. Natanial observed the bodies coolly. Singed hair. Raw, blistered skin. Tattered, still flaming clothing. One child ran screaming, naked, across the fallen bodies of three adults before a lashing vine caught it up and crushed it.

The tirajista was doing precise, surgical work. Natanial watched her, curious to see signs of distress or distaste, but she worked with furious concentration, deeply focused. Whirling vines tangled up the defensive units in the trees as well, and they began to drop like mashed insects to the forest floor.

After about a quarter of an hour, the bodies heaving up from the ground grew fewer and fewer, and the waves of fire and skewering vines came further apart.

"That's it!" Monshara called, and raised her fist.

Time to clean up.

Natanial sighed and got off his mount. He began to pull the children's bodies away from the others, making neat, long lines of them. It was grotesque, filthy work, and he began to question, for the first time, what the fuck he was doing here. Working for Saradyn had involved much distasteful work, but that work always felt purposeful. The death was leading somewhere. This was... wasteful.

Otolyn and three of her company arrived, herding a long line of young girls ahead of them. The girls were roped around the neck, six or seven of them. Otolyn slid off her bear and gave them a tug. The girls shrieked and sobbed at the sight of the bodies, all but two of them, who appeared struck dumb by the horror some time before.

Natanial went over to meet her and Monshara. "You know what she looks like?" Natanial asked Monshara.

"I do," Monshara said. "I'm looking for a little girl called Tasia," Monshara said to the girls. They huddled together, shaking and snuffling. Monshara peered into each face in turn. Lingered on one, a narrow-faced girl with big eyes and half her hair burnt off. One ear was slightly charred. "Tell me your name, child."

The child said nothing.

Monshara took off her helmet and knelt beside the girl. "What is your name, child?" she said, more softly.

Nothing.

"Child," Monshara said, "I can't take you back to your

mother if I don't know your name."

Another moment of hesitation. Then, "Tasia," the girl whispered. "I'm Tasia Sona."

"All right," Monshara said, and straightened. She released her from the rope and put a hand behind her shoulder, leading her back away from the field of dead and toward the open wink with Madah, who was getting an update from Monshara's second.

"What do we do with the rest?" Otolyn said.

"I bet I can guess," Natanial said. He gazed into each grubby face. He was going to get very drunk tonight.

"I liked it better when we were killing evil fucking Dorinah," Otolyn said. "These are just a bunch of fucking roaches."

"Greater rewards," Natanial said. "The fighting is almost done."

Otolyn spit. "That wasn't a fight."

Natanial couldn't argue.

"Some of them got away," Otolyn said. "None of them were kids, though. I sent a couple of people after them, but no doubt these roaches know the woods better."

"She only wanted the child," Natanial said. "I don't think she'll begrudge us a few extra lives."

"Yeah, well, I'm not counting on that."

He didn't want to stay and see what she did with the children, so he walked back over to Monshara. She had already handed the girl over to Madah. Natanial saw no sign of her.

"We need you to move north," Madah said as he approached. "We've discovered a larger camp there."

"Any more kids we need to kill?" Natanial asked.

"Possibly," Madah said, without hesitation. "We need the ground cleared here, though. You can take prisoners if you like, and interrogate them. Remember we're still looking for Yisaoh Alais Garika."

"Spoils of victory," Natanial said. "There was nothing worth taking here but human flesh. What am I supposed to do to keep my troops' morale up?"

"They are your soldiers, not mine," Madah said. "I'm sure you can think of something."

"It's going to take at least two days to clear this area," Monshara said.

"Yes," Madah said.

The wink closed.

"She's delightful," Natanial said.

"Like her mother," Monshara said. Natanial had no idea who Madah's mother was, but Monshara appeared wistful. Another dead woman? "The Empress will be pleased with this, though." She patted Natanial's arm. "It will be worth it."

She sounded very confident. She had been doing this a long time.

26

Kirana was in the baths when Madah brought the child down. Kirana heard the shrieking. The slap of flesh. More shrieking, raised voices. She knew who it was, and pulled herself out of the water and began to towel off.

Madah had the girl by one arm, and yanked her forward. "Is this her, Empress?" Madah asked.

Kirana wrapped the towel around her waist and took the girl by the chin. It was always remarkable, how much they all looked alike despite their circumstances, as if there remained some tenuous connection between them, despite the distance of their worlds. Kirana had not borne children, herself. And only Corina had been born of Yisaoh. Tasia and Moira had been born to Yisaoh's long-dead cousin, and Kirana and Yisaoh had fostered them since they were infants.

"Your name is Tasia?" Kirana asked.

The girl nodded.

Kirana released her. That was likely enough, but she wanted to be absolutely certain. No mistakes, this time, no lookalikes. "And who was your mother?"

"Lilia is my mother," Tasia said.

"Lilia?" That did not sit right. Then she remembered

the Dhai habit of calling any older woman who shared the household a *mother*. "I mean, who is the woman who birthed you? Could you tell me about her?"

Tasia shook her head. The girl's eyes filled. "Please, I want to go home!"

"You can go home," Kirana said, crouching before her. "But I need to know your mother's name. The woman who birthed you. You remember?"

"Please let me go home. I have a bird at home. A poppet called Jahin."

She was too frightened. And Kirana could not stomach any more of it. She recognized her well enough. "I have something for you. Turn around for me," Kirana said.

Tasia turned.

"I can do it," Madah said softly.

"No, no," Kirana said. "This was my promise. My family." She held out her hand.

Madah handed her a knife over the girl's head.

Kirana was quick. The blade flashed before the girl understood what had happened. A quick strike to the jugular. Kirana had not wanted to see her face. She held the small body against her as the blood pumped out over her arm and pooled on the floor, slipping across the tiles and making long crimson runnels that drained into the pool, swirling and dissipating in the water. The great living water spiders ballooned up from the bottom of the pool and came to investigate.

Kirana waited until the girl was still, the body drained, then rolled her toward Madah. "Have someone else come for that," she said.

Madah bowed and left her. Kirana took off her towel and

waded back into the pool. She floated out onto her back, gazing at the intricate details of the ceiling: happy, peaceful carvings and mosaics of birds and cats, sea creatures and snapping lilies, walking trees and great puffy seeds that navigated the air like something alive. A peaceful people, a peaceful country. Everything she wanted to build. But was it possible to come back from all this darkness? To establish a nation on war and genocide and then wean them off it, promoting peace and cooperation, understanding? She closed her eyes and thought of how she could work with Gian's people. More jistas to help with crops. More mouths to feed, yes, but Gian's people had brought stores with them on the ark. They could trade goods and favors with Aaldia, perhaps. Maybe the killing would be over.

At some point a few of her people came to take the body. She knew she should get out and go to her own Yisaoh, her own Tasia immediately and bring Tasia over. But she lingered. She had always known what saving her people meant. Some days, though, were easier than others.

A gaggle of new bathers arrived, loud and laughing until they saw her. They quieted, but the spell was broken.

Kirana got out of the great pool and dressed. Servants moved out of her way in the changing rooms; one old Dhai woman worked at replenishing the flame fly lanterns. All of the Dhai in the temples were warded; they could not commit physical harm against Kirana or one of her people, but those wards could be removed. Worse, she felt it made her people complacent, knowing the Dhai slaves could not physically harm them. They saw them as ghost people, hardly human, and though Kirana understood that was sometimes easier, she had learned to see every potential adversary clearly, especially those she kept under a fearful thumb. She knew love was a better way to rule than fear, but fear worked much more quickly than love, and she had not had time to woo any of them. It wasn't exactly a good time to start, either, with their food situation still precarious. They might end up eating Dhai bodies for dinner yet.

As she left the baths, a little runner arrived, gaze lowered. "Sai Hofsha has arrived," the boy said.

"She still in the foyer?"

"Just now, yes."

"I'll meet her there. Go."

The runner went ahead. Kirana took her time, and arrived just as Hofsha strode in, followed by two attendants. She had taken on a great number of slaves after the invasion.

"Empress," Hofsha said. She removed her hat and gave an overly dramatic bow. Hofsha was always one for drama and spectacle.

"You have news from Gian?" Kirana asked.

"I do. She has sent a gift."

Kirana eyed the girls.

"No, no," Hofsha laughed. "Nothing so droll. I told her the one thing we have in abundance is *people*."

"Come," Kirana said, "the Sanctuary."

Hofsha left her girls in the foyer and followed after Kirana into the Sanctuary. It was blessedly empty this time of day, used mainly as a gathering and teaching space.

Kirana closed the door and look around quickly to ensure they had privacy. She sat on one of the great green clothed benches. Hofsha did not sit, but gazed up at the great dome, beaming.

"It was not so long ago I first entered here," Hofsha said. "What a soft people, they were."

"Some other people may think us soft," Kirana said. "I hope not to meet them."

"That is not Gian," Hofsha said quickly. "She turned over storage goods, as you hoped. Enough rice to get us out of this hungry stretch."

"All of us?"

"Remarkably, yes, possibly. That is, I'm not the agricultural steward, but if we absolutely must, we can always stop feeding the slaves."

"I'd prefer to keep the labor."

"Oh, certainly, but–" Hofsha raised her gaze to the ceiling again, made a moue.

"Speak plainly," Kirana spat. She hated Hofsha's posturing.

"Gian has a request."

"Of course she does."

"She doesn't want to coexist. She'd prefer to take Dhai, and leave us with the rest of the country, after."

"And in control of these great engines that can break worlds? No, that would be mad."

Hofsha shrugged. "Well, we get to keep the rice, anyway."

"Is that a deal breaker? Surely she didn't think I'd agree to that."

"It will be difficult to approach her again without a counteroffer."

"Did you insinuate that I could burn up her entire ark at any time I'd like?"

"I did. And she insinuated that it was very well protected."

Kirana huffed. "Why did it have to be Gian? Why not

someone with less of a backbone? Aradan? Sovonia? They would have been kissing my feet on our first meeting."

"We may hear from them yet."

"Will she meet me here?" Kirana asked. "If she won't listen to reason, perhaps she will be swayed by seeing it. I want to show her the chambers. And the key passages of the book on how to use these machines are nearly translated."

"I can ask," Hofsha said.

"I don't need you to ask. I need you to persuade."

"Come now," Hofsha said, grinning, "I got a woman to betray her own son. This will be easy."

"Best hope so. Go on."

Hofsha bowed, sweeping her hat forward again, annoyingly, and stepped jauntily from the room.

Kirana went up the long slog of the stairs and knocked on Suari's door. He opened it, still bleary-eyed. She had kept him up the night before going over the translated diagrams from the Worldbreaker book.

"Upstairs," she said. "I need a wink to Yisaoh."

"Oravan is up there."

"I didn't ask for Oravan. I asked for you. Ten minutes."

She left him and went up to her office to prepare. Her secretary was already there, going through piles of missives, many of them sent by sparrows, others hand-delivered by those traveling by wink. The Dhai system of lifts had been largely destroyed by fire – hers and theirs, as she tried to cut them off from fleeing. But with Oma in the sky, travel and communication were very easy. That would not last, Kirana knew, and she already had surveyors out exploring various infrastructure projects that could connect her more quickly from here to the coast, as far north as Caisau and as far east as Janifa, in Dorinah.

Suari took almost half an hour to arrive. He strode up the steps just as she was considering whether to send her secretary down or one of the little Dhai bringing up tea. Oravan and one of her stargazers worked at one side of the table, going over their calculations for the billionth time. Para's rise was imminent, they said; every day they were better able to predict its reappearance, and last she heard, they were days away.

"Did you have other obligations?" Kirana quipped as Suari came through the archway.

"Shall we begin?" Suari said. He raised his hands.

"Do it," Kirana said. She would deal with him again later. If he'd been anything but an omajista, she would have had him strung up above the gates as a warning.

The air shimmered and thickened. Kirana rolled her neck and shoulders, preparing to meet with Yisaoh for the first time in several days. The wink rent the air in front of her, a little too close for her liking, and she narrowed her eyes at Suari.

She waited a beat for the jista on the other side to acknowledge the wink, but there was a long stretch of nothing instead. She gazed long at the dark wall.

Kirana approached the wink and bent to see further into the room. It was empty.

"Piss," Kirana muttered. Someone had left their station.

She called over a guard from the entry to the Assembly Chamber and sent her in to find their contact. The woman went quickly, pressing thumb to forehead and jumping through.

Kirana waited, pointedly ignoring Suari.

The guard reappeared, out of breath. "Something's happened to the consort."

"Fuck!" Kirana went to step in, but the guard held up her hands.

"Empress, caution! Someone has been here. Not one of ours."

"There's no one left alive on that fucking world," Kirana said.

"I don't think... I don't think they're from our world."

"Get back in here. You!" she yelled at one of the Dhai servants. "Go and get me Madah. Tell her I need a scouting party. Oravan!"

"Empress?"

"Relieve Suari. I want you on this wink. Suari, get me a sinajista for this side in case anything comes through."

This time, Suari picked up his pace as he hurried from the room.

Kirana went to her room and buckled on her armor. She held out her right hand, and let the blooming willowthorn weapon unfurl from it. It had been some time since she had needed it. Her heart thrummed. Sweat beaded her lip. Now was not the time to lose the woman she had done all of this to save.

Madah arrived with a force of thirteen, including three jistas. Suari brought a haggard sinajista up, one of the ones Kirana had working below.

"Madah, you have the floor here," Kirana said.

"You aren't... Empress, you aren't going in?" Madah asked.

"Keep the wink open. That's my family," Kirana said, and stepped through.

She unfurled her weapon the moment she was clear of the wink, and waited for the others to make it through. "I need three of you up here," she said. "We go through this room by room."

A tangled ruin of a body lay just outside the wink room; it looked as if it had been savaged by a wild animal, and had been dead at least a day. No, Kirana thought, I am not going to lose them. Not now.

She had told them to go room by room, but she found herself running down the hall, past slippery orange mold that oozed from the seams between the hold's stones. The vines they had used to shore up the place from the tremors and block out the charred air were shriveled and brown.

More bodies lay scattered in the hall, these ones... barely human, though she recognized them. Golden people, two sets of legs, and narrow waists like wasps. Green eyes in delicately featured faces. Like the Empress of Dorinah. Where had these ones come from? Surely not Raisa. Kirana had eradicated all of those who remained. Taking Daorian had been their last stronghold.

Other worlds were not supposed to come to hers, to this dying orb. She had never seen it happen. She came to the door of Yisaoh's rooms and threw herself against it.

"I have it! Empress!" the sinajista called.

"Carefully!" Kirana said.

The door charred from the center outward, blackening as it softened the integrity of wood. Two of her soldiers knocked the char out of the opening and stepped through. Kirana went after them, gaze sweeping the room.

"Mama!" The voice sent a dagger of pain through her heart.

Kirana fell to her knees. Tasia ran into her arms. She hugged her close, shoving her face into the girl's hair and inhaling the scent of her. "Your mother?" Kirana asked, raising her head.

Yisaoh lay in the bed. Kirana took Tasia by the hand and went to the bedside. She heard the ragged wheeze of Yisaoh's breathing.

"Oh, love," Kirana said.

Yisaoh sweated heavily, hands clutched around her middle. She was swaddled in the sheets, wrapped tightly and shivering.

"Tirajista!" Kirana yelled.

The tirajista came over quickly and gently pulled back the sheets. The smell of sweet rot filled the air. Kirana winced. A sour, oozing slash in Yisaoh's belly writhed with maggots.

"I'm... Empress, this isn't my specialty. I'm offensive, not rated for medical–"

Kirana hit her. The tirajista fell back. "Then go get me one who is!"

The tirajista ran.

Kirana bent over Yisaoh. Pushed her hair back. "Hey, love, can you hear me?" But Yisaoh's gaze was blank, so far away.

Tasia squeezed Kirana's hand. "I tried to help," Tasia said. "I locked the door."

"That was good," Kirana said. "What happened here?"

"The creatures came."

"Where's everyone else?"

"There's no one else. I think. We... Mam said to stay here. There was a lot of noise, and then... there wasn't."

"How long have you been here?"

"I don't know. I'm thirsty."

"You, get her some water," Kirana said to one of the soldiers. The woman passed over a bulb of water and Kirana urged Tasia to drink it, then lifted Yisaoh's head and tried to get her to wet her mouth.

Yisaoh coughed, but lapped up a little of it, her body responding even if her mind was addled.

"I'm so sorry," Kirana murmured.

The new tirajista arrived, and Kirana took Tasia into her lap and sat on a nearby chaise.

"Go clear the rest of the building. You, sinajista, and you, stay here with us and hold the door."

The scouting group moved out, and the sinajista and soldier took up a place at the door, far enough away that Kirana felt she could speak to her daughter with some amount of privacy.

Yisaoh gasped. The air grew heavy. The tirajista had a little bag of salves and potions with her, which rested near her feet.

"Mama, is she hurting?" Tasia whispered.

"She'll be fine, she's getting help. You did very well caring for her." Kirana smoothed back her hair. "I need to know more about these people who came here, though."

"They were scary," Tasia said. "I just ran."

"All right," Kirana said.

Yisaoh moaned. The tirajista had her drink something from a small green flask. Yisaoh's hand fluttered up, gripped it.

Kirana bent forward, waiting.

"Kirana?" Yisaoh whispered.

"I'm here." Kirana got up and stood next to the tirajista. The wound on Yisaoh's belly was closed, but the seam was still red. Hundreds of dead maggots littered the bedsheets.

The tirajista wiped the sweat from Yisaoh's forehead. Her black gaze was clearer now, alert.

Yisaoh reached for her. "Tasia?"

"I'm here, Mam," Tasia said. Yisaoh pressed her cheek.

"Good girl, my good girl," Yisaoh said.

"Suari was supposed to check on you daily," Kirana said. "Has he not?"

Yisaoh shook her head. "It's been three days. I thought… I don't know what I thought."

"I'll deal with him. Who came here?"

The tirajista wiped a greasy salve onto the red seam of the wound and began to pack up her things.

"Thank you," Kirana said.

The woman bent her head. "Anyone else?"

"Stay," Kirana said. "I have scouts looking for survivors."

The tirajista bowed her head and went to join the soldier and the sinajista at the doorway.

"It was sudden," Yisaoh said. She touched her belly, rubbed the greasy salve between her fingers.

"Why would any of them come to this world?"

"You know why," Yisaoh said.

"I'm sorry," Kirana said. "I can take Tasia this time, though."

Yisaoh's eyes filled. "Not me? Not me?" The tears fell freely. She gave a great heaving sob.

"Fuck," Kirana said. "Fuck, we're… soon. I–"

Yisaoh shook her head violently. "Take her," she said. "Take Tasia."

"No, Mam, I won't leave you!"

"Yisaoh, I'm… very close. We are–"

"Just go," Yisaoh said.

"I'm leaving this whole squad with you," Kirana said. "And I'll send more. You'll be protected. Gian has agreed to work together. We have more resources. I will–"

"Oh, Kirana." Yisaoh gestured for her to come closer. Kirana bent next to her. Yisaoh still wept, the tears would not stop. Kirana's heart nearly burst. "You know who pushed that weapon into my gut, Kirana, love? You know who Tasia barred the door against, though I told her to close her eyes, to look away?"

"Was it Gian? I will fucking murder her. I will murder her and all of her people. I will burn that ark–"

"No, no," Yisaoh said, and she pressed her lips to Kirana's ear. "It was you, love. You came here to murder us."

27

Roh still lay tangled with Kadaan, warm and muzzy-headed under a great bearskin, when he heard the shouting outside. He squeezed his eyes shut, willing the voice away, though it was familiar. He just wanted to sleep. He wanted to feel safe, just for another moment.

Anavha yanked open the thin membrane of the tent, and fell back when he saw that Roh wasn't alone. His eyes widened at the sight of Kadaan wiping sleep from his eyes.

"Zezili is here!" Anavha cried.

Kadaan pulled on his under clothes and reached for a weapon. Roh yanked on his tunic.

"Wait," Roh said to Kadaan, waving at the weapon. "What is it, Anavha?"

"Zezili," Anavha said. "My wife."

"Your wife? Here? Isn't that… good?"

"No, oh no, no." Anavha pressed his hand to his mouth. "Oh no! This is very bad, Roh. This is so bad. Something has happened to her, she looks… Maybe it isn't her? Could it be a Tai Mora? Maybe, maybe so. But she *knew* me!"

Kadaan handed Roh his tunic and said in Saiduan, "Is this a domestic matter?"

"I just need to calm him down," Roh said. "I'm sure it's fine."

Kadaan shrugged and kissed him. Roh held the kiss a moment longer than Kadaan expected. They leaned in together, still hungry, still warm.

"Please!" Anavha said.

Roh sighed. "All right."

He had expected that meeting Kadaan again after all this time, after all that had happened to him, would be awkward and terrible. Roh was no longer the dancer Kadaan had known. He had been a slave for a long time now. But they didn't speak about any of that. They drank aatai and Kadaan told him about how he had escaped Anjoliaa. Roh talked about how he had convinced Anavha into getting them out of Oma's Temple, and Kadaan found the story incredible.

They didn't speak much more that night. The speaking, the reliving of the horror, wasn't what either of them wanted. No talk of the past. No talk of the future.

In the wan light of day, Roh saw that Kadaan looked much older than he remembered. The bruises beneath his eyes were deep, and the lines around his mouth seemed to always draw his lips into a frown. But he was warm, and familiar, and for a little longer, Roh wanted to pretend nothing had happened to either of them. He pulled on his trousers, wincing at the sight of his mangled knees, and crawled out of the shelter.

The wind brought with it the smell of burning. Wisps of smoke curled through the air.

"Is that us?" he asked Anavha, but Anavha was already babbling again about his wife.

Saradyn still lay wrapped in a fireweed blanket, snoring near a banked fire. Roh could not see any other source of burning but the fires nearby, all of which were banked and nearly smokeless.

"Anavha, what's burning?" Roh asked again.

Anavha hugged himself; he was trembling. "I don't know about that. It's just, Zezili–"

A woman strode toward them, one with a tawny Dhai complexion but the flat features of a Dorinah. Roh saw something odd about her immediately. She moved too fast. Her skin was too clear. Something in her black eyes gave him pause. Roh limped forward and placed himself in front of Anavha. Anavha made some kind of strangled shriek and froze in place.

"Who are you?" Roh asked in Dorinah. "Anavha wants to be left alone."

"He's my husband," the woman, Zezili, said. Her black hair was long and shiny, twisted back from her face in a single loop.

"You don't own him," Roh said. "This is Dhai."

Behind him, Saradyn sat up, stretched, and yawned. Zezili's gaze moved to him, and her eyes widened. "You've got to be fucking kidding me."

Saradyn caught sight of her and laughed.

Zezili roared at him and bolted past Roh, knocking Roh and Anavha out of the way. She tackled Saradyn and punched him square in the face. His nose burst, spewing blood.

Roh, dumbfounded, watched them roll around in the turf.

Kadaan came out just as Saradyn bit the woman's cheek, spraying more blood.

"Do we want to break this up?" Kadaan asked.

"I don't know," Roh said. He glanced at Anavha. "What–"

"He cut off her hand," Anavha said. "And kidnapped me, I suppose. Well, it was Natanial, but it was for Saradyn."

Roh thought that interesting, as Zezili seemed to have both hands. Tira was risen, though, and Sina, and Oma. He supposed all things were possible. Why being kidnapped by Saradyn didn't seem to bother Anavha at all was puzzling, though.

A blazing ring of fire surrounded the two struggling adversaries, so hot it nearly singed Roh's eyebrows. He stumbled back, twisting his ankle on a divot in the ground, and fell. Kadaan reached for him.

Maralah came up to them, one hand out, face intent, little tendrils of fire dancing along her fingers. "That's enough! No violence in the camp! Enough! Get up!"

Two twining whips of fire lashed at Zezili and Saradyn, finally drawing them apart. Zezili sat back, snarling, her hair singed. Half of Saradyn's beard was a melted mess; the air filled with the smell of burnt hair. He was shouting things at her in Tordinian as he got up. Still raging, he smacked his hand against a tree, for all the good it did him. Blood poured freely from his nose, spilling down his front.

"Saradyn," Roh said. "Let it be." Kadaan helped him to his feet. A burning thread of pain shot through Roh's ankle. Just his luck.

"Attacked *me*!" Saradyn bellowed, in Dorinah.

"Sounds like she had good cause," Kadaan said.

Maralah stalked up to them. "What the fuck is going on here?" she asked in Dhai, though the word "fuck" was in Saiduan.

"Anavha?" Roh suggested, because he honestly had no idea.

"I'm his wife!" Zezili said, rubbing at her bleeding cheek. "I have a right to speak to my husband. But him!" she pointed at Saradyn. "This man is a fucking war criminal. A fucking warmonger. You cast him out or I'll fucking kill him."

"Is she real?" Anavha breathed. "Saradyn, you can see, can't you? Is she real? Is she some other Zezili? An imposter?"

Saradyn rubbed at his face again. Glanced at Roh. Roh tried again, speaking more slowly, "Is this woman from here? Or is she a shadow?"

"Ah," Saradyn said. He snorted. "Zezili. The same. Ours. Yes, same dumb cattle."

"Fuck you, Saradyn, you mewling shitfucking–"

"You'll shut your fucking face," Maralah said, and a wavering shield of shimmering heat surrounded her, so hot even Roh winced. "You get along or you leave the camp. We go by Dhai rules here. Woodland Dhai rules say no one owns anyone and nobody beats up anybody, no matter what you did outside this camp. I don't like it either, but that's how it is."

"Those are weak fucking rules," Zezili said. "You fucking kill *me*, then!"

"I might," Maralah said. "Don't test me."

"No one said anything to me about Dhai rules," Zezili said.

Maralah snorted. "Probably because 'don't murder the people who are providing you aid' should have been immediately obvious."

"Could you just agree to leave Anavha alone?" Roh asked. "He's clearly frightened of you."

Zezili frowned. "What? No, he's my husband. Anavha, you're not frightened, are you?"

Anavha, still shaking, did not look at her.

"Stay away from him," Maralah said. "And you–" she pointed at Saradyn, "–you stay away from *her*."

Three other Dhai approached her, elders from the Woodland camp. Maralah began explaining her use of her gift, and the tussle between Zezili and Saradyn. Roh wondered if they would be exiled. Saradyn had provided a lot of aid to him, and his ability to find spies among them was valuable. Perhaps if he could speak to them…

Roh tried to move away from Kadaan, but putting pressure on his ankle sent a fresh wave of pain. He sucked in a breath.

"I'll take you to the infirmary," Kadaan said.

"It's fine–"

"Tira is risen," Kadaan said. "They can repair the injury in a few minutes and relieve the pain. There's no need to suffer."

Roh heard the other part of that, too, and he admitted it made his heart a little lighter. "I suppose there are some things that can be mended," Roh said.

"Yes." Kadaan squeezed his hand. "We have time."

Yet, as Roh walked to the doctor's tent with Kadaan, he wondered how true that was. Did they have time? If they got onto that ship together and sailed south, if they left all of this to the Tai Mora and the various warring factions from other worlds, how safe would they truly be? For how long?

"This is Sola," Kadaan said, introducing Roh to a lean young Saiduan woman in the medical tent who wore a leather apron. She had long, bony fingers and a chin that barely emerged from her jaw, giving her the appearance of a turtle.

"Twisted ankle," Roh said, apologetic, because it seemed so small a thing to bother her with.

"Have a seat here, I'm just finishing with a patient."

Kadaan helped him sit on one of the cots. "I'm going to go and eat. I'll bring you something to break your fast," Kadaan said.

Roh sat at the edge of the cot, legs dangling. Sola stood a few paces distant with a young woman, administering what appeared to be a very bitter tea. When Sola moved away, Roh saw the grimace on the girl's face. She, too, sat at the edge of her cot, legs dangling, one foot twisted under slightly. She leaned to one side, and worked her weak left hand in her lap; it had clearly just been regrown.

She raised her head. Met his gaze.

There was a long moment.

Roh stared at her, dumbstruck. Her face was full of shiny scars, and her hair was much longer, her eyes somehow blacker, and her frown had clearly deepened, aging her face before its time. Her skin was sallow, sickly, and she was far too thin.

He wasn't sure what to say. He wasn't entirely sure it was her.

Something tugged at the corners of her mouth. A smile? Almost.

"We really have to stop meeting like this," Lilia said.

Roh burst into tears.

28

Kirana turned over the hourglass on her desk and watched the black granules slip through it for the fourth time in a quarter hour. Her daughters played in the waiting area outside her study. She did not usually want them up here, but after what had happened back on her world, she wanted them close. Wanted to hear the sound of their laughter.

She had left Yisaoh with a force of over a hundred to look after her, including several of her most trusted jistas. It was not a good time to be short of jistas, but if Yisaoh died… what was all of this for?

The sand ran its course.

She turned over the hourglass again.

Kirana had fought herself before, on this world. But that Kirana had been a sickly pacifist. That Kirana would never have considered leaping across worlds to hurt that which Kirana most valued. But the question that Kirana kept coming back to was… why? Why murder Yisaoh and Tasia? So she could bring across her own children to Raisa? But that would also mean that Kirana had to kill *her*, if she meant to come over. It made her head hurt.

Monshara had burned out the Dhai camp where they

found Tasia, but if Yisaoh, this world's Yisaoh, had been there, she had survived the attack, because her own wife could not come through. Yisaoh remained stuck, and time was, as ever, shorter and shorter. Never enough time.

And Suari was missing. She had relished the thought of torturing him slowly, over many days, but when she sent soldiers to look for him, he was missing, his meager belongings gone. Was he conspiring with her other self? For what purpose? Maybe the other version of her was nicer to her omajistas.

A knock at the door. "Kai? Commissar Gian has arrived."

"Send her up."

"Would you like the children to stay?"

"No, have the nanny take them to the library below."

The servant pressed thumb to forehead, and conferred with the girls and their nanny outside. That was a good little Dhai, that one. Kirana wondered if she were too good. She rubbed her face. Lies, backstabbing, betrayal. She was always waiting for one of them to ruin her, because so many clearly wanted to. Why now, though, when they were successful? She had saved their fucking lives, all her people, and the thanks she got was Suari fleeing like a fucking jilted lover.

She went back into her bedroom and changed into a clean tunic. Washed her face with tepid water from a little basin. When she arrived back into the assembly chamber, one of the Dhai had put out tea and wine. Her remaining stargazers, led by Masis, were laying out their work on the table. One of her line commanders, Yivsa, was in attendance while Madah managed forces on the plateau.

Gian arrived, escorted by another of Kirana's omajistas.

Gian brought with her the familiar faces from the ark, her lovers or seconds or cousins; Kirana had never asked. Kirana had permitted her to bring three of her own jistas, as well, making her party a rather large assemblage of seven.

The chamber was full for the first time since Kirana had taken it. Gian looked better after some doctoring and food. Her mouth was a thin line.

"Kirana," Gian said.

"Gian," Kirana said. "Will you sit? I apologize we don't have chairs for everyone, and I know it was a long series of steps."

Kirana sat first, gesturing for Gian to sit opposite. Gian hesitated a moment, then was seated. Her jistas kept at her back. One of the Dhai servants poured them all tea, but no one touched it.

"Thank you for attending," Kirana said. "I wanted us to better understand what we need to do together. Could you go through it step by step for us, Masis? For the benefit of our allies here?"

Masis laid out the translated pages of the Worldbreaker guide, each a detailed map of the underground chambers that she had discovered beneath each of the temples, as well as a diagram of the great lumbering beast they had dredged up, the fifth temple.

"The temples are engines," Masis said, "built for harnessing and focusing the power of the satellites. That's why all four satellites must be in the sky in order for them to work. The front matter is mostly myth and legend. It was written at least fifty or sixty years after the last rising of Oma."

"After they failed," Gian said.

"Yes." Masis pointed out the symbols next to each chamber diagram. "Four jistas, one to call each satellite, stand around a fifth figure, at the center, that must channel their power through each of the four temples to the fifth temple. We have been calling these people at the center 'conduits'. They can be any type of jista. But inside the fifth temple, the setup is different."

He tapped a different diagram, an intricately detailed room with multiple rings and intersecting lines labeled along the floors and walls. Here there were pedestals for seven figures. Four surrounding a fifth, around a massive orb at the center where the fifth would stand. The orb was labeled "Worldbreaker." "Guide" was written at the entrance to the chamber. Another placement, just in front of the central orb, was labeled "Key."

"So, the power is concentrated at this fifth engine," Kirana said. "Let's call them what they are."

"Correct," Masis said. "As we intuited, it's the person here, at the orb, that can use that combined power to… do anything, really."

"Define *anything*," Gian said.

Masis rubbed his chin. "Once they are fully powered, the Worldbreaker, or Worldshaper, depending on your translation of it, must manipulate the mechanism according to a set of rules that determine the outcomes."

"Slow down there," Kirana said. "*Worldshaper?* Why haven't I heard that translation before? Every text prior has referenced a *Worldbreaker*."

"This book is older," Masis said, "and the dialect is slightly different. I would not be comfortable saying it was one or the other."

Kirana nodded. "All right. What else?"

Masis continued, "The simplest way to use this device is to close the ways between this world, Raisa, and all of the others. Those instructions are in the book itself, here." He pointed to the page opposite the diagram of the fifth temple. "But it also refers to a more complicated set of instructions appearing in the appendix."

"What do those do?" Gian asked.

Masis gave a small shrug. "I'm afraid we don't know."

Even Kirana found that surprising. This, Suari had kept from her. "You don't know?"

"No, Kai… I mean, Empress. The book refers to an appendix. But I'm afraid the book has no appendix. It was torn out long before we received it."

Had Luna torn it out? Kirana thought, somewhere between the time ze washed up on the shores of Dorinah and when Kirana locked hir in the gaol? That tricky little ataisa.

"We'll have time to explore other ways to use its power," Kirana said. "Para should remain in the sky for a time, even after we use this combined power to close the ways. Is that still correct, based on your translations?"

"Yes," Masis said, "and for a much longer period than we suspected. While the engines themselves must be powered within the first two days of Para's rise, Para itself should remain risen with the other satellites for a full year, perhaps a little more."

"Good," Kirana said. "Let's concentrate on who we need to power this thing. What's this about a key and a guide? The Saiduan were looking for a worldbreaker. That can just be an omajista?"

"The engines themselves are sentient," Masis said. "They choose a key and a guide, we believe, but the Worldbreaker is simply one who harnesses that power. The only requirement seems to be that the Worldbreaker understand the instructions on how to use the mechanism and have some sensitivity to one of the satellites."

Kirana drummed her fingers on the table. "I have coteries of jistas now at each engine," she said, "waiting on my word to take their places the moment Para rises. No sleep until that fucking satellite goes down or we seal ourselves off from these invaders. But whom do I assign as a conduit? Does it matter? Any type of jista? Gian will need to know this, so we may decide how best to deploy our jistas."

"It doesn't matter in the text," Masis said, "but I'd put your most powerful in the role of conduit at each of the four other temples. They will need to be able to channel a great deal of power without burning out."

"You all seem to be skipping the most important thing," Gian said. "If these engines won't respond to Kirana, and if we still have not found a Guide or a Key, we could have three thousand jistas in each temple and not see a result."

"Well..." Masis said, nervously moving the diagrams around on the table. "There is this bit of translation that Talahina and I worked on. It's... a little poetic and strange, but–"

"Come, Masis," Kirana said.

He cleared his throat. "The book says the Key and the Guide will be *drawn* to the fifth temple. Through some supernatural or divine means? I don't know. Perhaps a pheromone the temple itself gives off? If this is true, well...

perhaps the Guide and the Key will... enter the fifth temple when Para rises. We have only to be there to follow them."

"That's trusting far too much in fate," Kirana said. "If you had not intuited, Masis, I am not a woman content to rely on fate."

"I understand," Masis said. "Talahina, will you present your idea?"

Talahina, the young stargazer who hardly ever spoke, squeezed her way past the jistas and soldiers to take a place at the table. She fluttered her hands nervously, and stared mostly at the table. "Yes, Empress," Talahina said. "We... That is, I have considered another way into the fifth temple."

"And?" Kirana said. She could not keep the irritation from her voice. Too much waiting. Too much disseminating.

"We have treated the temples as if they are inorganic," Talahina said. "I propose that we consider them as beasts, and approach them that way."

"They are beasts with very tough skins," Kirana said.

"Indeed," Talahina said. "But beasts... must breathe. Even underwater, the fifth temple had access to oxygen, certainly."

"Do we know that they breathe air?" Gian said.

"It's very likely," Talahina said, "though we suspect they intake it through either their skin, or the complex root systems at the bottom of each temple. Perhaps both."

"You want us to suffocate it?" Kirana said. "But what if we kill it?"

"I... We could consider starving it... slowly. Over time. They are sentient beasts. A few minutes here, a few minutes there, each time demanding entrance. I was... I apologize,

Empress, it was just a thought."

"An interesting one to come from a scholar," Kirana said. "I would have expected that suggestion from Madah." She turned over that idea for a few moments, then, "I approve of the attempt. We can do this without Gian's jistas, surely?"

Talahina nodded, and stepped away from the table, back into the anonymity of the crowd.

"Do you have more questions, Gian?" Kirana asked.

"Not at this time. Could we speak privately?"

"Of course." Kirana dismissed the scholars and jista.

Masis collected his diagrams and hurried away with Himsa, Orhin and Talahina, their soft robes brushing against the floor.

Gian's retinue stood and waited for her in the doorway, far enough to give them some privacy, but not so far that they could not keep an eye on her.

"How can I trust you with all this power?" Gian asked.

Kirana prickled. This alliance was already annoying her. She took a breath, remembering the stink of Yisaoh's wound.

"How could I trust *you* with it?" Kirana asked. "You understand that as part of this alliance, I am happy for your people to inhabit any region you wish. Any but this one."

"What's to stop you from using this power to murder all of us, once you figure out other ways to direct its power?"

"There isn't anything stopping us," she said. "That's why it's in your interest to have your jistas work together with mine in the belly of these engines. What I told you back at your ark is true. I'm weary of war, Gian. You don't want it either."

"How can I trust that?"

"You can't, there's no guarantee."

"There is a way."

Kirana felt heat move up her face. "If you think–"

"I want a warded promise," Gian said.

Kirana could not hide her own shock at the suggestion. She fairly reared back in her chair.

Gian leaned forward. "If you are so eager for peace," she said, "a warded alliance should be a small thing to ask."

"Wards can be removed."

"Not without the other party knowing," she said. "You and I will always know if the other has gone back on their word, or is preparing to."

"A ward still doesn't keep one of us from ordering the other killed," Kirana said.

"There is a far better type of ward," Gian said. "One you will greatly appreciate. Created by a tirajista and a sinajista. It ties our lives together. One to the other. If you die, I die, and vice versa. It ensures that neither party seeks to assassinate the other."

"What if your heart gives out? Or you drown? I won't be tethered to your bad fortune. No."

Gian stood abruptly. "Then we are done."

"What will you do without our alliance?"

"We will make a place for ourselves," she said. "We need you far less than you imagine."

"What do you have left?" Kirana said. "A thousand people? Many died in that fall."

"Which is why I won't risk more of them for a fool plan for which I have no guarantees."

Kirana shifted her hands into her lap and squeezed her fists. She knew what Yisaoh would say to this. Peace required sacrifices.

"I agree, then," Kirana said. "But I want the ward interrogated and understood and created in concert with my people."

Gian sat back down. "That is agreeable."

"How many can you send with us, to protect and to power each of these temples?"

"I will speak to my people. Your Sai Hofsha is still about. I can give her the message when we have decided. As you understand, the way we make decisions is communal, not tyrannical. It can take some time."

"You have until Para rises," Kirana said. "I'm sorry, I don't rule the heavens." Not yet, she thought, but there was a budding hope now, more than there had been in many months.

They discussed the temples and their engines for some time longer, and more urgent but boring issues, like where to house Gian's people; she preferred to keep them in the ark, which meant repairs, and constructing aqueducts. The infrastructure question was always top of her mind, right after food. Sanitation was becoming an issue.

Kirana felt the knot in her gut ease after several hours, when Gian finally drank from her cold teacup and asked for wine.

This is going to work, Kirana thought. The realization was a warm balm that softened her tight, terrified gut.

29

Lilia had never seen Roh cry.

"Roh?" she said softly. "Rohinmey? It is you, isn't it?"

He nodded, covering his face.

Lilia got up and sat next to him. "I'm so sorry, I–"

"Li." Light. "Can I have a hug?" he said.

She wrapped her arms around him. He trembled against her, sobbing. Lilia pressed her face against his neck. She wanted to feel something, but was mostly shocked. He sobbed for a long time, so long she realized it was not at all about her, but something else, something deeper, something very broken.

"Hush," Lilia said. "Hush now. We're all right."

"We're not," he said. "We're not, that's the problem."

She pulled away and regarded him. His hair was longer, braided back against his head, the tails tucked under and out of the way. His skin was cracked and peeling, the lips chapped, and his knuckles were peppered in scars. His eyes, too, were very different. He seemed so much older. Maybe she did too.

"What are you doing here?" she asked.

He touched her wrist. "I figured you would go to the Woodland," he said. "Some Woodland Dhai helped us track various camps of outsiders. This was where they pointed us."

"Ours was south of here," Lilia said. "You would have missed me. Well, it's a long story."

"They know about that camp here," he said. "I'd have found you. What I don't understand is why the Tai Mora didn't."

"The Woodland Dhai don't talk to Tai Mora," Lilia said. "They seem to be better at spotting them than many of us. The Tai Mora are especially bad in their understanding of the Woodland. I think it makes them stand out."

"How did you... Why are you here, then?"

"It's a very long story."

"Mine too."

They sat in awkward silence. Lilia had no idea how to even begin.

Sola interrupted them. "How do you know each other?" she said.

"It was a very long time ago," Lilia said. "I'm sorry, please help him."

"It's all right, I'm glad you're better too. You were just a bit dehydrated. The bone tree wounds healed cleanly."

Sola bent to tend to Roh's ankle, weaving tendrils of Tira's breath to mend him.

Lilia got up and went back to her cot. Her mind raced. What next? Where was Zezili? What to do with Roh? He was a parajista, he could help her. She just needed to convince these people, whoever was in charge...

Sola finished with Roh. He tested his ankle. Stood, put his weight on it. Lilia noticed his knees, then, how he had not fully bent them when he sat, and how he stepped gingerly now, more a hobble than a walk. What had the world done to all of them?

"Thank you," Roh said. He lifted his head. "Lilia, I want you to meet someone. Kadaan. My good friend."

Kadaan was a Saiduan name. Lilia had seen a few of them here, and met Maralah, the woman who insisted she wasn't in charge but who all of the Saiduan and many of the Dhai listened to, nonetheless. Lilia had immediately noted how much they looked up to her.

"Roh, there's something very important I need to do," Lilia said. It came out in a rush. "You remember when Taigan came to the temple? He thought I was gifted, and… that's a very long story. But listen, I think there's a way to… Oh, it's very complicated. Listen, I was in Tira's Temple. The temple… keeper, something, a creature, told me that–"

"What?" Roh said. He stiffened.

"Tira's Temple. There was this device… and… This fifth temple that the Tai Mora dredged up? It's not far from here, and I think, I really think Roh, that we could have a chance to take hold of it ourselves. It will take a great deal of coordination, and we don't have much time, but we have an element of surprise. She will never think–"

"Li, listen to what you're saying."

"No, you listen!" she nearly shouted. Stopped. Took a deep breath. "Roh, I'm not sure you understand, but there's something very important that I've been working toward. You are a parajista. You can help. We can use the temples to destroy the Tai Mora once and–"

"Stop," Roh said. "We need to back up a little. And take some time to talk. Really talk about this. You're talking about breaking the world. About powering the temples to push the Tai Mora back? Not just stop other worlds from coming here?"

"How did you–"

"Come," he said, holding out his hand. "Meet Kadaan, and we'll talk more."

She took his hand, but her heart was already betraying her, thumping loudly in her chest. She felt a tugging sensation to the west: Zezili. What was Zezili doing now?

Natanial and his people spent a day mucking through bodies, looking for a tall woman with a broken nose called Yisaoh. After a time, all the bodies looked the same to Natanial. He found himself drinking a little more wine at night, and another few slugs of it during the day.

"She isn't here," Otolyn said when he came over to her tent the evening of the second day. He collapsed next to her. Huffed out a long sigh.

"You stink," she said.

"So do you."

"Why don't we just fuck off?" Otolyn said.

"Can't," he said. "It's a long story. You're not bound, though. I know this isn't what you hoped for."

"Life isn't want I hoped for," Otolyn said. She brushed back an oily hank of hair from his face. "Poor bored thing, aren't you?"

"Just disappointed."

"Want to have sex?"

"Not really."

"Wine?"

"Yes."

She handed him her jug. He drank deeply. On the other side of the camp, near where Monshara's larger tent was staked, a wink shimmered into existence.

"Mother's calling," Otolyn said.

"Let her come to me," Natanial said. He drank more of the wine and set the mug between him and Otolyn. "What you think the sky will look like, when this is over?"

"About what it looks like now," she said, "just one more star."

"You're so very Tordinian."

"You're so very properly Aaldian. You don't even realize it."

"Don't I?"

"You were in love with that kid, weren't you? That omajista you found."

"Could we not?"

"Just saying, that's bad. Bring some dumb kid into this."

"Thank you. Very insightful. I see the error of my ways."

"Can't change them though, huh?"

"No."

"Natanial!" Monshara's voice. She waved at him from her tent.

"What if I pretend not to see her?" Natanial asked.

"Too late," Otolyn said.

Natanial struggled to his feet and wended his way through the camp to Monshara's side.

"We have another offensive," Monshara said. "I put a ranger on the tail of the survivors from this one, to see where they went."

"And?"

"Found another camp north of this one. They're using hazing wards of some kind. Not even a hundred people there, but some are Saiduan. That's concerning. Could have jistas. Sanisi. They aren't fun."

"No, they are not," Natanial said. "When do we go?"

"Dawn. Come in and let's sketch out the plan here with my line commanders."

Natanial wanted to groan, but it came out a grunt. He went into the stuffy tent and stood with Monshara and her line commanders as they plotted out the terrain of the camp. It lay perched on a great cliff overlooking the sea, and had an easy escape route at the center: a winding tunnel that cut through the cliff and led down to the sea.

"We circle them with winks, here, here, and these, here," Monshara said, marking out the areas with little brass circles. "Pour through here, overwhelm them. Sinajistas below, to catch any of the ones trying to escape through that sea cave. Be like sending dogs after rats. Easy enough."

"You said sanisi," Natanial said. "What about them?"

"The jistas will worry about them," Monshara said. "We aren't there for the sanisi. We're there for Yisaoh."

When she dismissed them all an hour later, Natanial went back to his tent, alone, and slept fitfully. Otolyn woke him, already grinning, the blistering ball of Tira's green glow just over her shoulder.

"Let's have some more fun," Otolyn said.

Natanial splashed his face with water and helped his fighters break camp, then rode up to join Monshara and the other line commanders to the wink where Madah, one of Kirana's generals, waited to give their final instructions.

"We're ready for you," Madah said, from the other side of the wink. She glanced behind her, to a rolling bank of greenery.

Natanial considered telling her his people weren't ready for *her*, but supposed his choices were limited at this point. What if he told her no? He would be burned alive like that unfortunate man under the temple dome.

"I'm thinking this isn't worth the money," Otolyn said, riding up behind him, voice loud enough for Madah to hear. With her she carried saddlebags stuffed with goods rooted out from the charred remains of the warren below. Food had been the most valuable loot in the aftermath of the slaughter.

Madah glanced back at them, glared at Otolyn.

"Better food over there?" Otolyn called.

"Less talking, more moving!" Madah said. "I've got winks opening on the next field. Clear your area there immediately."

Natanial called his forces together. "Circular assembly! Backs to the bonsa line!"

The great heaps of bodies they had collected and sorted through from the Dhai camp lay smoldering. The smell had been oddly appetizing, which he found grotesque, but hunger and lack of proper protein affected all of them. He had lost six soldiers in the two days they had spent at the camp, each one a blow to his esteem as a leader. In truth, he wanted to join them. Perhaps they were the smartest of all of them.

Natanial kicked awake a few of his hungover soldiers, and found two more were missing.

"Smarter than the rest of us," Natanial muttered as Otolyn paced him up on her bear.

"Maybe if we wait long enough it'll be over by the time we get there," Otolyn said.

Natanial got back onto his mount. "Go run your line."

"Yeah, yeah," she said, and turned her bear around to go inspect her portion of the troops. Such as they were.

"We ready?" Monshara called from the front, fist raised.

Natanial nodded to Otolyn. She raised their flag.

Three winks opened ahead of them.

30

Lilia had not been prepared for Roh's story of Saiduan, of the murder of Ora Dasai and the scholars, of his flight from the Tai Mora with his friend Luna and the Worldbreaker book, of his enslavement.

She found her stomach knotting as she sat over a bowl of cooling porridge with Roh and Kadaan at the center of camp. Kadaan was a tall Saiduan man ten years their senior who looked at Roh as if he were a precious star fallen from the sky.

"I can't... I'm so sorry, Roh," Lilia said.

"It's in the past," Roh said, but when he gazed past her she could not help but wonder who or what he saw there.

She leaned forward. "I'd like to talk about Caisau, though. It spoke to you, the way Tira's Temple spoke to me?"

He nodded. "It said I'm the... Guide. That I could get into the temples, that I could bring the Key and the Worldbreaker, and... I don't know, Li. I worked so hard to get here, thinking maybe we could do what the temples want, but... there's a real chance for us to have a life outside of Dhai. We could travel with the Saiduan, we could–"

"It's all right, puppy," Kadaan said, and took Roh's hand.

Lilia found Kadaan's nickname for Roh very annoying. "It matches what Tira's Temple told me," she said. "Don't you see? It's all coming together! You and I, together again. And so close to the fifth temple. These people with you? You said one is an omajista? And you're a parajista. All we need is a tirajista and a sinajista. I could operate the mechanism, I'm sure of it. I could figure it out. You'd be the Guide, we'd only need a Key, only–"

"That is still many missing pieces," Kadaan said. "It's a very desperate idea."

"These are desperate times!" Lilia said.

"The Saiduan are not part of this."

"You already are part of it," Lilia said. "You don't get to decide. All you have to decide now is what you're going to do."

"I'm going to create a home," Kadaan said.

"Well, you're a coward."

Kadaan raised his brows. A dark expression moved over his face, one that chilled Lilia to the bone. She had forgotten he was a sanisi.

He rose from the bench and said, "I'm going to help Maralah."

"I'm sorry," Roh said. "We'll speak later?"

Kadaan nodded.

"You didn't have to be rude, Li." Roh poked at his porridge.

"Come on, Roh! We are two of the three; I know we are! And surely... I don't know, we could do something with all these other allies we have here. What about Maralah? What kind of a jista is she?"

"Sinajista," he said.

"Look, then! We have a lot of what we need." Lilia
dumped out her porridge on the table.

"What are you–"

Lilia drew a rough circle and mapped out the chamber
in Tira's Temple from memory. "A parajista here. Kadaan.
A sinajista. Maralah. Your omajista friend here. We'd just
need a tirajista. Sola could do that, or Salifa! Oh, Salifa. I
wonder… I bet I could get her to join us. She wanted to
come, but Meyna and Yisaoh, and the Kai… The Kai is a
terror. We could *do* this, Roh."

Roh frowned at her gooey attempt at a plan. "You don't
have enough," he said. "You need a plan to get into one of
the temples. Step into my circle…"

"What was that?"

"It's what the creature told me… step into my circle.
There are two ways to get to the fifth temple, I think. Go
directly there, and just… walk in, I think, or get back to the
Assembly Chamber at the top of Oma's Temple, and step
through there."

"It would be difficult to get a gate opened at the fifth
temple," Lilia said. "No one's been inside it."

"Oma's Temple? Li, I just nearly died trying to get *out* of
Oma's Temple."

"I don't think we're all here because of luck, or
coincidence. I think Oma has drawn us here. I think we
have everyone we need."

"Oma is a brute."

"It is. But if it's asking us to come together here, maybe
we're here to–"

"Get revenge?" he said.

"No, I–"

"Because this whole time, what you sound like is someone who is really mad because she doesn't have any other life after the Tai Mora are dead."

"You don't need to be mean."

She saw Zezili approach from behind Roh. Her face was drawn. She scratched at something on her upper belly, just beneath her breasts.

"What is it?" Lilia asked.

Roh turned. "Oh no," he said. "You know Zezili?"

"She... It's a long story."

"Fuck," Zezili said, "the mouthy boy. Where did you pick him up?"

"We were in the temple together," Lilia said.

"He's trying to keep my husband from me. This whole camp is full of crazy fucking pacifists." Zezili dropped onto the bench beside Lilia. Grimaced at the mess of porridge. "You Dhai have shitty table manners. What the fuck is this?"

"Who is your husband?" Lilia asked.

"Anavha," Roh said. "The omajista." He pointed across the camp. Lilia turned. A big Tordinian man sat at a fire, taking instruction from someone showing him how to bind fireweed cord. Huddling beside him was a slight Dorinah man with a soft brown beard and sharp cheekbones who held a steaming cup of tea in his quaking hands.

"That Dorinah boy?" Lilia said. "Your husband is an omajista?"

Zezili looked genuinely shocked. "He's a *what*? That... no." She laughed. "No, that's not possible."

"He got us out of the temple," Roh said. "Opened a gate right there."

Zezili gaped. "What the fuck is happening?"

"Who's that man with him?" Lilia asked.

"Saradyn," Roh said.

"Fucker chopped off my hand," Zezili said, waving both hands at Lilia. "Called himself a king. Docile as a fucking lamb now, though. What the fuck did you do to him, kid?"

"Nothing," Roh said.

"He follows you?" Lilia asked.

"He listens to me," Roh said, but he would not look at her. "I don't know why. I asked him to look after Anavha."

Zezili snorted. "Fine irony, there." She scratched at her chest again. "Fucking shit," she said, and pulled up the tunic.

A raised red welt the size of Lilia's palm was pressed into Zezili's skin. The shape was instantly familiar: the trefoil with the tail, the one Lilia's mother had warded into her skin, the mark of the fifth temple, the one Kalinda had put into the box with Zezili's bones. The skin was rubbed raw and irritated.

"Itches like Rhea's cunt," Zezili said.

"Don't touch it!" Lilia said.

"What is that?" Roh said.

Lilia peered at the welt. Pressed her finger against it. The skin did not give. It was as if the silver trefoil Kalinda had put in the box had fused with Zezili's chest.

"A key?" Lilia said. "Kalinda put this piece in the box with you. She said we'd need it if we entered the fifth temple."

"Who is *Kalinda*?" Roh said.

Zezili waved a hand at him. "I've been asking her the same thing. Don't bother. Do you have any blood on you? Any you'd part with?"

Roh said, "There is something deeply wrong with you."

"No shit," Zezili said. "What the fuck are you two talking about?"

"Saving the *world*," Lilia said, tapping the symbol again.

"Fuck, enough!" Zezili said, jerking her tunic back down. "Why are we still talking about that? All these people are running the fuck away, which frankly, is a better fucking idea than any of the ones I've heard." Zezili grimaced at the porridge smeared all over the table. "That looks awful."

"Roh, if you've read that book, you know how to not just close the worlds, but... you know how to send the Tai Mora back, don't you? How to... kill them?"

Roh shook his head. "I... Li, if we're going to do this, it shouldn't be for revenge. If we leave it alone, the Tai Mora will close the ways between the worlds, and that's that."

"But, it can do so much more–"

"It can, but I don't think they'll figure that out. At least, I hope not."

"Hope is in short supply," Zezili said.

"I'm sorry, Li," Roh said. "I just... I really don't know. Let me think about this a little more, all right? Seeing everyone here has... I just need to think."

"Roh–"

"I'm going to help Kadaan."

"How? You're going to watch?" It came out crueler than she meant.

His face flushed. "Don't blame me," Roh said, "because you have nothing left to live for." He took his empty bowl with him and returned it to the kitchen tent. Then he stuffed his hands into his pockets and turned to the beach, the wind whipping his hair.

Zezili hooted. Slapped the table. "He must know you very well, to dig like that."

"We were friends once."

"I've never had friends."

"That doesn't surprise me."

"Nah," Zezili said. "We are just alike."

Lilia recoiled. "We are nothing alike."

"We get what we want. I do it with violence. You do it with deception. Weak little liar."

"I've never gotten anything I wanted!"

"I keep thinking I'll be like you, sacrificing myself for some bad cause–"

"Why, when there are so many good ones?" Lilia sneered.

"Don't cat-talk me, kid."

"I should have left you in your stupid box," Lilia said.

"I would have liked that. I wouldn't be so fucking itchy!"

"I'm not like you," Lilia repeated.

"Yeah, well, keep telling yourself that."

Lilia got up. "I'm going to go find someone in charge."

"Sure," Zezili said. She leaned closer to her. "Mind bleeding out a little here, into my cup, before you go? It's so good."

"Go murder something," Lilia said. She left Zezili staring morosely into her empty cup and made her way around the camp. She noted that the smell of smoke had gotten stronger. A few of the others commented on it; a runner had been sent out.

Lilia tried to figure out which of the Woodland Dhai elders to speak to, but everyone insisted there were no leaders. They were a collective. Lilia wanted to cry with frustration.

Maybe if she went back to Meyna... Meyna...! and Yisaoh with Zezili by her side, it would be more difficult to throw her out again. Zezili could protect her from the bone tree again. Lilia shivered at the memory. There was still time. She could make it right. She had come too far, given up too much, to stop now.

She walked along the edge of the camp, brooding. Lilia felt a prickling along her spine and turned, expecting to see Zezili creeping around, but Zezili still sat at the table, talking to another Dhai, probably attempting to weasel him out of his blood, or take it outright. Lilia swept her gaze across the camp as a cool sea wind tickled her hair across her face. What was that feeling?

And then Lilia saw him emerge from the woods, stepping on the heads of early blooming poppies. Behind him was a little figure, Dhai certainly, with tangled hair twisted back into braided knots. The Dhai person, she did not know, but *his* face she would never, could never forget.

Lilia stared.

He did not see her at first. Two of the camp's scouts accompanied him, and his gaze swept the camp, presumably looking for someone in charge.

He saw her.

Taigan touched his thumb to his forehead in Lilia's direction. That was a particularly cruel touch, she thought.

He crossed the camp and came right up to her, as if no time had passed, as if he had not abandoned her at the harbor wall, broken and burned out. As if they were good friends separated by circumstances.

"I suspected you outlasted them, little bird," Taigan said.

"We are both difficult to kill, it seems," she said slowly.

It came out more confident than it felt.

"Life is full of little ironies," Taigan said, and his mouth turned up at the corners. The figure behind him wore long tattered trousers and a short coat, both of Tai Mora make. The features, the slender figure, the dark hair and eyes, could be either Dhai or Tai Mora. Had Taigan brought around another spy? "I believe we can be of help to one another."

"I can't imagine," Lilia said, "how a burned out omajista you once threw off a cliff could possibly help you in any way."

"You would be serving yourself, of course. Ending this conflict with the Tai Mora. Isn't that what we both want?"

"Is it?" Lilia said. "You left me on the wall."

"I was compelled home. I was not my own, then. You understand."

"I don't."

"I have a very brilliant plan."

"I'm sure," Lilia said. "You always do."

"It is," Taigan said, "a brilliant plan, that is, but I can't take credit for it. Luna can explain it in more depth," and he acknowledged the figure beside him with a tilt of his head. "There's a… device that channels the power of the satellites. We can use it to close the seams between the worlds."

Lilia laughed. "I have heard of it. Is that why you came here?"

"That is a pertinent question," Taigan said, "one I also wish I had a different answer to. I was looking for the Saiduan allies that your little camp had made. You know your Catori, Meyna, she intends to run off with them."

"I don't have time for you," Lilia said. She turned away.

"Ah, wait," Taigan said. "I'm here because I know I was right all along."

"That was a revelation?"

"Let's say Luna is very familiar with how these temples, the engines, the beasts inside of them, operate. Luna has enlightened me during our many long days together."

"Roh is also familiar with it," Lilia said. "We don't need a second person."

"Roh?" Luna's eyes widened. It was the first thing they had said.

"Rohinmey," Lilia said, "yes."

"I need to find him, Taigan," Luna said, breathless.

"Down on the beach," Lilia said. "The path is there, middle of camp."

Luna ran. It clicked for Lilia, then. Was this the same Luna, the one Roh had fled south with? The other one who had originally translated the book?

Something the creature in Tira's temple had said came back to her. *The heavens themselves will draw them together.* She glanced up at the sky, the baleful eye of Oma, sparkling violet Sina, shimmering green Tira.

"Listen," Taigan said, leaning so close he startled her. "Luna was always a better translator than the boy. Suffice to say that though our people can power it, it was designed for one such as you to operate it. It's a bit complicated, but you have time to learn it."

"One such as me?"

"Someone motivated by revenge."

"Luna knows how to operate it?"

"More or less."

"That doesn't inspire confidence."

"Yes, well, what does these days?"

"I don't have any allies anymore, Taigan."

"You have me!" he said brightly. "What more do you need?"

"Taigan, the last time–"

"Yes, yes, the matter of the cliff. But this time I am much more confident. I have been proven right. I *like* it when I'm right."

"We can't do this, just the two of us."

"Three, with Luna! You are so hesitant. The Lilia I knew was bolder."

"She was also gifted," Lilia said.

"Not that you did much with it."

"You are so cheerfully unpleasant," Lilia said.

"What's the use of being miserably unpleasant, really?" Taigan said.

"I just… I don't know if we can do this without allies from Meyna, or Yisaoh." Lilia chewed at her fingernail. Taigan, Luna, Roh… she tried fitting all the pieces together. With Taigan they had one more omajista. With Luna – another person who could help navigate the temples, maybe? A Key and a Worldbreaker. Was Zezili the Key? Meyna and Ahkio were useless except in getting her access to more jistas. How to get into the fifth temple? That was the trick. How to convince Maralah and her people to help. What did Maralah have to gain? Everyone wanted to run away.

"Oh, well, you can ask them all about it soon," Taigan said.

"What?"

"You haven't heard?" Taigan snorted. "Oh, it's all the

Woodland Dhai can natter about. We stayed with some of them for a few days on the journey here. The smoke? The Tai Mora just invaded your little pacifist Kai's camp. Your Dhai friends are on their way here. What a happy reunion we'll all have!"

"What!" Lilia cried. "How did the Tai Mora find them? I worked so hard to protect–"

Taigan tilted his head to the sky.

"What is it?" Lilia asked, following his gaze.

"Well," he said. "This is interesting."

31

When Gian and her retinue had gone, Kirana went down to the Sanctuary to spend time with her children. They were alone at a far table. Their nursemaid was picking through the library stacks, presumably for something appropriate, considering their position here. As Kirana sat with them, Tasia nattered on brightly about what they had been learning, mostly Tai Mora history, which all three found fairly interesting, as it was largely about their immediate ancestors.

Tasia, Kirana thought, smoothing back the girl's dark hair from her face, *my* Tasia. Surely her children were the best versions possible. The only ones worth saving. Surely.

Corina and Moira, the elder two, were engaged in some memory game that Kirana only half paid attention to.

"When will Mam be with us?" Moira said as they finished their game. She had asked every day.

"Soon," Kirana said.

"You keep saying that," Corina said. "It's never happening, is it?" Brash, that one, little chin jutting toward her, dark eyes defiant.

"Hush, now," Kirana said. "I got you all over, didn't I? I saved us all, haven't I? When have I ever lied?"

Tasia smiled brightly. "You never did, Mama," she said. "You came for me too!"

Kirana kissed her forehead. "Of course I did. I always keep my promises. *Always.*"

Dhai servants brought in dinner, and they ate together under the light of Oma streaming through the dome above. When they were done, their nursemaid took them up for baths and rest. Kirana watched them go, and then sat alone in the vast chamber, relishing the silence.

Kirana did not believe in any gods. Perhaps that was her personal failing. They were useful ways to explain the horror of the skies, and the random chance that gave one person unconscionable power and another a terrible craving for drink that murdered their guts and ruined their lives. It wasn't fair. It was simply life.

She pulled over one of the books Tasia had been reading. Something about raising dogs. Kirana realized that what she wanted more than anything was simply to raise daughters who were happy farmers and herders. Maybe a village elder or two.

The light in the room flickered, as if a great cloud were passing over Oma's eye. She squinted, still peering into the book. The lights began to flicker more intensely. She had to cover her eyes, fearful of a headache.

Hurried footsteps came from the hall. She opened her eyes, shielding her vision as she closed the book. One of the big Sanctuary doors creaked open.

Yivsa came in, breathless. "Did you see the sky?"

"What?" Kirana raised her gaze to the ceiling. The sky seemed to be spinning. She had to look away, overcome by vertigo. "What is–?"

"It's time," Yivsa said

Kirana stood, still a little wobbly. The light in the chamber flashed: red, blue, green, purple lightning. She needed to get out of here before it made her sick. "Give the order. Get them all into place. Is Gian still here?"

"Already en route back to the ark, but I can get a runner."

"Do it. Tell Madah I want a report from her assault on that camp full of Saiduan."

Kirana cast one last glance back into the room. She rested her hand on the skin of the temple. "Let's finish this, you fucker," she muttered, and closed the door behind her.

The sky shimmered.

Lilia had to shield her eyes. Something winked at them, a flickering blue star. A cracking boom filled the air.

The ground shuddered.

When Lilia looked again, Para gazed back at her, the three satellites sitting diagonally in the sky, with the larger, spinning mass of red Oma whirling closer and closer to them, as if threatening to burst them apart.

A brilliant cascade of bluish-amber light filled the sky. It was eerie, like something from a dream. The great face of Oma winked at her as the other satellites began to fall into orbit around it, blinking and flashing like something alive. Tira, Para, Sina, three pieces broken away from a much larger object, lining up again for the first time in two thousand years.

Cries came from the camp, all around them. The world looked, collectively, to the sky.

The satellites began to pulse and dance. They aligned themselves into orbit around Oma.

"Oh no," Lilia breathed.

Zezili ran up to her, huffing. "What the fuck…?" she said, and moved to shield Lilia, as if she expected the stars to explode.

Maralah, from the head of the cavern trail, climbed back up into the camp. "We knew this was coming!" Maralah called. Behind her, Kadaan helped Roh up, both of them scrambling across the camp.

But no one could have known this was coming, really, Lilia thought. No one had seen this happen in two thousand years.

Sina, Para, and Tira began to slowly rotate around Oma, so near it was as if they were creating a new sun in the bleary violet sky.

"If those things collide, we might be fucked," Zezili said. "I mean, shit, nothing you can do now, huh?"

"The hand of Oma," Lilia said. "If only they would."

The three satellites, rotating around the fourth, instead came so close to one another's orbits that they had the appearance of a single flickering eye spilling ghostly red-violet light across the world.

Maralah strode across the camp toward them. Lilia took her gaze away from the sky, glanced back at Taigan.

"You!" Maralah said, and while the sky seethed, the air all around Lilia grew heavy as spoiled milk.

Taigan waved at Maralah. "Hello, Maralah! It's been an age. Isn't this delightful? No one has seen such a show in two thousand years! What a time to be alive."

Lilia's ears popped.

"Maralah!" Lilia called. "Don't! He's here to… help. Inasmuch as Taigan helps. Don't start using your gift here! Not now!"

Maralah stared at Lilia as if she were mad. "I'm not!" she said. "Who is… Are you pulling, Taigan? I'm not calling Sina."

The smell of smoke grew stronger. Lilia turned back to the woods. "Taigan?" she said. "How far back were those people coming from Meyna and Yisaoh's camp?"

"Oh, a day," he said. "But I told the scouts I encountered that it would be nice to blink them over here instead of making them walk. It turns out you have an omajista here who's very good with winks, they said. A Dorinah boy? Remarkable."

The air crackled. Voices came from the woodlands. The wind picked up.

Lilia shivered. The sense of foreboding had to do with more than the sky. All this power, all these omajistas in one place, these gates opening and closing… they were painting a target on this beachhead.

"Stop them," Lilia said. "Maralah! Have everyone drop their star! Stop pulling on your stars!"

As she cried out, the spill of refugees came up from the woods, bringing with them the smell of burnt hair and smoke. Kai Ahkio walked at the front, Meyna behind him. Ahkio carried a child – Meyna's? Lilia's heart clenched. Where was Tasia? Namia?

"Drop your call on the stars!" Lilia said, limping toward them, half-hoping for good news, for a miracle.

A roaring blur knocked into her, putting her onto her back. Namia lay on top of her, squeezing her tightly.

"Namia!" Lilia held her as the others streamed past. "Emlee?"

Namia made the sign for "taken."

"Tasia? Oh no, Tasia."

"Death," Namia signed.

Lilia got to her feet. Namia loped after her.

The smoke overhead grew lower and thicker as the wind shifted. Meyna, face blushed from exertion, sweaty tendrils stuck to her forehead, hurried to Maralah's side, one hand pressed against her burgeoning belly.

"Shao Maralah!" Meyna said. "You must know. We were attacked. The camp, the whole camp, as if they knew exactly where it was. Who would have told them, after all this time? We never–"

"You fool," Maralah said. "You've led them right here! How many are with you?"

"Not many," Meyna said. "Maralah, I know it's too soon, but our partnership–"

Maralah slapped her. Meyna fell heavily, clutching at her belly. Ahkio put the child down and ran to her, as did her husbands Rhin and Hadaoh. Hadaoh drew an infused weapon. Maralah burnt it from his hand. He cried out, clutching at his seared skin.

Lilia held Namia close.

"We were careful," Meyna said. "No one was–"

"You bloody fool," Maralah said. "As if you ungifted wretches would be able to tell if a Tai Mora scout trailed you."

The air thickened again, so heavily this time Lilia lost her breath.

This wasn't just the people in the camp drawing on the satellite's power, or even the Dhai refugees. This was something far worse. Far, far stronger.

Oh, Oma, she thought.

The air around the camp began to shiver and ripple like water. Lilia knew exactly what this was, and if she had any breath at all in her aching lungs, she would have screamed.

All around them, reality began to tear away. A dozen searing gates parted the woodlands surrounding the camp, cut tents in half, sawed through unlucky bystanders. Their yawning mouths vomited forth a wave of Tai Mora soldiers, all shiny in their chitinous armor, their infused weapons held aloft.

The smell of burning intensified. Lilia heard someone screaming, screaming. The trees above them lit up, instantly torched. Bits of char and winking embers rained from the sky.

Namia tugged at her hand, but Lilia found herself rooted to the spot, unable to move, frozen in some nightmare. It was all happening again, an endless cycle. One fiery raid after another, on this very spot, in some other world, and now here, with infused weapons: Kirana's army, invading world after world. She imagined a whole slew of Kiranas from a hundred thousand, a million worlds, cutting through these people, torching this same wood, again and again, as they had done to her people before, as they were doing to their people now.

Lilia reached. She was not sure what she reached for, something deep within her long lost. For so long she was filled with only revenge, hatred for these people. For everything they had done, were doing, again and again.

But as she watched it all happening again, here, on the same spot, she saw it for what it was. Something terribly broken. One people, ripped apart into a million, trillion pieces.

How could they ever be put back together again?

Screaming. The woods themselves were screaming.

32

It all happened very quickly, in a breath. Para rising. The incredible movement of the sky that awed and distracted. The winks opening. The air seething.

But Lilia was not awed. Not frozen. She had been waiting for this for a year. Waiting to fight back. Lilia *moved*.

"Roh!" Lilia yelled. "*Defensive wall!*"

Another parajista may have hesitated. One she did not know, maybe. One who had not been hounded and abused as Roh had after Para winked out a year ago.

But it was Roh, her friend Roh, the one who always wanted to be a sanisi, and so the shimmering wall of air whumped across the camp and smashed into the winks all around them an instant after her cry.

Kadaan raised a fist beside Roh. Dust rose from the ground. Bits of sand trembled and filled the air.

Lilia hurried over to them, calling to Zezili, "Get everyone with a weapon! Defensive line!"

Zezili leapt over the table. "Fucking *finally*!" she said and then, in Dhai, "Everyone with a fucking shield and a weapon, I want a defensive circle!"

"Taigan?" Lilia called back over her shoulder.

"There are fifty-six Songs of Unmaking coming through

those winks," he said, following her. He shrugged. "I can't hold them all."

"Try," she said. She pushed past the mobs of frightened and mobilizing fighters and others, trying to get to Maralah. Namia followed after her, silent. Lilia finally climbed onto a table and called, "Fighters to the outside! Those who can't fight, come to the middle! The center!" Panic could make people into mindless, self-destructive fools if no one took charge. Lilia had seen it before, on the harbor wall, and again during the madness of Kuallina.

Roh felt the air shift the moment he reached the trailhead. He was giddy, awed, already drawing deeply on Para. He and Kadaan had hugged back on the beach, delighted to be able to draw on their stars again, but Maralah was already running back to the camp, peering at the sky like some grim omen.

That had shaken him, and they went back up the trail after her, Roh using the delightful tails of Para's breath to speed himself along, fairly flying, no longer the shuffling final figure to crest the top of the trail.

But the air was wrong. He dropped onto the sand. Lilia shouted at him from more than thirty paces away. "Roh!" and he was already drawing on Para again, the Litany of the Palisade already half-formed in his mind, "Defensive wall!" He saw the gates opening in the next moment, already tying up his spell. He cast the defensive walls almost before she had finished, throwing up a hasty bubble of air around the camp as the twining blue bursts of Para's breath poured into the camp through the gates and attacked his defenses.

Kadaan reinforced his work, putting up a tougher defense on the inner layer of his.

"We need to layer these," Kadaan said. "You've done that?"

"No," Roh said.

"Watch me, then. This is the Song of Davaar, and the Song of the Proud Wall."

Roh was aware of the rest of the camp moving, and Lilia shouting. But he concentrated solely on Kadaan's voice and the purling lines of Para's breath he wielded. Even as they came together, Roh felt the hammering of their defenses, like physical blows that pushed the power of Para back under his skin. It might have startled him enough to break his concentration, a year ago, two years ago, but now he was far more used to pain and disappointment.

"It will get worse," Kadaan said, "as they realize how strong this wall is."

"I have endured worse," Roh said.

Lilia went to Maralah's side. Maralah stood rooted in place, hands raised, gaze fierce. A wall of flames licked up around the defensive wall of air, but Tai Mora were still bleeding through the edges of the winks, crowding around the outer edges of the defenses.

"Can you hold them?" Lilia asked.

Maralah did not answer. Lilia turned, surveying the camp. Fighters were moving to the outer ring of the camp, harangued by a gleeful Zezili. They were mostly Saiduan, who looked to Maralah before obeying. Maralah, for her part, gave them a nod.

Lilia broke away from Maralah, Roh and Kadaan. Taigan had said there were fifty-six Songs of Unmaking, that was fifty-six attempts to cut off their jistas from their satellites. The number of offensive spells that the others had to counteract would be far, far more. It would be all they could do to hold them.

She found Anavha cowered at the center of the group of civilians. "Where's Saradyn?" she asked.

"He went to fight," Anavha said.

Lilia leaned over him. Took his arm. Said in Dorinah, "Can you open a gate to somewhere safe?"

"I… in Dhai? I don't… the plateau, the temples… they are everywhere–"

"Somewhere else?"

"They are everywhere," Anavha said, and began to cry.

Lilia took a deep breath. "Somewhere safe. In Dorinah?"

"No, not–" he broke off, then, "Aaldia," he said, and that seemed to stem the terror, the tears. "I can take us to the farm in Aaldia."

"A farm? Good. That's good. No Tai Mora there?"

"No, but–"

"What?"

"It's all right. Nusi will understand."

"I'm sure they will," Lilia said, having no idea who Nusi was, nor particularly caring in that moment. "Can you do it now?"

"What if the defenses break? What if–"

"A great many things could happen between this moment and the next," Lilia said. "Including you getting us a way out. Can you do that?"

He nodded.

She stepped back, giving him space to work, and called away a few of the civilians near them. The last thing she needed was panic at the center. Panic at the center would make them all rush to the edges, and right into the Tai Mora.

Lilia spotted a reasonably calm young man and pointed at him. "You! Keep them away from him. Let him work!" The man nodded almost gratefully, as if pleased to have something to do.

She hurried back to the medical tent where Sola was frantically packing her things and yelling at people to move one of her injured patients.

"Sola!" Lilia said. "We are getting everyone out through a gate, there, at the center – see that young man, the one with the brown hair? You and your patients go first. We'll need you on the other side for injuries."

"Where–"

"It doesn't matter where," Lilia said, "it's safe." She said the last part with more conviction than she felt. She had to trust that Anavha had some idea of what he was doing, or she'd spend too long overthinking instead of moving. Their survival relied on fast movement, before the Tai Mora got a handle on their defenses. The parajista wall could go down at any time.

Lilia knew that nine parts of getting people to listen to you relied on confidence. Sola met her gaze, and she must have liked what she saw, because she nodded and called for another to help her move the injured.

"Zezili!" Lilia called.

"Fucking busy!" Zezili barked from ten paces away.

"Namia," Lilia said. "Come here, I need you to be my messenger, can you do that?"

Namia nodded.

Lilia grabbed Zezili, made her touch Namia's head.

"The fuck!" Zezili said. She handed over a weapon to a young woman.

"Namia," Lilia said. "Show her the sign for *retreat*."

Namia did.

"And show her, fall back. Good. And advance."

Namia gave the signs.

"You understand?" Lilia said. "Namia can give you orders."

"I can fucking manage this myself–"

"You can manage jistas and fighters against Tai Mora, in three different languages? No. Listen to me."

Lilia turned abruptly.

A roar of heated air blasted her from behind. Lilia pressed herself to the ground as a purl of flame licked overhead. One of the forces on the other side had broken through. Roh and Kadaan were already moving forward together, back to back, exchanging a few words as they sought to shore up the breach.

Lilia crawled back up. Namia came after her. Lilia went to Anavha, who was still struggling to open a gate. The air in front of him wavered, but did not part. He sweated heavily, and was trembling.

She leaned close to him and said softly, clearly, "The Song of the One Breath. You know it?"

He shook his head. "What's your litany?"

"Poetry. Tordinian?"

She wondered how he had been trained. Did they try to break him down, the way Taigan and the Seekers had tried to break her? Lilia didn't think she could feel pity anymore, didn't think she could feel anything at all, but watching this young man struggle to save them while the air pressure heaved and the air crackled, she remembered the feel of the Seeker Voralyn's stick when the Seekers captured her years ago, and the long freefall when Taigan pushed her over the edge of the cliff, daring her to fly. I am not you, Taigan, she thought. And this young man was certainly not her.

"All right," she said. "Find a point to focus on. That broken poppy there, see?" She pointed.

His gaze fixed on the trampled flower just on the other wide of the wavering air.

"Good," she said. "That's all there is. You and that… poetry. That song. The rest of this is nothing. It's not anyway. You want to focus on that, and where you want to go. Where do you want to be?"

"Not here."

"It has to be firm. Focus. See it. Taste it. Smell it." She closed her own eyes, remembering how she had sung the Saiduan Song of the Dead and burned the image of the Dorinah camp at the base of the Liona mountains into her mind, where Gian had waited for her. An age ago. Before Oma was lost to her.

Anavha smelled smoke. All he could see, when he closed his eyes, was the world burning.

"Smoke," Anavha said.

"Not there. There's no smoke there. What's there?"

He trembled. He felt the heat and rush of the wind again. Another breach in their defenses. Yelling, in Dhai and Saiduan. He couldn't understand any of it, only what Lilia told him in Dorinah, and that frightened him and soothed him at the same time.

Safe. Where had he been safe? He once thought safety

was a quiet house with Daolyn, when Zezili was away. Safety was sitting with Taodalain in the city, reading to her as her pregnancy progressed. He once thought safety was Zezili calling him *hers*. And for a time, yes, he had felt safe with Natanial, wrapped in his arms, ready to give him whatever he wanted because Anavha felt so *safe* there.

But when Lilia asked him where he felt safe, the image that bloomed in his mind was none of those places. Instead, it was rolling fields of golden grass. A house nestled among the hills that looked like a boat at sea. Safety was with Nusi and Giska and their rotating group of farm hands, called in during planting and harvest. Laughing at the table. Warm, clean beds. No violence. No raised voices. It had not been exciting, or dangerous. That made him anxious, those first few months. He kept waiting for the screaming. The flaring tempers. Getting locked in his room. Having things thrown at him. Fists raised to him. None of that happened.

"Nothing will happen to you here that you do not wish to happen," Nusi had told him, and the idea of that, the promise of it, was breathtaking.

"The farm," Anavha said aloud. "The planted fields. The dead man, from the sky. The hungry sheep. The dogs. I miss the dogs."

He opened his eyes. A small tear in the seams between their position and the next opened.

"A little more, Anavha," Lilia said.

Anavha concentrated on exactly where he wanted to be, the precise spot. The hill north of the farm, overlooking the house.

The tear widened into a great round door, so large he gasped a little and stepped back from it. On the other side:

a clear lavender sky, and rolling golden hills.

Lilia said, "Can you hold it open there, Anavha? I need you to keep hold of it."

"I have it," he said. And in a rush of awe, he realized that he did have it. The gate solidified. Did not waver. His hands did not tremble.

Natanial winced as the winks opened, and a shimmering wall of heat blasted their front line. The heat was unexpected.

"Hold the line!" Natanial called. The heat was enough to be uncomfortable, but not dangerous, as long as no one panicked.

Otolyn gazed over at him, questioning. He shook his head. Para was risen, and that did mean that a whole slew of parajistas had come back into their power. Natanial had a moment to wonder how Monshara would handle that. Four stars ascendant. Were there even existing battle strategies for that? Surely not.

"Forward!" Monshara cried, and the mass of bodies and bears and dogs was moving, groaning, creaking, yipping, growling.

The heat intensified, and as Natanial got closer to the winks, he saw a small but chaotic scene ahead. As he came through, a whirlwind of air and fire battered him. The spinning satellites made him dizzy, so he kept his focus on the ground. They were up above the sea on some spur of land. He smelled burning, yes, but the sea, too. Madah had opened a dozen winks around a small encampment. It couldn't have held more than sixty people, all of them grouped up in the middle.

Natanial tried to push forward, but his troops ahead were meeting resistance. Parajistas had a wall up, and waves of fire were coming off it, pushing his troops and all those surrounding them back against the winks.

"Hold the line!" Natanial yelled. Who was countering their attack? It should have been an ambush, no time to plan or retaliate. They should have crushed them here as easily as they had back at the other camp.

Natanial scanned the figures at the center of the camp. Whoever their jistas were, they were in no formation, no line. He could not identify a leader of any kind. Two rings of fighters had formed around those in the center, though, which meant the center likely held both civilians and jistas.

"We're useless until they break the jista defenses!" Otolyn yelled.

Natanial growled. He hated foolish orders and confusion. She was right. Madah had gotten ahead of herself. His mercenaries were going to break and bolt at the next wave of fire; he knew his people weren't high on the list of those Monshara's jistas were going to protect.

"Retreat and regroup!" Natanial called.

Otolyn swapped flags and blew into the horn attached to her saddle.

His troops were not dignified or orderly. They simply turned and ran, breaking hard for the winks behind them.

A shrieking above the din of frantic soldiers, the huff of wind and fire. Natanial peered ahead as his soldiers streamed back through the wink all around him. The defensive barrier around the Dhai camp was shrinking, contracting. The ring of defensive fighters moved back with it.

How were they retreating? Where?

Natanial caught a glimpse through the shimmering defensive wall of air, and thought his eyes must be deceiving him.

There was Anavha, moving among the heads of the others – he could not mistake that willowy frame, that long face, and the silky brown hair, so out of place among the black-haired Dhai and Saiduan.

And standing next to Anavha – though it was impossible, as impossible as the blinking quad of satellites in the sky – was Zezili Hasaria.

When the winks appeared, Ahkio saw his moment. He sought out Caisa. There, near to him, as she had always been. He ran from Meyna's side in all the chaos and reached for Caisa's hand.

"Do you trust me?" he whispered, urgently.

"Kai, what–"

"Come with me," he said. "Take my hand. I need you to help me draw out Yisaoh."

"Catori Yisaoh? Why?"

"Please, Caisa. Trust me one last time."

Winks were opening all around them. Ahkio scooped up Hasao, as Rhin and Hadaoh were now trapped by the press of fearful people, all pressing together toward the center of camp.

Ahkio looked for Yisaoh. Nodded at her. "Come! Yisaoh, this way!"

He charged through the gap between two winks, heading for the cover of the woodlands. Hasao screamed, the loud, piercing scream of a fearful child. The screaming child and the smoke made him think of the way his mother had screamed when he tried to save her.

The air assaulted him. A blast of it took him off his feet. Yisaoh yelled and tumbled beside him. Caisa reached for Yisaoh to help her up.

Ahkio let the child go; she tottered a few paces and then sat in the brush, still screaming, frozen. The child, at least, would live. Something would outlast him.

Ahkio rounded on Yisaoh before she had time to get up. He hit her on the nose stunning her.

Caisa gasped. "Ahkio!"

"Help me hold her!" Ahkio said.

"But, I–"

"Caisa!"

Caisa ran to him and twisted Yisaoh's arms behind her back. Yisaoh was strong, and it took the two of them to hold her down.

"You fucking traitor!" Yisaoh screamed at them, and kicked him.

The Tai Mora swarmed forward from the winks, enveloping the camp, oblivious to them behind the main line of winks. Ahkio yanked Yisaoh up. "This is the only way!" he said.

A Tai Mora noticed them, then, blade drawn.

"We surrender!" Ahkio said, raising his hands, releasing Yisaoh. Yisaoh tried to twist away, but Caisa still held her, mouth an open moue, confusion still twisted on her face. "Kirana. I need to see Kirana. I'm her brother. Do you understand?"

The soldier hesitated.

Two more came over. "I'm her brother!" Ahkio insisted. "I have someone she wants!"

Ahkio spotted a woman on a bear, someone with far more authority than this group, and bolted past the soldiers.

"I have Yisaoh!" Ahkio yelled at her. "I have Yisaoh!"

The woman leaned over and took him by the collar. "Where?" the woman said.

Ahkio pointed.

Lilia gestured to Sola. "Go, now. Fast as you can."

After Sola came the children and their parents, running over in groups of two, three, six.

When they were moving well, without panic, she turned her attention back to the jistas. They were all still rooted at the top of the path leading down to the beach. Kadaan and Roh had shifted only a few paces.

Taigan made his way over to her, but his look was more intense than she had ever seen it.

"There are more omajistas coming," he said. "I'm holding thirty-seven Songs of Unmaking right now. Whoever they are bringing through is very powerful. I can feel them pushing already."

"Anavha has a gate," Lilia said. "I need to figure out… We'll need to start compressing the circle, falling back to the gate."

"We can't let them see where we're going," Taigan said. "They will be able to follow."

"I need every jista we have," Lilia said. "I can't leave any of them."

"Not even me?"

Lilia turned away from him. "Not even you, you fool," she said, and then, to Maralah, "We need to pull back to the gate! We have a gate!"

"Namia," Lilia then said. "Go to Zezili. Tell her, fall back. Tighten the circle. You may need to… show her that one. Go, please."

Namia raised her head, cocked it, sniffed a long moment, then ran in Zezili's direction.

"Maralah!" Lilia called again. "Pull back to the gate."

Maralah shook her head, the barest movement. "Move the gate."

"I can't, Maralah. He can barely keep it open as it is. It would take too long for him to open–"

"If we pull in these defenses," Kadaan said, "it will let more of them in. We won't be able to hold–"

"We won't have to," Lilia said. "Pull back quickly. Speed. Speed, all right? We only have speed and surprise. You understand."

Kadaan looked to Maralah.

Maralah was clearly in pain. The amount of power she was pulling had to be much more than Lilia had ever tried, certainly more than she'd ever attempted without burning herself out. But she moved her chin, once.

"Stages," Kadaan said to Roh. "Ten paces. Break for one. Ten paces."

"Start moving to the gate as you pull it," Lilia said.

Namia returned as Lilia went back to the shimmering gate. Lilia asked, "Is she coming?"

"Unknown," Namia signed, which didn't bode well. Zezili had been switching back and forth between speaking Dorinah and Dhai, and it was possible whatever response she'd given Namia had been full of Dorinah curse words that Namia wouldn't understand.

"She'll figure it out when the defensive walls move," Lilia said.

Zezili had not had this much fun in some time. She delighted in the opportunity to boss around the Saiduan, though she was not oblivious to the fact that Maralah had given them leave to listen to her. Some fool had given her a sword, and she held it aloft in her strong right hand, gripping the hilt like the cock of a long-lost lover. She kissed the blade. How had she gone so long trying to murder people with her left hand? This was fucking excellent.

She yelled a lot in Dhai, which she hated, but she knew only three words in Saiduan, and they were all filthy curses. She deployed those liberally, too.

"Everyone with a shield, start a defensive line!" she called, and demonstrated with two Dhai defenders and their paltry shields. She slammed the bottoms of the shields into the dirt, just a pace away from the shimmering air of the defensive wall. "There will be breaches! Cracks! You will murder every fucking thing that breaches! Nothing will get past you! You are the final line!"

Zezili was relieved to see the Saiduan had better weapons. She found she needed to pull the ring of fighters back ten more paces, though, because she did not have enough to make a tight circle right up by the wall. She didn't like that.

As she pulled them back, she saw a boiling mass of movement at one of the gates to her left. A woman on a bear shouted something and was pushed into the defensive wall so hard her helmet came off, revealing a tangle of black hair knotted in white ribbons. Gray eyes, a rounded face with a broad nose and narrow jaw. *Monshara?*

Monshara barked at her troops. Zezili found herself rooted, captivated by the spectacle. Monshara, as if sensing her, raised her head. Their gazes met.

A beat, no more, and then Monshara turned again, yelling at her troops, forcing them to pour around the defensive wall instead of getting stuck back through the gate behind it. She took hold of someone near her bear's head and bent over.

Zezili thought it was a Tai Mora, but no, she recognized his face, too: Ahkio. Monshara shook him.

How the fuck had Ahkio gotten himself stuck outside the defensive wall?

Namia darted to Zezili's side and tugged at her sleeve. Zezili shrugged her off and yelled at two soldiers with a break in their shield line.

Namia signed at her again, huffed, and ran off.

Zezili spotted a break in the wall of air and darted over to help the collection of fighters. Six Tai Mora squeezed through, and the line broke up, trying to surround them.

"Hold that fucking line!" Zezili roared in Dorinah, and switched to Dhai as she plunged into the fray, yelling at her line to reform.

She slashed the throat of the nearest Tai Mora and heaved the body onto the one behind. The wall had sealed up again. Zezili hamstrung a heavy man and chopped at his head. Her sword wasn't sharp enough to sever it, but blood gushed from his jugular, and he fell, tripping up the one behind.

Zezili stabbed the one who'd fallen and landed a palm strike to the woman coming up behind her. A knife glanced off Zezili's elbow. She knocked the wielder in the chin with her other elbow and dipped forward, stabbing at the fourth attacker just as one of her fighters got a spear into the Tai Mora's ribs.

When she came up, sword raised across her body, her fighters stood around the little mound of bodies, staring at her.

"What are you looking at?" she demanded. "Reform the line!"

The wall of air behind her knocked into her back. She swore and came forward. The defensive wall was moving.

"Back ten paces!" Zezili shouted. As the fighters moved, she knelt quickly next to the man she'd hacked in the neck and drank a handful of sweet, sweet blood. It felt magnificent going down her throat, like a restorative liquor. She grinned.

As she leapt over the bodies to retreat ahead of the wall with her fighters, she noted the pain in her elbow. Brought it up and regarded it. A long slash in her flesh, gooey. It oozed a pale greenish fluid, thick as old blood. Zezili shivered and looked away.

Whatever the fuck had happened to her, she was going to enjoy the time she had left.

33

Refugees from Lilia's old camp were passing through the gate now, pouring through to the other side. Lilia knew many of their faces, and found herself still looking for Emlee and Tasia.

Meyna stood just to the other side of the gate, ushering her people through. Lilia caught her gaze; Meyna looked away first. A bruise was forming on her cheek from where Maralah had hit her.

"Where are Ahkio and Yisaoh?" Lilia called, trying to peer at Meyna through the crowd.

"I don't know," she said. "I lost them in the panic. Ahkio took up our child and ran. Yisaoh followed. My husband Rhin found Hasao, but said Ahkio and Yisaoh were being led the other way, by... the Tai Mora."

"Hasao was the child he carried into the camp, as well?"

"My child," Meyna said. "His and mine. She's safe."

The last of the soot-stained refugees made it past them. "You go," Lilia told Meyna. "The fighters are next."

Meyna glanced back at the ring of fighters. They had moved in ten paces, and so had the defensive wall. Even as they both watched, the ring of fighters moved in another five paces, and the jistas began making their way to the gate, rapidly.

Meyna nodded and went through. One of her husbands helped her on the other side.

Big Saradyn came up with some fighters. "Go through," she told him, but he stood rigid, peering at her.

"Go!" she said.

"No ghosts," he murmured, in Dorinah.

"Please," Lilia said.

"Impostor," he said, pointing a large finger at her.

"Who? I'm not… I don't…" Oh no, Lilia thought, Roh had said the man could tell who was from this world, and who was not. He was far larger than her, muscled and menacing. She had no recourse against him.

"Roh is my friend," Lilia said. "If he is your friend too, then we can be friends together."

Saradyn's eyes narrowed. "Patron-killer," he said. "Wait."

Lilia had no idea what he meant, but he turned to watch Roh advancing when he said it.

The fighters streamed past her. Zezili took up a position opposite her at the gate now, yelling at everyone in Dhai to hurry. "When are we going?" Zezili asked her, because of course they would have to go through together.

"After Roh," she said, glad to see that Saradyn was still distracted. "The jistas. They'll be able to hold the wall."

Beside her, Anavha said, "We need to hurry." The gate wavered, wrinkled and snapped back open, like a blinking eye. One of the fighters lost the end of her spear, which thunked at their feet.

"Go, go!" Lilia urged the last four fighters, and then they were down to the jistas. Maralah, Roh and Kadaan were just steps away. Taigan stood beside Zezili already, muttering something darkly as the surging mass of Tai Mora spilled from the other gates, so many and so fast that they were a living wall of flesh.

"You last," Lilia said to Taigan. "As soon as you drop, they will cut you all off. Maralah, go."

Maralah shook her head. Gestured to Roh and Kadaan.

Kadaan grimaced, but took Roh by the sleeve and dipped through the gate. They continued to hold the defensive wall from the other side. As long as they had line of sight–

A burst of air knocked Lilia back. She fell against Namia and grabbed the edge of the gate to right herself. The edges of it were a physical thing, like the frame of a window. Maralah burned up six Tai Mora who had broken through the air wall.

"That's it!" Maralah said. "Taigan, a burst! Distract and retreat."

Taigan smiled, one of his delighted and frightening smiles. "Bird," he said, "go now."

"Anavha," Lilia said, "come through with me. Keep it open for them. Can you move and keep it open?"

He nodded.

Lilia took Namia's hand and stepped through the gate, stumbled. Zezili came after her, and grabbed her arm to help her regain her balance. She went past Roh and Kadaan, still holding their defensive walls through the rent in the world. Lilia reached back for Anavha. Grabbed his hand and encouraged him to come through. The edges of the gate wavered again.

Anavha was through.

Maralah and Taigan blocked the other side of the gate, working a spell in tandem that Lilia could not see, but she could sense. The air on this side was as heavy as the other. The pressure in her ears was so intense it affected her hearing. It was like being underwater.

Of course Taigan despised Maralah, but then, he despised a good many people.

He had also fought beside her for over two decades. Not so long, by his reckoning of time, but long when he considered how many other people he had been forced to put up with for any length of time. When it was just the two of them remaining, facing down twelve open gateways pouring hundreds of Tai Mora at them, well, he had an idea of their choices in such a situation.

She no longer had a ward on him. He could do to her what he liked and walk away, burning through all of these foreign jistas and running off merrily into the woods or swimming endlessly across the sea, if he chose.

Taigan had a long, bitter memory. In this moment, facing the seething hordes of Tai Mora, he was reminded of Aaraduan, and how the black, slithering plant flesh swarmed the blue walls of the hold, even as the living hold spat and hissed at them. Para, Lord of the Air, had not protected them then. The satellites had abandoned them. The Patron was dead. What were they in this moment, two cursed figures without a country, saving a bunch of pacifist cannibals? To what end?

Maralah tilted her head at him. The air was so heavy it felt like drinking soup.

He snorted at her. Raised his hands. Called for Oma, as much and as quickly as his body allowed.

"Five second delay?" Taigan asked.

"No," Maralah said. "One hundred paces out, though."

"That will hurt you."

"I thought you'd like that."

"I do."

They called upon their stars, and wove a deadly burst of power in the air twenty paces out, right up against the wall of air.

Maralah made a sign, most likely to Kadaan, behind them. Taigan recognized it.

Drop the wall.

Taigan released his tangled spell, and braced for the blowback.

A massive blast of heat and air rushed through the wink, sending Taigan and Maralah with it. Lilia didn't have time to move out of the way. The blast took the nearest of those at the gate off their feet, throwing them ten paces or more away.

Lilia landed in a tangle of others, ears ringing. She pushed her way back to the gate – it was still open. A great crater of fire consumed everything on the other side, but already figures were moving out of it.

"Anavha!" she called, but even to her own ears, her voice was muted, far away.

Anavha was key to everything. Without him they were stuck here, with no time to get back before Para left the sky. How would she manage that? Ships took days, days they did not have, not now.

Lilia stared out at a great rolling horizon; golden fields of grass as far as she could see. She pivoted, taking in the sheer breadth of it. She had never seen so much open space.

As she came round again, a farmhouse came into view,

or rather, she assumed it was a farmhouse; it looked more like a ship, strung with riggings on which plants twined their way up from sod gardens to insulate the roof. The house itself was half-buried in the ground and carved with totems, like those on the prows of Aaldian ships, but these totems were charred, and the grass on the sod roof, too, had burned, as well as a good chunk of grassland out behind the house.

She caught sight of Anavha's brown hair and slender form, and hurried over to him. He lay in the broken grass, staring at the charred house.

"Oh no," he said. "Oh no."

He got up and ran for the house. Lilia called after him, but he kept running. She would never catch him, so didn't attempt it.

Behind her, the gate was still open; smoke and heat poured from it, swirling up and up into the great lavender sky. The Tai Mora lines were advancing, swarming over their fallen comrades.

"Taigan!" Lilia said. He sat up. His eyebrows were singed, and blisters formed on his hands. Beside him, Maralah was vomiting.

"Where is he?" Taigan rasped. "He needs to shut this."

"He's run to the house."

"Undisciplined children," he muttered.

Lilia glanced through the gate. "They're coming," she said. "If they know where we are–"

"They won't," Maralah said. She released another wave of fire, less strong than the first, and pulled out her blade. She began to hum softly. Her blade glowed deep red, then violet.

The attackers on the other side fell; one, then another, a fourth, a sixth…

The gate winked shut.

Maralah fell to her knees, letting her blade fall beside her.

"What was that?" Lilia said.

"Souls," Maralah said. She shook her head. "Sometimes drawing on and releasing souls can upset the stability of the gates."

"You just… you made a guess about what might work?"

Maralah snorted. "You didn't? How did you think so quickly? Most people, even sanisi, panic and freeze. You *moved*. You knew where each of us were. Knew the strategy for jistas and fighters. Or you just guessed!"

"I took the measure of the camp when I came in. I was already looking for allies and making plans. That's… what I've been doing for a year now."

"What plan?"

"There is nowhere you can run," Lilia said carefully. "Have they showed you that yet?"

Maralah curled a lip at her and turned on her heel. Lilia's shoulders sagged. She took in the measure of who had made it to the other side.

Meyna stood apart with her family, directing the Dhai, answering questions. The Dhai from her camp had moved a little apart. The Saiduan collected near Maralah.

Lilia limped over to Meyna. "There's a well," Lilia said, pointing it out beyond the dog pens. "I think there are some sheep on the other side as well. The Saiduan will make neat work of that. But there may be something in the cellars."

Meyna did not look at her. "Thank you," she said, "we are aware."

"There aren't even two hundred people here, Meyna," Lilia said. "You lost them all. Will you listen to me or not? We aren't working at cross-purposes."

Meyna rounded on Lilia and moved away from the others, so they could not be overheard. "I won't let my people be used in some–"

"And how did that work for you?" Lilia said. "I am not here to be spiteful. I will tell you that being left for dead in a bone tree is not great fun. But you see it now, don't you? They won't stop until we're dead."

Maralah interrupted them. "Come with me. Roh, Kadaan, you too. And Luna. Yes, I see you, little Luna. The house, there."

"I'm coming," Zezili said, pushing her way through the crowd. "Don't try to leave me with these Dhai."

Lilia followed after Maralah, Namia at her side and Luna trailing after them both. They arrived inside the house, which bore a great charred hole in the ceiling where the sod roof had been burned and collapsed. She did not see any bodies, though, and the place had clearly been ransacked.

Anavha sat weeping in the back hall. Taigan sat at the great table in the center, eating a raw tuber from a bag. Soot covered everything.

Lilia went to Anavha and said, "This was your home?"

He nodded.

"Do you… see them?"

Anavha shook his head. "No one. No one's here."

"That's good," Lilia said. "That means they probably got away."

Roh approached her, gesturing for her to go back to the table with Maralah and the others. He sat next to Anavha.

"Why waste time with that boy?" Taigan grunted.

"Without him all of us would have been killed," Lilia said.

Taigan shrugged. "*I* would have been fine."

"We need to discuss next steps," Maralah said. "Where can he get us to next?"

"Only places he's seen," Roh said. "Anavha can't get us to Hrollief, or anywhere else. We could try Dorinah? But that's all Tai Mora territory now. Where is there to run? They've conquered everything!"

"No more running," Lilia said. "You've seen what they can do. Let's stop them now. Aren't you tired of running? I am."

Maralah peered at her. Sooty, weary, certainly bone tired, after the energy she had exerted on the beachhead. "What's your plan then?"

"What's yours?" Lilia countered.

Maralah grimaced. She pressed her hands to the table. "If I do this, with you and… Taigan, fine, *Taigan*, then the rest of my people–"

"They can stay here," Lilia said quickly, "if nothing else. We can do that now. It's as safe as we can make them for the duration. Clearly someone has been through here already. Let's hope they won't be back for a while."

She recreated the diagram of Tira's Temple again, this time in the sooty layer of the kitchen table. "Here's how we do it. We get our people into this fifth temple before Kirana, we control it, we hold it. Here's what I'd be doing in precisely this moment, if I were Kirana. I'd be getting my jistas, five for every temple, into these other four temples. Immediately. And working to get into the fifth temple by any means necessary."

Taigan laughed and slapped his knee. "Fifth temple? It's teeming with jistas. Likely the Empress herself has given them a visit and pissed all over it to mark it hers."

"Give me a minute," Lilia said.

Roh approached them, Anavha behind. Anavha was more composed now, but only just. Roh said, "We don't need to go through there to get to the fifth temple, remember? Oma's Temple can take us."

All gazes turned to him.

"Because you are the Guide," Lilia said. "All right, let's consider that. We just need to get you to Oma's Temple."

"As if that is easier!" Taigan said.

"With the Worldbreaker and the Key," Roh said. "Lilia, I know you said you could figure out the mechanism, you could play the role of worldbreaker, but... Li, I just think–"

"What are you talking about?" Maralah said. "A Key?"

Roh said, "The Key is... it's what channels all the combined power from all of the temples, and... I assume the Key is the person who can filter all that, so a worldbreaker can use it. We just need someone very powerful who can withstand that."

Lilia glanced over at Zezili, who sat on the rail outside, licking a tuber and wincing. "I thought it might be Zezili, she has this... this symbol? A missing piece that a woman named Kalinda gave me. She said it would help us in the fifth temple. I don't know. Maybe Zezili *could* endure all that power. We can find out?"

Luna came forward tentatively, slipping hir slight form

between Taigan and Maralah. "The symbol?" Luna asked. "Is it a trefoil with a tail?"

"Yes," Lilia said.

Luna traced the symbol over the center of the diagram, where the Worldbreaker would operate. "I would put her here. You may not want her to work the device, but that thing inside of her, you will want that here. Both of you need to be there, for it to work. There's nothing in the book about a missing piece, but if there is one, it would sit there."

Lilia sketched out a drawing of the orrery she had seen in Tira's Temple. "This is the device, I think," she said. "Tira's Temple… showed it to me. Have you seen anything like this in the book? Anything about an orrery?"

Anavha leaned over the drawing. Frowned.

"Nothing about an orrery," Luna said, rubbing at hir forehead. "I didn't see any device like this in any of the drawings, but… the instructions for closing the ways, they are mathematical equations that could easily be applied to the heavens. Oh, yes, I can see this now."

"That looks like the game of spheres," Anavha said, in Dorinah, though he certainly hadn't been able to follow any of their other conversation.

"You've seen this before?" Lilia asked, in Dorinah.

"Something like it, yes. All different colors of orbs, though. It's a game, a tavern game here. You have to match all of the orbs so they are correct pairs. Knowing the correct pairs is difficult because it isn't by size or shape, but distance. There's math involved, a lot of strategy."

"I want to know more about this game," Lilia said. "Can you set it up here?"

"It's better to go to one," Anavha said. "Then maybe you can see if it's really like what you saw."

Lilia translated for the others.

Maralah dug into the bag of tubers. Taigan tried to pull it back. She snarled at him.

"The Key is more difficult," Luna continued. "For a long time, I assumed it was the Kai."

"Tira's Temple said it wasn't," Lilia offered.

"Right," Luna said. "Instead, it's someone who can channel all that power into operating the orrery. Yes, all the jistas at every temple are channeling power, but the one here, in the fifth, has to take in all that power and feed it back to the temple to power that... machine. That must be what it looks like, an orrery. It's... a lot of power. Enough to destroy pretty much anyone. These are organic machines, with the people acting as parts. It makes sense that the Key is a person, an organic part."

"Maralah, do you think–" Lilia began, and stopped. Her gaze settled on Taigan instead, who was gnawing on a tuber while making faces at Maralah. He noticed her looking, and grimaced.

"Oh no," Taigan said. "Don't even say it."

"There's only one person here who wouldn't have died back there," Lilia said. "You admitted it yourself. Who else could get torn apart by the power of every satellite and not die?"

"You need an omajista! I will be the useful omajista. Blow someone else up."

"Our omajista is Anavha," she said. "You're the Key, Taigan."

"I so look forward to more pain and discomfort," he said.

"You wanted to help," Lilia said. "Isn't that why you came back? This is how you can help."

"Killing, helping, as long as they're the same," he said.

"I'll talk to Anavha," Lilia said; at his name, he perked up, but she didn't want to share her theory with him, not yet, so she continued in Dhai. "I think others should learn too, though, in case something goes wrong. Luna? You seem to know more about what these can do than anyone."

"Me?" Luna said. "I... suppose I could, but... I don't want to stand up there."

"Maybe you won't have to," Lilia said. "I just don't like the idea of any of us being singular. We only have once chance at this."

"There's still the matter of getting *into* Oma's Temple," Roh said. "We can't just open a gate in there. The jistas will sense us and be on us immediately. Anavha and I barely got out when he opened a gate. It's like they have some kind of alarm that senses when power is used."

Anavha, frustrated at being excluded, asked for a translation. Roh provided one.

"I have several contacts there," Lilia said. "One in particular is very high up. Is Caisa here?"

"Who?" Roh asked.

"Never mind," Lilia said. "I still need to see who made it from Meyna's camp."

"There's also Saronia. Do you remember her?" Roh asked.

Lilia grimaced. She did. "That bully?"

"She does the laundry," Roh said. "Carts it in and out of the temple, across the bridge, from the plateau. We could come in through the cart."

Maralah shook her head. "It's too many people. A bare minimum of seven must go down, and you will want others, as you said, in case something happens to any single person. I would not attempt this with fewer than twenty. You can't get them all in through the fucking *laundry*."

"We could have Anavha open a gate at the base of the plateau," Lilia said, wiping away the diagram of Tira's Temple and drawing a map of the plateau and the spur of rock that held Oma's Temple. "Maralah, you could set the plateau on fire, at night to draw their attention. That's a good distraction. The darkness will help confuse them."

Roh pointed at the temple. "We need to get to the Assembly Chamber," he said. "That's where the temple told me to bring the Key and the Worldbreaker. The ceiling of that chamber is glass."

"Right," Lilia said.

"Para is ascendant," Roh said. "When you've drawn their attention to the plateau, a lot of other jistas will be pulling on their stars to put that fire out. Kadaan and I can get Anavha in on a wave of air, break in through the glass and make sure the area is secure. When it's clear, Anavha can open a gate and get in the rest of you. That will be much faster."

"Why can't Anavha just open a gate inside the Assembly Chamber?" Maralah said, rubbing her head. "This is overly complicated."

"We have no idea who will be in that chamber," Lilia said. "Kirana might have dozens of jistas in there. If Anavha opens a gate directly in that chamber, they will immediately sense his power and send everyone running up there before Roh and Kadaan can secure it, and we'll be through. Even with Roh and Kadaan coming in first, I still think we will need a bigger distraction than burning the plateau if we really want to make sure the Assembly Chamber is empty. If we can get those guards and jistas below, we can cut them off from their stars."

"I can cut them off," Taigan said. "A Song of Unmaking. After that little lark on the beach, I can say for a fact that I can cut off fifty-nine jistas at a time, at least. I'm very good at distractions."

"And how do you propose to get in?" Lilia said. "We are all very… obvious."

"I propose that I walk right in and offer that Empress something she would like very much indeed. *That* will get her and her jistas and guards out of that Assembly Chamber, and anyone else."

"What could you possibly offer that they'd want badly enough to swarm you for?" Roh said.

"I would give her Lilia Sona, the upstart kitchen girl leading the rebels."

"No," Lilia said. "They would cut you off from Oma the moment you walked in. And murder me, certainly."

"They would try. I've discovered that your people and hers are bad at the Song of Unmaking, at least when it comes to unmaking *me*."

"It's a very big risk," Lilia said. She chewed her thumbnail. "Maybe we won't do it at all. Maybe we should just risk–"

"Oh, how touching," Taigan said. "I would be fine. I'm always fine."

Roh said, "Taigan, do you really think you could get into the temple with Lilia, cut everyone off from their stars, *and* get yourself upstairs to the Assembly Chamber after?"

"I'd tell her Lilia knows how to work the machine,"

Taigan said, "that she is the Worldbreaker, and she needs to take us upstairs. You'd have the room secured by then, surely."

"What if I didn't know how?" Lilia asked.

"*Especially* if you didn't," Taigan said. He leaned toward her. "You know what that angry murderer is doing right now, with the moments that Para is in the sky ticking away? She is throwing jistas into those machines, all four of them, and frantically trying to murder that fifth temple. Her moments are numbered. She knows it. If you and I come in the front of the temple, she will meet us, and I will get us to the Assembly Chamber. I relish the challenge."

"You're very confident," Lilia said.

"I'm always confident," Taigan said.

Maralah said something to him in Saiduan. He snapped back at her. The air tensed for a moment, and Lilia waved her hands at them. "Let's not!" Lilia said. "We need to mobilize very, very quickly. Are we all aligned with this plan? If we do this, it *must* happen tonight."

"It still needs some refining," Kadaan said, from beside Roh. "Too much relies on… I'm sorry, Taigan, but we all know how you are. And we know very little about how many people are in this temple. She could have that chamber warded, and if so, there's no way we could enter, by wink or anything else."

"I agree this is mad," Maralah said, "but Lilia is right. We lose our window when Para winks out. But it's a good reminder that we need two of everyone. There's too much that could go wrong. You best go find out about this game of spheres, and make sure two of you know it! I'm going to get us a few more jistas. We still need a tirajista."

"I think I have one," Lilia said. If Salifa had lived. If any of the jistas from her camp had lived.

"And another in reserve," Taigan said. "This isn't your first turn with an impossible attack, bird. And we know how those turn out."

Heat rose in her face, but she said nothing, and Taigan did not continue.

"All right," Maralah said. "I need to go make sure these can eat. Kadaan, let's see if we can get ourselves some of those sheep."

The room cleared. Taigan lingered, munching on his tuber. Lilia stared at her messy drawings in the soot. Her dirty fingers.

"You have failed at how many assaults now, bird?" he said brightly.

"Go soak your head, Taigan."

"Let's count them," he said, and held out a finger. "There was the harbor, of course. Where you lost the wall and burned yourself out, despite my admonitions." He held out a second finger. "There was Kuallina. Ah, Kuallina! What a delightfully absurd mess that was, on all levels, when you lost your little Gian and–"

"Shut up, Taigan."

He held out a third finger. "And of course, you lost your little regiment of rebels in the woods. To a dead man, no less! That is still something extraordinary, let me say. This plan is overly complicated *and you know it*. You're relying on too much good luck, and we all know your history of luck."

Lilia pounded the table with her fist. "Enough!"

"Oh my," Taigan said, pressing a hand to his chest. "Did

I strike a nerve? Was it the dead man? Or Gian?"

"I know what I'm doing this time."

"You know what you're doing even less this time. You know why you keep failing?"

"You aren't very successful yourself."

"It's because you are so driven by your own desires. Finding your mother, first." He rolled his eyes. "A fool's chase that was. She never wanted you to find her, and for good reason. And when she was dead, what was it then? It was getting revenge on the Tai Mora, certainly, but we both know it's Kirana you really want. To hurt her as you have been hurt. To destroy her as you've been destroyed."

Lilia seethed. "Why are you here, if I'm such a self-destructive failure?"

He shrugged. "What else do I have to do?"

"You could go annoy someone else. Destroy someone else's life."

"Me? I did not destroy your life." He rose and popped the last of the tuber into his mouth. Wiped his hands on his tunic. "Never forget, bird," he said, "*you* chose to come with *me*. You chose to sit at the table with Kirana and your little girlfriend, oh yes, I heard about that. You chose to keep antagonizing the Tai Mora forces, instead of retreating a year ago. No one made those choices for you."

He sauntered back out the door, leaving her in the charred kitchen, alone, with the smell of burnt hair and bits of crumbling sod falling from the ceiling. She dropped her head to her chest, and her eyes filled with tears. She was so tired.

"Hey, what you doing? You still in there?" Zezili called from the door.

Lilia wiped at her face. "I just need a few minutes."

"The sky isn't waiting on any of us," Zezili said.

"Get out!" Lilia yelled.

Zezili grinned. "Look at you! All right, all right. But I can't go far so hurry the fuck up." She went back outside.

From the kitchen window, Lilia watched Zezili alight on top of the fence that held in three or four dogs, easy as breathing. Saradyn shuffled past the fence, yelling something at Zezili. He raised his head and peered inside. When he spotted Lilia he made a sign at her, something obscene or profane, and yelled, "Impostor!" in Dorinah.

Lilia grimaced and moved away from the window. She hated Zezili in that moment. Hated her easy confidence and health, her seeming detachment from everything around them. She had died once, hadn't she? She had nothing to fear from death. But Lilia feared everything. Because Taigan was right. She had done nothing but fail from the very beginning. Failed her mother. Failed at the harbor. Failed Ahkio and Yisaoh, failed Meyna. Failed the refugees from Dorinah.

This time, she always vowed, every time, *this time it will be different.*

But she knew, knew it in her bones, that as long as she kept making the same choices, nothing would change at all.

34

Ahkio had waited years to see his sister again.

Beside him, as they waited for their audience with the Empress of the Tai Mora, Caisa was wringing her hands, her eyes questioning his decision for the thousandth time, but she was loyal, so loyal, and he didn't feel he deserved it.

He did not deserve it.

But here he was.

He hadn't told Liaro what he hoped to do. Liaro only wanted to live. Liaro didn't understand Ahkio's sister.

An omajista led Ahkio upstairs. "What about Caisa?" he asked.

"She'll wait," the omajista said. "We've confirmed your prisoner is who you said she is. You can join her upstairs and wait with the Empress, but this one stays with us, for now."

Some of the color drained from Caisa's face.

"I really insist–" Ahkio said.

"Move," the omajista said, and pushed him. Ahkio gazed back at Caisa. His stomach churned. Caisa began to weep.

Had he made a mistake?

The omajista sat him down in the Assembly Chamber to wait. Everything in the chamber was different. Piles of books and papers, and jistas, so many jistas, and Dhai slaves and running feet. He had not seen the temple so bustling in his entire lifetime. Kirana had done this. She had always been a better leader. Yisaoh sat at the other end of the table, her steely gaze fixed on him, hands bound, two Tai Mora guards beside her, and a sinajista, though by all accounts Yisaoh was ungifted. She simply inspired caution in people. He knew that better than anyone.

"Fucking traitor," she muttered.

Kirana entered the Assembly Chamber from the stairs, which he had not expected. He stood. She came up the steps and regarded him, and he didn't know what to think of her. This woman, this warmonger, this mass murderer, was not the sister he knew, though she shared her face.

Her gaze did not seek his, though. She crossed the room to Yisaoh. As Kirana moved, he tried to see something in her that he remembered. He sought some shadow of his sister there, in her face, her walk. But this Kirana's walk was bolder. Her eyes flat and black: no mirth, no kindness. She had the gaze of a predator.

Kirana took hold of Yisaoh's chin. Yisaoh spat at her. Kirana laughed and stroked Yisaoh's cheek. Released her. "She is a good likeness," Kirana said, rounding on him. "How do I know this isn't some lookalike? We all thought you dead, Ahkio. I caught them fishing your fucking body parts out of the sewer dregs."

Ahkio shivered. "I have no memory of that."

"I bet," she said. "Sina is risen, and Para and Tira now too, so I suppose miracles are possible. But so is treachery."

"I've brought you who you wanted."

"I admit I wasn't certain you would come," Kirana said, "after all this time." She gestured at the soldiers beside

Yisaoh, and they advanced and took hold of Yisaoh and dragged her back down the stairs. Yisaoh tried to bite Kirana as she passed, but Kirana paid her no mind. "You promised me Yisaoh at Kuallina, and never delivered her."

"You tyrant!" Yisaoh yelled. "And you, Ahkio, you Sina-cursed traitor! Sina will burn you for this. Oma will crush your bones!" She continued shouting as they took her down the hall.

"I have no memory of that either," Ahkio said, turning back to Kirana. "But I've heard that, yes."

"If you are truly the same Ahkio, I wonder why it is you brought her here now, finally. Did it take you this long to consider my proposition?"

"I've been changed," he said. "I have heard people say it. I'm not the same man. Maybe that is true. Maybe I'm some construct. But I've been shaped by what's happened since then. I want peace, Kirana. And the sister I knew would keep her word when it came to peace. I don't know how much of that Kirana is within you, but it's my dearest hope that this war is over. We can work together to build something better. We don't need to be enemies any longer."

"I can't believe you would forgive what's been done," Kirana said. "I wouldn't."

"We are very different," he said. "I see what continuing down this road will do to us. To you, and to me, and the people I still lead. We simply want you to release the people you have here, and let us all go. You never have to see any of us again."

"We need the slaves here," Kirana said, "for another season yet."

"Then let us work as equals, not slaves."

"And murder us all in our beds? No. I am not a fool, Ahkio. Not like you. Tell me, what were you all doing out there, trying to run away?"

"To build a new life, yes. Catori Meyna and I were working with the Saiduan to find peace. I wanted to ensure they would be safe on those boats before I came to you, but… then you arrived. What I want to know is how you got word we would be there."

"Magic," Kirana said. "I'm sure you can appreciate that."

"I want to stop all of this," he said. "It's gone on too long and I can't watch any more of my people die. I can be the person who holds out their hand to you. All you have to do is take it."

Ahkio held out his hand. It trembled, just a bit, and he worked hard to still it.

Kirana stared at his proffered hand. "I don't remember peace," she said. "The world was dying from the time I was born. I knew what had to be done."

"I understand," Ahkio said.

"Do you?" she said. "No, you couldn't. You don't know what it is to have a world dying around you, and your family trapped on the other side. You don't know what it is to have to become everything you despise to save your people. You don't know–"

"On the contrary," Ahkio said. "I know very well what it is to compromise one's principles. I know about difficult choices. I am here, Kirana. I've betrayed my own people to give you want you want. I've sacrificed one of my own so you can save your wife, your Yisaoh. And in return, a family has lost a daughter, a sister, a lover, here. Take my hand, Kirana. Please. Let's end this."

35

Kirana saw his hand shaking, and she knew it was with fear. In that moment, she admired him: this simple, naive young man who was clearly much braver than her own brother had been. She stared at his burned hands, wondering what he had done to them on this world, in his time. She was caught, again, in that terrible limbo between this reality and the other, one world and the next.

"Let me tell you about my brother," Kirana said, and he lowered his hand a fraction. "You know what I did to my brother? I used him as a pawn. I sacrificed him in front of your birth mother, Nasaka, so she could see how serious I was in my intentions. My own mother does not know that. Nor does our Nasaka, because of course, I had to kill her very early in the conflict. She was scheming and far too powerful, just like yours."

Ahkio pulled his hand away. "I suspected you had something very awful over her."

"Oh, she wanted power," Kirana said. "Make no mistake. But she did try to protect you, and that's more than I've done, on my world or this one. There was no path to peace, here, for your people and mine. Only the end of your people. Always."

"There is time to change your mind," he said. "While we are alive, there is always time, Kirana."

Kirana felt a tug toward him. Ahkio had always been so naive, but his naivety was honestly touching. She took a step forward and gently took his hand.

His palms were soft, just like her Ahkio, but unlike her true brother, he bore terrible scars on the fingers, knuckles, his wrists – every part of his hands that had been exposed as he tried to drag his mother from a burning building. There would have been no way to save her brother, to bring him here and pretend he was another, because it was impossible to replicate those scars. She knew. She had tried, with several of her captives, to see if they could do it correctly.

Kirana drew him into an embrace, and she held her brother, this version of her brother, tightly against her. He was taller and thinner than her. She pressed her face to his shoulder and took in the scent of him; that, too, was the same. He was very beautiful, in this world and the next, in all of them.

"I'm sorry," she said.

He did not ask for what. There were legions of things she could be sorry about. But she was sorriest for what she was apologizing for now.

Kirana drew away from him. She kissed his forehead and pushed his hair back from his eyes. What he saw in her gaze, she did not know. She hoped he saw grief, remorse.

"I'm sorry," she said again. She slipped the utility knife from the sheath at her side and jabbed it neatly into his neck, piercing the carotid artery.

His eyes bulged. He grabbed at the wound, reflexively

trying to stopper the gout of blood. It usually took a few minutes to bleed out, but he was thin, weak, starving, and his knees buckled and he collapsed in her arms in less than a minute, eyes still wide, lips moving, but making no sound.

Kirana gently pulled him to the ground, staying with him until his gaping ceased and the hopeful flicker in his eyes went out.

She still stood there when Yivsa came back up the stairs and paused in the door. The others, too, had ceased their work to stare at her. One of the Dhai servants was crying softly. The others were very still, perhaps shocked. Many had known her brother.

"There is nothing I will not do," she said, raising her voice for them all to hear, "to ensure our survival here. Don't ever doubt that."

She wiped her bloody palms on Ahkio's body and stood. "Yivsa?"

Yivsa cleared her throat and came forward. "It's done," she said.

"I need to see the body."

"I thought–"

"I have to see it."

Yivsa led her to one of the small libraries on the floor below. Yisaoh's body lay inert on the floor, throat still tangled with a garroting wire. Her eyes bulged, staring blankly. Her tongue lolled, just touching the stone floor.

Kirana got down on one knee beside her and checked her pulse, to be sure. She had no more times for mistakes. There were any number of people she could kill, whole worlds, but this killing she had known she could not do herself. Killing Tasia, even, a child not of her own womb, but of her heart, had been easier than Yisaoh, who *was* her heart.

"Where's Oravan?"

"Below, working to power the engines. All the omajistas are engaged."

"Well, I need to unengage him. Come with me." She pointed at one of the soldiers preparing to move Yisaoh's body. "There's another upstairs," Kirana said. "I want them both prepared properly."

She and Yivsa hurried down the stairs, down and down. Kirana's heart thumped loudly in her chest. She tried to keep her breathing even. She was so close. So very close. As she came down into the foyer, she realized she didn't even care if they could power these blasted temples or not. With Yisaoh, *her* Yisaoh, by her side, she could keep fighting them for two more decades. She would find the strength.

They passed through the basements and into the great cavern with the fibrous tree roots. The moment she stepped down into the room, the air shifted. Became dense as milk. She took a deep breath and forged on. Muted sounds came from the engine chamber below: the voices of her jistas and stargazers.

Kirana went down the ladder, Yivsa just behind her, and had to shield her eyes from the light. The four pedestals around the central one each held a jista captured in a massive beam of light the same color as the satellite they channeled. The central pillar glowed green, and four of her stargazers and two more jistas conferred over it.

Oravan saw Kirana and rushed over to her.

"What happened?" Kirana asked.

"As soon as they stepped in, it…" Oravan gestured. "It won't let them go."

"Well, I hope they're hydrated," Kirana said. "Have Gian's people seen this?"

"I'm afraid so," Oravan said. "She sent observers to each temple."

Kirana waved a hand. "What have you tried to get them out?"

"Everything. It burns anyone who tries. Masis had the flesh burned off his whole right hand."

"Well, he doesn't need a hand to chart the stars," Kirana said. "The central pillar?"

"I… Suari would have been the best–"

"Suari isn't here."

"Perhaps one of Gian's–"

"You don't want to do it?"

Oravan winced.

"It's fine," Kirana said. "I need a wink to Yisaoh and our people there. We're bringing them all home. There are another half dozen jistas there you can throw into the machine."

"What's a good staging area?" Oravan asked. "I recommend the Sanctuary."

They walked back up to the main floor together and gathered in the Sanctuary. Yivsa closed the doors and guarded them.

"Open the wink," Kirana said.

The air between them parted.

On the other side, another omajista waited. Kirana confirmed the day's password with her and stepped through. Yivsa accompanied her, and told the omajista they were conducting the final retreat. The toxic air smelled of sulfur, and made her cough.

Kirana found Yisaoh in the great hold kitchen, regaling two sinajistas and a fighter with a story of how she had once broken another soldier's skull after a particularly gruesome battle in the early days, before she and Kirana were married, before Kirana deemed it far too dangerous for Yisaoh to continue soldiering, especially under Kirana's command. Too many understood that Yisaoh was Kirana's weakness; Yisaoh could be used against her.

"What's the news?" Yisaoh asked as Kirana came in.

Kirana grinned. She could not help it. "You're coming home with me today," she said. "We're all going home."

Yisaoh clapped her hands and spread wide her arms. They embraced. "All of us?" Yisaoh said.

"All of us," Kirana said. "Let's go see the children."

They walked hand in hand back to the open wink. Kirana gave orders for the others to follow. She gave one last look back at the old, dying world, and squeezed Yisaoh's hand.

Yisaoh did not look back, and it was one reason Kirana loved her so.

Kirana held her breath and stepped through, holding tightly to her Yisaoh. She would not be separated again.

And then they were through the wink and standing on the other side back in the Sanctuary, both whole.

"I told you," Kirana said. "I told you. I promised."

"You did," Yisaoh said. "You did." She began to tremble, as if cold or frightened. Kirana rubbed her wife's arms.

"Food, tea, and a bath," Kirana said softly. "That will cure anything."

Kirana wanted to leap and shout and show her around the temple, but she saw the shock and exhaustion on Yisaoh's face. She needed rest. The other soldiers began to come through, all the jistas and fighters Kirana had left to guard Yisaoh. Even in her rush of pleasure at having Yisaoh at her side, she could not help but also be grateful to see her forces surge again. She needed those jistas for the work ahead.

After baths and food and being reunited with the children, Kirana took them all up to the big bedroom behind the Assembly Chamber and drew the curtains. They all piled into bed, the whole family reunited at last.

"I can't believe we're all here," Yisaoh said. Tasia lay her head onto Yisaoh's stomach, and was asleep almost immediately. Corina and Moira curled up with one another at the center of the bed. Corina's fingers were tangled in Yisaoh's hair.

Kirana lay next to Yisaoh and stared at her face, absently stroking her forehead. "I'm sorry it took so long," she said.

Yisaoh knit her brows. "Did you… was it you who…?"

"No," Kirana said. And that was why she had not done it, because she knew Yisaoh would ask, and she would not be able to lie to her. "But it's done."

Yisaoh's eyes filled. Her eyelids fluttered, and the tears wet her face like dew.

"Hush," Kirana said. "We're safe now. All of us. Every one. They can never separate us again."

Through the seam of the curtains, the light of the pulsing satellites danced across the floor.

36

Aaldia was a country of games. Anavha knew that well, but he had not expected this particular game to play such an important part in the end of the world. As the dusk settled, he walked out the back porch and had the other jistas form a circle. The night was cool, lit by the spinning satellites and triad of moons.

Anavha raised his arms and carefully spun up the twinkling illusion that was the game of sphere. Hundreds of orbs twinkled to life in front of them. A whirling collection of spinning spheres formed in a myriad of colors. The smallest was no larger than his thumbnail, the largest as big as his head.

"We move to the center," Anavha said, gesturing for Lilia and Luna.

Both gaped at the game. Lilia recovered first and said. "You... They just have this map, the same one each time?"

"Not always the same," Anavha said. "There are different end states."

The three of them moved to the center of the spinning orbs, which moved lazily along their elliptical orbits.

"Did it look like this?" Anavha asked. "What you saw in the temple?"

"Something like this," Lilia said. "What's the purpose of the game?"

"Each projected sphere is called a door," Anavha said. "Now you will see a second set of pieces come up." He gestured, and a sparkling net of additional spheres joined the first. Two hundred different pieces then, total. "These are the board pieces," he said. "The goal is to match the doors and the pieces."

"But…" Luna said. "There's… I'm not seeing a difference between the board pieces and the door pieces."

"This is the math part," Anavha said. "It has to do with geometry, and where they sit on the board."

Lilia followed a series of spheres along their path. "A three-dimensional game board, then?"

"Exactly," Anavha said.

"How many ways are there to play?" she asked.

"What do you mean?"

"The doors and pieces… I have an idea of what the end game for that would be. Pairing like and like. Other worlds and their people, maybe. But what else? How else do you win?"

Anavha considered that. "Well, there are other ways to play it, but they aren't very sporting."

"Teach me those ways," Lilia said.

Anavha said, "I'm not sure–"

"Teach me," Lilia said. "Luna, are you taking notes?"

"I… yes. This is just very similar to something I know."

"What?" Lilia asked.

Luna shook her head. "I'll tell you later."

"Then let's begin."

Anavha made a sweeping motion with his left arm, and

all the board pieces furled toward him and collected in a great sphere above his head. He moved his right arm in the opposite direction, and the door pieces joined them, all whirling together in the massive sphere.

"What was that?" Lilia asked. "What you just did?"

"Oh, that was nothing," Anavha said. "That just resets the game."

The twinkling spheres blinked back into their orbits.

It was a beautiful little game. Anavha loved it.

Three hours later, her mind spinning with glowing orbs and violet light, Lilia announced that she was done, and they could delay no longer. She had lost the game sixteen out of eighteen times. Namia had fallen asleep on the porch behind her.

"We don't have time to go again," Lilia said, gazing at the moons as they began their descent.

Luna shivered. The winking orrery went out.

Saradyn and Roh still sat outside with them on the soft grass; Saradyn snoring like a great bear, Roh nodding in and out of sleep.

Lilia wished for sleep, but knew she didn't have time for it. Two days, Luna had said, maybe a bit more, maybe a bit less. How far had Kirana gotten already? Had she gotten into the fifth temple? Convinced the keepers to make one of her jistas a guide and worldbreaker? All she had to go on was this game and its various outcomes. Pull in the spheres, remake them, reshape them, put pieces back into the worlds they belonged. There had only been two hundred pieces here, though, and her memory of the orrery was that there were far more. And if they represented worlds, all these many versions of the worlds all colliding together… there could very well be millions. Trillions. She did not say that out loud, but it made her head ache: a pulsing pain behind her left eye.

Anavha yawned. She didn't want to pause their plan for sleep, but realized it would be safer if he, at least, did so before opening a gate. Too much relied on the gates.

Meyna had bedded down all of the Dhai in the surrounding fields, and a few scouts with flame fly lanterns kept watch on the hills around the farm. The Saiduan had claimed the barn, since there were fewer of them.

But a few other Dhai were still up, and one came over to Lilia, catching her before she went inside.

"Li?" Salifa said.

"Ah!" Lilia said. "You're alive! I'm sorry. It's been–"

"I know," Salifa said. "I wanted to say I was sorry I didn't go with you."

"It was my fault," Lilia said. "I was embarrassed to tell you all that I burned out. And the rest, well… Meyna does not like me, does not like the white ribbons–"

"I heard you need a jista."

"I do," Lilia said.

Salifa touched the ribbon at her throat. "Avosta won't speak to you. He says he hates you now. Harina never came back, and Mihina–"

"Salifa, I'm not asking you to go with us. Death is–"

"I know," Salifa said. "What I'm telling you is, they all died to get us here. It's foolish for me not to help now, here at the end."

Tears wet Lilia's cheeks. She wiped at them.

Namia yawned on the porch, rolled over, and came over

to her, crooning to comfort her.

"It's all right," Lilia said. "Thank you, Salifa. Two hours? Come inside and I'll have Maralah show you how this works."

Lilia walked in and introduced Salifa to Maralah. "A tirajista," Lilia said. "Could you show her?"

"You show her," Maralah said, turning her back on Lilia.

Lilia sighed and went over the diagram with Salifa. "When we are in, this is where you will be. Me and Zezili, here. Taigan, that annoying sanisi, here. Maralah here. Anavha. And Kadaan, the Saiduan man, there."

Salifa nodded. "If we don't survive this," she said, "I hope Sina takes our souls and does something very useful with them."

"Me too," Lilia said.

A scuffle from the hall caught her attention. Anavha leaned against the doorframe leading back to the bedrooms. "I'm afraid," he said.

Lilia went back outside and woke Roh and Saradyn. "Roh, can you and Saradyn sleep in the room with Anavha?" Lilia asked. "There are six good rooms here, and three beds."

When she went back into the house, she found Taigan already asleep in one of the back bedrooms, breathing contentedly, as if he didn't have a care in the world. Lilia noted that he slept with his boots on though.

She entered his room. His eyes snapped open.

"Two hours," Lilia said.

He grunted and rolled over.

When she returned, Salifa had gone, and Maralah stood over the kitchen table with Kadaan. They had wiped away the old diagrams and sketched out new ones. Roh skipped over to them on a little puff of Para's breath. Said something to them in Saiduan. Lilia could not help smiling at seeing him use his gift again.

"You have everything sorted?" Lilia asked.

"You have a tirajista?" Maralah countered.

"I can have Salifa," Lilia said.

"That's only one tirajista," Maralah said. "We need two."

"That's what we have," Lilia said. "Anavha helped me send word to my contact in the temple earlier. My contact will meet you inside, in the Assembly Chamber, when the moons set."

"That's in two hours," Maralah said.

"That's what I said. We're out of time," Lilia said. "Kirana is ahead of us."

Roh said, "We can trust your contact?"

"Yes. She's the one who's given me all the information I have from Oma's Temple so far."

"I'm worried about how fast this needs to happen," Roh said.

"We have one chance," Lilia said. "If we don't take it now, we lose it forever. Or at least for the length of our own lives."

"I think we should wait," Maralah said. "Roh is right. We are all tired. Tired people make mistakes."

"We have to get our people into that fifth temple before Kirana does," Lilia said. "If her people end up taking those places… I don't know that we'll be able to get them out."

"We know so little," Maralah muttered.

"It's more than Kirana knows," Lilia said.

"You can't guarantee that," Roh said.

"I'm willing to take this risk," Lilia said. "I'm going to walk in the front with Taigan to buy you some time. With Kirana sleeping in the Kai quarters, surrounded by jistas... she could murder you all coming out of the wink in that Assembly Chamber. We have to call her down below. A distraction that rouses the whole temple. A spectacle."

"We need sleep," Maralah said.

"Then sleep," Lilia said, turning away so she didn't have to see Maralah's face. "Two hours."

Roh came after her. "Li, listen."

"I need to sleep," Lilia said. She paused at the door of the room she was going to share with Namia and Zezili.

"Maralah made a good–"

"We go in two hours or we don't go," Lilia said. "Those are the choices."

"That's garbage, Li," he said. "There are more than two choices. It's not all good or evil, this or that. We have the power to find other choices. If I learned nothing else in Saiduan, it was that. I... You don't know what happened there. How I lived, and others... It was very bad. I thought I had two choices, always, but there were more than that, always. And I... made mistakes. Don't make those mistakes."

"I'm not going to make any more mistakes," Lilia said, and closed the door.

37

Lilia woke with the light of the swirling satellites in her eyes, peeping in through the window of the bed she slept in. They had not winked out in the two hours she had tried to sleep.

It was Namia who woke her. "Going?" Namia signed.

"No," Lilia said. "You're staying here. I told you that." She heard Maralah, Roh and Kadaan already awake and conferring in the kitchen, in Saiduan. She hated it when they spoke Saiduan together because she knew so little of it.

Zezili lay beside her, not asleep but staring at the ceiling.

"Do you sleep at all?" Lilia asked.

"No," Zezili said. "I don't think so. I never feel tired. It was nice to just sit here for a minute, I guess."

Lilia went to the rear bedroom and woke up Taigan. "It's time."

"It's not even light."

"That's the point."

He grumbled, but got out of bed.

Lilia found Saradyn and Anavha asleep in another room, and got them up as well. She sent Namia out to round up the other jistas and fighters they needed. When Lilia saw

Salifa with them, she dared to have a little hope.

"Thank you," Lilia said.

Salifa inclined her head. "It's an honor, Li."

Lilia counted them all up, and Maralah confirmed it.

"Are you worried what Meyna will do when you're gone?" Roh asked. "That maybe she will... I don't know."

"I don't care," Lilia said. "It's always been about this, about striking back. Either we come back victorious, or we die trying. Either way, what comes after is up to Meyna, not me. I want no part in it."

Roh raised his brows, but said nothing.

"Anavha?" Lilia said. "You take Maralah first. Roh and Kadaan next." She doubted he could do two gates at once, and she wanted to keep things simple.

Anavha took a deep breath. Closed his eyes.

The gate wavered just outside, through the open back door.

Maralah muttered something in Saiduan. Taigan laughed.

"One last great adventure," Taigan said, in Dhai.

Lilia thought she should give some speech, something beautiful and a little melancholy, but she was too tired. Whatever was going to happen was going to happen. She had to keep moving forward.

Maralah stepped through the gate and onto the plateau, and set the world on fire.

38

Roh stood in the woodland behind Oma's Temple, Kadaan at his side. Anavha shivered behind them, though he was wrapped in a large dog-hair coat. Saradyn had insisted on coming, though Roh could not think of anything in particular he could help them with. Intimidation, maybe. An extra fighting arm. Though Roh knew that if it came to close combat, they would have already failed. With only one chance, though, Lilia and Maralah had insisted on many redundancies.

"You didn't have to come," Roh said to Kadaan in Saiduan.

"You needed a parajista."

"We had a number of other parajistas," Roh said softly. They were waiting for the spread of Maralah's fire to wake up the temple and distract the Tai Mora. Lilia had wanted them to move immediately, but Maralah urged them to wait for the temple to light up. From here, the top of the temple appeared very far away.

Roh held out his hand. "After, I'd like–"

"Let's not talk about after," Kadaan said. "We go forward."

Roh watched the top of the temple again. Lights began

to flicker in the long series of slanted windows that marked corridors and foyers. Flame-fly lanterns roused to wakefulness.

"Another few minutes," Kadaan said. "If we move too quickly, they'll still be close enough to reach us."

"Are you ready, Anavha?" Roh asked in Dorinah.

He nodded.

Kadaan was the more skilled parajista, so he pulled Para first, weaving an intricate web using the Song of Davaar and the Song of the Wind. Roh held out his hand for Anavha. Saradyn grimaced, but came forward, and Kadaan wrapped them all into the blue mist of Para's embrace.

Anavha closed his eyes and began to tremble. He wouldn't be able to see the threads of Para any more than Roh could see Anavha using Oma's.

Roh sent a second thread of Para's power across the vast distance, tying it off at the crenulation that marked the end edge of the glass over the Assembly Chamber.

Then they were flying, weightless, with alarming speed. Anavha held onto Roh. Saradyn gaped at the ground as it disappeared beneath them.

"Wonderful!" Saradyn yelled in Dorinah.

Roh kept his gaze on the temple, looking for defensive threads of Para's power. On the other side of the temple, over the plateau, a great bloom of blue mist crackled. Roh felt the wind it generated, and pulled Para to try to counteract it, but Kadaan hissed at him.

"Don't do that again," Kadaan said. "I have it."

They alighted on the slippery glass of the Assembly Chamber. As Kadaan released his spell, Roh called a focused tornado of air and smashed through the ceiling while also damping the sound of the crash of glass. It was eerily silent.

Kadaan swung down first, weaving a defensive wall spell as he leapt.

Saradyn went next, landing heavily on the table at the center of the room. Roh stuck his head further in, trying to see who was inside. Kadaan held the defensive wall in place; someone was yelling. Roh heard it through the defense.

"Stay here," Roh told Anavha. "I don't want to risk you."

"I don't want to be here alone," Anavha whispered.

"I'm right down here!" Roh said. He sent a whirl of Para's breath below him to break his fall, and landed softly on the table.

Kadaan held a shimmering defensive wall around the table, pressing back a single woman who was nearly crushed against the far wall. Roh thought it was supposed to be empty, though.

"Where are Lilia and Taigan?" Roh asked.

Saradyn pointed at the door to the chamber. Smoke swirled under it from the stairwell.

"What's burning?" Kadaan said.

39

Taigan stepped through the gate and onto the plateau outside Oma's Temple. The garrison there was already on fire, a great billowing blaze that was quickly consuming the whole plateau, sending bits of charred grass into the sky that trickled onto the woodland below. More blazes would begin, burning out more of the Tai Mora. That pleased him.

"Remember," Lilia said, huffing behind him, "we need to be enough of a distraction to get that chamber clear. If Anavha's wink draws all the jistas here up there, and if Kirana is still there–"

"Oh, fear not," Taigan said. "My distraction will be much more… dramatic."

The fire had also drawn away the guards at the stone bridge leading to the temple. They were halfway to the garrison already.

Taigan strode ahead of Lilia and Zezili, straight for the bridge, already spinning a powerful song to surprise the guards on the other side. He went across the bridge without pausing for them to catch up, though Zezili kept harping at him in Dorinah.

Lilia wanted to distract these people, to cut them off

from their stars and hobble them, to buy Anavha and Roh and the others time in the rooms above. But Taigan had other ideas. Hobbling was not enough. Not nearly enough.

The guards inside the temple reached immediately for their respective stars, and six more guards came in behind him from the gardens, shocked at his passing. Taigan cut the jistas off neatly from their stars and immobilized the regular guards with an easy binding song.

"I have a gift for your Empress," Taigan said as Zezili caught up to him.

"The fuck are you doing?" Zezili said in Dorinah.

He pretended not to understand her.

"She has gotten a good many gifts lately," the older jista said. "What makes yours special?"

"Do you want to risk angering her now, so close to the end?"

"You can wait in the gaol."

"We can wait where the guests wait," Taigan said. "Where is that?"

Lilia finally came through the doorway, breathing hard. She narrowed her eyes at Taigan.

"Guests wait here," the jista said.

Taigan flicked his wrist, and snapped every bone in her body. She fell to the floor like a broken puppet.

Lilia gasped. "Taigan!"

He set the rest of the guards on fire. They screamed.

Zezili grabbed his shoulder. "What–"

Taigan immobilized her in a neat net of Oma's breath, spinning a little prison around her to keep her out of his way. She hung just above the floor, spitting and yelling.

"What are you doing? This isn't the plan!" Lilia said.

Taigan shrugged. "These people murdered my entire country," he said. "I didn't think I was terribly upset about it until just this moment."

"But… what did you tell me about revenge? This is–"

"I am very bad at taking my own advice," he said, and burned up the next wave of soldiers and jistas coming down the stairs. He set everything on fire that would burn: the tables and chairs in the banquet hall. The doors. The drapes. The occasional wooden or otherwise organic panel. The carvings on the stairs. The portraits.

Lilia choked and gasped behind him, but he had come here to satisfy a very deep craving, and he was far from being sated.

He took the stairs two at a time, burning Tai Mora and Dhai without distinction. It simply did not matter to him. He paused on the third floor, far ahead of Lilia, and sent a tendril of Oma's breath back down to pick her up. She yelled.

Taigan set her down beside him.

"Murder me too," she gasped. "Just get it over with. Is that what you're here for?"

"Not at all," Taigan said, as the black smoke crept up the stairs. "But if we fail at this little venture, and bird, you have a divine history of failure, I want to ensure I murder as many of these people as I can before the end."

He kept climbing, sending fire down every corridor, extinguishing the lives of every breathing inhabitant his star's power could unearth. He marveled that there appeared to be no omajistas in the temple; without one, there were none who could counter him.

"Kirana was as rash as you!" Taigan called down to

Lilia. She had paused halfway up the fourth flight of stairs, huffing for breath.

Ah. The smoke, of course. He considered leaving her. Certainly, she knew how to operate the device, but so did Luna. Taigan smirked at that. All this time, he had been searching for a worldbreaker, scouring one continent after another for the right person, for some chosen one, when it turned out all they'd had to do was *train* one. Oh, the irony. The years of wasted shit and toil.

"She must have all her omajistas engaged in the temple!" he yelled down again.

Could she hear him at all? Who knew? She was surely drowning, gasping for breath, her vision no doubt tunneling out. Oh well.

He turned away to go up the final stair to the Assembly Chamber. How long it had been since he stood there, trying to convince these foolish pacifists that this was all coming, that this was how it would all end.

"None of you listened!" he yelled at Lilia again, but he could not see her anymore. With everyone and everything burning around him, he had no audience to appreciate his work.

Taigan sent a purl of Oma's breath back for her, tapping along to the rhythm of the crackling flames as he waited for her arrival.

The body he brought up was limp, barely breathing, but alive. He focused his power on her bruised and battered lungs. He eased the smothering inflammation and repaired the oxygen-starved tissue. It was all just so much easier with Oma risen. He felt like the most powerful person in the world.

Lilia gasped and sat up. She clutched at her chest. Stared at Taigan.

"Just this way," he said brightly, holding out his hand.

"You're monstrous," she said.

"I never pretended to be anything else. We are a lovely group of monsters, Lilia, you and me and that construct you call Zezili. One has to be monstrous to do what we are about to do."

He released the tangle of Oma's breath that held Zezili immobile in the foyer, assuming that she had yet to die, or that his resurrection of Lilia had also affected her. A curious binding, that one.

Taigan was proven correct as he pushed open the door to the Assembly Chamber and Zezili came barreling up the stairs, yelling at him, hardly winded.

"Did you even look back?" Zezili shouted.

He waved at her. "Good of you to join us. So much confusion down there!"

"Fuck you, you fucking–"

He came up against the parajista barrier inside the door and called to Kadaan, "Would you let us pass? There's a great deal of burning down here." All of them appeared to be intact, inside: Anavha and Roh, Kadaan and Saradyn. A strange group of companions, no matter what the sky was doing.

"Thanks to *you*," Zezili said.

"You're welcome," Taigan said.

"Saradyn," Roh said. "Grab her and keep her quiet when we drop the barrier."

Saradyn lumbered to the other side of the room where a woman was pressed against the wall by the barrier.

Taigan had not anticipated her being there. He sighed. "Oh dear."

Lilia put a hand to her mouth, clearly recognizing Gian immediately.

The barrier dropped.

Lilia was exhausted, her chest still sore. She wanted to murder Taigan where he stood, but when she saw Gian on the other side of the room, she forgot it all for one brilliant moment.

She would know Gian's face anywhere. The woman who had taken her out to Fasia's Point on a vain quest to find Lilia's mother. And again, a different Gian but always the same Gian, in her memory: the Gian whose leg she had mended, whose hair she had brushed and braided, the Gian who loved her when she was no one, nothing, just a filthy, stinking scullery girl. Gian, the lovely face in the dark.

Gian, the one she had lost because of her own terrible choices.

Even as she was overcome, Saradyn picked Gian up and wrapped a big hand around her throat.

"Don't kill her!" Lilia cried. "Wait, just. Let me think." Her breath came quickly. "Let her be, just a moment, I–"

"Anavha!" Kadaan said. "It's time. Lilia! Get back here!"

Anavha raised his hands.

Smoke still poured in from the stairwell and escaped through the shattered hole in the ceiling.

Roh said, "Lilia, come in. I need to block that smoke."

Anavha's gate winked into existence. The others jumped through the wink above the table: Maralah first, then Luna, Salifa and the rest.

Salifa immediately ran up to Lilia, white ribbons streaming from her hair. "Are you all right? What's–"

"Go!" Lilia said, pointing back at the table. "Get in place. I can handle this."

Salifa winced and retreated.

Taigan chuckled. "She isn't even the right Gian, bird."

"Shut your face!" Lilia said. Her hands trembled. The memories tore over her. Gian's face as she gagged and fell over at the table they had shared while trying to parley with Kirana, so long ago, at Kuallina. The spray of black bile. Gian convulsing, another dead Gian. All dead.

"Not this one!" Lilia said firmly. "Not. One. More."

Taigan was right. This was another of her overly complicated plans. This wasn't going to work. She had put them all in danger. She was failing them, just like she had failed Gian. How many more would she sacrifice because she just wanted… to win? To be *right*?

Gian stared at her, wide-eyed. Lilia crept toward her, hesitant.

"You know me?" Lilia asked.

"I do," Gian said softly.

"Don't scream," Lilia said, "or this big man will harm you. I won't stop him."

Gian nodded again.

Lilia said to Saradyn, in Dorinah, "Release her, all right? Just loosen your grip so she can talk."

Roh called to the others, "Make a circle here around the table. Lilia! We need you and Saradyn! Let her be!"

"How do you know me?" Lilia asked.

"I know your face," Gian rasped, "as it seems you know mine. Some other you, though. She died."

"Most versions of me seem to," Lilia said. She remembered gasping in the foyer and blacking out, left to die for the millionth time by Taigan.

"And me?" Gian asked.

"You've died a lot too," Lilia said. "I'm very tired of watching you die."

Lilia turned back to the others, who had made a circle around the table.

"Let her go, Saradyn," Lilia said.

Saradyn grunted, said to Roh, "You say?"

"Lilia, she'll tell them–" Roh sputtered.

"They can't follow us," Lilia said. "They don't have a Guide or a Kai."

"Fine," Roh said. "Do as she says. Just... take that woman's sword. *Lilia*, hurry!"

Saradyn took Gian's sword and shoved her back against the wall, knocking the breath from her.

Lilia made her way to the circle, and stood between Salifa and Taigan.

"Hold hands!" Roh said.

Taigan smirked and took Lilia's hand on one side, Luna's on the other. "Are we going to sing religious songs now?"

"All right," Roh said. "Everyone step onto the ring into the floor, on my mark. Now." Roh stepped onto the circle of temple flesh in the floor. The others followed. Lilia felt the warmth of the temple's beating heart beneath her feet.

Nothing happened.

For a long moment no one said anything.

"Well," Taigan said, "I'm glad I murdered as many of them as possible. This was certainly an excit–"

They fell through the floor.

40

A banging on the door. Kirana shifted in her sleep, pushing away sticky dreams. Shouting. She roused herself and sat bolt upright. Threw off her coverlet. Why did she feel so woozy? Her head ached. Was that the smell of smoke?

Yisaoh wiped at her eyes. "What is it?"

"I don't know."

The door opened.

Kirana let loose her infused weapon. It snapped out of her wrist. She pushed herself up. The flame fly lanterns came alive at all the movement and noise.

Gian stood in the door, panting, one hand pressed against her chest as if she'd been knocked about. "A bunch of Dhai came up here," she said. "They just came in through the ceiling in the Assembly Chamber and dropped through the floor."

"And… you're alive?"

"There's… a girl with them. I… knew her, in some other life. She was weak. That's our one advantage. She said only a… Guide, or a Kai could follow them? Does that make any sense to you?"

"Where's Yivsa?"

"I have no idea. I was alone in the chamber."

"What were you doing in *there*?" Kirana released her weapon and tugged on her trousers.

"The children–" Yisaoh said, getting out of bed.

"Stay with them," Kirana said. The noise had woken Tasia. She was already calling to them from the adjoining room. Kirana rounded on Gian again. "What do you mean, you were the only one there?"

"There wasn't any other guard. Someone called them away. There's something happening downstairs."

"Madness," Kirana muttered.

When she was dressed, she rushed into the chamber. Broken glass littered the table; a gaping hole had opened in the ceiling. How had she not heard that?

"What...?"

"They used sound barriers," Gian said. "They had at least one, maybe two parajistas with them. You wouldn't have heard anything, but you might have a headache from all the air pressure. It blocked the smoke, too."

"Where the fuck is everyone?" Kirana muttered. Smoke poured in from the stairwell. "What did they burn?"

"Everything, I think," Gian said. "The fire has cut us off. They'll need to clear it out before we can get reinforcements up here."

"We need to leave immediately. Yisaoh! Bring the children!" Kirana darted back into her office.

The children were bleary-eyed and whining. Kirana took Tasia into her arms. Yisaoh took Corina and Moira by the hands.

"I need you to stay close," Kirana said. "There's a fire, you understand?"

"Don't try the stairs," Gian said. "I can get us out."

"You?"

"I have some skill with Para," Gian said. "We can go out the way the others came in." She pointed at the ceiling.

Kirana exchanged a look with Yisaoh. Smoke continued to fill the chamber.

Gian said, "We are bound, Kirana. Murdering you risks me as well. You wanted to be allies. This is something allies do."

Kirana took Yisaoh's hand, and Gian bundled them all up into a puff of air and sent them flying through the tear in the ceiling. The children shrieked, and Kirana held onto them.

Gian brought the group back down on the plateau, just in front of the bridge leading to the temple. The plateau, too, was burning, though the blaze there had been contained to the garrison. Kirana noted a number of parajistas working along the edges of the blaze to contain it.

Gian alighted next to them.

Kirana found Yivsa organizing those fleeing the temple, and asked what had happened.

"A breach," Yivsa said. "Some omajista."

"Far more than that," Yisaoh said. "The Assembly Chamber was breached. Parajistas."

"Fuck," Yivsa said. "The omajista was a fucking distraction."

"The basement. Is Oravan still–"

"Yes, Empress, they've remained at their posts. The fire was contained to the upper floors."

"I need my wife and children moved."

"Of course. We're re-housing key personnel at Para's Temple."

"Good, fine. Do we have an omajista?"

"Oravan has a wink waiting, here. We sent three people up for you."

"None of them made it," Kirana said. "I want to know what happened to my guards. The Assembly Chamber door was open, and six guards missing."

"We'll look into it immediately, but it's highly likely they were drawn downstairs when the fires started, and the omajista… Well, there are a lot of bodies."

"I don't care what other issues we had to deal with," Kirana said. "The security of this temple was paramount."

"Yes, Empress."

Kirana seethed, but knew that yelling at Yivsa in the middle of the crisis wasn't going to solve anything.

She got her family off to Para's Temple, and made Yivsa personally escort them to safety. Kirana, for her part, lingered behind with Gian.

When her family was gone, Kirana said, "What were you doing up there?"

"I'd come to see you," Gian said, "but all the guards were gone. I even knocked at that chamber door. It was already open. They must have had someone on the inside."

Kirana narrowed her eyes. "What did you want to discuss?"

The double helix of the suns was just beginning to rise, washing the eastern mountains in a warm red glow.

"Progress on the People's Temple."

"In the middle of the night?"

"I thought you'd be up."

Kirana peered at her, but could detect no deception.

"We're close," Kirana said, shifting her attention back to

the rising suns. "If the Dhai infiltrated the temple, it will have something to do with that. How did they... ah, the boy. He sank himself through the floor here. I wonder..."

"I'll need to gather my people," Gian said. "I left them waiting in the gardens."

"Better that than the banquet hall," Kirana said, and grimaced again at the smoke rising from the shimmering temple.

She went to the ring on the floor, the raised bit of the temple's flesh.

"Yivsa?" Kirana asked, toeing the smooth surface. "Where did that soldier put my brother's body?"

41

Lilia fell heavily down and back, tweaking her left leg. She howled. Pain ran up her knee and through her hip like a dagger. The air was damp. She pushed against the spongy floor, trying to get her bearings. A thin film of water covered the ground, soaking into her clothes. She bumped into someone else in the darkness.

"Light?" Roh's voice. "Maralah?"

A flicker of orange light brightened the immediate area. Lilia had a sense of a great deal of space, but all she could see in the ball of flame in Maralah's palm was the outer edges of their group, all tumbled around inside a large greenish circle on the floor that mirrored the one in the Assembly Chamber. The reek of rot and damp permeated everything. Lilia wrinkled her nose.

"Is this it?" Maralah asked, clearly disappointed.

"Raise the light higher," Lilia said.

Maralah released the ball of flame, and it floated above her, three, four, six more paces, then doubled in size, tripled, until its light finally reached the shadowy walls that enclosed them, if not the great bones of the ceiling.

Lilia gaped. It was not like the other temples. This chamber was at least four times the size, and each of the compass points had a circle on the floor like the one they stood within. Massive ribbed columns stretched from the circumference of the walls all the way to the center of the room, where they dipped beneath a massive pool of water and twisted up again, winding around a giant dais that glistened with damp and something more substantive, alive? The floor was off-kilter, and liquid pooled on the other side of the room; the drip of water sounded all around them. The air tasted stale.

She stared at the floor. It pulsed beneath her, moist and blue-black, pebbled with tiny bumps like the papillae on a tongue. Lilia walked out of the circle, following the downward tilt of the floor toward one of the columns that looked more like a fibrous band of muscle in this light. As she left the circle, the whole room began to glow. She gasped and froze.

"Don't move!" Roh said.

A blue band of light appeared at the edges of the floor and the ceiling. The muscular colonnades gave off a faint green glow, and the floor sprang to life, a roiling field of deep crimson so dark it was almost black. Above them, the ceiling seemed to move. The great eye of Oma appeared there, illuminating what had been hidden: the ceiling here mirrored the ceiling in the Assembly Chamber, only on a much grander scale. The blinking eye of Oma shed light onto a glistening raised platform. The rest of the ceiling came alive: blue Para, over another dais; green Tira; and purple Sina, its light bleeding across another pedestal. Twinkling stars speckled the ceiling, glowing faint blue and red and white. As Lilia watched, they began to move, orbiting around the top of the chamber.

"It's like it's… like we woke it up," Lilia said.

Roh slowly came after her, stepping gingerly on the spongy floor. "It matches the drawings," Roh said.

"You have any idea where to start?" she asked. "We don't have much time. I… Everyone, get into the places with the right symbols!"

Luna trailed after Lilia, quiet as a ghost. The others fanned out across the squelching floor, examining the strange architecture.

Roh snatched at Lilia's sleeve. "Li," he blurted. "Oma's Temple said something to me, when we came through the floor."

"It talks to you?"

"It said you were going to destroy them, the temples. That you were here to ruin everything. Is that true?"

"No. I'm here to turn back the Tai Mora and close the ways between the worlds. That's all. That's our plan. Whatever you're hearing… I don't know what gave it that idea." But what he said made her doubt herself. Was she going to do something wrong? Maybe it *was* best he didn't give her the other options.

Roh said, "Maybe… maybe we should have Luna operate the mechanism instead. You said the Worldbreaker could be either of you, anyone who could learn."

"It's been decided, Roh, and planned. I'm not changing it. The temple was wrong. I know what I'm doing."

Roh met her look for a breath, then turned away. "There should be marks for the jistas," he said, limping over to one of the knobby pedestals. "Here they are. Sinajista here. Maralah?"

Kadaan said, "I want to make sure we have defenses up.

If they come down through the floor like we did–"

"I don't think they can," Roh said, "not without a Kai or a Guide. But there are certainly other ways they could get in, too. It's entirely possible we're underwater now, and they'll pierce the dome here and swamp us. It's likely they came to Fasia's Point because it's the closest land mass to the temple mark on the map."

Lilia stood at the edge of the pool of water surrounding the central dais. Luna came up beside her.

"That's not easy to get up on," Luna said.

"Let alone stay on," Lilia said. The dais was easily as high as her shoulder. Had people been taller in the past?

"Maybe it was meant for giants, or Saiduan," Luna said.

"Well, they have *us*."

Maralah went to the dais marked with the sinajista sign and wrinkled her nose. The dais bloomed, opening like a flower and revealing great red petals. She sniffed at it. "Smells like apples. What kind of device is this, really?"

"I don't know," Lilia said. "I don't need to. I just need it to work."

Kadaan said, "There's something wrong."

"What?" Lilia asked.

He still stood in the circle, one hand raised. "I can feel something... here. There's a good deal of power."

"Let's bring more," Lilia said. "Salifa, you're there. The one with Tira's mark."

Salifa tentatively approached another pedestal, which glowed brilliant green and unfurled long, slithering green tentacles that wrapped the base of it. "Is this... safe?" Salifa ventured.

"We'll find out," Lilia said. She was still eying the large

pedestal over the water. "Roh, can you just… use Para to get me up there?"

"Yes," he said. "Ready?"

She nodded. An invisible twist of air circled Lilia's waist and propelled her to the top of the dais. Roh set her down carefully, but she still stumbled, and went to one knee. The pedestal was warm beneath her hand, and had the same smooth texture as the skin of the temples. But it did nothing when she touched it.

"Everyone get in place!" Lilia called.

Maralah said, "You had best be ready. Once we are locked into this, there's no going back."

"I've been ready my whole life," Lilia said.

Maralah stepped up into the center of the petaled dais, and raised her hand. The air thickened.

A searing jet of purple mist enveloped her. Her body went rigid, back arched, mouth agape, as the mist suspended her six paces above the dais.

The others recoiled, and Lilia had to direct them. "Salifa, Kadaan, Anavha! It's time!"

Kadaan exchanged one last look with Roh. "Hold the defensive wall?"

"I have it," Roh said.

Kadaan stepped onto Para's dais as it purled open, revealing slick blue leaves that trembled as he stepped onto them. Blue mist engulfed him, and he, too, became caught in the whirlwind of power, rising from his place.

Salifa closed her eyes and stepped up onto her pedestal. Pulled on Tira. Lilia held her breath, fascinated to see the multicolored breath of all the satellites herself for the first time.

Zezili shouted at the fighters, instructing them to take up defensive positions around the outer circle of pillars.

"Anavha!" Roh said. "We need you to step in, Anavha."

Anavha trembled as he approached Oma's dais, a great black knobby thing that began oozing red fluid, thick as mud, as he came forward.

"I can't!" Anavha said.

Roh called to Saradyn. "Help him!"

Saradyn took Anavha by the waist and hauled him up onto the dais. Anavha shrieked, but settled onto it, exchanging another look with Roh.

"You can do this," Roh said.

Anavha closed his eyes. Raised his hand. Oma's crimson breath swirled up from the bottom of the pedestal and blanketed him.

Lilia waited, expecting something to happen to her dais, but nothing did. "What are we doing wrong?" she called to Luna.

"We need the Key," Luna said. "Taigan? Do you see it?"

Taigan stood just outside the ring of columns, frowning. "I see what looks like a very uncomfortable cage," he said.

The position for the Key was a twisted white structure that bisected the room, floor to ceiling, just behind where Lilia stood. It looked like a great tendon with a body-sized gap at the center.

"Taigan," Lilia said, "you're the last one. You want to burn them all up? This is how to do it."

"Who's to say I couldn't just go back and–"

"Taigan! Please!"

He shrugged and sauntered over to the great quivering mass of the web.

The air trembled. Lilia felt a deep groaning beneath her, as if the whole room were shifting.

"What is that?" Zezili yelled.

The circle on the floor they had come through glowed a brilliant green.

"Oh no," Roh said, "someone's coming through."

"Hold the line!" Zezili called.

Lilia screamed, "Taigan!"

Taigan heaved a great sigh, and climbed up into the great gory cage. The moment he stepped inside, a burst of brilliance emanated from the other pedestals, blinding Lilia.

The dais beneath her heaved like a ship at sea. Her stomach churned. And then something in her – she could not say what it was, or where it had been – something within her opened, some vital connection that had long been burned closed.

She gasped.

Taigan's clothes and hair were instantly incinerated. His body – the flesh, the tendon, muscle, bone – burst into a fine red mist that spun around in the chamber, coagulating together into a fiery red eye of blood.

Lilia's stomach heaved. The blood rippled, became flesh, great gobs of it roiling and flexing like sticky cheese. His body was trying to remake itself.

The gobs of flesh burst again, imploded back into the red eye, the gory mist. A blinding white light pierced through the organic cloud of ephemera that had once been Taigan as the form began to flush with new skin again, roiling and bubbling with half-formed, inhuman shapes before breaking again under the incredible power being drawn from all five temples.

The light shuddered through the great tendon and through the water all around Lilia, crawling up her dais as she began to rise from it, as if caught up by the hand of a god.

She spread her arms, and light burst from her fingertips, flooding the room. All around her, a massive shifting orrery bloomed, bursting into being as if it had been there all along, and she had simply not been equipped to see it. She found herself floating inside a multicolored sphere of power, and struggled to stay upright.

The game, the game, how to start the game?

She raised her left hand and concentrated on the nearest sphere, a great red orb. It hummed through the air and floated just above her palm. When she gripped it, her fingers found purchase. It was solid. She thought she would see her reflection in its shimmering surface, but no – instead she saw great armies, all marching toward the center of the world. She recoiled. Released the sphere. It floated back into the whirling orrery.

"I don't think I need the piece!" Lilia called down at Zezili. "It's responding without that symbol! I can do this myself!"

Her attention was so fixed on the spheres that she heard Zezili's voice only dimly.

"They're here! They're sending more! Defenses up?"

Lilia felt a little smile creep across her face. "Let them come," she whispered, and called on more power.

Her shadow fell across Luna, below, who trembled.

42

Kirana brought them all together in the Assembly Chamber – Gian and her jistas, Yivsa and twenty of her best soldiers. She had one of the stargazers, Talahina, there as well. She wanted a scholar with them, just in case. She had two of her own omajistas, Mysa and Shova, standing side by side. The smell of smoke still permeated the air. Much of the temple's interior still burned, but had been contained by four very exhausted parajistas. She had called them all from the coast, winking them here quickly from their failed attempts to smother the People's Temple.

Yivsa poured a large jar of Kirana's brother's mud-thick blood onto the ring in the floor. The ring of flesh glowed softly blue, just as it had done when the boy, Roh, had stepped into it and disappeared through the floor as he held the book.

"Let's see what we can do," Kirana said. "Yivsa, take Mysa and Shova with you and ready your weapons. Gian, we'll wait until they are in place and open a wink to us from… wherever this goes. I don't want to risk this entrance for all of us. You said they had twenty people?"

Gian nodded. "I had time to count them. They joined

hands and stepped onto that circle. They will no doubt have defenses in place."

"Then let's prepare to break their defenses," Kirana said. "Remember, we don't care about who they have in the niches, those four jistas. They will be locked in until this ends. We want to control the center."

"Who will operate it?" Gian asked.

"I will," Kirana said. "We know enough to do the minimum. Close the ways between the worlds. The rest, we can do in time. In thirty hours, this will be over, one way or another."

Yivsa raised her hand. "You heard her. Mysa, Shova, to me, one on either side of the circle." She gave orders to the others, and then they stretched out their hands and clasped them.

Yivsa stepped onto the glowing blue ring. The others followed.

Kirana took a breath. Nothing happened.

"Maybe it doesn't respond to him?" Gian said.

"He's yours, temple," Kirana muttered. "Fucking take him."

And Yivsa and the others sank through the floor.

Kirana smiled. Those remaining in the chamber shifted uncomfortably. One of Gian's little parajistas gasped.

"Now what?" Gian asked.

"We wait," Kirana said.

The air shuddered a moment later. A wink opened just above the Assembly Chamber table, and brilliant white light poured into the room.

Kirana recoiled.

On the other side, Yivsa yelled at her to come through.

"They're already in place! We need to overwhelm them!"

Gian strode through first, much to Kirana's annoyance. Kirana didn't want her to take some fatal blow so early in the day.

A hot wind emanated from the wink. Kirana waited for Gian's parajistas to put up defenses, then stepped through with her tirajistas beside her.

Mysa and Shova had both opened winks. The second wink looked out onto the sandy peninsula where Monshara's soldiers waited to reinforce them.

Kirana stumbled on the sloping floor. Yivsa held out a hand, but Kirana ignored it, transfixed by the flaming figure at the center of the room. She knew exactly who it was, the ghost of a girl who had come to her before Kuallina, and sat her down later over a poisoned meal, the little rebel girl all the Dhai proclaimed the next Faith Ahya, their prophet-god.

"Can you hold…" Kirana shouted at Yivsa as a great rumbling shook the chamber. The floor tilted and heaved. The temple itself moaned. Water began to bubble up from the floor's lowest side. Were they… sinking? Had the temple shifted off the sand bar?

A great ball of light rolled off Lilia, hurtling itself toward Kirana.

"Fuck," Kirana said.

Zezili kept low; there were too many jistas in the room and too much power. What she needed were more projectile weapons to distract the jistas. The tangled defenses and offenses were mostly parajista and sinajista, air and fire, and the best defense against both was to wait for a gap in their casts. She saw Kirana immediately, and barked, "Her! That's the one! Kill the head and the beast dies!"

A blast of heat crackled, burning up three fighters and one of the jistas.

Zezili came up quickly, hunched over, yelling at her people to close the line.

Something thudded into her shoulder. She went down.

Shocked, winded, Zezili looked around, sword raised. People were coming through the second wink, the one that opened onto the plateau. She recognized the man with the bow immediately. Natanial. That fucking fuck.

Behind him, waving through more jistas, was Monshara. Oh, Monshara, how long ago that acquaintance had been. And here Monshara was, still fighting for these awful people.

Zezili pushed herself up. Fuck them. Fuck Natanial. She heaved herself toward him, breaking the line.

Kirana surged into the air, brought aloft by a spinning rainbow of powerful light. She whirled toward the central pedestal and the burning figure of the girl there.

The girl's face was a bitter rictus. "I want to murder you!"

"Do it then!" Kirana shouted. "You'll murder yourself, too. Did you forget that? Forget you're one of us? Kill me, and you kill yourself, and you kill your little friend Gian too. Did you see her? Fallen from the sky, far tougher than that little nymph you brought to the table. Send us all back to our dead world, and you'll be there with us, hacking your guts out."

Invisible bands of power constricted Kirana's body. She gasped.

"Not the Tai Mora," Lilia said. "Not all of us. Just you, Kirana. Just. You."

"Gian and I are… bound…" Kirana gasped. "Kill me… you kill her too… How many… more times… will you… kill her?"

"I want to murder you!"

"Do it. Do it, you coward!"

"I want you to suffer as my mother suffered."

"No one can suffer that much."

Lilia screamed.

Natanial let loose another arrow; it slammed just below the first into Zezili's left shoulder. She kept coming, like an angry bear. He backed up; she was too close now. He shouldered his bow and pulled his sword.

Zezili tackled him. They both went over. Behind her, her lines of fighters broke, one after another, in the face of overwhelming offenses. Monshara and Natanial had brought a fucking army with them. Far more than Lilia or her Saiduan had ever anticipated.

Natanial's hands found her throat. Her grip found his as well. They lay locked like that, grunting and gasping, splashing around on the cold floor.

A knife of cold fire went through Zezili's body. She gaped. Natanial punched her, and she went over.

Zezili gazed up to see Monshara standing over her with a great infused weapon, eyes blazing.

"Wait!" Zezili said.

A massive cracking filled the room, and water from the lower end of the temple rushed in, faster and faster as the temple continued to plunge deeper into the sea. Water began to pour from the ceiling. How far under were they already? Death by Monshara's hand, or the sea's?

Death on all sides.

Lilia was aware of Gian breaking through the defenses. Roh had fallen. The shield of air lay broken. Gian's forces were already attacking Anavha and Kadaan, trying to loosen them from their pedestals.

Saradyn was the last defense around Roh, and Gian cut through him like his raging, bearish body was nothing. She was fast, determined. Her hair had come undone, and blew back across her face; Gian, my Gian, Lilia thought. No, no, she is just another Gian. Who Gian could have been, in another world. I destroyed my Gian. I destroyed them all.

"Lilia!" Gian yelled. She came to the edge of the water and raised her weapon. "Don't do this! There's another solution. We can–"

"You're a liar! You're all liars! She's taken everything!"

"Lilia!"

Lilia screamed, and squeezed.

Kirana's back bent, her mouth open in a silent cry. Blood burst from Kirana's eyes and nose, splattered her mouth.

Gian crumpled like a puppet with a cut string. Tumbled into a heap on the floor. Water rushed over her body, growing deeper and deeper.

Lilia sobbed and released Kirana. She fell into the water surrounding the pedestal, floating face down, not so much as a bubble of breath escaping her lungs. Blood sank swiftly through the water in whirling tendrils.

The temple shuddered again.

Lilia released the wave of power, the same way she used to release Oma's breath. But the orrery still whirled around them, locked into orbit, waiting for someone to break the world. Or perhaps put it back together again. Was that possible? Lilia thought. Was that ever possible?

Her heart hurt. She saw Zezili flopping around on the floor like a breathless fish. Lilia sank to her knees. Luna, just behind her, shouted, "Lilia! Lilia, you haven't stopped it yet!"

Lilia gazed at the bodies of Gian and Kirana. She cried, great gasping sobs that racked her body.

Behind her, Luna waded across the water and began to climb up the pedestal. Luna, breathless, pulled hirself onto the dais and took Lilia by the shoulders. "Lilia? You hear me? We aren't done."

"I'm done," Lilia sobbed. "I'm done."

"We're not here for revenge," Luna said. "We're here to save the worlds."

Lilia got to her feet, shakily. The chamber heaved again. Kirana's people rushed to her body. Someone raised a bow, notched an arrow.

"Let them," Lilia said. She raised her arms. "Go ahead!"

Light suffused the platform again, a burst of power so great it blew Lilia off the pedestal and into the water below. She gasped and paddled, crawling up beside Kirana's body. Gazed up.

Luna drew deeply on the mass of energy, body shivering with power. Luna began drawing globes together; they crashed and sparked.

Lilia sobbed. What came after closing the ways between the worlds? Nothing. No future, for her or for any of them.

She pushed over Kirana's body and stared into her bloody face.

"You did all of this," Lilia said. "Now you and I are done."

Several of the Tai Mora came to the edge of the water, weapons pointed at Lilia. Lilia pulled Kirana's head into her lap. "Let us alone," she said.

There was a stir behind them as the orbs crackled overhead. Something... else was coming through the wink.

Great, golden-skinned figures with wasp-like waists and bulging green eyes tottered through the wink. Lilia had a long moment of dissonance, unable to comprehend what she was seeing. The figures walked on four legs, and they were tall, so tall, like giants! A woman rode through after them on a chariot pulled by two more of the figures, her eyes blazing, a misty whirlwind of power making the air around her shimmer like a soap bubble.

"No!" Lilia yelled.

Lilia had killed Kirana. She had murdered her. The body, here... Lilia held Kirana's head, gazed into the sightless eyes, and raised her gaze to meet the piercing stare of this new version, this more powerful version, whose terrible soldiers were tearing apart Lilia's companions and the Tai Mora with equal relish.

By killing this Kirana, all Lilia had done was free another to take her place.

A man rode the great chariot behind this new Kirana. He stepped off as it came to a halt a few paces from the pedestal.

"Suari!" this new Kirana said. "Get that one off the dais! Keep the others in place! I want control over this!"

This Kirana spoke accented Dhai, not Tai Mora.

Lilia gaped at her, but this Kirana paid her hardly a glance. A sneer at the body of the dead Kirana, but no more. Her forces were intent on controlling the device.

What did I do? Lilia thought. What terrible thing did I do? She had killed this Kirana... only to unleash another one. A darker one. Opening the way again and again to another Kirana...

Oh no. Oh no...

A wave of fire rolled toward her. She shrieked, knocked back into the water. She splashed around, and finally crawled out the other side.

Suari was riding a wave of power to the top of the dais. He knocked Luna off with a great burst of fire. Luna fell, landing hard on the stones. Lilia heard the crack of Luna's skull. Saw the blood.

Lilia struggled out of the water, crawling toward Roh and Saradyn. The gleaming orrery shivered, waiting for another worldbreaker to operate it.

Not me, Lilia thought. It was never me. *I chose wrong.*

She got to her feet just as a passing Tai Mora swung her blade, catching Lilia in the side. Lilia gasped, stumbled. Blood bloomed from her belly.

43

Roh's defenses burst. He lost his hold on Para and slid across the wet floor. Three arrows seethed through the broken defenses and sank into his guts. He rolled over, gasping. A wave of Tai Mora came at him. Saradyn roared and positioned himself in front of Roh, shielding him. The orbs of the orrery shimmered and danced in the room, obscuring his view, causing confusion and chaos. The trickling sound of water had become a constant stream, the mutter of multiple waterfalls. The water rose around him.

A wave of chittering figures burst forth from the wink that opened onto the plateau. Saradyn roared and threw himself at the figures. They hissed and broke around him, as if fearful or in thrall to him. He laughed, a great guffaw.

Saradyn grabbed Roh by the arm and hauled him up. Blood wept from Roh's guts. Pain made him woozy.

"The circle," Roh said. He looked back to where Lilia sat, weeping. "Get Lilia. I can go a while on my own."

The wasp-waisted figures continued to ignore him and Saradyn. Saradyn kept hold of Roh's arm, dragging him painfully through the water.

Saradyn looped another arm under Lilia's. Roh noted

her wound. Gave one last look to the pedestals where Kadaan, Maralah, Anavha and Taigan were locked into the device. Luna's crumpled body was just visible on the other side of the main pedestal. The man this new Kirana had called Suari stood atop the pedestal, hand outstretched to the new Kirana.

Saradyn got them within six paces of the great green circle on the floor before an ax took him in the back. He went over, dropping them both.

Roh fumbled at the arrows in his guts. Snapped off the ends of them, and took Lilia by the collar.

"What did I do?" Lilia cried. "What did–"

Roh dragged Lilia back into the circle where they had arrived while the temple heaved around them. The stones groaned. Water continued to rise all around them. It was as deep as his shins now, rushing up faster and faster.

Roh took Lilia by the shoulders and shook her. "Listen to me! Would you listen? I told you."

"I didn't… I did the right–"

"You did the *selfish* thing," he said. "Don't you understand yet, Li? There's always another monster, another and another, behind them. You kill them, you become them, you lose everything you ever cared for." He was crying too, remembering what he had done to the Patron of Saiduan, and the path that had brought him here. All the selfish, terrible choices. "We made poor choices, Li. We are terrible, selfish people. We aren't Dhai at all."

Another surge of water rolled over them. Lilia gasped and spit water. Roh's knees weakened. He sank to the floor, arms wrapped around Lilia.

He closed his eyes. "I need to go back," he said. "Please,

back to Oma's Temple. Not the Assembly Chamber... somewhere we can hide... please, can you do that, keeper? Can you hear me at all?"

Nothing. No voice. No help. After all this time, all this work getting them here, and they were going to let them die?

"Temple keeper!" Roh said. "You made me your Guide. We're dying! We're going to–"

The floor swallowed them.

Darkness.

An absence of pain. Relief. Oma, he was so relieved, he was nothing but a wave of warm emotions.

My Guide.

"We failed," Roh said, or thought he said, because all was blackness and he could not feel his body.

Everyone does, my Guide. Perhaps we always choose wrong.

"You don't," Roh said. "We do."

Always the same choices.

"Give us another chance."

I can't do that. I'm just a beast.

"We can make better choices."

It's not your choice, the temple said. *It's hers.*

"Then give her another chance."

You believe in her?

"I always have."

A glimmer in the darkness. Brilliant white light.

44

Lilia gasped and rolled over onto a cold floor, right next to a gaping hole that dropped into a chamber beneath her. Light flickered from below, illuminating the tangled roots that stuffed the chamber. The basements? The temple of Tira? Or Oma? Were they the same?

She felt a weight around her, a heavy… Roh?

Lilia shook him. "Roh, are we–" He did not move. His body was cool. Blood continued to ooze from his wounds.

"No, no, no," Lilia cried. "No, no."

She panicked. Her wound throbbed. She crawled across the floor, working her way toward the tangled roots. They would be looking for her, and for Roh, that other Kirana and her strange soldiers. Lilia needed to hide, needed to get away, needed to tend her wound. How long could she hide here?

She took hold of one of the tree roots and heaved herself up. Blood gushed through her fingers. She felt light-headed, light enough to fly.

Lilia stumbled through the darkness. She got painfully to her feet and hobbled across the floor, winding her way through twining roots. Blood continued to escape her fingers. I'm going to die down here, she thought, I'm going to die here with Roh and Gian and all the rest of them.

A cry came from behind her. The sound of boots on stones. They were looking for her. How had they known where she was? They must have felt the surge of power when they came through from the fifth temple.

This had to be Oma's Temple, didn't it? Why had the temple deposited them here instead of back in the Assembly Chamber where they had come through?

She leaned against a massive root, spitting blood. She tried to ball up her tunic and stem the flow of blood, and her hand wrapped around something, what was... The blood. The little vial of muddy blood from the child, the one Ahkio had raised to Li Kai.

Some old memory tugged at her as she pulled herself under and around root after root. Ahkio had... lost time here. Here, he had said, roots... A stone. Placing his hands against it to call the temple keeper, only to find himself pushed forward in time... while another version of him... went *back*.

Her breathing came loud and fast in her ears. Ahkio had... lost weeks of time, one Ahkio. But another Ahkio had lost only a day. He had gone back a full day.

He had made different choices.

It was at the very bottom of the temple, Ahkio had told them, the obelisk, tangling among heavy roots. Would it work the same way if she placed her hands on it? Push some version of her forward and another, please, Oma, perhaps another version... back? To start again?

To make better choices.

Lilia choked on a desperate sob. How foolish to even consider some future, when she was very likely to die in a few minutes.

All she had now, as her life dripped along the floor, was this. Ahkio could have been lying about everything. He was probably an impostor. But as she bled out, the story he had told kept her moving, kept her breathing, kept her searching for the broken stone of time.

It is hope that keeps us going, she thought, sliding around in the darkness in her own blood. Everything looked the same. So many shadows.

The shouting grew closer. She saw the light of a flame-fly lantern. They must have found the trail of blood. Black spots danced before her vision. She caught herself on one of the roots, leaned over it with all her weight, trying to stem the flow of blood. One foot. Another foot.

We are all stories, she thought dimly, *moved by stories, pushed forward. We have to believe we can live. We have to believe there are choices. May your…* what was the old Dhai proverb? *May your choices be shaped by your hopes, not your fears.* She felt the rage and despair bubble up in her again. She had been ruled by fear. She had murdered everyone she ever loved. Roh was right. She had not fought monsters. She had become one.

The lights behind her gave her enough light to see just ahead.

A large broken stone lay on its side; it had settled there in the twisting mass of rocks. If nothing else, she thought it looked like a nice grave marker. A good place to rest. She was sweating heavily. Her palms were slick.

She pushed herself through the tangle of roots. Lilia crawled the rest of the distance to the stone, watching the blood leave her body. Nausea overcame her. She dry heaved.

I put my hands on the stone, Ahkio had said. *I went back a day.* What a stupid story. What a mad thing.

But he was Kai, had been Kai.

Lilia pressed her hands to the cold stone. It stayed firm. She laughed, and coughed up a little blood. She set her cheek against the stone. Blood.

More shouting, nearer now. Again. Someone was hacking at the tree roots. She lay on her back as the blood pumped from her body.

Lilia dug into her pocket. Fumbled at the little vial of blood. She twisted at the cap. Her hands were so weak. So very weak. The cap popped off. Rolled next to her.

Lilia pressed two fingers into the gooey blood.

A lantern swung overhead.

"Here she is!" someone cried, in Dhai.

Lilia pressed her fingers to the stone.

A chill went through her bones.

The floor rumbled.

I need to go back, Lilia thought, please, *Oma, give me one more chance, like you gave Ahkio.*

And then the world was filled with light.

45

"We've stemmed the assault," Suari said. "We're pursuing the last two, a boy and that girl who was working the orrery."

Kirana Javia Garika, Empress of Dorinah, Queen of the Tai Mora, Captain of the Seven Realms and ruler – finally! – of the known worlds, pressed her hands to the wood of the great Assembly Chamber. She could not keep the smile from her lips. She had achieved her decade-long campaign to defeat her Tai Mora double and usurp her from power over Raisa, and she felt fucking fantastic about it.

She admired how similar this table was to the one she had planned and plotted out this assault from on her own world, so very, very near to this one. Her soldiers worked busily through the temple, assuaging fears and rumor. She didn't know who had burned so much of the temple's interior here, but her allies assured her it was well contained, and the temple secure. She had murdered all of the other Kirana's soldiers inside the fifth temple, keeping her own identity safe, for a time.

"That girl and boy are a problem," Kirana said. "I know them from our side, or one very like her. Lilia, the girl – I want her killed as quickly as possible."

"Could I ask–"

"She always ruins my fucking plans," Kirana said. "I want her body. What about Luna? You got Luna fixed up? Closed the ways? If that's done, we can start handling the next phase of this assault."

"It's already done," Suari said. "I got Luna mended and back on the pedestal. The seams between every world but ours have been closed. We no longer need to worry about assaults from other worlds, but we can still bring our people through. There are instructions on... many other things that can be achieved with that power, though. We are interrogating Luna now. We may find a way to keep Para in the sky for far longer. Unlimited power for decades! All yours."

"Good," Kirana said. "Let's bring up that whole fifth temple again, though. All that quaking very nearly sent it to the bottom of the sea again. Put it out there on the plateau. It will be more stable.."

"Very well," Suari said.

"You did well, Suari," Kirana said.

"Being bound to you," he said, "meant I was also bound to her. That deception worked in our favor. Remarkably well."

"Told you, didn't I? Keep the faith, Suari! Get the rest of those Rhea-worshipping allies of ours into the other temples," she said. "I want to move quickly."

Despite her stated urgency, Kirana did not go immediately to find her own Yisaoh when Suari closed the wink. She still needed to ascertain where the former Kirana's Yisaoh and children were being sheltered, without giving herself away as... well, a different sort of Empress.

She traversed the temple, nodding to those who pressed thumb to forehead, and a little Dhai ran up to remind her that she had agreed to meet her mother for tea in the garden. Her real mother, of course, who had been here all this time, keeping her abreast of her counterpart's plans.

Spies, indeed. This world's Kirana had had no idea of the extent of it.

She met her mother in the garden as the double helix of the suns rose. Her mother peered at her.

Kirana laughed, and used the pass phrase they had agreed upon. "The ways between the worlds are ours."

Her mother clapped her hands and stood. Embraced her. Used her appropriate response: "Happy day! This is so joyful."

What an incredible thing, Kirana thought, to save herself and her own world from… well, herself.

"Mother, it's going to be so grand," Kirana said. "The power, the world. You've done so well. Thank you."

Her mother leaned over and pressed her forehead to Kirana's.

"I am so proud of you," her mother said. "No one else could have done this. No one else could have saved us."

"I did what had to be done," Kirana said. She finished her tea and rose. "I suspect I should announce it to our people here. And I'll need to find where they've hidden their version of Yisaoh and the children."

"I'm sure you'll make short order of it."

As Kirana stepped down from the little raised tea table, the air suddenly became cold, so cold it hurt her bones. She paused. Stared at the sky.

"What is it?" her mother asked.

Kirana grimaced. Her bones knew, knew because she had felt this before, in some other life. Knew because something that she thought had come together was now pulling apart.

"I don't know," Kirana said.

The ground trembled.

And there was light.

46

Lilia gasped. She woke with the light of the swirling satellites in her eyes, peeping in through the window of the bed she slept in: the Aaldian farmhouse. She knew the pane of the window only too well.

She grabbed at her stomach where her wound was, but found her tunic untouched, her skin whole. No blood. No torn clothing. Silence, outside. Then the bark of a dog. A breath of wind. The creaking of the old house.

Namia barrelled into the doorway, signing at her: "Going?"

Lilia's heart pounded hard. Sweat soaked her back. "Namia!" she said, and hugged her close. Namia wriggled from her grasp.

"Going?" Namia signed again.

Lilla stared at the window. Still dark, very dark, the same time she had woken the morning before.

She heard Maralah, Roh and Kadaan already awake and conferring in the kitchen, in Saiduan. Zezili lay beside her, not asleep but staring at the ceiling.

"Are you ready?" Zezili asked. "I never feel tired. It was nice to just sit here for a minute, I guess."

Lilia just lay there, trying to still her racing heart. Namia shook her again.

"Not yet," Lilia said. "Just… sit here with me awhile."

"I'm so bored," Zezili said.

"Go kill something," Lilia said, slipping her shoes on. The floor was cold. "Just… Not a person. And not too far away, obviously."

Zezili sighed.

Lilia went out into the kitchen where Maralah, Roh, and Kadaan stood. Maralah and Roh held cups of hot tea.

"Awake already?" Maralah said.

"I've changed my mind," Lilia said. "Maralah was right. We need the sleep."

"But everyone will be awake, then," Roh said.

"It's all right," Lilia said. "I've learned… I know that there aren't any omajistas in the temple, not in the Assembly Chamber. They've been called away. And if we wait, well… if we wait, there will be even fewer people in the temple, come morning. We can all go in together. We don't need a second distraction."

"When did you learn that?" Maralah asked sharply.

"Trust it," Lilia said. "Taigan and I won't go in by ourselves. We'll come through the gate with the others. I know for certain no one will be there."

Maralah and Kadaan exchanged a look. "This is all very unexpected. Did you have some kind of vision? Or have you lost your nerve?" Maralah asked.

"It could be called a vision, maybe. I just… I have new information. You were right. Anavha needs to sleep. You, the men, all of us. Tired people make mistakes."

"When do we move then?" Maralah said. "You said yourself we're very much out of time."

"Just before noon," Lilia said. "Most people will be going

down to the banquet hall for the noon meal."

"That's… a lot of missing hours, Li," Roh said. "You were so urgent before."

"Please, just… could you trust that I know better? Maralah agreed."

"I agreed that we needed more sleep," Maralah said, "especially Anavha. But another ten hours or more?"

"What do you suggest?" Lilia asked.

"Dawn," Maralah said. "That's another three hours."

"Roh?" Lilia asked. "Kadaan? Do you agree?"

"I'm good with dawn," Kadaan said. "I'm heading back to sleep, then. Roh?"

"In a minute," Roh said.

Maralah shook her head. "You can't go shifting this plan around," she said. "Any more changes–"

"It's going to need to be flexible," Lilia said. "There's so much we don't know."

"To bed again with me, then," Maralah said, eyeing them both one more time before she left.

Roh said, "What happened?"

"I can't… I can't really explain it."

"Try."

"You won't believe it."

"There's a good many things I wouldn't have believed two years ago," he said. "I'd believe them now."

She sat next to him at the table, so they almost touched. Reached for Maralah's abandoned cup of tea. Sipped it. Bitter.

"We lost," she said.

"We seem to do that."

"No, I mean… It was like I'd done it, the whole plan. And it went terribly."

"A dream?"

She rubbed her hand against her stomach, where the wound had been. "I don't think so."

"So, you have a better idea of how to do it this time?"

"I know how to do it differently."

"Did we live? Any of us?"

"No."

"Well," he said, standing. "Whatever we do this time will certainly be better than that."

"What if there's no way out, Roh?" she blurted.

He paused. "What do you mean?"

"What if this is all one big loop, one long cycle, that can't ever be broken? What if we are fools to try?"

"We'd be fools not to," he said.

Lilia fell asleep at the table. It was Zezili who woke her, just before dawn.

"Hey," Zezili said. "Everybody said you delayed the plan?"

Lilia yawned, trying to snatch at her dreams, but she had slept soundly, no echoes or memories.

"That's right," she said. "Be flexible."

Lilia woke Taigan up. He stretched and yawned and stilled as she told him the new plan.

Taigan frowned. "You and I won't go in the front?" he said. "That's so disappointing."

"I'm sure," Lilia said, giving him a long look that only made him shrug. She shivered at the memory of him burning the temple down around them, nearly murdering her on the stair. Taigan, ever the same in his unpredictability.

The others gathered around the table, making tea and

pulling yams and turnips from the coals where they had been roasting since the evening before.

Lilia erased what they had mapped out a few hours earlier and said, "I've had some time to think. I still agree that the fire on the plateau will draw them out and create a distraction. But I don't believe it's necessary for Taigan and me to pull Kirana out. If we wait long enough, she will have left her chamber for the day."

"Probably for the fifth temple, though," Maralah said. "If she beats us to it–"

"We want her to."

"Why?" Roh said.

"Because once her jistas are in place, they're locked into the mechanism. And that also means she can't use them."

"How the fuck do you know that?" Zezili said.

"I have... sources," Lilia said. "All of her jistas are going to be concentrating their power there. She won't be thinking about defense in there because we won't have shown our hand too early. She'll have no idea we're coming."

"We still have to make sure no one is in the Assembly Chamber," Roh said. "It will be busier during the day."

"Not if Kirana is gone," Lilia said.

Maralah shook her head. "We don't know that."

"The Kai's living quarters are there," Roh said. "Her family could be there, and soldiers to guard them–"

"My contact can clear out the soldiers," Lilia said.

"Her family–"

"If they are there, we'll deal with them," Lilia said. "They are the least of our concerns. We still go in through the ceiling. We still step through the circle."

"Are we agreed in this?" Maralah asked.

Lilia held her breath.

Zezili said, "I'll do this whatever way kills the most of them."

Roh leaned over to Anavha, translating.

"How precise can you be?" Lilia asked Anavha. "Could you open a gate right on top of the table? Or right inside the door?"

Anavha considered that. "I could get you onto the table, yes. Or very near it."

"We act quickly," Lilia said. "If we are fast enough, focused enough, they will have no time to counter us. I know that now. I was… overthinking. I'm sorry. Kadaan and Roh go through Anavha's gate first, pushing out a defensive wall to mask the sound and keep others out. The rest of us, we make a circle around the table. There will be a raised green circle beneath it. Step right onto it and hold hands."

Taigan snorted. "And then what, we sing religious songs?"

The phrase sent a knife of fear through Lilia. She thought of the loop again, the possibility that all of this was going to end the same way. "Fast," Lilia said. "No thinking. I want to practice it, right here, around this table. Anavha?"

"Are you serious?" Roh said.

"Yes," Lilia said.

Anavha took them all outside, and opened a gate just above the kitchen table. They ran through the exercise three times. The third time, they were all through and in place in just twenty seconds. Lilia chewed at her fingernail after she finished the count the third time, wondering if that was going to be fast enough. Perhaps, perhaps not.

Surely it would be fast enough to keep Taigan from burning the whole temple down around them. She could hope.

"That's as fast as it's getting," Maralah said. "We're losing time. If someone else gets up on that dais before you–"

"If someone's up there when we get in," Lilia said, "we'll have enough free jistas to knock them off. Our focus is on getting me on that pedestal, no matter the cost."

"And then we close the ways?" Maralah said.

"Yes," Lilia said. She didn't know what else to say, because she had no idea what she was actually going to do this time, knowing precisely what came next.

47

Kirana lay in bed with Yisaoh, absently stroking her temple while the light of the satellites streamed through the windows and the double helix of the suns made their slow bid for dominance of the sky. She wanted to linger much longer, but she already heard the children awake in the next room, laughing. And the sky waited for no one.

She pulled off her coverlet and dressed just as someone knocked at the door and peeked in. A little Dhai servant, come to stoke the fire and set out tea.

"Come in," Kirana said.

"Shall I let in the children?" the Dhai girl asked.

"Give Yisaoh a few more moments to sleep."

"Yes, Empress." The girl set the tea tray on the table at the window and went to tend the banked fire.

Kirana had dreamed of death, of fighting herself in a large dark cavern as it slowly filled with water. She stood at the basin of water on her dresser and peeled off her sweaty shift. Wiped the stale sweat from her chest, under her arms, beneath her breasts. She gazed long at herself in the polished metal mirror, her face so thin and ravaged by worry and hunger that she could have been looking at a stranger. How would she know?

Another knock at the door.

"Yes?"

"Madah has urgent news from the beachhead."

Kirana pulled on her shift again and opened the door. A little Tai Mora page stood there, fairly shaking. "She opened a way into the Assembly Chamber?"

"Yes, Empress."

"Tell her I'll be a moment."

Kirana dressed. Kissed Yisaoh. Yisaoh murmured something, but did not wake.

Kirana went through her office and into the Assembly Chamber where Madah already waited, pacing the room with Mysa Joasta, one of the omajistas Kirana had assigned to her.

"News?" Kirana asked.

"The sand bar has become unstable," Madah said. "I don't suggest we try and brute force our way in any longer. I can move the temple, if you give me a few more jistas, but I'm worried it relies on the sea water. That it breathes it."

"I have a better idea," Kirana said. "I'll have Yivsa bring a gift, one the temple may well recognize."

"The boy's blood?"

"Oravan said it worked downstairs, to wake the temple keeper. They got little out of it, though. Just more nonsense about a guide and a key."

"You think it will recognize you, with his blood?"

"I will make it recognize me," Kirana said. "You have everyone assembled on the beachhead?"

"We're ready."

"Give me a few minutes to prepare. I want Himsa and

Talahina to come with us."

When she had gathered her stargazers, Mysa opened a wink between the temple's Assembly Chamber and the sandbar about fifteen hundred paces from the shoreline where Gian and her jistas waited for them.

"This is quite an undertaking," Gian said.

"I expected nothing less," Kirana said.

The seething leviathan of the temple pulsed so strongly the water rippled around it; the sandbar trembled slightly.

Kirana freed the blood inside her jar and smeared it on her palm. She peered at the gooey creature and smiled grimly. "Let's see what you say now, friend." She pressed her palm to its skin.

A tremor. A sigh.

A seam opened in the side of the leviathan, and a gush of seawater poured out, soaking Kirana's shoes.

"In!" Kirana called to those behind her. "I want to open another wink between this temple and the basement in Oma's Temple so we can communicate with them there. Are the jistas still locked into the other temples?"

"Yes," Madah said. "No change."

Kirana waited for her force of jistas and fighters to enter ahead of her; many were the same trusted people she had left with Yisaoh back on their world. When Kirana finally slipped through the slit in the temple's skin, Talahina was already ordering around the jistas and getting them up onto pedestals. The great cavern sparkled with light; the constellations on the ceiling began to move and shimmer.

Kirana gaped, taking in the measure of the cavern. Her feet splashed in the water beneath her. "An organic machine," she said.

Gian, beside her, said, "Like our ark. Something built, awakened, and left... sleeping, for a time."

"Now we wake it up," Kirana said.

Her parajista stepped onto a glowing blue pedestal and a surge of power bent him nearly double. His mouth opened in a silent scream.

The tirajista and sinajista were next. Talahina conferred with Oravan, and they argued over something.

Kirana came over to them. "What is it?"

"We need someone to go in there, the Key," Oravan said, gesturing to a great white webbing that bisected the cavern. "These last two pieces we were... less certain about. Let's ask Mysa."

"I don't want to risk too many omajistas," Kirana said. "I don't want to get stuck in here."

"Suari would have been–" Talahina began.

"We don't have him," Kirana snapped. "Does it have to be a jista?"

"Yes," Talahina said.

"Gian?" Kirana said. "You have a strong jista?"

Gian frowned. Nodded. She called up three of her people and gave them over to Oravan.

Oravan instructed the first to get up into the webbing and then call on his star.

There was a brilliant flash of white light, then a sound like a burst melon. Bits of flesh and blood, broken bones and gooey viscera, splattered them all as the jista was obliterated by the combined burst of power.

"Well, that... didn't work," Oravan said, staring at the fleshy bits of what was left of the jista.

"Try another until it does work!" Kirana said. "I'm

getting up on that pedestal."

Talahina said, "Are you sure? What if–"

"If anyone's going to break the world, it's me," Kirana said. She climbed up. Once standing there, she wiped her palms on her tunic. Below, Gian looked less than impressed.

"How much of this are you guessing at?" Gian called.

Kirana said, "Have *you* done this before? Make a good suggestion or get out of the way."

A sound behind her. A gasp from the jistas nearby. Oravan swore.

Kirana swung her gaze to the other side of the chamber where a group of around two dozen people were already scrambling to their feet. They had simply… appeared. No wink, no–

She felt the wave of air headed toward her, too late. Kirana tumbled off the pedestal and into the water below.

48

Lilia did not know where or when she lost the little container of Hasao's blood, but she knew the moment she realized the little vial was missing from her tunic pocket. Blood was the key to everything, and it was missing.

She stepped through the wink and into the Assembly Chamber just behind Zezili. Distracted, Lilia squeezed at her pockets even as the others leapt off the table and assembled quickly around it. Kadaan had a wall of air up to shield them; Lilia knew they only had a few precious seconds before someone sensed them here.

"What are you grabbing at?" Zezili asked, helping her down from the table and keeping hold of her hand as they got into place.

"I had… a small jar of blood here, in my pocket."

"Oh," Zezili said, "yes, I ate that. It was terrible, not as good as fresh, but I did feel better."

"You… what?"

"When you came back to bed. I could smell it."

"Step forward!" Roh called.

Lilia and Zezili stepped forward with the others. Lilia pressed her feet to the circle. "This isn't good," Lilia said.

Maralah said, "Ready Songs of Unmaking. I want any

jista in there immediately cut off."

"What's a little old blood, between colleagues?" Zezili said to Lilia.

"No, no, no," Lilia said. She squeezed Zezili's hand. "We can only do this once, now. We can't–"

A cry came from the other side of the room, a familiar one.

"Stop! What are you–"

They began to sink through the floor. Lilia's ears popped as Kadaan dropped his shield. She was aware of someone running up behind her, from the direction of the Kai's old study, but she dared not look back, dared not because she feared it might be Gian and this was all going to go wrong again.

A hand gripped Lilia's collar, yanking her head back.

Lilia had just enough time to realize it was Yisaoh holding her tight, falling in after them, before the light winked out.

Lilia struck the cold, wet floor just as hard the second time as the first. She clawed her way up, hands slick against the tongue-like surface. It was not dark this time, and not empty. Far from it.

The air fairly sparked with power. Her head swam; her vision was dazzled by the blazing lights. All of the jista pedestals were filled, their jistas captured in the twists of power. Beside Lilia, Yisaoh lay on her side, coughing and wheezing.

Kadaan, Maralah and Taigan were already up.

"Songs of Unmaking!" Maralah called, but it was already done. Lilia knew because the two winks leading outside the room went out.

"Luna!" Lilia called.

Luna scrambled after her as she began limping to the great dais at the center of it all.

The figure at the top of the dais flew off and fell into the water below. Lilia had a feeling it was Kirana. Who else would be arrogant enough to get up there? Just Kirana. And Lilia.

"Zezili!" Lilia said. "Watch that woman in the water, but don't kill her! Just make sure she doesn't come after me."

And there was Gian, gaping, surrounded by powerless jistas, all cut off from their stars. Her people raised their weapons.

"Don't! Wait!" Kirana splashed over to them, arms raised, staring at something behind Lilia and Luna.

Lilia turned and saw what Kirana did: Yisaoh, getting to her feet beside them. She looked dazed. This wasn't Lilia's Yisaoh. She could see that immediately. The hair was too short, and she was too thin. Kirana's Yisaoh. Somehow Kirana had gotten her Yisaoh through.

Ahkio, Lilia thought. That traitor.

"Zezili!" Lilia called. "Grab that woman! Grab Yisaoh!"

Zezili came back around and took Yisaoh's arm. Yisaoh punched her; Zezili's face came away grinning and bloody. She twisted Yisaoh's arm behind her, forcing her over. Yisaoh cried out.

"Let her alone!" Kirana said. "Please. You aren't here for her. She's nothing. You're here for me, aren't you?"

The old anger rose in Lilia, the rage that had made her snap this woman's back. Lilia grit her teeth. "Step away from the dais," Lilia said. "Keep your hands above your head. I know you have a weapon there in your wrist. Don't come near me or Zezili will murder Yisaoh, your Yisaoh.

Because you already murdered ours, didn't you?"

"It's the way it is," Kirana said. "Every cycle, the worlds come together to murder each other. And the cycle will keep going on, Lilia, you and me and those who come after us, again and again, cycle after cycle. In some other world, you did the same as I did."

Lilia shivered, because Kirana was right, wasn't she? *I was the monster*, Lilia thought, remembering the terrible influx of golden women with green eyes.

"Get up there, Lilia!" Roh called. "Taigan?"

"This is ridiculous," Taigan said. "I'd prefer to burn them all where they stand."

"Don't you dare!" Lilia shouted. She pointed to the great white cage where he needed to be. "You wanted to break the world, Taigan, or maybe save it? It's time."

"Oh, there's, ahh…" the little Tai Mora man near the webbing began. His companion hushed him. Lilia noted the splattering of flesh and viscera all around them. How many people had they tried to feed to it?

Lilia needed to get to the top. "Roh!" she called. "Can you get me up?"

A gentle wind enveloped her and took her to the top of the pedestal, far more softly this time. Perhaps Roh was not as frazzled. And he had Kadaan and Anavha and Maralah with him this time; the other pedestals were already powered by Gian and Kirana's people.

Lilia gazed down at Gian as Taigan climbed into his niche. Lilia's shadow loomed over the cavern as the brilliant white light enveloped Taigan behind her. Lilia's feet and fingers tingled. This time, she stared at the floor beneath her, and saw the symbol: the trefoil with the tail. The missing piece?

"Luna!" Lilia said. "A missing piece. What do you know about a missing piece?"

"What?" Luna cried, splashing in the water below.

Lilia raised her arm and stared at her wrist where her mother had warded that symbol into her flesh. What if she chose to just flood this whole temple, and end them all? How could they live beside these people? How could they possibly make a future together? When her ancestors broke the world, they had left their descendants to put it back together. Lilia resented them all, resented their arrogance and hubris. Lilia hated those old dusty jistas who had made the temples, but she hated the future more. Why did the choice come down to her, the choice to continue some terrible cycle or break it? All on...

"Can you do it?" Luna called.

Lilia shook herself out of her dark thoughts. Not all on her. She had believed it was all her choices that led them here, but that, too, was arrogant. As arrogant as her ancestors had been. Luna chose to be here. Taigan, even. And Anavha! That poor boy should have stayed on the farm, what was he thinking? Roh, dear Roh, who had traveled so long and so far, fuelled on what? On hope. Hope that they could get here. That they could change something, instead of just continuing the same cycle over and over again.

Many worlds, Lilia thought. A multitude of choices. She was thinking narrowly, without understanding the rules of the machine. They were all mucking about in this big thing, trying to make it work, trying to save themselves.

"Luna!" she said. "Do we have to break the world?"

"What do you mean?"

Lilia could feel the power beckoning to her to open herself to it, calling, calling… She closed her eyes. Clenched her fists. "It's called the Worldbreaker, the book, and… the person up here. But do we have to break the world? Can't we… couldn't we… put it back together?"

"I… don't know!" Luna said. "There are… There are trillions of worlds here, Lilia, too many choices. I… yes, you can! I took those pages out of the book! The instructions! I'm sorry! I don't remember them."

"You think you can live next to these people?" Zezili said, twisting at Yisaoh's arm again. Yisaoh fell to her knees. "Send them all fucking back. Murder every last one of them. You can't build a future next to fucking murderous–"

"Like you?" Lilia said. "We can't go back to what we were. We can't keep doing this over and over again."

Zezili snarled at her. "I don't have any interest in getting out of here alive either. You're the one who called on me, remember? Because you needed a fucking brute. Don't pretend your hands are ever going to be clean. You're as bad as I am, and you know it."

Lilia straightened.

Roh yelled something. A wink was opening on the other side of the room: Kirana's people, most likely, trying to re-establish a connection here. The room groaned and trembled beneath her.

Lilia closed her eyes and opened herself to the power of the satellites.

The warm burst of power channeled through her; the orrery popped into existence, a dizzying array of orbs. So many choices…

"You're right," Lilia said to Zezili. She held out her arm to Zezili. "We *are* alike. We'll do this together."

"What?"

"Roh, send her up here!"

Zezili yelled as a wave of air twisted her away from Yisaoh and propelled her to the top of the pedestal. She landed next to Lilia and grabbed at Lilia for balance, nearly going over again.

"What the fuck are you doing?" Zezili said.

"I don't need the instructions," Lilia said. "My mother gave them to me, and Kalinda."

"What?"

Lilia pressed at Zezili's upper belly. Zezili hissed and clutched at where the symbol lay twisted within her flesh.

"It's broken," Lilia said. "Like the worlds. Like us. We have to put it back together."

Zezili followed Lilia's gaze to the symbol in the floor, the one that neatly mirrored the one in her flesh. "Oh, fuck," Zezili said, "fuck."

"If I try and put people back where they don't belong," Lilia said, "the game ends. Just like the game of spheres. Who knows why? Maybe it's not allowed. Maybe it destroys worlds. Annihilates universes. You put the Tai Mora back, and who are we? We are them. And it's true, what Saradyn said. You are from this world. I'm not. I need you to help me do this."

Zezili grimaced.

The spheres continued spinning, their lacey orbits whipping out behind them like tails of smoke. Could she stand here forever, just waiting? No, no. If she closed her eyes and listened, she could hear Roh and Kadaan yelling as their defenses began to give way, just like the last time.

Below her, Yisaoh was free, running across the great room to Kirana's arms. If Lilia killed Kirana she would summon a future far worse than this one.

Zezili pulled off her tunic. The silvery symbol beneath her flesh glowed faintly blue. "This is going to hurt," Zezili said.

She pulled a knife from her side and jabbed it into her belly, working it around the piece stuck in her flesh.

Lilia felt an echo of the pain, a deep ache that helped her focus. She reached for the little green orb nearest her. It was real in her hand. It barely had weight at all, much like having a bird land on one's palm: all softness and air, brittle bones, no mass. Such a small thing to hold, this ball that represented not only her own life, but the lives of all the Tai Mora and their allies, all at her mercy now, after so long. She didn't know why that occurred to her, why it was this world, this small green orb, that felt so much like her home.

Her eyes filled with tears, as Zezili tore the piece of the temple from her flesh and held it in her hand.

Lilia remembered her mother. Her mother cut down by Kirana's weapon. And her mother, again, fused with the mirror that was to bridge their worlds before Oma's rise. Her mother had safeguarded her and protected her, tossed her into some other world so that she had the chance to live. She had done what Kirana had done; they were motivated by the same things, weren't they? They loved their families. They wanted to live. It was the determination of every creature: those two things. To survive, to reproduce. Who was to say she would have done any differently, in Kirana's place? She had been selfish, arrogant, since the worlds began to come together, and she had nearly destroyed everything.

And isn't that where she sat now, the power of life or death in her own hands? The terrible choice, to let them live here alongside the Dhai they murdered and enslaved or to cast them out to their dead world where they would all be consumed by fire? Two choices. The Dhai choice was to let them stay, to survive, but what then? Hope that they could live beside their oppressors? Those who murdered their kin? That was worse than death. The Dhai, her Dhai, did not deserve that. But the other choice was to be a Tai Mora, to do the very worst thing. The genocide of an entire race.

Two choices, two choices.

Shouting, close. Roh's voice. "Hold them! Hold them!" The clash of weapons. More voices. She could not go back and do this again, not now. There was no way out, no way to buy more time.

She had to make her choice.

"Lilia?" Zezili said. "You hear me? Take it! Take the fucking thing!" She held the bloody trefoil with the tail in her hand. Her blood dripped on the dais beneath them.

Don't become them, Emlee had said. Lilia closed her eyes and saw the little girl cut in two by the seam Lilia had ordered drawn in the world. The dead she left in Tira's Temple. She had done terrible things. She deserved this death, to cast herself and the people she had come from back to their rotting husk of a world. She had done all of this, everything, seeking this end. There was never any way back. She had pushed on, committing greater horrors, becoming all that she was fighting, so she could end it here.

She opened his eyes. Took a deep breath. Infinite worlds purled out ahead of her, casting up and up; when she looked down, they spread low and long beneath her, too.

She hefted the green sphere that was her life, the Tai Mora lives, and in her other hand she made a motion, like grasping for a hanging branch, and the whole map pivoted, rushed forward. If the Aaldian game of spheres was any indication, she had only one chance at this. If she chose poorly, it wasn't just she who would die, but also everyone here. Roh and Anavha, Maralah and Kadaan, and Gian, whom she loved despite knowing it was a stupid compulsion.

There were infinite worlds, and infinite choices. She had only to let herself see them.

One choice. Choose, Li.

Li.

Light.

"Lilia!" Zezili yelled. "Ah, fuck!" She slipped on her blood, nearly toppling from the pedestal.

Lilia was rooted in place, transfixed by the orrery. There, curled at the center of a whirl of spheres, was a softly winking white world. White, like the martyr Faith Ahya.

Choose.

"Where will we go?" she murmured. Would the Tai Mora murder people there as they had here? Would there be any people at all? Who was she, to further break them apart? Divide them? Division had created this terrible cycle in the first place.

They had been arguing all this time about whose was the right face, about which body belonged where. But they were all the same people, weren't they? Broken apart by their foolhardy ancestors, using power they didn't understand. They were all the same bodies, the same people. Just different choices.

The realization made her lose her breath. They had broken it all apart. Someone needed to put it back together.

They were nothing without each other.

"Fly, fly, little bird," she murmured. She released the green sphere and let it float back into its orbit.

She slid to knees, painfully, and took the trefoil with the tail from Zezili's slick hands. Lilia pressed the missing piece into the base of the pedestal. The light all around them intensified. Zezili screamed. A great wave of power took Lilia into its embrace, lifting her from the pedestal as if she weighed nothing. For one glorious moment, she felt light as air itself, without pain, without doubt.

Suffused in the power of the combined satellites, an infinite number of endings and beginnings before her, every choice imaginable, she brought up her left hand in a long sweeping motion. The billions of worlds drew closer to her, skipping from their paths to collect around her in a great whirling mass. The light intensified again, sparking and hissing. One more move on the board, the last move.

Worldbreaker, or Worldshaper?

Lilia swept her right arm out and brought it toward her. The infinite worlds, infinite stars, infinite possibilities, collided.

And she reset the game.

49

Roh saw her move the orrery: a long sweep of stars. No one else was watching. Kirana's reinforcements broke his defensive wall so forcefully he lost his grasp on Para. The room seethed and buckled, tilting wildly beneath their feet as the temple slid off the sand bar and deeper into the sea. Water rushed in from massive cracks in the walls. Roared from the ceiling. They were going to drown in here.

"Lilia, don't!" Roh lurched toward her. She was going to murder the Tai Mora, murder herself.

Lilia held the green piece aloft, and glanced over her shoulder. For the rest of his life, he would think about the expression he saw in her face: fear, triumph, resolution, defeat... All of them, and none.

"Li!" He reached for her, fingers grasping, trying to make it across the distance as fast as his legs would carry him, breaking apart the misty worlds, his skin bathed in pinpricks of light.

Li.

Light.

Zezili hung from the platform, screaming. The light suffusing the pedestal became nearly blinding. Lilia was lifted high in the air, hair streaming behind her.

She released the sphere back into its orbit, and swung her left arm around, drawing all the smaller orbs up into a whirling mass above her head. The ground trembled beneath them. She stumbled, but did not fall. Raised her right hand, and pulled the larger set of spheres from their orbits as well.

The misty worlds all collided above her.

Light.

Roh covered his eyes. The light was so powerful it overwhelmed. It pierced his consciousness even through his closed lids. Pierced him to the bone, like a physical force. But there was no boom. No rush. Just blazing light.

Then... darkness. Water rushing up below him, carrying him. Saradyn shouting, grabbing for him. Roh called to Kadaan, trying to draw on Para, finding... nothing.

Roh opened his eyes, but the light had been so intense that he was still blind. He blinked, reaching, swimming back toward the dais where Lilia had stood. His fingers met the lip of the dais, and as his vision returned, his sight confirmed what his fingers discovered – Lilia was no longer there.

The great beast of the temple was tilting, tilting, collapsing under its own weight, sliding off the sandbar and back into the ocean whence it came.

He swept his gaze across the room, now dim and dull, lit only by a ring of blue and green phosphorescence along the ceiling, the orrery only a brilliant memory. Others bobbed and gasped in the water all around him. Light pierced his vision again, light and pain in his head.

He gasped. The sea rushed in from the crumbling wall, pushing him and the others across the cavern. Roh bobbed and splashed, forced against the far wall, which gave under the pressure.

He was sucked out of the chamber and into the sea. Heaving, desperate, he tried to swim, but he was dizzy and overwhelmed. He vomited. His mind became clouded. Memories. Vertigo. Flashes of something, light – memory:

He was a farmer in a field, married to Kihin. He nursed his mother Naori through the yellow pox. He died in Saiduan, cut through by Kadaan and torn apart by bears. He and Luna ran off together across the tundra and lived to be old people, settled alone along the far northern sea. His father barred him from going to Saiduan, and instead he died next to Kai Ahkio, fighting shadows in a clan square while the world burned around them.

Split apart, he thought. They split us all apart.

Lilia hadn't murdered them.

Lilia had pulled them all back together.

Every single one of them.

Roh tried to reach for Para – and found… nothing. Panic seized his heart. Para! He reached again, but could not even sense his star. Had it winked back out of existence? Was it descendant again? Who had an ascendant star?

He was going to drown.

Strong arms around him, moving him up, up, up. His lungs were near to bursting.

I'm going to die, he thought. What a time to die.

50

Kirana splashed through the rising waters, screaming. That was how she became aware of herself. Cold, screaming. The taste of salt. A rush of memories overcame her, tangling in her mind like hopelessly knotted nets.

She was cutting down a woman called Nava Sona. Murdering her coldly. Marrying her. She was a cobbler, like her mother, drowned early in the toxic rain that fell from the sky. Her brother was pulling her from a burning building, poor little Ahkio, his hands, his hands... poor Ahkio, whom she loved, whom she had to protect, because Oma was coming and he would not be prepared. He was too fragile for this world. She loved her country. She hated her country. She had no country, a refugee from some other lost star, stumbling into this world during the last two years of Oma's rise.

She was all of these things, and more, an infinite number of selves, of memories, of choices, all colliding painfully, overwhelmingly.

The water filled the room, pushing her toward the far side of the cavern. People were missing – far more than could have been lost already. Zezili was gone, but there, there! Yisaoh!

Kirana reached for her. Took her by the arm as she whirled past.

"Yisaoh!" Kirana cried, and embraced her, but Yisaoh pulled away, her eyes so very black, gazing at her as if she were a stranger.

"No, no," Kirana said.

Yisaoh punched her in the face.

Kirana reeled back in the water, nose burst, bloody. The sea rushed in and pushed her under and out through the back wall of the great structure.

She screamed under water, bubbles rising all around her. Kicking, up, up, what about her children? Would they know her for what she was? Who would they be? Which version? No, no, she knew who she was, didn't she?

Poor Ahkio, too soft, and her mother, too soft, and Nasaka, always scheming. Nasaka...

No, I am not that woman! Kirana wanted to cry, but there was only the ocean around her, the sea. She flailed, bumping into a bit of detritus: a bit of wood already rising to the surface.

She came up out of the water and gasped. Spit, choking on seawater. She splashed all around. There were others not far away, heading toward the sandbar. Her mind seethed with memories, hers and others, so many others. I murdered my brother. I murdered my country. I destroyed everything and everyone that mattered to me.

"No!" Kirana screamed. "I'm not... I did this... I'm not that woman. I'm not a fucking monster, I'm not..."

Another wave of memories overcame her. She lost her grip on the piece of wood, and splashed further away from the sandbar. She would go back, start over, go to Saiduan, where she had been queen, where she had married the Patron, where her children became gods...

What life? In what world? In the memory of the worlds, of all her desperate choices: choices that she could no longer flee from.

51

Roh burst through the surface of the water, paddling madly. Waves rocked softly against a sandbar nearby, and he made for it as quickly as he could, terrified that the dissolution of the temple would pull him back under.

"Roh! Roh!" Luna, just behind him, splashing. "I can't! Roh!"

He took hold of Luna, slipping an arm under hirs. "Kick!" he said. "The sandbar! Saradyn, help Luna too!"

They gasped and splashed their way to the sandy rise. Roh vomited saltwater. Luna burst into tears. Roh did not ask what hodgepodge of memories Luna was struggling with. He could barely cope with his own.

The body of a woman, face down, floated nearby, and Saradyn splashed out to haul her in. It was Yisaoh. He pushed her over and smacked at her back. She coughed and heaved. Blinked up at him.

"Roh?" she said.

"You know me?"

"Many of… a lot of me does. Does that… I can't…"

"She brought us back together," Roh said. "It's… I can't describe it either."

"I've done terrible things," Yisaoh said. "So many terrible things."

"Who..." he hesitated. Why ask her which or who she was? She was all of them, wasn't she? Their Yisaoh, the one who had caught him on the stairs, and Kirana's Yisaoh, and more besides. All and none.

More stragglers made it to the sandbar, many weeping, some hollow-eyed and unresponsive, too shocked to speak, all stunned by whatever lives were warring for dominance in their heads.

Kadaan and Maralah came up onto the beach, dragging Anavha with them. Anavha was crying, calling for Zezili and Natanial.

"Has anyone seen Taigan?" Maralah asked.

"No," Roh said. "Lilia?"

Maralah shook her head.

Saradyn pointed.

Roh turned, hoping to see Lilia, but it was Taigan, sloshing onto the sandbank, one hand pressed against his head. His beard was gone, and a great deal of his hair, burned or yanked out, Roh could not tell.

"That was memorable," Taigan said. He pulled his hand away from his head.

"Taigan?" Roh said. "You're... bleeding."

Taigan stared at the watery red tail of blood snaking down his hand. "I... indeed I am. Oh, that *is* interesting." He brought up his hands and marveled at the fine cuts and scratches, which still marred his hands, bright and bleeding. "I may even have some bruises!" he cried. He squeezed a bit more blood from the wound on his hand, inspecting it with wonder. "Look at that. It's not healing!

How extraordinary." He furrowed his brows. "Wait, how long should this last?"

"For normal people?" Roh asked. "It depends on how deep it is."

"Oh my," Taigan said. "My, my."

"Put pressure on it," Roh said. "Press hard. That helps."

"I don't think I've ever bled this much from a single wound," Taigan said. "This is very curious. Can I die now? That would be... remarkable."

"Better not test that out," Roh said.

Taigan glanced around the sandbar. "Where's Lilia?"

"She... disappeared," Roh said. "After she... I don't know. Brought us all together. Do you... are you feeling strange? Do you have memories?"

"Memories?" Taigan said. "Only the ones I've always had."

"What does that mean?" Luna said. "I... I have..."

"Me too," Roh said.

"Ah," Taigan said. "How... interesting. You carry memories of... other lives? Other worlds?"

"You don't?" Roh said.

Taigan grinned. Clapped his hands. "How incredible," he said. "I am unique! Perfectly singular to this world. How delightful. I always knew I was terribly special."

Maralah said, "Don't get ahead of yourself, Taigan. You're bleeding. What bleeds can die, now."

"Oh, how lovely," Taigan said. "After all we've been through, after all this, you want more death?"

"No," Maralah said, gazing back at the beached Saiduan ship. "I want to go home."

"What happens now?" Roh said.

"Now," Taigan said, "I will go off and have some excellent adventures, and hopefully never see a single one of you again."

Anavha lay on the sandbar, sobbing, hugging himself, rocking slowly back and forth. His mind was crowded with memories, from this life and so many others. Zezili, so many versions of Zezili; he had loved her, she had killed him, he had killed her, Natanial had killed her, her sisters had killed her. Zezili, dying by the Empress's hand. Death, over and over.

But in nearly every memory of his own life he lived. He married Taodalain. He married Natanial. He married Nusi. He lived alone in a print shop in Aaldia. He became a tailor. He had children. So many children! Oh, how he had wanted children.

The wave of memories overcame him. He lay on the sand, eyes squeezed shut.

"Anavha?"

Was that in his head, or here?

Anavha rubbed his face and looked up. There was Natanial, crouched nearby, mop of wet hair hanging into his face. "They aren't real," Natanial said, "they're just memories. Let them come." He brushed the hair away from Anavha's face.

"I don't know what to do!" Anavha gasped.

"I do," Natanial said. "I… Every version of me does. I've been very selfish, Anavha. No better than the others."

"Where is Zezili? Please, I have to know!"

Natanial cupped Anavha's cheek. "Is she always there? Every memory?"

Anavha nodded.

"Not in this one," Natanial said.

"You didn't see her?"

"She isn't on the beach, Anavha. I don't think she made it out of the temple. Neither did that girl operating the mechanism. They're both gone, together."

"Natanial, I can't feel Oma anymore. Is it... did it go away?"

"It did."

"I don't miss it. Natanial, it's a relief not to feel it." Anavha squeezed his eyes shut again, seeking that fine sliver of power, the nagging breath of Oma. But there was nothing. Just him and all of his choices.

"What do you want, Anavha?"

"I want to go home," Anavha said.

"All right," Natanial said, and lifted him up.

52

The seams between the worlds had closed. That much seemed certain, in the aftermath of the shattered temple and broken heavens.

The satellites had disappeared, leaving the sky empty, save for the double helix of the suns during the day and the three warbling moons at night.

Had Lilia made the satellites come back together into a single form? If so, where had it gone? Where had *she* gone? Sent somewhere else? Blinked out of existence, like so many of the other people that had been brought together from across so many worlds? Whole armies had gone missing, villages scoured of inhabitants. Those who remained went mad, struggling with a rush of disparate memories, of lives lived and unlived.

The world of Raisa had come back together. They had won. But to win, they had broken the world they knew. They had broken the sky.

A nascent world began that day. What that world would look like, though, no one knew. That was a future none of them had lived, not in any memory, not on any world.

It was something entirely new.

53

Roh felt a deep sense of loss as he stepped onto the repaired Saiduan ship with Luna, Maralah and Anavha. It had been three weeks since the sky broke, and not a single one of them had an ascendant star. He still woke at night, aching for Para, reaching for a power that was not there.

There was no more magic in the world. Just people who used to wield it. People who remembered it.

Over time, the memories of his other lives began to fade and flicker. He was aware of them most often in his dreams, when he experienced some bickering fight with Kihin, or when he woke sweating beside Kadaan, convinced that he had killed him, only to realize that was in some other life.

Yisaoh met them on the deck of the ship as the wind whipped around them. "I can't believe you're going back to Aaldia," she said. "I thought you'd change your mind before today." She rubbed her fingers together, as if longing for a cigarette that was no longer there. Roh suspected she would need to find a new habit.

"I like Aaldia," Roh said. "And I think we could build a life there. A different Dhai. I'm sure Meyna will be back, soon. You know you'll have to work something out, with whoever is in charge of the Dhai here."

"It's just as well," Yisaoh said. "I keep expecting Mohrai to show up, some version of her resurrected by... all this. Wouldn't that be interesting?"

"That's a word for it," Roh said. "But let's hope not."

For Roh, there were too many memories here, too many burned out orchards and clan squares and death and battle and violent politics. He had no illusion that a Dhai he helped create in Aaldia with the survivors from the Woodland would be much different, but he hoped the past would not haunt him there as it would here.

"Lots of Dhai still in the valley," Yisaoh said. "Lots of madness, too. Lost Tai Mora."

"You think you can build a peaceful society that includes those Tai Mora?"

"I think we can build... a different one."

"Good luck."

"To you, also, Roh. You think we're the lucky ones?"

"Yes," Roh said. "We get to live. The ones who live get to shape what comes next."

Luna held out a hand to him, and Roh took it. Kadaan walked up behind him and took his other hand. For the first time in years, Roh felt comforted. Safe. For once he did not mind being merely a passenger, a follower.

He wanted to go to Aaldia and plant an orchard. He wanted to become a farmer, and die old there in his own grove, back pressed against the warm bark of a tree he had nurtured with his own two hands. He wanted to create something, to build something, because he was weary of destruction.

And as he gazed over at Luna and up again at Kadaan, he had a moment of audacious hope that such a life was possible, that he could build a home with the people he loved, and that there would be generations of Dhai and Saiduan or whatever they called themselves next, and that their children, and children's children, would never have to experience what they had. Never again.

Natanial did not board one of the Saiduan ship to Aaldia, though Aaldia was certainly the only home he had ever truly known. Instead he watched the ships launch into the clear, sun-kissed sea. He stood on the beach, alone, peering out at Anavha's dark head there on the deck for as long as he could before the ship's distance swallowed him.

Saradyn waited beside him, turning his face up into the double suns and smacking his thick lips.

"Why didn't you go with them?" Natanial asked. "I thought you'd follow that boy forever."

"He was very powerful," Saradyn said, pulling at his lip. "But now... Now, I can't see his ghosts." He peered at Natanial. "Or yours, for that matter. My head feels... clearer. I feel... more myself."

"Which self?"

"Ah, that is the question." He peered back at the suns, and Natanial wondered what he saw there; the Thief Queen he had murdered, maybe, or married, in some other life. The children he didn't kill, the life of a tavern keep, or a drunkard, instead of a king. Natanial did not ask because he did not want to know, did not want to get all those versions of Saradyn mixed up with the monstrous self-styled former king who stood before him. It could be easy to forget who was friend and who was foe, when the world had been unmade and remade again.

"I think I'll take up a trade," Saradyn said. "Making something." He held up the arm still missing a hand. "Go into making fake hands! Ha! An art!" This seemed to please him, and he began to grin and snort.

"You're in a good humor."

"What's left? I've already gone mad, once. I prefer humor. But you… You'll want to get back to your men."

"Will I? Half of them have probably gone mad, like you. It's a long journey out of the Woodland to the valley, and I'm not sure what we'll find there."

"We are all mad, now. Now you know what it's like."

"There will be power upsets," Natanial said. "You could go back to Tordin and be a king, truly. Unite Tordin like you always dreamed."

"That was some other man's dream."

"What does this man dream?"

Saradyn furrowed his brows. "I don't know."

"I think I'll go down into the valley," Natanial said. "That Gian woman is bound to fill the void here, and she'll need good fighters beside her."

"You will still fight?"

"I don't know how to do anything else."

Saradyn guffawed. "You get after that pretty boy for following, but you are just like him."

"Maybe that's why I tried so hard to set him free. You make a habit of following others, thinking they will take you some place new, reveal something about you, give you some meaning. And when they don't, you find you're stuck in the same circle, trying to find comfort in servitude."

"Can't relate."

Natanial sighed. "I didn't expect you to." He gazed

one last time at the blot of the ships along the horizon, wondering what kind of life Anavha would live without him or Zezili, without the burden of being an omajista, existing as a foreign man in a foreign land. He hoped it was a different life than the one either of them had led up to this point.

"Goodbye, Saradyn," Natanial said. "You have enough water to make it back?"

"Always enough," Saradyn said. "Just going to sit here for a while. I enjoy watching the sea in silence. Did you know, Natanial? The children have stopped screaming."

Natanial hefted his pack and turned away from the ocean. He forged back up the beachhead and entered the cool, dark wood.

Taigan settled into the warm arms of a bonsa tree, near enough the coast to watch the Saiduan ships disappear over the horizon. Taigan snoozed there until the suns began to set, considering what came next. Taigan rubbed at her itching crotch; she'd gotten another yeast infection, which made urinating painful. It appeared Taigan would mostly present to the world with female sex organs and a downy beard that Taigan found most pleasing. Taigan had tried on ataisa pronouns for a few weeks while helping the others repair the ships, but found being "she" fit just fine, for however long Taigan lived in this newly rotting body.

Would she transform again? Who could say? But the wounds she had received in the slimy temple had scabbed over and healed slowly, as if she were some mundane body, just another anonymous refugee on Raisa, not special at all, not chosen.

She very much enjoyed being herself, belonging to herself, in a way that had never existed for her, not in the many centuries of memory that she could still recall.

"Fly, fly, little bird," Taigan called to the suns, and, though she had succeeded in avoiding such thoughts in the weeks after the satellites winked out of the sky, Taigan thought of Lilia. She considered writing a memoir of this time. Perhaps she could call it: *Pretty Little Cannibals: My Life Among the Dhai*. That made her laugh out loud. A good laugh that shook her chest and made it ache.

Foolish Lilia, the ungifted worldshaper, the headstrong burnout, the child she had thrown off a cliff, but who had nontheless become the masterful architect of this new world.

A world without the satellites. A world without magic. Without immortality. A world where they had only themselves. Taigan thought it would be a duller world, but she had found that bleeding and coughing made the experience of being alive far more exciting than it ever had been for her before.

She could die now. *Really* die. If she chopped off someone's limb, it would stay chopped off, forever. She had watched a man in the camp fall off the ship and break a leg a few days before, and the tirajista who ran to help him had a look of utter horror and confusion as she realized she could do nothing but set the bone and bind the leg. A new world. A broken world.

Taigan slid down the tree, scraping her hands as she did. She marveled again at the little flakes of skin, the small beads of blood. How extraordinary. The prick of pain, the warmth of the tree's bark, the tangy smell of the sea: it all felt somehow more brilliant, more beautiful, knowing that any moment could be the last she experienced of anything.

Mortality. What a wonderful gift.

EPILOGUE

She lay in a field of heavy-headed poppies, staring at an empty lavender sky. Her body felt light, only a little painful. When she pressed her hand to the place where her wound had been, her tunic was still cut and crusted with blood, but there was no scar. The air was warm, like the last breath of low summer moving to high fall. The trees above her scattered a few heavy brown leaves, but were otherwise in their full splendor.

Her last memory of this life, in this world, it had been spring, heading into high summer. Where had all the weeks gone? She did not know. But that other one, the Kai... Ahkio, yes, he had woken missing weeks, too, hadn't he? After going back in time, he leapt forward...

Memories skipped across her mind. She remembered bringing the worlds together. But she remembered many other lives as well. She was killed by Kirana as a child, plucked from her mother's arms in the burning village. She died tumbling from a tree before she learned how to read. Taigan pushed her off the cliff, and it broke her, really broke her, and Gian did not save her. Gian, Gian... She had memories of so many Gians. The Gian who had escorted her away from Kalinda's. The Gian with the maggot-infested leg, whom she had nursed back to health. The terrible Gian who worked with Kirana. Lilia had the memory of knowing that Gian too, of an arranged marriage they had both thought they would hate, but loving each other anyway. Of walking and running without her twisted foot, but tumbling anyway, pushed from the top of the ark by one of Gian's rival generals.

And more, others, but no good endings, no death where they were two old women, drunk on too much hard tea and each other. Lilia's memories were all of an early death, in every world.

It was why she was still trying to understand why she had woken up again in this one.

A cry came from nearby. She slowly rose, and gazed across the field of poppies. She should have known that her view from here would be of Oma's Temple. Oma did have a sense of humor. Oma, or… whatever beast or creature had helped guide them.

The shrubbery parted, and Namia came racing through, standing entirely upright now, making a murmuring sound in her throat, and signing over and over, "Lilia!"

Namia grabbed hold of her, knocking her back over, and Lilia grunted, the breath squeezed from her. Namia released her and kept hold of her with one hand while signing frantically with the other, so fast Lilia could not keep up. Namia was taller, Lilia noticed, her face rounder, her gangly limbs more robust. Her hair had grown, and been expertly braided with ribbons in a very lovely style that reminded Lilia just a bit of Dorinah.

"Namia?"

Another figure came up the hill, pressing through the poppies, and Lilia knew the voice.

Gian halted when she caught sight of her. She, too, had filled out, and it gave her more softness than Lilia had seen in any of her memories. She had cut her dark hair short in the back and looped the rest up behind her into a topknot. She held a large walking stick in one hand and the lead of a large brown dog mount in the other. The dog moved its ears forward and gave a little yip.

Namia signed Lilia's name again, this time in Gian's direction.

"Yes, yes, I see her," Gian said. She came forward slowly, parting the poppies. "We weren't going to come up this way. It's far off the path to Mount Ahya, but Namia insisted. I see why."

Lilia said, "You look well."

Gian laughed at that, and then Lilia laughed too, because it was a foolish way to start, after so much time, in so strange a place.

"How long has it been?" Lilia asked.

"When did you get here?"

"I... don't know. I remember... all those lives... do you? And I remember the orrery. Did everyone live?"

"Everyone lived," Gian said, "and they carried all of their other selves, too. I suppose, then, everyone, on every world, lived. Some more so than others. Not everyone liked what they remembered."

"You remember me?"

"I remember all of the versions of you that you remember of me."

Lilia felt her face warm, and pressed her hands against

her cheeks. What a strange reaction. A foolish notion.

Gian laughed. "You just got even darker!" She sobered. "We thought you were dead. A lot of people simply... blinked out, like the stars. We have a theory those were the ones who hadn't survived in most of their other lives. It's a question that will keep philosophers busy for ages. Found new religions. Which we will need, of course."

Lilia gazed again at the sky. "How long has it been?"

"A little more than a year."

"A year... That's so much time... more than..."

"You have no memory of this last year, in any life?"

"No."

Gian nodded behind her, at the great hulking form of Mount Ahya. "That's not so bad," she said. "I settled all of my people in, and the Kai has been easy to work with."

Lilia opened her mouth to ask who the Kai was, and then realized she didn't want to know. She had never wanted to be involved in any of that; politics and games were a means to an end, to revenge. Now she felt... relief. But also an emptiness. What drove you on, after you put the world back together?

Gian said, "I've a mind to climb Mount Ahya. Did you want to come? I have a... memory of us doing that, in some... other life."

"Mount Ahya? It touches the sky."

"Indeed. I'd like to touch the sky again."

Namia signed at Lilia, "Come."

"What do you remember, Namia?" Lilia asked.

"Many things," Namia signed. "All here."

Lilia embraced Namia again. "I'm so sorry for everything."

"Don't be sorry," Gian said, "you saved more of us than

I ever thought possible."

"What do you think it was?" Lilia asked Gian. "The satellites? What do you think they broke?"

"I think it was nothing we were supposed to understand. I think we meddled with something very old, far older than us, and misused it."

"Do you think it's been trying all this time, to put us back together?"

"I'm not a god, Lilia. Just a woman."

Lilia struggled to her feet. Gian moved forward to help her. Lilia took her offered hand; warm and calloused, with long, lean fingers. Their gazes met. A tumble of memories. Gian would have them too. All those lives, all those deaths. They both should have winked out, if death was what destroyed the others, but here they were. Oma's sense of humor.

"Maybe we'll live this time," Gian said.

"Everyone dies," Lilia said, "it's just a matter of choosing what you do between now and then."

"Let's climb mountains, then."

They turned toward Mount Ahya, fingers entwined, heads no longer raised to the sky, but to each other.

GLOSSARY

Aaldia – Country on the southwestern shore of Grania, led by a conclave of three queens and two kings, each representing one of the five former independent states of the region.

Aaldians – The people of Aaldia, a country on the southwestern shore of Grania, known for their passion for mathematics.

Aaraduan – Far northeastern city in Saiduan, home to one of the infamous "living holds" of the western half of Raisa. Before the Saiduans, the city was called Roasandara, and was part of the ancient Dhai empire. The city was destroyed by the Tai Mora.

Aatai – Saiduan liquor.

Abas Morasorn – A Saiduan dancer at Kuonrada.

Adenoak – A type of yellowish hardwood tree commonly grown in Dhai.

Ahkio Javia Garika – Son of Javia Mia Sorai and Rishin Garin Badu. Li Kai. Brother to Kirana Javia Garika.

Ahmur – The largest of Raisa's three moons.

Aimuda Mosifa Taosina – Elder Ora of the Temple of Tira. Masura's cousin.

Alaar Masoth Taar – The Patron of Saiduan; eighth in the country's current line of rulers. A tirajista.

Alais Sohra Garika – Birth mother to Yisaoh Alais Garika. Married Garika clan master, Tir, and Moarsa, and Gaila.

Alasu Carahin Sorila – A Kuallina militia member found dead in Clan Sorila.

Albaaric – A city in Saiduan on the coast. Home city of Maralah Daonia.

Alhina Sabita Sorai – Mohrai's cousin.

Almeysia Maisia Sorila – An Ora and the Mistress of Novices at the Temple of Oma. A very sensitive tirajista who can call upon her powers even when Tira is in decline.

Aloerian – A city in Dorinah near a dajian camp.

Alorjan – An island nation currently claimed by both Saiduan and Dorinah forces. Both nations removed their forces to deal with Tai Mora matters.

Amelia Novao – A Dorinah Seeker. Recruited and bound by Lilia to help her get the dajian refugees across the Dhai border.

Anavha Hasaria – Zezili Hasaria's husband. Son of Gilyna Lasinya. The Empress awarded Anavha to Zezili as a token for her service.

Anjoliaa – A port city in southern Saiduan.

Aradan Foswen – A leader in an alternate version of Raisa.

Arakam Solaan, Ren – An ataisa sanisi.

Aramey Dahina Dasina – A Dhai scholar. Married to Lanilu Asaila Sorila.

Arasia Marita Sorila – Temporary keeper of Liona Stronghold.

Arisaa Saara – One of Alaar Masoth Taar's wives. Known

as his most formidable wife, Arisaa is the mother of Alaar's most beloved sons and provides him with valued advice.

Asaolina – A small village in Dorinah.

Ashaar Toaan – A Saiduan scholar.

Asona Harbor – Harbor on the Hareo Sea, in Clan Sorai. This defensive structure was built by Faith Ahya and Hahko in anticipation of raids from Saiduan and Dorinah.

Avosta – A former member of Ghrasia Madah's militia.

Azorum – A dead people conquered by the Tai Mora on their world.

Bael Asaraan – Record-keeper for the archives at Kuonrada. Native of Caisau.

Battle at Roasandara – A battle between the Saiduan and the ancient Dhai at the city of Roasandara, taught to every member of the Saiduan military.

Bendi – A strategy game played in Dhai.

Bleeding pen – A pen made from the stamens of claw-lilies.

Blinding tree – A tree that emits a deadly acid that numbs flesh and can eat through skin, bone and armor.

Bone Festival – One of the winter festivals held in Saiduan.

Bone tree – A tree with yellowish bark and spiny branches, made of bone. It catches small animals in its branches, and secretes a poisonous sap that kills its prey.

Bonsa – Large, yellow-barked trees trained to become living establishments in Dhai. Saplings are also used to create weapons infused with the breath of Para.

Book of Dhai – A written set of religious practices, codes and laws followed by the Tai Mora. The book states that when Oma rises, one world will die and another will be transformed. In the book, omajistas are referred to as the hand of Oma, and will decide the fate of the worlds.

Book of Laine – The holy book of Tordin.

Book of Oma – A written set of religious practices, codes and laws followed in Dhai.

Book of Rhea – A written set of religious practices, codes and laws followed in Dorinah.

Borasau – A Tai Mora, one of Roh's captors.

Broodguard – The Patron of Saiduan's personal guards.

Caisa Arianao Raona – Novice at the Temple of Oma now working as Ahkio's assistant. Parajista.

Caisau – A city in Saiduan just south of Isjahilde. Caisau's hold is a living building, but has been repaired so many times over the years that it is a patchwork of organic and inorganic material. 2,000 years ago, Caisau was the seat of the Dhai empire.

Caratyd – A city in Tordin.

Casa Maigan – An old acquaintance of Dasai's who has talamynii blood and can read old talamynii. Was part of Alaar Masoth Taar's harem in Isjahilde. Casa was left behind by the prior Patron, and inherited by Alaar.

Casalyn Aurnaisa – Empress of Dorinah. Long ago, her people crossed over from another world, but many were left behind. She seeks to bring the rest over now, with the help of the Tai Mora. Other titles – Eye of Rhea, Rhea's Regent, Lord of the Seven Isles.

Castaolain – A city in Dorinah.

Catori – Spouse of the Kai. The current Catori is Mohrai Hona Sorai.

Chali Finahin Badu – Brother of Roh; they share two mothers and three fathers but are not related by blood.

Cholina – A city in Dorinah, located northeast of Daorian.

Clan Adama – Named for one of Hahko and Faith Ahya's children, Clan Adama's primary exports come from its orchards, generally in the form of olives, apples, cherries, and apricots. Also known for its rice production.

Clan Alia – Primary exports of Clan Alia include textiles. Also known for its rice production.

Clan Badu – Clan bordering Clans Garika and Sorila, in Dhai. Politically close to Clan Garika.

Clan Daora – Clan Daora, like Clan Badu, has a skill with forged pieces, including tools and weaponry, though it is much more well-known for its craftsmanship and attention to detail. Their jewelry pieces are highly sought after in Saiduan and Aaldia.

Clan Garika – Known as the most powerful single clan in Dhai, Clan Garika is the birthplace of three Kais and four Catoris. Often at the center of challenging the power and autonomy of the Kais, the clan is also an economic center and trading hub for the whole country. Goods coming up from the harbor in Sorai are generally brought to Garika for distribution and sale across the clan. Much of the population makes a living as merchants, traders, and in other skilled professions such as plumbers, hedge doctors, and clan law specialists.

Clan Mutao – Smallest and least economically powerful of the Dhai clans, Clan Mutao provides some exports in mushrooms, coal, and copper, but mostly ends up working in reserves overseen by neighboring Clan Nako. Their status as a dwindling clan requiring subsistence from others to survive has led to a petition in recent years to combine clans Nako and Mutao.

Clan Nako – Neighboring Clan Mutao, Clan Nako holds much of the country's wealth in copper and other metals. The sale of these materials is regulated by the clan, which manipulates supply and demand as necessary to ensure the best exported price. Such market manipulation for goods meant for sale within the country are not permitted, but exports are exempt.

Clan Osono – Central clan in Dhai. Chief commodity is sheep.

Clan Raona – Originally comprised of two different clans—Riana and Orsaila—Clan Roana is just a century old, and was created in an effort to tamp down the fierce feuding between the Riana and Orsaila clans, which resulted in nearly a dozen deaths, the most unnatural deaths outside of war time that the country had ever experienced. Clan Roana is loosely aligned with clans Saobina and Taosina. Primary exports include rice and wine. Raona also raises most of the sparrows used as messengers in the Dhai temples.

Clan Saiz – Dhai clan. Chief commodity is timber and artisanal goods.

Clan Saobina – Clan Saobina exports timber and plantstuffs – including herbal aids and medications – which it grows and mixes in its own fields and workshops. The clan borders the woodlands, and so its members tend to be called on to consult on poisonous or dangerous plant outbreaks between the clans.

Clan Sorai – Named after the powerful son of the third Kai, Clan Sorai is often allied with clans Adama and Saobina in political affairs. They are also the clan responsible for the safety and security of Asona harbor, the country's single largest trading link to the outside world. The clan is generally allied closely with the Kai, and has a notorious rivalry with Clan Garika. The clan's leader is Hona Fasa Sorai.

Clan Sorila – Clan nearest the Temple of Oma, in Dhai. Primary export is timber.

Clan Taosina – Named for Faith Ahya's second daughter, clan Taosina – like clans Saobina and Sorila - borders the woodlands. Pottery and complex, plant-derived technologies such as bioluminescent floor or ceiling lighting solutions, self-cleaning fungus floors and the like are generally created and installed by Taosina crafters.

Concordyns – A province in Tordin.

Cora – A dajian who lives with Emlee.

Corina Yisaoh (Tai Mora) – Yisaoh's daughter, being raised by the Tai Mora versions of Kirana and Yisaoh.

Coryana Puyak – A friend of Natanial's who trains gifted on how to draw on the satellites' powers.

Dajian – In Dorinah, enslaved Dhai people are called dajians. Often they are branded with the mark of the family that owns them.

Dakar – Zezili Hasaria's dog mount.

Daolyn – Owned by Zezili Hasaria, housekeeper and dajian.

Daorian – The fortress seat of the Empress of Dorinah. A city of the same name rose up around the fortress on the ruins of the former Saiduan city of Diamia.

Dasai Elasora Daora (Dhai) – An elder Ora, over a century old. One of Ahkio Javia Garika's teachers. In

Dasai's youth, he was a slave to the Patron of Saiduan at that time.

Dasai Elasora (Tai Mora) – Tai Mora magistrate in charge at Caisau.

Dayns – A runt dog belonging to Saradyn.

Dhai – Small country located on the northwest corner of the island of Grania, an island at the far tip of the Saiduan continent. Also the name of the people inhabiting this country. Modern Dhai was established 500 years ago by former slaves fleeing their masters in the neighboring country of Dorinah. It's said the satellite called Sina was especially powerful during that time, allowing Dhai sinajistas, who outnumbered sinajistas among the Dorinah, to escape their servitude.

Dhai has been led by a series of leaders given the title Kai. The title is hereditary and passes through the mother's lineage to the child with the greatest ability to call on the power of the satellites.

Dhorin – A unit of currency used in Dorinah.

Dorinah – A matriarchal country on the northeast shore of Grania, ruled by a long line of Empresses. The country is roughly 1800 years old, and relies on the enslaved labor of Dhai people – known locally as dajians – to sustain its infrastructure and economy. The flag depicts the Eye of Rhea on a purple background.

Driaa Saarik, Shao – An atasia sanisi. Sent to Alorjan to shore up the island for Saiduan's retreat. Recommended by Maralah to meet with the Dhai party sent to Saiduan. Born in Tordin.

Dryan – A city in Dorinah.

Elaiko Sirana Nako – An Ora at the Temple of Oma and

assistant to Nasaka Lokana Saiz.

Emlee – Gifted healer and midwife in a dajian camp, now liberated.

Empresses of Dorinah – The line of Empresses in Dorinah began 1800 years ago, when a green-eyed foreign sorceress expelled Saiduan from the fortress of Daorian.

Enforcers – Members of the Dorinah military who capture wandering men or dajians and return them to where they belong.

Esao Josa – Granddaughter of Nirata Josa. Esao is killed when a gate summoned by her grandmother closes on her.

Etena Mia Soria – Ahkio Javia Garika's aunt, Etena was driven mad by her own power and supplanted as Kai by her sister, Javia Mia Sorai. Exiled from Dhai.

Everpine – The scent of this tree dissuades bugs and most sentient plants. Travelers through the Woodland apply the scent to sleeping rolls and other supplies they want to remain undisturbed.

Fasia's Point – A fingerling peninsula in the Dhai Woodland that juts into the sea.

Faith Ahya – Faith Ahya is regarded as the mother of the newest incarnation of the Dhai nation, founded five hundred years before when she led an uprising of Dhai slaves in Dorinah. With her lover Hahko, she established the Dhai nation in one of the most contaminated areas on the planet, one few other nations would touch. For five hundred years, the descendants of her eldest and most gifted children have ruled Dhai as the Kai, or "First Dhai."

In the dajian version of the legend, Faith Ahya is

betrayed by her lover Hahko, killed, and hung from the ramparts of Daorian. She then ascended to the peak of Mount Ahya and was engulfed by the light of Sina. It is said she will return to the world when she is needed.

In a story in Fifteenth Century Dhai Romances, Faith Ahya was a slave from Aaldia. She carried the child of an enslaved Dhai, and was a pitiful and self-serving character.

Faith's Rally – A Dhai song about Faith Ahya establishing the first clan.

Faralis Mosa Daora – A member of the Liona militia.

Farosi Sana Nako – A militia man, leader of a group of Oras and militia sent out to search Dhai for assassins. His group located and killed five of the assassins. Head of the militia at the Temple of Oma.

Faythe – A story from Fifteenth Century Dhai Romances, in which Faith Ahya was a slave from Aaldia. She carried the child of an enslaved Dhai, and was a pitiful figure.

Faytin Villiam – A Tordinian historian who recorded events during the time of the Thief Queen.

Fellwort – A plant trap that consists of a pit filled with poisonous green bile.

Festival of Para's Ascendance – A festival held on the day when parajistas are at the height of their power.

Fifteenth Century Dhai Romances – A book of Dhai history written by Dorinahians. Includes the story "Faythe."

Finahin Humey Garika – One of Roh's mothers.

Flame flies – Flies that create light, used in lanterns.

Floxflass – A yellow, thorned plant that moves to constrict prey in its tendrils.

Forsia tubers – A tuber that is poisonous if not deveined. Root of forsia lillies.

Foryer Galind – One of Anavha's guards in Tordin.

Fouria Orana Saiz – A Kuallina militia member found dead at the bottom of a well in Clan Sorila.

Fox-snaps – Plant defenses used outside Woodland Dhai homes to protect them from dangerous wild plants.

Gaila Karinsa Pana – Near-mother to Yisaoh Alais Garika. Married to Alais, Tir and Moarsa.

Gaiso Lonai Garika (Dhai) – Elder Ora of the Temple of Oma in Dhai. She was responsible for the overall functioning of the temple and care of the people therein. Cousin to Tir Salarihi Garika. Replaced by Ora Soruza Morak Sorai.

Gaiso Lonai (Tai Mora) – Tai Mora parajista company general. One of Kirana's four line commanders.

Gasira – A city in Tordin; the seat of Saradyn's power.

Ghakar Korsaa – Dance teacher at Kuonrada.

Ghrasia Madah Taosina – Ghrasia's mother was originally of Clan Mutao, but relocated to Taosina and named Ghrasia for that clan. Ghrasia went on to become a hero – the Dhai general who defeated the Dorinahians during the Pass War. She is currently the head of the military forces stationed at Kuallina Stronghold and Liona Stronghold. An old friend and lover of Ahkio's mother, Ghrasia is allied with him.

Gian Mursia – Former dajian servant in Daorian with latent skill in calling on the satellites.

Gian Mursia Badu (Tai Mora) – A tirajista Tai Mora raised on Raisa prime in Clan Badu, and directed to accompany Lilia Sona by Kalinda Lasa.

Giska – An Aaldian, one of Nusi's siblings.

Gonsa trees – Great trees which are hollowed out by tirajistas for use as homes in Dhai.

Gorosa Malia Osono – Head of the hold at Kuallina.

Grania – The island continent that is home to the countries of Dhai, Dorinah, Aaldia and Tordin, located at the far tip of the Saiduan continent.

Guise of the Heart – A Dorinah romantic political thriller set in Daorian a century ago.

Hadaoh Alais Garika – Husband to Meyna Salisia Mutao and brother to Rhin Gaila Garika, Lohin Alais Garika and Yisaoh Alais Garika.

Hague Gasan – Steward at the Gasiran hold.

Hahko – Hahko was a former slave in Dorinah, and aided his lover Faith Ahya in leading the uprising of the Dhai slaves from the scullery of Daorian. The two became the first rulers of the independent Dhai state, the first in over eighteen hundred years, after the defeat of the Dhai by the Saiduan roughly the same time ago. Like many slaves in Dorinah before and since, Hahko had only one given name.

Halimey Farai Sorila – A young parajista who works with Ghrasia to look for Tai Mora assassins living in Dhai. A member of the Liona militia.

Haloria Tarisa – Syre Storm's second in command.

Harajan – A city in Saiduan, south of Kuonrada. Contains an old hold built by the Talamynii that borders an underground sea.

Harina Fiaza Taosina – Newly appointed Ora. Sinajista.

Hasao – Meyna's child, Li Kai.

Himsa – A Tai Moran scholar.

Hirosa Mosana Badu – Clan leader of Clan Badu.

Hona Fasa Sorai – Leader of Clan Sorai.

Honorin Sholash – A Tai Mora military leader.

Hrollief – Southern continent on the western half of Raisa.

Huraasa Firaas, Ren – Sanisi in charge of shoring up the Saiduan retreat to Anjoliaa.

Isaila Larano Raona – Tir Salarihi Garika's apprentice clan leader at Clan Garika. Her mother was clan leader before Tir. Isaila was given the clan leader seat after Ahkio exiled Tir and his family.

Isjahilde – A city in northern Saiduan, Isjahilde has been the country's political center for thousands of years.

Isoail Rosalina – A powerful parajista living near Lake Morta in Dorinah. One of the Empress of Dorinah's seekers.

Jakobi Torisa Garika – Ahkio's third cousin. Chosen to accompany Ahkio to Clan Osono to meet with the clan leaders.

Janifa – A city on the coast in Dorinah.

Jasoi (Januvar) of Lind – Native to Tordin, Jasoi's title among the Dorinah is Syre. She is Zezili Hasaria's second-in-command,

Javia Mia Sorai – Former Kai of the Dhai. Ahkio and Kirana's mother. Javia became Kai after exiling her sister Etena, who was so gifted that she went mad.

Joria – An outer island to the north of Dorinah.

Jovonyn – A coastal city in Dorinah.

Kadaan Soagan, Ren – A sanisi, and one of Maralah Daonia's first students. Left hand of the Patron of Saiduan. Called the Shadow of Caisau. A parajista.

Kai – Honorific used for the leader of the Dhai people. The title of "Kai" means "First," and was used in reference to the eldest daughter of former slaves Hahko and Faith Ahya, who are credited with founding the country. The line follows the most gifted in a family, no matter their sex or gender. Though the Kai is the leader of the Dhai, they do not have absolute rule in the country; they are held accountable to clan leaders, their Ora advisors, and the people themselves. The Kai's duties are as a religious and political figure, negotiator of contracts with other countries, and arbitrator of disputes between the clans.

Kai Saohinla Savasi – Kai sometime before Kirana. Visited the heart of Oma's temple after the battle of Roasandara.

Kakolyn Kotaria – A legion commander in Dorinah whose estate was sold off to pay her debts. Her title in the Dorinah military is "Syre." Kakolyn was ordered by the Empress to purge Seekers from Dorinah.

Kalinda Lasa – A parajista Tai Mora who has traveled to many worlds. She was the keeper of a wayhouse in Dhai on the road to Garika, and was killed by Tai Mora. Kalinda grew up with Nava Sona, and aided Lilia when she was separated from her mother.

Karoi – One of four kinds of nocturnal scavengers in the Dhai Woodlands. The karoi is a vicious black raptor.

Karosia Soafin – Local priest and tirajista in the region of Zezili Hasaria's estate in Dorinah.

Keeper Takanaa – Keeper of the Patron of Saiduan's house.

Kidolynai – A city in Dorinah.

Kihin Moarsa Garika – A novice at the Temple of Oma. Tir Salarihi Garika's youngest son. He was killed in

Saiduan.

Kimey Falmey Nako – Defensive forms teacher in Clan Osono.

Kindar – A cooperative game of strategy played in Dhai. Pieces are wooden figures that represent family members.

Kirana Javia Garika (Dhai) – Former Kai of the Dhai. Sister to Akhio Javia Garika. Daughter of Javia Mia Sorai.

Kirana Javia (Tai Mora) – Kai of the Tai Mora. Said to be the savior of the Tai Mora, this version of Kirana seeks to save her people from the destruction of their world. A tirajista with some sensitivity to Oma.

Korloria Fanis – Tai Mora attendant to the slaves translating texts in Caisau.

Kosoli Mashida – One of Roh's captors.

Kovaas Sorataan, Ren – A sanisi in Maralah's trusted circle.

Kuallina Stronghold – Hold where Dhai militia are stationed, captained by Ghrasia Madah Taosina.

Kuonrada – A mountain city in Saiduan, built for cold weather and strong defense.

Ladiosyn – A city in Dorinah.

Laine – The god that many pray to in Tordin, and the preferred religious figure of King Saradyn Lind. The satellites are known as Laine's Sons. Oma is called Laine's Eye.

Lake Morta – Lake in a remote part of Dorinah. The lake is the subject of many Dorinah stories, and is considered to be a holy place blessed by Rhea. It is a spot where it requires less energy to travel between worlds. As a result, people from other worlds often appear here.

Lake Orastina – A lake north of Lake Morta in Dorinah.

Laralyn Maislyn – A seeker who ends up in the same dajian camp Lilia is in. Recruited and bound by Lilia to help her get the dajian refugees across the Dhai border.

Larn – A dajian who lives with Emlee.

Lasli Laodysin – See Syre Storm.

Li Kai – Successor to the Kai.

Liaro Tarisa Badu – Ahkio Javia Garika's cousin.

Lilia Sona – Scullery maid (drudge) at the Temple of Oma, originally from mirror Raisa. Daughter of Nava Sona. An omajista.

Line – A sort of living transportation system in which people travel in chrysalises.

Liona Stronghold – Hold that occupies the pass next to the valley that cuts through the mountain range separating Dhai and Dorinah. The building itself is a construct of parajista-shaped stone and tirajista-trained trees and vines. The forces stationed here are captained by Ghrasia Madah Taosina.

Litany of Breath – A litany that helps focus the user to draws on the power of the satellites.

Litany of Sounding – Defensive litany used by parajistas.

Litany of the Chrysalis – A litany that condenses the air around a parajista into a solid bubble.

Litany of the Palisade – A litany recited by parajistas to construct shields made of air.

Litany of the Spectral Snake – An offensive litany.

Litany of Unbinding – A litany to break a binding trap set by another jista.

Livia Hasaria – Zezili Hasaria's mother. A tirajista who specializes in the creation of mirrors infused with the power of Tira. Resides in the city of Saolina.

Lohin Alais Garika (Dhai) – Husband to Kirana Javia Garika. Brother to Yisaoh, Rhin and Hadaoh. Former Catori of the Kai. Killed in an attempted coup.

Lohin Alais (Tai Mora) – A Tai Mora infantry commander's squire and intelligence officer.

Lord's Book of Unmaking – A book with appendices that include love poetry written to Oma by a sixth century Saiduan scholar.

Luna – A Dhai bound to Saiduan and a scholar of Dhai matters. Once a Woodland Dhai, Luna was caught by a Dorinah raiding party and sold to the Saiduan.

Madah Ghrasia Mutao – Ghrasia's daughter.

Madah Ghrasia (Tai Mora) – One of Kirana's four line commanders in the Tai Mora army.

Mahinla Torsa Sorila – A dying woman from Raona.

Mahuan powder – An herbal treatment for asthma, mixed with water and then ingested.

Maralah Daonia, Shao – Sanisi, one of the Patron of Saiduan's generals. Sinajista. Sister of Rajavaa Daonia. Also known as the Sword of Albaaric.

Mardanas – Brothels in the religious quarter of Dorinah cities where male prostitutes serve Rhea by pleasuring women. Also called "cat-houses."

Marhin Rasanu Badu – A Kuallina militia member, lover of Ahkio, found dead in Clan Sorila.

Marister Fen – A Tai Mora infantry member, originally from a country called Osadaina there.

Masis Avura – A Tai Mora stargazer.

Masoth Chaigaan Taar, Shas – A sanisi and Alaar Masoth

Taar's eldest son.

Masura Gailia Saobina – Elder Ora of the Temple of Tira, Masura oversees everyday management of that temple. Was once a lover of Javia Mia Sorai.

Matias Hinsa Raona – Ora and doctor at the Temple of Oma. Now deceased.

Mays Krynn – A guard at the Gasiran hold in Tordin.

Mey-mey – Meyna's eldest daughter.

Meyna Salisia Mutao – Ahkio Javia Garika's housemater and lover. Wife to Hadaoh Alais Garika and Rhin Gaila Garika. Meyna and her family were exiled from Dhai by Ahkio, for their kinship to Tir Salarihi Garika.

Mihina Lorina Nako – Parajista.

Moarsa Fahinama Badu – Near-mother to Yisaoh Alais Garika. Wife to Tir, Moarsa and Alais.

Mohrai Hona Sorai – Catori of Dhai, married to Ahkio. Daughter of the leader of Clan Sorai, Hona Fasa Sorai.

Moira (Tai Mora) – Kirana and Yisaoh's child. Adopted from Kirana's cousin.

Mora – The small red sun in the sky over Raisa.

Mordid – Village in Tordin with about 300 residents.

Morsaar Koryn – Rajavaa Daonia's best friend, lover, and second in command of the what remains of the Saiduan army. Started his military career as an assistant cook for the army when he was young.

Morvern's drake – Broad leafed plant which grows in boggy areas whose roots are crushed and used as a sudsing agent for scouring and cleaning.

Mount Ahya – A mountain in Dhai, located to the east of the Temple of Oma.

Mundin Mountains – Mountains at the northern border

of Tordin.

Mur – One of the three moons of Raisa, Mur is irregularly shaped.

Mysa Joasta – Tai Mora omajista.

Nahinsa – A Tai Moran woman and Keeper Dasai's secretary

Naldri Fabita Badu – Elder Ora of the Temple of Para.

Namia – A young girl who travels with Lilia

Naori Gasila Alia – A powerful parajista. Ahkio's third cousin once removed.

Nasaka Lokana Saiz – An Ora at the Temple of Oma. Ahkio Javia Garika's aunt. Religious and political advisor to the Kai. Sinajista.

Natanial Thorne of Yemsire – A Tordin man who kidnaps Anavha Hasaria.

Nava Sona – Lilia's mother, from the world of the Tai Mora. Led a rebellion that took 200 omajista children and hid them across many worlds.

Nirata Josa – An omajista. Kin to Gian Mursia Badu.

Novoso Mora – The Tai Moran name for the country that was once Dhai.

Nusi – An Aaldian.

Ohanni Rorhina Osono – A parajista and dance teacher at the Temple of Oma.

Old Galind – A city in Tordin.

Oma – The dark star, a heavenly body which appears in the above Raisa every 2,000 years (or so). The light it shines is red.

Omajista – Sorcerers with the ability to channel Oma. Those with this power can open gateways between worlds and across distances, raise the dead, enhance the powers of others, call fire, and perform many other feats as yet unknown.

On Violence – A political philosophy book by Empress Penelodyn, former ruler of Tordin. Saradyn had it translated and carries it with him.

Ora – Title/honorific for a Dhai magician-priest, who is able to channel the power of Oma, Sina, Tira, or Para. Oras often act as teachers in the temples of Dhai.

Oravan – A Tai Moran servant.

Orhin – A Tai Moran scholar.

Osadaina – A country on Empress Kirana of the Tai Mora's Raisa that has no equivalent on prime Raisa.

Otolyn – A Tordinian woman and Nataniel's second.

Pana Woodlands – A woodland area in Dhai near the Temple of Oma.

Para – Para, Lord of the Air, one of the satellites that appears sporadically above Raisa. Para's light is blue.

Parajista – The common name for sorcerers who can channel Para when it is ascendant can manipulate the air levitate, effect weather, or form shields, barriers, or vortices. In Tordin they are often called wind witches.

Pasinu Hasva Sorai – Nasaka's new apprentice. Near-cousin to Mohrai, on her third mother's side.

Pass War – A war in which the Dhai, led by Ghrasia Madah Taosina, defeated Dorinah. The war started when 800 dajians escaped Dorinah and came to Liona Stronghold, begging for mercy and entrance to Dhai. Ghrasia would not let them in, and they were slaughtered by the pursuing Dorinah.

Patron of Saiduan – Leader of the Saiduan. Powerful Saiduan families have traditionally gone to war for the

Patron seat. Since it was established, eighteen different families have ruled Saiduan. When a new family rises to power, the prior family's adults are killed and the children raised as slaves.

Patron Osoraan Mhoharan – Patron of Saiduan before Alaar Masoth Taar.

Penelodyn – Sister to the Empress of Dorinah. Ruled Tordin before being unseated by the Thief Queen.

People's Temple – Also known as the fifth Dhai temple, long lost beneath the sea.

Pherl – A dajian man with a flesh-eating disease who is cared for by Emlee and Lilia.

Pol – A boy in Old Galind who gives away the rebels to Saradyn.

Rainaa – A slave of the Patron of Saiduan.

Rajavaa Daonia – Maralah Daonia's brother, and Captain-General in charge of a Saiduan military regiment. Rajavaa becomes Patron after Alaar Masoth Taar is killed.

Ranana Talisina Saiz – The defense forms teacher at the Temple of Oma.

Rasaa Goara – Saiduan man who pursues Luna.

Rasandan Parada – A dancer at Kuonrada.

Rasina Tatalia – Tai Mora infantry commander. Lohin's mother through marriage.

Ren – A title among the Saiduan sanisi indicative of relative talent. Most powerful are Shao, then Ren, Tal and Shas.

Rhea – The goddess of Dorinah religion. Para, Sina and Tira are said to be her daughters. The Empress of Dorinah is also known as Rhea's divine. In Dorinah scripture, Rhea's Eye is a name for Oma.

Rhin Gaila Garika – Husband to Meyna Salisia Mutao

and brother to Hadaoh Alais Garika, Lohin Alais Garika and Yisaoh Alais Garika.

Rimey Lorina Riona – A former student of Ahkio's from Clan Osono. Relocated to the Temple of Oma to serve as Ahkio's assistant.

Rishin Garin Badu – Javia's Catori and Nasaka's brother.

Rohandaar – A dead city from Tordin's history.

Rohinmey Tadisa Garika – Novice parajista at the Temple of Oma, with the ability to see through wards. Son of Finahin Humey Garika, Tadisa Sinhasa Garika, and Madinoh Ladisi Badu. Brother of Chali Finahin Badu.

Romey Sahina Osono – A former student of Ahkio Javia Garika's, whose body was found in a sheep field in Clan Osono. Presumed to have been killed by Tai Mora agents.

Rosh Mev – A young woman who started a rebellion in Old Galind.

Ryn – A city in Dorinah.

Ryyi – A leader among the Seekers.

Sabasao Orsana Adama – Assistant to Ora Una.

Sagasarian Sea – A sea to the north of Dorinah.

Sai Hofsha Sorek – Emissary of the Tai Mora.

Sai Monshara – One of the top generals of the Tai Mora, Monshara is tasked to work with Zezili Hasaria to eradicate the dajians in Dorinah. Monshara is the daughter of the former Empress of Dorinah on the Tai Mora version of Raisa. One of Kirana's four line commanders.

Saiduan – Large empire which rules the northwestern continent on Raisa. The continent itself is also called Saiduan. The empire is led by the Patron, the eighth in the country's latest family line of rulers. Powerful

Saiduan families have traditionally gone to war for this seat. Since it was established, eighteen different families have ruled Saiduan.

Salifa – A Tirajista traveling with Lilia.

Sanctuary – A room at the heart of the Temple of Oma where the Dhai clan elders traditionally meet to discuss issues of government.

Sanisi – The conjurer-assassins of Saiduan. Sanisi carry weapons infused with the power of the satellites.

Saofi – The Empress of Dorinah's dajian secretary.

Saolina – A small town in Dorinah where Zezili Hasaria's mother lives.

Saolyndara – A dajian camp in Dorinah.

Saradyn of Lind – King of Tordin, he is struggling to unite the constantly warring factions in the country. Can see "ghosts," which he believes to be a cursed power bestowed on him by one of the satellites.

Saronia Sasis Sorai – A former novice Ora.

Saurika Halania Osono – Clan leader of Clan Osono.

Sazhina – A dajian. Pherl's sister.

Screes – A strategy game played in Dhai.

Sea of Haraeo – The sea that separates Dhai and Saiduan.

Seara – A winter month in the Dorinah calendar.

Sebastyn – An outer island to the north of Dorinah.

Seeker Sanctuary – The training location for Dorinah's gifted. Seekers in Dorinah have their licenses to practice magic renewed here.

Seekers – The Empress of Dorinah's assassins. The seekers have the ability to channel the satellites, a rare talent in Dorinah.

Sel oil – A flammable oil.

Shanigan Saromei Dasina – A senior Ora and mathematics teacher at the Temple of Oma.

Shao – A title among the Saiduan sanisi indicative of relative talent. Most powerful are Shao, then Ren, Tal and Shas.

Shas – A title among the Saiduan sanisi indicative of relative talent. Most powerful are Shao, then Ren, Tal and Shas.

Sindaa Mokaa, Shao – Commander of the sanisi at Harajan.

Shar – The large double helix "sun" in the sky over Raisa, actually twin stars which exchange mass as they rotate one another. Also called "the sisters."

Shodav – A dancer and old friend of Dasai and Luna. A former slave.

Shoratau – A prison in Saiduan, located northeast of Kuonrada. Shoratau houses prisoners who were thought to possibly be useful later.

Shova Hom – A Tai Mora omajista.

Siira – The Dhai name of a winter month of the year.

Silafa Emiri Pana – A young, newly appointed Ora, part of Ahkio's most trusted circle.

Sina – A satellite that appears over Raisa, also called the Lord of Unmaking. Sina's light is violet.

Sinajista – Sorcerers who can channel the power of Sina when it is ascendant. Their abilities may include calling fire, raising the dead, transmuting or transforming substances, removing wards, and prophecy.

Sloe – A runt dog belonging to Saradyn.

Sokai Vasiya – A seeker who ends up in the same dajian camp Lilia is in. Recruited and bound by Lilia to help her get the dajian refugees across the Dhai border.

Sola – A young girl refugee on boat escaping Saiduan with Luna.

Song of Davaar – A song used to focus power to creates an intricate net.

Song of One Breath – A song used to control the power of Oma, taught to Lilia by Taigan.

Song of Sorrow – An omajista litany.

Song of the Dead – A litany of remembrance.

Song of the Cactus – An attack litany.

Song of the Mountain – An offensive litany.

Song of the Pearled Wall – A defensive litany.

Song of the Proud Wall – A defensive litany.

Song of the Water Spider – An offensive litany.

Song of the Wind – An offensive litany.

Song of Unmaking – Litany that cuts a person off from their ability to draw on a satellite. Temporary, and easy to counter once one has become skilled.

Sorana Hasaria – Zezili's youngest sister.

Sorat – Emlee's nephew.

Soruza Morak Sorai – Replacement for Gaiso in overseeing Oma's Temple. A jista from the Temple of Tira.

Sorvaraa – Saiduan city south of Harajan.

Soul stealer – Saiduan term for a sinajista at the height of their power. Some sinajistas can capture and harness the soul or life essence of those they slay in their infused blades.

Sovaan Ortaa, Ren – A sanisi.

Sovonia – A seer and rebel leader on another version of Raisa.

Storm, Syre – The Empress of Dorinah's only male legion commander. Not permitted to fight, but commands others. Given name – Lasli Laodysin.

Suari Febek – A Tai Mora stargazer.

Sulana Ofasa Daora – Parajista and Ora.

Tadisa Sinhasa Garika – One of Roh's mothers. Also mother of Chali Tadisa Badu.

Taigan Masaao, Shao – An outcast sanisi aligned with Maralah, bound to her with a ward, after she was able to spare Taigan's life when Taigan betrayed the Patron. Taigan has since been tasked with finding additional omajistas to help the Saiduan fight the Tai Mora.

Tai Mora – The invaders. The Tai Mora seek to escape through a permanent gate from mirror Raisa before their world is destroyed by the ascendance of Oma.

Tal (person) – A dajian. Pherl's sister.

Tal (title) – A title among the Saiduan sanisi indicative of relative talent. Most powerful are Shao, then Ren, Tal and Shas.

Talahina – A Tai Moran scholar.

Talamynii – Former allies of the Dhai, when the Dhai were a powerful nation. The Talamynii tamed wolves and used them as mounts. More fearsome than the Dhai, they were wiped out by the Saiduan. The few who remained intermarried with Saiduan people and their culture was subsumed by the broader one.

Talisa Gaiko Raona – Leader of Clan Raona.

Tanasai Laosina – Near-cousin to Zezili Hasaria. Tanasai was raised as part of Zezili's family after the death of her mother, but was seen as a burden by Zezili's mother.

Tanays Heydan – Saradyn's second in command.

Taodalain Hasaria – Zezili Hasaria's sister. Daughter to Livia Hasaria.

Tasia Gohina Garika (Dhai) – A young girl separated from her family.

Tasia Gohina (Tai Mora) – Kirana and Yisaoh's child. Adopted from Kirana's cousin.

Temple of Oma – A temple dedicated to Oma. Located in Dhai at the tip of the Fire Gate peninsula. The building itself is a living thing, made of some unknown combination of organic matter.

Temple of Tira – A Dhai temple located deep within the Woodland. Somehow repels nearby dangerous plants. Its grounds contain the most renowned gardens in Dhai.

The Cage – A mountain range in Dorinah, near Lake Morta.

The Lament of Hahko – A very old Dhai ballad.

Tumbleterrors – A semi-sentient plant that propels itself through the woodland using massive tentacles. Moves in packs.

Thief Queen – Unseated Penelodyn and attempted to take power in Tordin. Was killed by Saradyn Lind. Also known as Quilliam of the Mountain Fortress, Quill of Galind, Quill the Thief Queen. Was once Saradyn's ward.

Ti-Li, Keeper – The keeper of Oma's Temple.

Tir Salarihi Garika – Clan leader of Clan Garika. Father to Yisaoh Alais Garika, Hadaoh Alais Garika, Rhin Gaila Garika, Lohin Alais Garika and Kihin Moarsa Garika. Exiled.

Tira – Name of the satellite also referred to as Lord of the Living. Tira's light is green.

Tirajista – Sorcerers who can channel the power of Tira

when it is ascendant, which gives them the power to heal flesh and grow/train plants and other organics. Tirajistas are also skilled in the creation of wards.

Tolda – A dajian.

Tongue Mountains – Mountains in Tordin.

Tordin – Country on the southeastern shore of Grania, led currently by a King named Saradyn Lind. Constantly in a state of civil war. Was led by the Empress of Dorinah's sister, Penelodyn, before she was unseated by the Thief Queen. The country is difficult to unite because of its geography – cities are far apart, and the terrain is hilly. Dangerous plants spring up again quickly after being cut.

Tulana Nikoel, Ryii – Leader of the seekers hiding in the dajian camp where Lilia is held. An omajista.

Una Morinis Raona – Gatekeeper of the Temple of Oma.

Vestaria Mauvia – A Tai Mora at Caisau.

Voralyn Jovyn – A Dorinah Seeker recruited and bound by Lilia to help her get the dajian refugees across the Dhai border.

Water lily spiders – Semi-sentient plants that filter water when they breathe.

Willowthorn – Thorny weeping tree with small leaves which grows up to 175 feet tall. Saplings are infused with the power of Sina to create infused weapons.

Wind witches – Name for parajistas in Tordin.

Woodland Dhai – Those who have been exiled from – or who chose to exile themselves from –the Dhai settlements in the valley. The Woodland Dhai have a different dialect than those in the valley.

Wraisau Kilia, Ren – A sanisi.

Yisaoh Alais Garika (Dhai) – Yisaoh once contested Javia Mia Sorai for the title of Kai. Daughter of Tir Salarihi Garika. Sister of Rhin Gaila Garika, Hadaoh Alais Garika, Lohin Alais Garika and Kihin Moarsa Garika.

Yisaoh Alais Garika (Tai Mora) – Married to the Tai Mora leader, Kirana Javia.

Yivsa Afinisla – One of Kirana's four line commanders.

Zezili Hasaria (Raisa Prime) – Captain general of Dorinah's eastern force. Zezili's mother, Livia Hasaria, is a titled Dorinah and her father a dajian, making her half Dhai. Her title is Syre.

Zezili Hasaria (Mirror) – Incited a revolt against the Tai Mora and killed Kirana Javia's Tai Mora father. Worked on the massive mirror the Tai Mora created to facilitate entry to prime Raisa, but was eventually killed for refusing to cooperate.

Zini – The smallest of Raisa's three moons.

ABOUT THE AUTHOR

KAMERON HURLEY is an award-winning author, advertising copywriter and online scribe. She has won the Hugo Award, Kitschy Award, and Sydney J Bounds Award for Best Newcomer; she has also been a finalist for the Arthur C Clarke Award, Nebula Award, Locus Award, BFS Award, the David Gemmell Morningstar Award, and the BSFA Award for Best Novel. Her non-fiction has been featured in *The Atlantic*, *Locus*, and the game-changing collection *The Geek Feminist Revolution*.

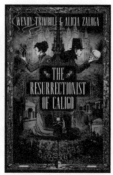

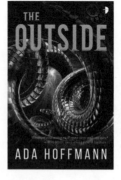

Science Fiction, Fantasy and WTF?!

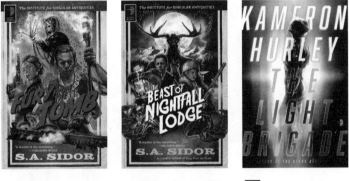

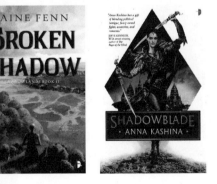

Complete your WORLDBREAKER SAGA *collection...*

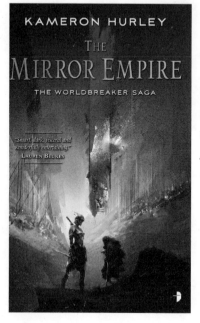

When a shadowy force threatens their world, an orphan blood mage, novice fighter, and an illegitimate ruler must unite fractured nations – and confront their own darker natures.

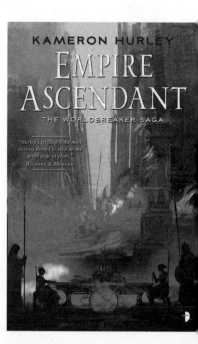

The nation of Dhai is under siege by enemies newly imbued with violent powers from the dark star, Oma. Their only hope for survival lies in the hands of an illegitimate ruler and a scullery maid with powerful – but unpredictable – magic...